Last Train to Lime Street

Last Train to Lime Street

Mersey Murder Mysteries Book VI

Brian L. Porter

Dedicated to the memory of Leslie and Enid Porter
Sleep sound, Mum and Dad.

Acknowledgements

I always owe a debt of gratitude to one particular lady when I write any of the Mersey mysteries and *Last Train to Lime Street* is no different to those that have gone before it. So, my thanks go to my friend, my researcher and proof reader, Debbie Poole, who has spent many hours driving around Liverpool and its suburbs in search of and checking locations for the book. She was joined on this venture by her friend Dorothy (Dot) Blackman, who became her erstwhile assistant researcher and joined her on her ongoing investigative 'Car Trek' around the city. The names kind of go well together don't they, Poole and Blackman. I can picture these two intrepid ladies motoring around the city like a pair of latter-day Jane Marple's, sticking their noses into all sorts of unlikely places as they searched for relevant places for 'body dumps' and other necessary scenarios for the books. My undying gratitude goes to them both.

As always, I owe thanks to Miika Hannila at Next Chapter Publishing, not just for his ongoing belief in, and support for the Mersey Mystery series, but for helping to advance the series' exposure by having negotiated a contract to have the books made into audio books, having been approached by one of the UK's largest producers of the media. It's yet another exciting step forward in the development of the series.

I have to add my thanks to all my readers, who this year have helped book three in the series, *A Mersey Maiden*, to win the prestigious 'Best Book We've Read All Year Award' from Readfree.ly. I was delighted to have won the award and very grateful to receive the beautiful glass trophy that came with it.

Of course, I always save my dear wife Juliet to last when writing my acknowledgements. She puts up with innumerable hours of me being 'incommunicado' as I sit engrossed by my story and characters who do tend to almost take over my life as the books progress. Her support is unwavering and she is always my first and fiercest critic, correcting me if she thinks I'm going 'off-track' with any of my stories. I couldn't do it without her.

To the People of Liverpool

As I was about to start working on Last Train to Lime Street, my researcher/proof reader, Debbie Poole came across a poem which kind of sums up how many people whose origins may lie on that great city that stands proudly on the River Mersey feel about the place. Although the original poet is as far we can ascertain, unknown or anonymous, I have recreated it here, and willingly give credit to the poet.

Liverpool

Of all the cities in the world,
London, Paris, Rome,
You won't find any finer,
Than the one that I call home,
She is a part of who I am,
My flesh, my blood, my bone,
When you are born a scouser,
You'll never walk alone

Looking out across the Mersey
Her three graces steal the show
You won't find any finer
No matter where you go
She's changed a bit since I was young
Time does that to a place

But she never lost her magic
I'm still held in her embrace
She has a style all of her own
Its seen on every street
You can hear her in the voices
Of the people that you meet
And wherever your life takes you
All the world around
She's there on every jukebox
With her distinctive Mersey sound
The Beatles and The Searchers
And of course. the Merseybeats
Gerry and the Pacemakers
A sound straight from her streets
The Iron Door on Temple Street
I remember way back when
And of course The Cavern Club
It was swinging there back then

We'd go dancing in The Grafton
The Rialto and Coconut Grove
At supper time a pan of scouse
Would be waiting on the stove
Looking smart in brand new kecks
With grease to style your hair
You'd stand under Dicky Lewis
And hope she'd meet you there

A day out over the water
Was as far as we would stray
We'd watch the Punch and Judy show
New Brighton for the day
Windswept on the Mersey

As the quay and I did part
But I knew I'd be returning
So I left behind my heart

With two very fine Cathedrals
Her skyline has been blessed
She also has two football teams
Much better than all the rest
Everybody loves the footy
Whether red or Blue
Both our teams are dynamite
We fetched home a cup or two

Laughter was born in this city
Our humour is unique
With Sir Ken Dodd and Mickey Finn
Even bleak times weren't that bleak
This place has launched a thousand ships
And she's built a fair few too
Her Liver birds watched over
Every vessel passing through

Everybody loves a bevvy
In this place that I call home
We love to let our hair down
And we don't do it alone
Whether after work or Friday night
Or of course, after the game
We'll raise a glass together
We all love that just the same

From the Albert Dock to Scottie Road
From The Echo to the Philly
I love every single inch of her
I don't care if that sounds silly
The old and new, the been and gone
Where else would I want to be?
From now until my dying day
It's Liverpool for me.

Anon

Introduction to the Series

Welcome aboard *Last Train to Lime Street,* the 6th instalment in what began as a single standalone novel, with *A Mersey Killing.* Such was that book's success however, that the decision was taken to begin a series of books featuring Detective Inspector Andy Ross, Detective Sergeant Izzie Drake and their colleagues on the fictional Merseyside Police, Special Murder Investigation Team. This elite squad is brought in to solve what appear to be extra-difficult or mysterious killings in the large metropolitan area covered by the Merseyside Police Force. Of course, much of their work is concentrated in and around the city of Liverpool and in creating the characters that populate the books, in particular Ross and his team, I decided to make them as 'real' as possible by basing a great deal of their personalities and personalities of members of my own family, as recalled from my younger days as a boy in Liverpool, and those who have read *A Mersey Killing* will realise why I had to use my memories of them as they were in the 1960s in order to make things work.

When the second book in the series, *All Saints, Murder on the Mersey,* performed equally as well as the first, and book 3, *A Mersey Maiden,* won a 2018 Book of the Year Award, it looked as if the characters were doing a pretty good job.

They were followed by the equally successful, award-winning *A Mersey Mariner* and *A Very Mersey Murder,* and believe it or not, by then, some of my characters were attracting fan mail of their own, as I received a number of communications from readers who have their favourite characters and seem to have developed attachments to them and their lives and actions, much as TV viewers often do with the characters in their preferred soap operas. Newlywed Detective Constable Derek McLennan watch out, you have a female fan following!

As always, my thanks go to the people and the city of Liverpool, without whom none of the Mersey Mysteries could exist.

Glossary

Some of the Words and terminology use by the people of Liverpool can be confusing, even for fellow Brits, so it's hardly surprising they are sometimes confusing for my American readers in particular. Some U.S. readers have criticised the grammar, but must realise that it would be extremely rare for a Liverpudlian police officer to say, for example, "Izzie and I are going to see a witness," and would generally say, "Izzie and me are going to see a witness," which though grammatically incorrect, is the way people actually speak, and so, that's how it will appear in the dialogue in the book.

La' - a contraction of the word, 'lad' popularly used in the local Liverpool dialect.

'ould – a local version of the word 'old' pronounced as 'owld' e.g. 'My 'ould man," = "My father."

Z Cars – a hugely popular British TV series set in the fictional town of Newtown based on Kirkby, near Liverpool. It ran from 1962-1978 and popularised the ubiquitous Ford Zephyr 6, as used by the officers in the series.

Boot (of a car) – what Americans call the trunk.

Oppo – opposite number, as in partner or assistant

Scrote – Slang for a worthless, obnoxious, contemptible person

999 – UK equivalent to 911

S.I.O. – Senior Investigating Officer

D.C.I. – Detective Chief Inspector

D.I. - Detective Inspector.

D.S. - Detective Sergeant

D.C. - Detective Constable

Scally: Local Liverpudlian description (from the word scallywag), used to describe a ne'er-do-well, a mischief maker or small-time thief or hoodlum.

There may be a few words I've failed to mention, but I think you'll get the hang of the 'Scouse' accent after a while. Speaking of the word 'Scouse'

Scouse/Scouser, a common term to refer to the natives of Liverpool, derived from the once popular dish 'scouse,' served in Liverpool households for many years, though not so much nowadays a' a contraction of the word, 'lad' popularly used in the local Liverpool dialect.

Author's Note to my American Readers – English/American Spelling/Grammar

It has occasionally been mentioned by my U.S. readers that the spellings and grammar in the Mersey Mysteries is, in their minds, incorrect. I must remind you that although we share a language, our usage of it differs greatly from one side of the Atlantic to the other. Being English, my books are therefore written in English as spelled and spoken by those of us on my side of the Atlantic and I am aware that this can be quite confusing to those in the USA. We also tend to use different forms of grammar as well, but please be aware, these do not constitute errors. They are simply the way we speak and use the English language here in the United Kingdom.

Contents

Chapter 1   1

Chapter 2   8

Chapter 3   14

Chapter 4   22

Chapter 5   30

Chapter 6   36

Chapter 7   46

Chapter 8   54

Chapter 9   60

Chapter 10   69

Chapter 11   78

Chapter 12   95

Chapter 13   108

Chapter 14	114
Chapter 15	124
Chapter 16	130
Chapter 17	142
Chapter 18	148
Chapter 19	154
Chapter 20	166
Chapter 21	173
Chapter 22	180
Chapter 23	190
Chapter 24	198
Chapter 25	207
Chapter 26	211
Chapter 27	219
Chapter 28	225
Chapter 29	238
Chapter 30	254
Chapter 31	261
Chapter 32	270

About the Author   276

From International Bestselling Author Brial L Porter   278

Chapter 1

The Wedding

Saturday, 15th December 2005 would long live in the memory of Detective Constable Derek McLennan. It was, after all, his wedding day and as he and his bride, nurse Debbie Simpson walked out of the Cotton Exchange Building on Liverpool's Edmund Street into the crisp winter sunshine, having tied the knot in front of their families and friends, Derek considered himself the most fortunate man in the world. He and Debbie had met when he was hospitalised after being shot while attempting to foil an armed robbery of a jewellery store during his off-duty hours. Now, he stood nervously, wearing a brand new navy-blue three-piece suit specially bought for the occasion, while Debbie was dressed in a beautiful, cream strapless, knee length silk dress, with a lace overlay. She wore a Chantelle Lace bolero over her dress, which she could remove for the reception, letting her feel like she was wearing a different dress. In her cream, 3-inch stiletto peep-toed shoes to match her dress, Derek thought she looked like a fairy tale princess. Her ensemble was topped by a waist length veil, removable for the reception, held in place by a simple tiara. She carried a small bouquet of her favourite flowers, cream and pale lemon Gerbera Daisies and Carnations. Debbie had a nice surprise for Derek for later, too. Her slim legs looked stunning in ten denier stockings, (he didn't know they were stockings of course), which were topped off with a lacy blue garter. She planned to make their wedding night very special for him.

All too quickly, the happy couple had exchanged their vows and were promptly declared man and wife, to the delight of their small group of guests who applauded as Derek kissed his new wife in time-honoured fashion.

Debbie had been one of the team of nurses who had helped Derek in his return to health after being operated on to remove the bullet that had lodged in his chest. As he endured the inactivity forced upon him by his time in hospital, she had spent many of her off-duty hours sitting and talking to the young detective until, almost inevitably, romance blossomed between the young couple and by the time Derek was discharged from hospital he had faced his biggest fear to date; proposing to the pretty young nurse who had stolen his heart. He later confessed to his colleague, D.C. Lenny (Tony) Curtis, that he was more afraid of being rejected by Debbie than he was when confronting the armed robbers, unarmed, on the day he was shot.

Following the wedding, the happy couple and their guests, including their families and most of Liverpool's Specialist Murder Investigation Team, headed for the reception at the Adelphi Hotel, where Tony Curtis, his closest friend on the squad, delivered the traditional best man's speech. Some of the team had expected Curtis to produce a flippant and jocular speech that fitted in with his usual daily persona, but instead, Curtis delivered a masterful and almost tear-inducing speech that focussed on his friend's dedication to duty, his willingness to put himself in the firing line to protect society in general and his colleagues in particular. Much to Derek's surprise and embarrassment, Curtis made a great and impassioned reference to Derek having received the Chief Constable's Commendation for bravery following his selfless attempt to foil the jewellery store robbery, finally leading to an injection of humour by saying,

"I've seen some weird and whacky ways of guys trying to meet the girl of their dreams, but Derek just had to take it to the nth degree. I mean, who else goes out and gets themselves shot just so he can meet a gorgeous, sexy nurse and fulfil almost every man's fantasy?"

This was greeted by a round of polite laughter with Derek, seated beside his best man, managed to surreptitiously, playfully thump his best friend's thigh in a successful attempt to shut him up. Derek's ploy worked for a moment, until his best man delivered his final embarrassing fact relating to the groom.

"Of course, we all know just how committed Derek is to the job, don't we? Who else would stand in a back alley, snogging a sergeant, just to provide cover for a spot of covert surveillance?"

Curtis was referring to their last case, when Derek and the squad's on-loan German detective, Sofie Meyer had played the part of a courting couple in an impromptu attempt to obtain a visual sighting into the rear of their suspect's home while the rest of the team converged on the front. Derek still blushed when he recalled Meyer saying, in a voice not to be denied, "Kiss me Derek." Debbie had laughed when he'd related the incident to her later, telling him how brave he was and how proud she was that her husband-to-be was so dedicated to his job that he'd risk a slap from his fiancée in order to catch a criminal. For a minute, he'd thought she was serious, but then her face crumpled in laughter and Derek joined in, still slightly embarrassed by the whole thing.

Finally, Tony Curtis came to the end of his speech, wishing the happy couple a long and happy life together. As he sat down, the assembled guests gave him a rousing round of applause, and, unusually for him, he blushed. Truth be told, he'd been absolutely terrified at the prospect of delivering his best man's speech and was relieved it was over and that he hadn't managed to make a fool of himself.

As soon as he was seated, and the applause died down, Derek leaned across to him and whispered in his ear, "Thanks a lot mate. I'll fucking kill you later, shall I?"

Curtis laughed and replied, "What else did you expect when you asked me to be your best man?"

"True. I should have known you wouldn't be able to resist putting the knife in and making me look a right pillock."

"Ha-ha," Curtis laughed. "Lighten up man, they loved it, and you are the luckiest copper in Liverpool. Debbie's a real cracker mate. I envy you, and that's a fact."

Smiling, Derek turned to his friend, shook his hand and said in a heartfelt voice, "Thanks, Tony. I mean it. From the day I joined the squad, you've always had my back."

"Aw, shut up, man. You do the same for me and everyone else on the team. That's why we work so well together."

Soon afterwards, with all the speeches over, and before the dancing began, Debbie's father, John Simpson stood up and asked everyone to join him at the hotel's main entrance, where he announced, a special present awaited Derek and Debbie. Nobody had noticed when Debbie's brother, Neil, had quietly left the room while Tony Curtis had been making his speech. It was his job, arranged by him and his father, to bring the surprise present to the front of the hotel. As Derek, Debbie and their guests dutifully gathered at the Adelphi's entrance, a quizzical look on their faces, a gleaming, black, beautifully restored Ford Zephyr 6, Mark III, familiar to fans of the old TV show, Z-Cars, pulled up right in front of the entrance, and out stepped Neil Simpson. Debbie's father placed a hand on Derek's shoulder, and said to his new son-in-law, "We know you love classic cars, Derek, and you know Neil earns a living restoring old vehicles, so we thought you and Debbie might like this."

"It's for me? I mean us?" Derek beamed with delight.

"All yours, son," said a smiling John Simpson. "Enjoy it."

Neil walked up to Derek, shook his hand and handed him the keys to the Zephyr.

"All the best to you both," he said as Derek took possession of the keys to the finest wedding present anyone could have given him.

"Thank you, Neil, and you too John. God knows how much it must have cost you to restore her, but she's beautiful."

"Only two owners since she was first registered in 1965," Neil said, proudly. "It was a pleasure doing her up for the two of you."

"Are you happy to be seen in this old thing, Debbie?" Derek asked as his wife stood smiling beside him.

"Of course I am, you twit," she replied. "I told Dad and Ian how you're mad about old cars, and they planned all this without a word to me, but just look at it. It looks like it's brand new. How could anyone not want to be seen in it?"

"Here's a set of keys for you too, Sis," Neil said as he presented a second set of keys to his sister. "Just don't fight over who's going to drive it now, will you?" he laughed.

"No chance of that Neil. Derek will be using it more than me. It's got one of those old-fashioned column change gear sticks. Not my thing really. I'll stick to my little old faithful mini, thanks."

Debbie's brother laughed, and then, beckoned by Derek, he joined his brother-in-law and together they proceeded to take a quick drive to Lime Street station and back, finally driving around to the hotel car park, where they parked the car for the time being.

"Will you take care of it while we're on honeymoon?" Derek asked as he parked his wonderful wedding present from his in-laws.

"Of course," Neil replied. "It'll be waiting for you when you get back from Majorca."

"Thanks, Neil, for everything. I couldn't have wished for a better present, or a bigger surprise. Debbie knows I love these old cars, and if anything proves how much your sister loves me, it's that she suggested this to you."

"She thinks the world of you, mate," Neil told him. "Thinks the sun shines out of your arse, she does. I'm sure I don't have to tell you to take care of my little sister, do I?"

"You've got no worries there. She means the world to me," Derek assured him.

"I kind of realised that from the way you look at her. I really hope you'll both be truly happy together, Derek, and if you get any trouble from the car, you let me know, okay? Don't be going to no garages or service stations, promise?"

"I promise," Derek replied. "I wouldn't dream of letting anyone else handle her."

"Good, that's settled then. We'd better get back to your reception before Debbie thinks we're run away together with the Zephyr."

The two men, both ardent car enthusiasts, laughed together as Derek locked his precious car and the two of them returned to the wedding reception.

Before long, the clock approached the time for the happy couple to make their way to the airport to catch the flight that would carry them to their honeymoon destination.

One by one, Derek's colleagues came and wished the couple happiness and prosperity. D.I. Andy Ross and his wife Maria were first to wish them well, followed by Detective Sergeant Izzie Drake and her husband, Peter. They were soon followed by Detective Constables Nick Dodds and Samantha Gable, and their German colleague, Sofie Meyer. Derek was delighted that his former colleague, D.C. Keith Burton had accepted their invitation to the wedding. Keith had been shot soon after Derek, while on the job, but his injuries had been more severe and he was currently reassigned to a desk job within police headquarters. It was not known if he'd ever be fit enough to return to his previous role, but they all lived in hope.

Missing from his colleagues in the Specialist Murder Investigation Team were Detective Sergeant Paul Ferris and the team's admin assistant Kat Bellamy, left in charge of the team's squad room. Anything could and often did happen during daylight hours in a city the size of Liverpool, and someone had to man the desks while the wedding was taking place. Ferris was represented by his wife Kareen and his young son, Aaron, who had survived a kidney transplant at a young age and was now growing into a strapping young lad, almost the spitting image of his father. At 9 years of age he could easily be mistaken for a boy at least two to three years older. Kareen hugged both the bride and groom and planted a kiss on Derek's cheek, and Derek hugged her back and made Aaron's day by shaking his hand as he would a grown man and telling him to pass the handshake on to his Dad later. Aaron Ferris positively beamed his pleasure and Debbie McLennan felt a surge of love for her husband for helping to make the lad feel important.

When the 'cab' to take them to the airport arrived, Derek was surprised once more as the car that awaited the couple was a silver Mercedes, driven by no less than a fully-liveried chauffeur, who Derek easily identified as Stan Coleman, the former D.I. and now owner of one of the city's largest cab companies. Coleman had been helpful to the squad in helping to track down the killer in their last major case and now he was here to drive Derek and his bride to the airport to catch their honeymoon flight.

As the car pulled away, accompanied by much cheering and waving, the guests drifted back into the bar where some continued to party into the night. A few left early, ready to fall into bed, happy and tired, knowing that work was never too far away. They were right of course, though nobody knew it at that moment.

Chapter 2

Last Train to Lime Street

Sixty-year old Bob Fraser had grown up with a single-minded ambition. As he proudly replied to anyone who asked the question "*What do you want to be when you grow up?*" he'd say, "*An engine driver.*" From the age of five, he'd been obsessed with trains and the railways in general. Driving a train was his single-minded obsession and nothing would prevent him fulfilling his sole ambition. He'd fulfilled his ambition by the time he reached his twenty-fourth birthday and in the intervening years, he'd driven virtually every type of locomotive seen on the railways of Britain.

Now, he sat at the controls of the last train of the day from Manchester Piccadilly to Liverpool Lime Street. The Type 155 'Sprinter' diesel multiple unit, built by Metro Cammell, and capable of a maximum speed of 75 mph, was one of the most frequently seen locomotive units on the British Railway system and though not quite as large and powerful as some of the locos he'd driven over the years, he was happy in his work and no matter what he was asked to drive, as long as he could feel and hear the vibration and the 'clickety-clack' of the train as it moved along the permanent way, Bob was in his element. In all his years at the controls, he'd never had an accident and was confident he'd reach his impending retirement with his perfect record intact.

Now, just four miles from Lime Street, he had slowed his train as he passed through Mossley Hill station, bang on time. As he cleared the platform he increased speed slightly as he approached the bridge that carried Rose Lane over the railway just a few yards from the station. Suddenly, in the locomotive's headlights, designed for illuminating the tracks directly ahead of the train, his eyes caught a momentary sight of an object falling from the bridge, directly in front of his train. With little or no time to apply the emergency brakes, Bob did so anyway, in a forlorn hope of avoiding disaster. A sickening thud quickly told him he'd been wholly unsuccessful in his attempt. As the train slowed, Bob felt the awful sensation of the thing that has fallen under his train being dragged along under his locomotive for at least a quarter of a mile as he brought the two-coach unit to a halt. Despite not having had a clear view of the falling object, Bob's instincts told him he had just struck a human being and dragged the body along under his train.

As the train came to a halt, Bob took a moment to compose himself before daring to open the driver's door to inspect the damage his train must have caused to the unfortunate person who had fallen under the wheels of his train. As he stepped down from the cab, he was joined by Ray Warren, the conductor, who'd guessed their train had hit an obstacle, and who'd leapt from the rear carriage the second the train stopped. Ray had shouted to the thankfully few passengers on the train to stay on board as he attempted to ascertain the cause of the hold up to their journey. He had to hope they'd obey his instruction.

"What the fuck was that, Bob?" he asked the driver.

Even in the dark, Ray could see that the driver's face was ashen, and it looked to him as if Bob was about to be sick.

"I think we hit someone, Ray," he managed, before falling silent as he felt the bile rising again. "I saw something fall from the bridge and then felt the thump as we hit it."

Ray Warren switched on the large torch he was carrying and together the two men began searching the front and the underside of the two-car multiple unit. Seeing blood on the front left side buffer, they proceeded to carry out their search, bent almost double as the torch picked out the darkened underside of the train.

"What's this?" Ray asked, seeing something hanging from the rear bogie of the driving unit.

Peering along the beam of the torch, Bob looked closely and then almost jumped back as his eyes focussed on the unmistakable sight of a human arm, neatly sheered off at the shoulder, sliced neatly by one of the locomotive's wheels.

"Oh fuck," he exclaimed and with that single expletive spoken, he rushed to the side of the tracks, where he promptly vomited.

Ray left him to it, giving him the respect and dignity that would allow him to do what he had to do without adding any fuss to what a nightmare scenario for the two men was already. As Bob threw up the contents of his stomach, a head appeared from the rear door of the leading carriage and a voice called out, "Hey, what the hell is happening here? Why have we stopped?"

"Please, remain on the train," the guard/conductor called to the man. "We have an emergency situation to deal with here."

"What kind of emergency?"

"Just, please, stay on the train. We'll give you more information as soon as we can."

Bob completed his retching and vomiting and stood up, ready to re-join his colleague.

"Are you okay?" Ray asked the driver.

"Not really," was Bob's reply as the two men resumed their search. Within seconds, Ray felt, rather than saw, something to his left and shone his torch on the clump of bushes that grew beside the tracks.

"Oh, shit," he blurted out, followed by "Holy Mary, Mother of God."

In the bushes, they could clearly identify what remained of a human being, obviously thrown to the side when the brakes had been applied and the wheels had momentarily locked, sending it flying up and out from under the rear bogie to land where they now saw it, mangled and bloody.

Bob retched again but his stomach contained nothing more to throw up.

"Get on the blower, Ray. Call it in, now!"

Ray Warren lost no time in calling in to the Northern Rail Operations Centre in Liverpool, who gave orders for him and Bob to remain with the train and ensure no passengers left before the police arrived. The ops centre would notify the British Transport Police immediately and their close proximity to Lime Street would ensure the railway police would be with them in minutes. Responsible for the security and safety of those travelling on Britain's railways the BTP were on the scene within fifteen minutes, a uniformed inspector, a sergeant and two constables arriving in two cars, their sirens and flashing emergency lights dominating the scene around Mossley Hill as they screeched to a halt outside the station.

Within minutes Inspector Dave Hood had assessed the situation and sent for reinforcements. He quickly sent the two constables in the two cars at their disposal to block off both ends of the road where it crossed the bridge and from where the body had apparently fallen to the tracks. Sergeant Billy Carter took charge of the train's interior, and after gathering the smattering of passengers together in the rear unit of the train, he informed them that, with apologies, they would have to remain on board until statements could be taken from the twelve of them. He knew they could in all likelihood offer nothing useful in terms of information, but procedures had to be followed. Once Hood's small emergency response team had been reinforced by the arrival of another four constables, despatched from Lime Street, arrived on the scene, the inspector began his assessment of the situation.

It didn't take him long to realise that the body, easily identified as a male and reduced as it was to a number of separate parts, distributed either beneath the leading locomotive unit or in the bushes beside the track, was lacking one vital thing which might have helped him to arrive at a fast identification. Whoever the deceased might have been, he was completely naked. There wasn't a stitch of clothing to be found, either trapped beneath the train or on what remained of the body in the bushes.

"Do you think it's a suicide, Inspector?" an ashen-faced Bob Fraser asked the policeman after he and his men had made their initial examination of the scene.

Hood seriously doubted that the deceased would have thrown himself naked from the bridge to land purposely in front of the approaching train, so late at night. Plus, his men had found no trace of any potentially abandoned vehicle close by, where the man may have left his clothes if he had decided on such a strange method of ending his life. For now, though, he remained cautious in his reply to the driver.

"I can't say for certain at this point," he replied. "We can only say for sure that the deceased was male, naked, and is lying in various pieces under and around your train."

Bob immediately felt sick again at the inspector's rather graphic way of stating the facts but managed to hold it in on this occasion.

"What do we do now?" the driver asked.

"We have your statement, and that of Mr. Warren, so we'll arrange transport home for you both, though we're sure to have more questions for you later. We have brief though bloody useless statements from your passengers too, so the same applies to them. We couldn't expect any of them to have seen anything to be honest. It's a bloody bad business, that's for sure. It's not every day we have a churned-up body under one of our trains, after all."

Bob's cheeks puffed out as he gagged again and this time he did run to the side of the tracks, where he promptly threw up again.

Once he, Ray Warren and the passengers had been dispatched to their homes or final destinations, Dave Hood, Billy Carter and their men began a further, painstaking investigation of the area, both from the bridge and the rail tracks, without, Hood lamented, finding anything he considered remotely helpful. It wasn't until the arrival of the duty police surgeon, Doctor William Nugent, who carried out a quick examination of the body parts in-situ, that Hood finally realised, almost with relief, that this was a case that might just require some specialist investigation and that he would in all probability be ordered to hand it over to someone better placed to carry out the type of investigation that was now so clearly required.

After all, he thought, *suicides don't usually slash their own throats from ear to ear before jumping from a railway bridge to land conveniently under the wheels of a passing train.*

Chapter 3

Sunday, Bloody Sunday

The harder he tried to kick his way clear of the cloying morass, the more he felt the power of the undertow that was slowly threatening to pull him down, deeper into the mire. His arms clawed at the side of the trench, yet they were so smooth his grasping fingers failed to find a handhold.

Andy Ross felt as though he was clawing his way out of a deep trench but was being held back by a deep layer of mud that acted like quicksand on his scrambling legs, pulling him ever deeper. Another loud, squelching, sucking noise assailed his ears as his legs sunk another few inches into the all-powerful mud. He was losing the battle and there was nothing he could do to prevent it. Buried up to his waist, he continued to try and think of a way out of his dilemma, when he suddenly saw a face appear at the top of the trench, about ten feet above him.

"Derek?" he called out as Derek McLennan's smiling face looked down at him. "Get me out of here, there's a good lad."

Instead of replying, Derek reached over the lip of the trench and slowly lowered a bottle of champagne, tied to a rope, to his boss.

"What the hell do you expect me to do with this?" Ross screamed in anguish as he sunk another six inches into the mud.

"Drink it, of course, Boss," Derek eventually replied, grinning from ear to ear.

"Then what?"

"Then we can have a real party"

"Derek, get me out of here, for fuck's sake," Ross shouted again.

A loud bell rang, almost deafening the floundering man. As he tried to block out the sound by placing his hands over his ears, it sounded again.

The trench shook, almost as if someone had taken hold of him and was shaking him.

"Andy, ANDY," the voice of his wife, Maria sounded in his ear. "Answer your phone, please!"

Opening his eyes, Andy Ross realised he was coming out of a dream, well, a nightmare really as he reached across to his bedside cabinet, picking up his mobile phone as his fingers made contact with it.

Maria stroked his back as he turned over, aware that her husband had been caught up in a nightmare when he'd begun talking to newly married Derek McLennan in his sleep.

"Ross," he almost shouted into his phone, relieved to be free of the cloying, sticky mud of the dreamworld. He listened carefully as the voice on the other end of the line spoke and finally responded.

"What time is it, Sergeant?"

On receiving the reply, he looked at his left wrist, confirming that it was indeed two o'clock in the morning, Sunday morning, when he should have been off work, relaxing after attending Derek's wedding the previous day.

"And D.C.I. Agostini wants me there right away?"

"Yes sir, the duty sergeant replied. He said he needs you and Sergeant Drake there asap. Said something about wanting to reopen the railway lines as soon as possible, it being an important commuter line and all that."

"Have you notified Sergeant Drake yet?"

"Doing that next, sir. I wanted to notify you first."

"Okay. Tell her to meet me at Mossley Hill as soon as she can, and Sergeant?"

"Sir?"

"Thank you."

Thinking Ross was being sarcastic, the duty sergeant just mumbled in reply to the inspector, little realising his call had helped put an end to Ross's nightmare, one he'd been having a little too regularly in recent weeks.

Turning to Maria, he spoke quietly, "Sorry love, body on the tracks at Mossley Hill. Nasty one by all accounts."

"And just why do they want the specialist murder squad out there at this time of night?" his wife queried.

"Seems he fell, or was pushed, naked from a bridge and fell under the wheels of a train. The body's in pieces all over the tracks. The transport police woke Oscar up and he must have decided it was one worth waking me and Izzie for too."

"You were having that nightmare again, weren't you?" Maria changed the subject quickly.

"Mmm, yes," he replied. "God knows where it's come from or why I'm having it. I've never had bloody nightmares before."

"We'll find a way to stop them," his doctor wife replied. "Can't have you losing sleep when you've important work to do."

"Right, whatever you say, Mrs. Ross." he smiled for the first time since waking up.

Ross quickly dressed and felt relieved he hadn't stayed and drunk too much at Derek's wedding reception. Arriving at Mossley Hill station just before 2.45 am, he was pleased to see his partner, Detective Sergeant Izzie Drake already there waiting for him. Dressed in a khaki-coloured parka, jeans and a pair of knee-high boots, with a Russian-style furry hat to combat the cold, Ross thought she looked a completely different person to the svelte, smartly dressed woman who he'd danced with at McLennan's wedding reception just a few hours earlier.

"No comments about the hat, please," she grinned at him. Despite it being a cold December night, Ross had grabbed the first things he'd come to before leaving the house, and was shivering violently in his black trousers, and turtle neck sweater, topped off by a black leather jacket and a blue Everton Football Club baseball cap.

"Hey, I don't mind what you look like as long it keeps you warm. I'm bloody freezing. Have you had a chance to check out the scene yet?"

"Inspector Hood from the Transport Police gave me a quick sight of the remains, well, most of them anyway. Our friend Doc Nugent is down there already. Apparently, he's been hard at work for over an hour and a half."

"On his own? Where's his oppo?" Ross referred to the pathologist's regular assistant, Francis Lees, often cruelly referred to as looking more cadaver-like than some of their 'clients.'

"Seems poor Francis had a few too many at the reception. Word is he doesn't drink much, and some joker spiked his drinks liberally with vodka."

Ross did his best to repress a smile at the thought of poor Francis Lees staggering around in a drunken stupor. He almost wished he'd stayed to see the sight of the poor fellow, staggering around in a drunken fugue, before someone kindly put him out of his misery and took him home. He was surprised when Drake informed it had been their own Tony Curtis who'd ferried the pathologist's assistant home. Ross had a feeling Curtis might have been the prankster who spiked Lees's drinks in the first place and then took pity on the man through some latent feelings of guilt when he saw the state of him. He held his tongue, however, this being neither the time nor the place to discuss the matter.

"Right, well who's he got taking his usual hundreds of photographs?"

"Some dolly bird who he called out of bed. A new assistant to his 'death squad' as Drake laughingly referred to the doctor and his assistants.

"So, let's go see what we've got," Ross said, and Drake led the D.I. into the station proper, walked to the end of the platform and then down onto the tracks, perfectly safe as Northern Rail had already suspended all trains running through Mossley Hill.

William Nugent, wearing a blue, heavy, quilted and padded coat that appeared to double his already prodigious size, looked up at the sound of approaching footsteps and smiled ruefully as Ross and Drake drew closer to his position, beside the bushes where the majority of the victim's remains lay. Not for nothing was he privately known among Ross's team as 'Fat Willy.' To one side, a young woman, who must be his stand-in assistant was busily taking photographs, using a high-powered flash. Little more than her face was visible, though Ross could tell she was in her twenties and appeared to be an attractive girl, from what he could see. She was slightly built, and he couldn't help thinking that next to Doctor Nugent, almost any member of the human race would appear slim.

"Ah, the good Inspector Ross and the delectable Sergeant Drake," he spoke in a quiet voice. Here, in the dead of night, following the incident that had brought them together, a whisper could have been heard ten yards away. "Not the best way to follow on from the festivities of Detective Constable McLennan's nuptials, is it?"

"You can say that again, Doc. I've been told it's a bad one." Ross spoke in an equally soft, almost reverential tone.

"Aye, you could say that, alright. Poor chap has been virtually chopped and pulped into little pieces and spread all over the tracks. Mind you, that's hardly surprising when ye consider he was struck by about seventy tons of train travelling, so I'm told, at about 40 m.p.h."

"And where did you get such precise information about the weight of the train and its speed?" Izzie Drake asked, and before the pathologist could reply, a voice from behind the little gathering answered the question for her.

"From me," said Inspector Hood, who had been with his men, marking and cataloguing each identifiable item of the body to the best of their ability in the dark, aided by torches and a couple of arc lights that had quickly been supplied and erected by the local track maintenance depot, which was luckily manned 24 hours a day, in case of any and all contingencies that might arise on a busy rail network. "I was given the weight and speed by the driver himself before I sent him home. Poor bugger was as pale as a ghost, kept throwing up, so I had my sergeant take statements from him and the conductor and sent them home in one of our cars. They'll be available in the morning if you want to speak to them."

Hood walked the last few feet to offer his hand to Andy Ross, who shook it and Hood then performed the same introduction with Drake.

"Not the best way to spend your night eh?" the inspector asked Ross, who shook his head solemnly.

"Definitely not my preferred place to be at this time on a Saturday night cum Sunday morning," Ross replied. "What are your thoughts?"

"Poor bastard was murdered, no doubt about it, and that's confirmed by Doctor Nugent here, correct, Doc?"

"Aye, that's a yes for sure," Nugent replied, his Glasgow accent creeping into his speech as it often did when the rotund pathologist was working under pressure. "It's nay likely your victim stripped himself, hid his clothes somewhere, and then cut his throat from ear to ear before somehow finding the strength to mount the parapet of yon bridge before throwing himself in front of a conveniently passing train."

"That seems a reasonably accurate and precise denial of any chance of it being an accident, thanks Doc," Ross smiled ruefully at Nugent.

"Aye," the pathologist agreed. Turning to his female assistant, Nugent asked, "Are you nearly finished, Sarah?"

"Just about," she replied. "Hello, by the way, I'm Sarah Neve," her comment directed to the two detectives.

"Och aye, I'm sorry," Nugent interjected," Ah didnae introduce you, did I? This is Doctor Sarah Neve, just joined my staff. Thought it would be good experience for her to help me on this one, so I dragged her away from her work on the boring old night shift at the morgue to assist me, seeing as how one of your detectives helped poor Francis into a state of blathering intoxication."

"You mean he got drunk at the reception and can't even stand up," Ross smiled at the pathologist.

"Drunk? The poor chap was inches away frae alcoholic poisoning the last time ah saw him," the Glasgow accent coming out stronger as Nugent became more irritated.

"Well, never mind poor Francis," Ross used the phrase mockingly. "What can you tell us about this poor sod?"

"Aye, well, I'd say he was a man in his late thirties to early forties, going by the appearance of the torso and other complete limbs we've found. Also, the torso allows me to guess at his height, which I'd put at around five feet, ten inches to six feet. The head is pretty badly damaged, but the neck was sufficiently intact for me to determine the poor bugger had his throat cut pre-mortem, and probably bled out and was dead before being tossed from the bridge."

"Any blood on the bridge?" Drake asked.

"Not enough to suggest he was killed there," Nugent replied.

The two detectives looked at each other, similar thoughts running through their minds, until Izzie Drake voiced what they both now believed.

"So, he was killed elsewhere and brought here to be dumped. Is that what you're telling us, Doc?"

"I'm afraid so," Nugent responded. "It's just made your job a damn sight harder, hasn't it"?

"Too right it has," Ross grumbled. "Now all we have to do is search the whole of bloody Liverpool to find out where he was killed and butchered."

"Sorry, Andy," Nugent said, feeling sorry for the D.I. It wasn't often the pathologist referred to Ross by his first name, despite the pair having known each other and worked together for many years.

"Not your fault, Doc. I want a full forensic team here at first light, Izzie. Miles Booker and his team will need to go over this area with a fine tooth-comb, just in case anything's been missed in the dark. What's the situation regarding keeping the line closed, Dave?" he asked the Railway Police Inspector.

"I'll make sure the tracks remain closed until you've done what you need to do. It's a murder enquiry after all. The travelling public are used to moaning about the rail service, and it's about to get whole lot worse, temporarily at any rate."

"Thanks. I'd hate to think of one our Scenes of Crime team ending up in a state like this poor bugger. Next question we need to deal with is, of course, who the fucking hell is he?"

"Without clothes or a wallet, credit cards, driving licence, that's going to be a herculean task, Boss," Izzie commented.

"Ye may find his teeth helpful," Nugent offered. "His jaws escaped most of the damage, so we may be able to trace him through dental records if he's local."

"And if he isn't? Ross let the question hang, and Nugent could do nothing more than shrug his shoulders. He knew the task that lay before the detectives and didn't envy them. Having said that, he also knew that crimes like this were exactly what Ross's specialist squad had been set up to deal with. He knew that if anyone could solve the riddle of the nameless victim, it was Andy Ross.

With the body parts, (the ones they had managed to locate), catalogued, gathered and secured in individual body bags, William Nugent supervised their loading into a waiting ambulance which would ferry the various limbs etc to the mortuary, where his detailed examination could commence, after he'd snatched a few hours' sleep of course.

Ross made arrangements with Inspector Hood who'd agreed to place a police guard on the station, the bridge and their environs, until Ross and his team, plus Miles Booker's forensic specialists from the Crime Scenes Unit could commence their examination of the scene in daylight. Ross knew there was too much chance of the crime scene being contaminated by having a team of Crime Scene Technicians blundering around in the dark, so he thought it best to leave Booker and his people to enjoy an unbroken night's sleep. Things would look better in the morning, Ross thought.

Chapter 4

Bits and pieces

It was hard for Ross and his team to comprehend that less than 24 hours earlier they'd been enjoying themselves at the wedding of their friend and colleague, Derek McLennan. Now, with the December frost eating into their frozen extremities, most of them found themselves sifting through the detritus that littered the trackside of the railway line just outside Mossley Hill Station in the company of Miles Booker's forensic team.

"This is fucking mind numbing. I can hardly feel my fingers," Detective Constable Nick Dodds moaned as he rummaged under a trackside bush, alongside D.C. Gary (Ginger) Devenish, the newest member of the team.

"Almost makes me wish I was back working with the Port Police," Devenish replied, echoing Dodds' sentiments. "I mean, why are we doing this anyway, Nick? Surely Miles and his people are the experts in this sort of thing?"

"Oh, they are Ginge," Dodds confirmed, "but the boss wants to be sure we're involved to make sure there isn't the slightest chance of any piece of evidence being overlooked."

"By evidence he means bits of this poor sod's body, doesn't he? I don't fancy coming across a piece of churned up intestine or maybe even the poor bastard's prick, if you know what I mean."

"No chance of that happening," the voice of Miles Booker replied, surprising the two men as he came up behind them. "One of my lads found that particular appendage a few minutes ago. Just in time to stop a crow from picking it up and taking it home for Sunday lunch," he quipped.

"Are you serious?" Dodds asked the head of the Scenes of Crime team.

"Deadly," Booker responded. "There can't be much more to find, so you boys shouldn't be here much longer."

"Hey boys, just heard from the boss," D.C. Sam Gable announced as she hurried up to stand beside Booker. "He called from the morgue."

"God, even the morgue would seem warm after this," Dodds observed.

"So, what's the latest from the house of the dead?" Devenish asked.

"Seems Doc Nugent is happy enough with what they found last night, to have reached some conclusions. He thinks our man could be foreign."

"Oh yeah, like, how foreign?" The question came from D.C. Lenny 'Tony' Curtis, who had also joined the group as they stood shivering beside the tracks.

"Yeah, I mean foreign could mean almost anything, like Eastern European foreign, American foreign, Asian foreign, blah, blah, blah, know what I mean?" Curtis quipped.

"Irish, even," said Devenish and then, on receiving odd looks from Gable and Dodds, "Well, the Republic of Ireland is officially a foreign country."

"As is Germany," came another voice from behind them as Sergeant Sofie Meyer, the team's German temporary two-year secondment from the *Bundeskriminalamt* arrived to complete the complement of detectives from Ross's team.

"Quite right, Sarge," Curtis nodded. "Have any of us found anything of any possible bloody use in the time we're been ferreting around on our knees in the freezing cold?"

"Mostly, we have found various pieces of flesh and internal body organs that were expelled by the force of the impact of the train's wheels with the body," Meyer replied. "The forensic people now have everything bagged and it will all be sent to the pathologist for examination, but I fear it will be a waste of time and effort. After all, we know he was struck by the train, but killed elsewhere so this is, as far as I am concerned, more of a clean-up operation the anything else."

"Yes, I agree," said Curtis, "But back to my question, how does Doc Nugent know our guy is a foreigner?"

"It would appear his new assistant pathologist is trained as an orthodontist. It's her considered opinion that the dental work carried out on the victim is possibly American. Said something about an 'American smile,' all crowns, and straightened teeth and too white to be real," said Meyer. "I suppose the boss will tell us more, later."

"So, what do we do now?" Dodds asked the obvious question.

"We return to headquarters, of course," Sofie Meyer smiled at her group as she spoke.

"Thank God," said Sam Gable.

"Amen to that," Nick Dodds added.

"Time to get warm again," Ginger Devenish added.

The whole mood, however, was summed up by Tony Curtis.

"Thank fuck for that!"

* * *

Back at the mortuary, Ross and Drake were watching as William Nugent and Sarah Neve attempted to put the various body parts of their victim into some semblance of order. In some instances, it appeared to be something akin to doing a jigsaw puzzle with pieces of human flesh, bone and gristle as they slowly and methodically pieced together an approximation of a human cadaver.

At one end of the autopsy-suite table was the almost intact, though decapitated head and neck, ghoulishly displaying the long, obscene gash that had probably been the cause of the victim's death. Next came the badly damaged torso, with, beside it, various organs that had been ripped and torn from the body's innards by the wheels of the late-night train. Still in polythene bags were various pieces of flesh and bone, mostly sections of rib and the sternum, that had been forcibly wrenched from their natural position by those terrible, sharp wheels. Being pulled open by the force of the impact and the dragging along under the engine's bogies had performed devastating damage to the man's torso, and the two pathologists were, in truth, struggling to put the man back together. As Nugent had commented when Ross asked how it was coming along,

"This isn't Humpty Dumpty, Inspector, nor are Doctor Neve and I all the Kings Horses and all the Kings Men. I can tell you that it appears his throat was cut from left to right, leading me to believe his attacker was right-handed and was behind him when he made the fatal knife wound. Will that do for starters? Ah cannae perform miracles in a few hours, especially with so much damage to the poor man's remains."

As he and Neve placed one entire severed leg, the left one, only minus its foot, beside the three sections of recovered leg tissue that made up the right leg, foot present but badly smashed and now mostly broken bones and pieces of hanging flesh and gristle, Ross grimaced and Izzie Drake couldn't help feeling a moment of nausea as she imagined the train colliding with the falling body and the combined effects of that collision as the body was dragged, at speed under the travelling wheels of the powerful locomotive unit.

"I know that Doc," Ross replied. "I have a bad feeling about this one. I just don't see how we're going to I.D him if we can't come up with some form of documentary evidence, and you haven't been able to come up with any fingerprints for us, or have you?"

Nugent's face had exhibited a sly grin for a second, as though he knew something Ross didn't which was true of course, as so far, Ross knew nothing about the victim.

"Even though the hands were severely mangled by the impact injuries, Doctor Neve was able to find one finger which wasn't totally obliterated and yes, we were able to lift a partial print from our victim,"

Nugent sounded almost triumphant, at having found at least something that might help Ross's investigation.

"Well done Doctor Neve," Ross was almost effusive in his praise of the new assistant pathologist, who smiled coyly in return.

"We got lucky, Inspector," Neve stated, "but if the victim was American, unless he had a record here in the UK a fingerprint may not be much help to you after all.

Ross couldn't help but agree with Neve.

"Well, for the time being, we'll get that print over to Paul Ferris at headquarters and see if he can come up with anything. Sergeant Paul Ferris was Ross's computer expert and together with the team's admin assistant, Katrina (Kat) Bellamy, the D.I. knew that if their victim was anywhere in either the PNC, (Police National Computer), system, or his print was recorded in any shape or form with any other UK agencies, Ferris was the man to find it.

"What about facial recognition, sir?" Izzie Drake asked. "We're lucky the head wasn't too badly damaged. What about getting the Press Liaison Officer to put out of those '*Do you know this man*' photos to the press?"

"Your problem there, Sergeant, is that the left side of his face is relatively undamaged as you can see, but if you come round to this side," Nugent indicated for Drake to walk round the table to join him, "you can see there is quite a bit of damage to the other side, so a full frontal photo wouldn't be a great idea."

"I see what you mean," Drake agreed as she stood beside the pathologist, looking down at the severed head of their unknown victim. Maybe, he thought, they could make up photofit based on the undamaged portion of the face.

"You know, Izzie," Ross ventured a new opinion. "We should also get one of the team to look into recent reports of missing persons. If this poor bugger lived anywhere in the Liverpool area, there just might be a chance of his already being in the system. Of course, we can also access the national computer records to see if anyone matching his description, such as it is, is recorded as being reported to any other force around the country."

"Good idea," Drake agreed. "Maybe things aren't as bleak as we at first thought."

"Exactly, and we've still to see if Miles and his Crime Scenes technicians have found anything of value at the station or on the bridge and the tracks at Mossley Hill."

"Aye, well, I can see you have a lot to do," Nugent observed, "so if there's anything else we can do for ye, we'll get on with doing our best to put this poor bugger back into some semblance of looking human."

"Sure Doc, we'll let you get on with it. Oh, just one other question?"

"Aye, go ahead," Inspector.

"Have you got the stomach? I just thought, if you have it and it's intact you may be able to tell us what he ate for his last meal. It might also give us something to go on."

Nugent pointed to a stainless-steel dish on a separate steel table a few feet behind him.

"Your wish is my command, Inspector Ross. We have it over there and Sarah will give it her best attention very soon. Once we have the results, I'll call you. Will that be acceptable to you?"

Ross smiled at his old friend, though they rarely exhibited what would normally be termed 'friendship' in the accepted sense of the word, but years of working together had brought about a special working relationship between the acerbic pathologist and the dedicated detective.

"I'll wait for your call, then, Doc," he replied as he and Drake left the two pathologists bending intently over the assorted organs and lumps of flesh and bone that made up all that was left of their murder victim.

As they were leaving the building the two detectives stopped briefly at the office of the mortuary supervisor, Peter Foster, Drake's husband. Izzie had decided, with Peter's agreement, to retain her maiden name at work after their marriage, her relationship with Ross having been built over several years of working together. As such, she didn't want to confuse others in the force by making them think Ross had lost his long-time assistant and been landed with a new, less experienced sergeant.

"Hello, you two," Peter smiled as the pair pushed open his office door and strode into his own working domain.

"Hi Honey," Drake said in response to her husband's cheery greeting.

"Peter," Ross added by way of a greeting.

"You're on the jigsaw man, I see," Peter commented, not having seen or spoken to Izzie since she'd left their home in the early hours of the morning.

"Jigsaw man?" Ross asked.

"That's what the staff are calling your unknown victim," Peter replied. "So many pieces for Doc Nugent to try and put together, hence, the jigsaw man."

"Oh my god, Peter, please try and make sure that name doesn't leak outside this building," Izzie said, with a look of horror on her face. "We don't want that getting out to the press who could then start sensationalising the case before we've even got started."

Andy Ross, impressed with Izzie's quick thinking and her assertive words towards her husband, merely added, "Yes, do your best to keep a lid on it, Peter, will you?"

"Don't worry about it," Peter replied. "I've already told the staff they will probably lose their jobs if they repeat that name anywhere outside this building, even on their phones."

"Good man," Ross nodded at him.

"We just popped in so I can let you know I might be late getting in tonight," Drake informed her husband.

"When I heard what they'd brought in, I knew it was the case you were called out to in the night, so I already assumed this could be a very long day for you. Don't worry, I'll have something ready for you to eat when you get home. Just give me a call when you can to give me an indication of when that might be, okay?"

"Okay, see you later," Drake said as she bent down and gave her husband a kiss on his cheek, and she and Ross then left him to get on with his work as they headed back to police headquarters. As Peter Foster had succinctly observed, they knew this was likely to be a long, long, working day.

Chapter 5

Identity

"At least the trains are running again," Tony Curtis commented at the end of the latest team briefing.

Two days had passed, and Ross and his people had still been unable to make a positive identification of the victim of the bloody body dump at Mossley Hill Station. The partial fingerprint had proved of no use to them, as the victim, as far as could be ascertained, had no police record anywhere in the UK, adding credence to Ross's belief that the man had been, as Doctor Neve suggested, an American, based on the dental work present on the man's disfigured but still intact jaw. Sarah Neve had taken the time to explain to Ross that, contrary to popular belief, human teeth are not, in fact, pure white as is popularly supposed but are in fact a shade of off-white, almost cream in colour. The beautiful, pristine white teeth so beloved of models and film celebrities are in fact a result of cosmetic vanity, as also perpetrated by expensive dentists on anyone eager with the money to be able to afford to emulate their favourite actors and their toothy role models. In fact, she'd pointed out, in general, the teeth of the average UK citizen were in fact regularly found to be healthier, overall than those of their American counterparts. This, she asserted was a scientific fact. As interesting as this might be, it did nothing to help Ross's case and he mentally filed it under 'useless information.'

Having reached a compromise with Doctor Nugent regarding photographing the cadaver on his slab, the police photographer had been allowed to take a photograph of the face in profile, the section of the neck exhibiting the fatal knife wound having been airbrushed out before being passed to the Police Liaison Officer. Ross's old friend, George Thompson had sent to the local news-hounds a press release which together with the photo, asked the question, *'Do you know this man?'*

So far, they'd drawn a complete blank and Curtis's quip about the trains running again through Mossley Hill being nothing more than a poor attempt to lighten the mood of doom and gloom and general despondency that had befallen the detectives. They were not used to finding it so difficult to identify the victim of a serious crime, especially murder.

"Yes, they started again last night," Dodds confirmed, a soon as Miles Booker gave the scene a forensic all-clear."

"Didn't they find anything at all?" Ginger Devenish asked.

"Nada, zilch, bugger all," Sam Gable added.

"Very lady-like, "said Curtis.

"Alright, cut it out," came the voice of Detective Chief Inspector Oscar Agostini, the overall commander of the Specialist Murder Investigation Team, who'd entered the room quietly as Ross brought the briefing to a close.

"Morning, sir," Ross spoke in greeting to his one-time partner, now his boss.

"Morning Andy, everybody," he replied.

The assembled squad members acknowledged the D.C.I. in various phrases and hand waves.

"To what do we owe this pleasure?" Ross inquired.

Agostini smiled and walked to the front of the briefing room where he stood beside Andy Ross and Izzie Drake.

"I just received a call from a D.I. Newcombe at Birkenhead. He thinks he may have a name for our railway victim. A woman walked into the station over the water to report her husband missing. Seems she hasn't seen any newspapers or TV news bulletins over the last two days. Newcombe is pretty convinced she's probably been out of her head on drugs of some kind. He said she looks a bit 'tarty' as he put it, but the general description of her husband seems to fit with our unknown victim, and... he's American."

A ripple of comments and murmurs circulated around the briefing room as Agostini's news seemed to bring the squad to life. Andy Ross felt a quick adrenalin surge at the thought of finally getting to grips with the case.

"That's good news," he said to Agostini. "What the victim's name, sir?"

His name, Andy, is Joey Slimani, a native New Yorker. His wife is a bit of a looker, according to D.I. Newcombe, but I couldn't help a bit of a laugh to myself when he told me her name."

"Okay, I'll bite, what's her name?" Ross asked.

"The widow's name, ladies and gents, is Trixie Mae Bluebell Slimani, known professionally as Trixie Mae Bluebell."

The room burst into almost unanimous laughter at Agostini's news.

"What the hell kind of name is that?" Tony Curtis fired at the D.C.I.

"Sounds like a porn star to me," Nick Dodds offered at which Oscar Agostini held a hand up to call for silence. Andy Ross caught on quickly.

"That's what she is, isn't it?" he looked into Agostini's eyes, receiving the confirmation he required from the look he received in reply.

Agostini gave a kind of forced cough, and then spoke again.

"D.C Dodds is actually right on the nail," he said. "Mrs. Slimani did in fact refer to herself to D.I Newcombe as an actress, 'in the adult entertainment industry' as she put it.

"A porn star then," Dodds repeated.

"Isn't that what I just said, D.C. Dodds?"

"Yes, of course you did, sir," Nick Dodds grinned.

"What about her husband, sir? Izzie Drake asked the important question. "What did he do for a living?"

Agostini managed to look slightly embarrassed as his face reddened. Andy Ross could feel his friend was uncomfortable but could do nothing to help him out.

"It would appear her husband was well known in the pornography world," Agostini almost stumbled over the words. In his younger days he was an actor and went under the name..." he hesitated... "erm, Dick Hardman."

The room exploded into raucous laughter at this revelation. Even Sam Gable, Sofie Meyer and Izzie Drake failed to suppress the giggles that accompanied the D.C.I.'s words. Agostini wasn't finished, however. "According to the wife, her husband had given up appearing in front of the camera when they married four years ago. He then began a new and quite lucrative career as a producer and director of what she described to Newcombe as high-grade adult movies. He used the name Joe Slim Productions for his new company and apparently, he has become a very wealthy man as a result of his new venture. His films are in great demand, it would seem."

"I bet they are," Curtis quipped.

"Anyway, Agostini continued, "It seems Joey left home on the morning of his murder, saying he had an important meeting planned with a new contact, who could help in expanding the distribution of his 'products' as she described them. She never saw him again."

"Why didn't she report him missing earlier?" Ross asked.

"Well, Andy, D.I. Newcombe asked the same question and she said it wasn't unusual for her husband to disappear for a day or two now and again, if he found what she called 'interesting people or developments' during the course of his work."

"In other words, he was either off his head on drugs somewhere, or laying some prospective star for his next porno production," Ross responded. "I'm expecting Doctor Nugent to call me with the results of the toxicology report on the remains later today. That could be very interesting."

"I think you're right about that, Andy," said the D.C.I. "Anyway, it was a little unusual when it got to this morning and she still hadn't heard from him. She tried his mobile phone, got no answer, in fact it appeared to be turned off, something he never did. She looked in his work diary and found the number for the person he was supposed to have met and guess what?"

"No reply and phone turned off," Izzie Drake suggested.

"You've got it in one," Agostini confirmed.

"So, it looks like our victim was lured to a meeting by someone as yet unknown who had him set up for murder, again, for reasons also unknown," Ross conjectured.

"That's how I see things, too," Agostini nodded to Ross. "I suggest you and Izzie hightail it across the river to Birkenhead and see what you can glean from Mrs. Trixie Slimani."

"Right you are, sir," Ross beckoned to Drake who rose from her seat and moved to join him. Before they left the room, he turned to the rest of the team.

"Paul, Kat," he said to Ferris and Bellamy, start an in-depth search on those super-computers of yours. Find out all you can about Joey Slimani, Dick Hardman, Joe Slim Productions and Trixie Mae Bluebell."

"Right sir, we're on it," Paul Ferris replied.

"What about the rest of us, sir?" Sofie Meyer asked.

"Okay, Sofie, I want you, Tony and Nick to hit the local sex shops. There's a fair few in the city. Find me some samples of any *'Joe Slim Productions'* and bring them back here, unopened, of course."

"Okay, sir," Meyer nodded, while Curtis and Dodds looked a little disappointed at Ross's last words."

"Sam and Ginger, take out a pool car and follow Izzie and me to Birkenhead. Once we arrive to interview the widow, I want the two of you to make a few discreet inquiries with the nearby residents. See if you can build up a picture of what our pair of pornographers were like as neighbours. Did they have a lot of visitors, any odd comings and goings at odd times of the night, that kind of thing. We're all assuming that just because they were in the porn industry they must also have been into the drugs scene. Don't assume anything. We need facts before we go busting the balls of local known suppliers. Did D.I.

Newcombe tell you if he's done anything about arranging official identification of the remains, sir," the last question directed at Agostini.

"Sorry, no, Andy. As we're taking over the case he thought we should take charge of that little job too."

"Great," Ross grumbled. "That's not going to be a very pleasant job. Right then, everyone, let's go to it."

Ross and Drake left the briefing room first, followed quickly by the rest of the team, as they all went in to action to begin their investigation in earnest. Now, at least, they had a name and something to build their case around. Truth be told, Curtis and Dodds couldn't wait to get to grips with the case now. There was, after all, something intrinsically titillating about having to carry out an investigation into the pornographic industry, at least from the two red-blooded males' point of view. Knowing how their red-blooded minds would be working, that was the reason he'd sent them with Sofie Meyer to trawl the city's sex shops. With the sergeant in charge, they would be forced to keep their minds on the job.

In no time, once they'd all departed, the only sounds that could be heard emanating from the nearby squad room were the tap, tap, tap of the fingers of Paul Ferris and Kat Bellamy as they began their computer search for anything and anything to do with the victim, his wife and his movie production company.

Chapter 6

Trixie Mae Bluebell Slimani

Weak winter sunshine greeted Ross and Drake as they emerged from the Queensway tunnel, connecting Liverpool with Birkenhead. With Ross at the wheel, they followed the A552 for a short distance before turning onto Storeton Road, officially the B5151 heading in the direction of South Mersey Golf Club. Following directions provided by D.I. Newcombe from the Birkenhead Station, they soon reached a left turn that led them along a narrow lane, which opened out to reveal a large, almost mansion type private home dead ahead of them, partially hidden by a row of Elm trees, that held between them a pair of wrought-iron gates, painted in quite garish, metallic gold, gloss paint. A sign attached to one of the two supporting concrete gate pillars read, *Paradise Found.*

"Bloody Hell, now that can only be the home of a porn king and queen," Izzie Drake commented as they stopped at the closed gates.

"Would you like to do the honours?" Ross asked his sergeant, as he indicated the presence of an intercom affixed to the passenger-side gate-supporting pillar.

"Bit weird to have it on the left side, don't you think? Drivers would have to get out of their car and walk around to operate it," Drake observed.

"Hmm, unless," Ross mused.

"Unless what?"

"Two possible reasons I can think of. One, he was American, so it could be a basic design flaw in as much he had it placed there as if he was back home, where they drive on the right. So, drivers would be in the left-hand seat and therefore it would make sense to him to have the intercom there. Two, maybe it was deliberately put on that side to make sure that any lone driver would have to exit their vehicle and walk round to the intercom, placing them in full view of the security camera I just noticed mounted on the trunk of that tall tree over there,"

"And there's another one over there." Drake pointed to a tree on the opposite side of the driveway, beyond the gates. Not waiting for further comment from Ross, she exited the car and walked up to the intercom, cleverly mounted high enough to ensure the occupant of a car would have to leave their vehicle to reach it, thus revealing themselves clearly to the camera, pressing the button to request entry to the property.

After identifying herself and Ross to a mechanical-sounding voice over the intercom, the gates slowly swung open and with Drake once again seated beside him, Ross slowly drove along a long, sweeping driveway that curved first to the left and then to the right, cleverly designed so that the house itself only came into view when visitors were almost on top of it, figuratively speaking. That is, because the house itself, with a circular, gravel driveway, that adjoined the tarmacadam main drive, sat like something like from a Disney fantasy, towering above them. Before reaching it, they both marvelled at the softly gurgling marble fountain that stood in the centre of the gravel parking area, before Ross pulled up next to a gleaming red Ford Mustang, with private plates which read TR 1XE, clearly the property of the lady of the house. The house itself was what Ross could only describe as "Bloody horrible."

Three stories high, it appeared to have been built from genuine Cotswold Stone, fashioned to resemble a crenelated mansion, but with a mixture of styles that did nothing to impress the policeman or his partner. Gargoyles hung from the walls, and chimneys looked as if they'd been stuck on to the black-tiled roof randomly, as if most of them had no connection with the rooms below. The upper floor was fitted with windows that resembled something from Castle Dracula, arched and fitted with leaded lights, reducing visibility for anyone looking out. The windows on the two lower stories were large but, from the outside, Ross failed to see how, if at all, they could be opened from the inside. He sincerely hoped the Slimanis had air-conditioning.

As he and Drake walked up to the front door, a black solid wood monstrosity that would have looked quite at home at the entrance to the aforementioned Castle Dracula, Ross reached out, ready to use the brass door knocker, shaped like a Chinese dragon, to announce their presence, but was saved from doing so as the door swung slowly open.

Ross and Drake simultaneously did a quick double-take as they were greeted by a man they presumed to be some sort of manservant. He was aged between forty and fifty and wore a uniform that resembled a butler's traditional attire, with certain differences. Instead of a collar and tie, the man wore a black, studded dog collar and his jacket, which had shorter than normal sleeves revealed wrists which were clad in black leather cuffs, which had steel rings in them and which could clearly be used as some form of restraint, if required. His face was almost expressionless as he spoke in a deep, gravelly voice, reminding Ross of a character from an old TV programme he used to watch, *Tales of the Crypt.*

"And you are?" Ross had to ask.

"Jennings, sir. I'm the mistress's personal manservant."

"I just bet he is," Drake whispered to Ross as they followed the man across the expansive, marbled entrance hall, both not failing to notice the curved, marble staircase that led off from the hall towards the upper floors of the house,

"In here, please," Jennings beckoned the pair as he opened a large, panelled door and stepped to one side to permit them to enter before him. As the detectives entered, he quietly closed the heavy door behind them, he announces in that distinctive voice, straight from the graveyard of Ross's dreams, "Detective Inspector Ross and Detective Sergeant Drake, Mistress."

The use of the word 'mistress' rather than 'madam' 'ma'am' or some other traditional form of servant to employer address, left Ross wondering just what other services Jennings might perform for Mrs. Trixie Slimani, who now walked towards them from where she'd been standing beside a large fireplace, which housed a roaring log fire, and warmed the large room more than adequately.

The first thing that struck Andy Ross about the newly-widowed Mrs. Slimani was her size, she was tiny, no more than five feet tall, slimly-built, no more than a UK size 8, with breasts that bore no relation to her height and build. It was clear, even to Ross, that the woman had undergone breast augmentation surgery, probably as an aid to her career in the adult movie industry. The woman looked, at first sight to be no more than about twenty to twenty-five years old, but as she drew closer, Ross could see was in fact a few years older than he'd first thought. Make-up had done a wonderful job in knocking years off her age, he decided. Wearing a short black mini-dress that was struggling to cover her bottom and all points south of her bikini line in fact, with high-heeled black patent-leather shoes, she was clearly doing her best to achieve a widow-look, though somehow not quite carrying it off.

Izzie Drake, meanwhile had taken a quick look at the woman as she approached them, but also allowed her eyes to wander to scan the walls and furnishings of the room in which they stood. The marble floor, identical to the one in the entrance hall, was covered in thick, plush carpeting and various rugs in an eclectic mix of colours, ranging from black to bright yellow to pale, pastel cream. On the walls, which were stark white with black panelling every few feet, hung several pictures, though not the type one would normally expect to find in a typical home. Izzie could barely pull her eyes from the selection of what appeared to be promotional posters for what she presumed to be several of her husband's movie productions, or in a few cases, perhaps stills from some of Trixie's own career in the porn industry.

This is like being in some perverted sheikh's harem, she thought to herself.

"So, you guys are the police?" Trixie said, the question being wholly rhetorical as Jennings had already introduced them as such. She held a hand out to Ross, who wasn't sure if he was expected to shake it or kiss it. He settled for a quick handshake and couldn't help noticing that the woman held on to his hand a little longer than would be consider usual in such cases.

"Yes, Mrs. Slimani, I'm so sorry for your loss," he said, his voice as sympathetic as he could make it.

"Yeah, poor Joey. I'm in total shock. Who the hell did this to my husband, Mr. Ross? You guys got any ideas yet?

"I'm sorry, as we only found out your husband's identity when D.I. Newcombe from the police station here in Birkenhead contacted us, I'm afraid our investigation has really only just begun."

"Yeah, I guess that's to be expected. What can you tell me about how he died? The guy, Newcombe, he wouldn't tell me much, except to say he's found dead on a railway track near Liverpool, but Joey never used trains, Mr. Ross. He has a damn fleet of cars and two limos at his disposal."

Ignoring the woman's repeated use of the term Mister, while addressing him, Ross tried to steer the conversation into productive mode.

"You told D.I. Newcombe that the last time you saw your husband on the morning of the 15th, he was heading to a business meeting. Is that correct?"

"Oh wow, I love the way you guys talk. Yeah, well, sorry, oh yeah, that's right. He left at around eleven that morning. I never heard from him again."

For the first time, there appeared to be tears forming in Trixie's eyes.

"Do you know who he was supposed to be meeting?" Drake asked her.

"No, he just said it was important. I never pried into Joey's business. He knew what he was doing, see."

"Did he say when he'd be back?"

"No, the last thing he said to me was, "See you later, Babe. Keep it warm for me. That was kinda our own little private joke, if you know what I mean."

"I think I catch your drift," Drake nodded, knowing exactly what Trixie meant.

"How long had you been married to Joey?" Ross inquired.

"Three years last August," Trixie replied. "We met on the set of one of his movies. He liked what he saw, and with Joey, well, it was a case of what Joey liked, Joey got."

"How many, erm…movies did you make with Joey?" Drake asked.

"I made fourteen movies under Joey, and twenty-six before we met."

"And how old are you, Mrs. Slimani?"

"Twenty-six," she replied.

"And Joey was?"

"Thirty-five," which came out sounding like *"Thuyty-five,"*

"You're from New York, I take it, Mrs. Slimani," Ross observed, having placed her accent.

"Yeah, that's right. Born and raised in Manhattan."

"Think carefully now," Ross went on. "Can you think of anyone who might have had a grudge against your husband, a reason for wanting to harm him."

"My Joey, no sir. He was a real pussycat, everyone loved the guy, even his ex-wives."

Ross's ears pricked up at her words.

"How many ex-wives did Joey have?"

"Two," the widow replied. "There was Mary-Beth, she was number one, but goes by the name of Mary Honey professionally, and then Lana, she's Lana Love in the business."

"I take it they were both porn actresses too?" Drake asked her next.

"Yeah, they were. Mary-Beth and Joey married while he was acting, you know? He told me they did some scenes together and felt like they had this kinda chemistry between them, so they got hitched when he was twenty-five, and she was, like nineteen. Trouble was, she was a real popular girl, and Joey, who never believed he could get jealous, just couldn't handle her fucking all those guys once they'd tied the knot."

"So, why didn't he ask her to give up the movie scene?"

"Listen Sergeant, it's obvious you guys got no idea about our business. Do you have any idea how much money a girl can make in a year, compared to a guy?"

"I have no idea," Drake admitted.

"Okay, let me explain. When guys watch a porno film, what do they wanna see? Pretty girls, right? Pretty girls spreading their legs, bending over, whatever. Doing it with well-hung studs, or maybe with other girls. Do they give a shit who the guy is or what he looks like? No way. So though there are some well-known studs in the business, most of them big black guys, well-hung and with muscles like Schwarzenegger, it's the girls who earn the big bucks. The guys earn peanuts compared with the girls. I've known girls of eighteen, nineteen, earning over a hundred grand a year, depending on how many scenes they're prepared to do, and just what skills they're prepared to show."

"I'm sorry, I'm not sure I know what you mean by 'skills' in this context," Ross queried and then almost wished he hadn't.

"You really are a bit naïve Inspector, ain't ya? Look, a girl who just does straight sex ain't ever gonna make the big bucks okay? No, the audiences these days want more, anal, oral, two or three-way sex, double penetration, girl on girl, orgy scenes, and for those who are willing to do cream-pie scenes there's real big money to be made."

"Cream-pie scenes?" Izzie asked, already blushing.

"Yeah, you know, girls who will let the guy ejaculate in them on camera, maybe in her pussy or in her ass. Real big bucks there, let me tell you."

Ross and Drake didn't know where to look. They were both totally embarrassed by Trixie's quite open and explicit description of the porn industry and it's workings.

"Yes, well, I suppose what you're saying is that Joey kind of lived off the earnings of his wives, is that right?"

"You got it," Trixie nodded her head, "but once Joey had enough cash, he set up by himself, producing and directing his own shit, you know? He was darn good at it too. Made some real classics and you know what? He still took care of Mary-Beth and Lana."

"And you didn't mind that?"

"Hell, no. We had plenty, just look at this place. Those girls were like me in many ways, they'd earned whatever he could do for them. Hell, Inspector, honey, they were still making movies with him. Why would they wanna hurt him?"

Ross could scarcely believe it.

"And you, Trixie? Are you still...?

"Making movies? Why sure, honey, why not? You don't think I'm gonna give up making those big bucks while I'm still young enough to demand big fees, do you?"

Ross couldn't think of a suitable reply to that one so instead tried to change the subject.

"Do you know where his two former wives are right now?

"L.A. New York, who knows? They are both working, I do know that, 'cos Joey has showed me some of their work. There's a big market for older women you know? What we call MILFs. Mary-Beth did a lot of BDSM stuff at one time. I guess she's still doing it. That's *Moms I'd like to f...*"

"I get the picture," Ross cut her off, though he guessed both women would be, at most, late twenties or early thirties, not exactly old, but then, he imagined this must be predominantly a young person's business. As for the BDSM reference, that was one term he was aware of.

"Have either Mary-Beth or Lana remarried, Trixie?" Drake asked, having been mostly silent throughout the interview. In truth, she'd found most of what Joey Slimani's widow had told them so far to be shocking in its content, and indeed in the woman's honesty in describing the business in which she and her husband had made a very obviously lucrative living.

"No, well not at least as far as I know. If they had, Joey would have known about it and he'd have told me."

"Well, anyway, Trixie, I know it won't be nice for you, but the law here in England requires an official identification of your husband's body and we were hoping…"

"Yeah, sure, I understand you got your laws and such. When d'you want me to do it?"

"Will tomorrow be okay?" he asked.

"Yeah, sure. Just tell me where and when?"

"I'll call you later if that's okay. I can arrange a car to come and pick you up and take you to the medical examiner's office if you'd like."

"Hell no, don't you go troublin' yourself with things like that. I can find my own way there, or if I don't feel like driving, I can get Jennings to drive me there."

"One last question for now," Ross had saved this till last. "Why did you and your husband decide to settle here in England?"

"Hell, that's easy. We were in L.A, Inspector, where most of the industry is centred, but it's a real cutthroat business and the bigger producers and studios were squeezin' us dry. Joey said Europe was the place to be. We get girls from Russia, Germany and France and from good old Great Britain too, so we looked around and found this little piece of land and Joey had this place built. It was supposed to be our dream home. We even have our own recording suite up on the top floor. Do you guys want to see it?"

"Not just now, thanks," Ross replied, "but we may want to take a look at some time in the future."

"No problem," Trixie was actually sobbing quietly now. "You say when, I'll show you around."

"Before we do anything else, I'll make arrangements for you to be met at the mortuary, if you'll be kind enough to let me know what time you expect to be there. Then, I'd like it if you would accompany the officer who meets you there to police headquarters where we can take a formal statement from you," Ross said, summoning as much sympathy as he could for the woman. Whether he approved of her lifestyle and choice of career was irrelevant, he reminded himself. For now, she was the widow of a murder victim and would be accorded the respect her position demanded.

He and Drake then wrapped up the interview with Teresa (Trixie) Slimani as quickly as possible and were soon heading back through the Mersey Tunnel to Liverpool, and, as they both saw it, a semblance of normality.

"Was that real?" Drake asked as they drove along at a sensible speed, trying to assimilate all they'd learned about the world of their victim.

"I know," Ross agreed. "All that stuff about how those women make their money, and how leeches like Slimani virtually live off their earnings, like bloody high-class pimps."

"She would never see it that way though, would she?"

"No Izzie, you're right. To her, it's a career, having sex with God knows how many men in a year, simply because, as she sees it, it's all part of the bloody movie business."

"I've never had reason to get involved with the porn industry before, but it strikes me those girls are even more exploited than the poor women who are forced into prostitution on the streets."

"You'll never convince them of that, Izzie. To be fair, it sounds like they make a whole load of money, and I don't think anyone really forces them into it."

"Maybe not where Trixie comes from, but what about the Russian mafia and all these Eastern European gangsters that are coming over here and causing mayhem? We know they force girls into virtual slavery as prostitutes, so I wonder how many end up being forced to make porn films too?"

"Good point," Ross was forced to agree, and the pair fell into a silent reverie as they completed the short journey back to headquarters, where they first reported the results of their interview with Trixie Slimani to D.C.I. Oscar Agostini. Ross was also eager to learn whether Sam Gable and Ginger Devenish had discovered anything during their own visit to Birkenhead.

Chapter 7

Golf Club Blues

"Looks like we've got a tricky one on our hands, Andy," D.C.I. Oscar Agostini said, after Ross and Drake had spent just over twenty minutes filling him in on their meeting with Trixie Slimani. "I can honestly say even I'm a little in the dark when it comes to the porn movie industry. I know it's all legal and above board nowadays, but there still seems to be a hint of sleaze attached to anything to do with it, at least in my mind, anyway. Or, am I just being prudish?

"Hell no, Oscar. Me and Izzie couldn't wait to get out of that house, right Izzie?" Ross replied.

"Too right," Drake agreed. "The way that woman spoke, sir, it was like she and her husband didn't even think there was anything strange about her having sex with dozens of men a month, simply because they look on sex as a saleable commodity and the fact that they make a hell of a lot of money from it seems to lift them out of the normal moral restrictions most of us would feel at the thought of it. I mean, who has bloody great posters of themselves having sex with different men plastered all over the walls of their home?"

"A very good point, Sergeant Drake, who indeed" Agostini agreed. "So, what do you plan to do next, Andy?"

"I've already got two officers making enquiries about the Slimanis over in Birkenhead. They should be back any time soon. I want to see what Paul Ferris has found out from his computer search and we might have to get in touch with the police in New York and Los Angeles, because we're going to have to speak to the two ex-wives. Who knows what motives either of them might have had for wanting Joey out of the way?"

"But I thought the wife said her husband was still taking care of them?"

"With the money these women can make from their 'acting' careers, my take on Joey 'taking care' of them could well mean he's been active in making sure they got plenty of work in the business," Ross replied.

"I was thinking the same thing," Drake added. "Maybe we should have asked Trixie if he employed Mary-Beth and Lana in his own movies."

"We can ask her tomorrow when she comes in to give her statement," Ross decided.

"Okay, Andy," Agostini brought their meeting to a close. "Keep me posted on progress and please, keep those calls to the USA to a minimum. You'll be costing the force a fortune in international calls if this case goes on too long.

Ross laughed and promised to do his best. Before long, he and Drake were back in his own small office, where they'd been joined by Sam Gable and 'Ginger' Devenish, recently returned from their fact-finding trip to Birkenhead.

"So, tell me, what, if anything did you manage to learn from the locals?" Ross prompted the pair, and it was Sam Gable who immediately replied.

"Not too much, I'm afraid," she began. "As you and Izzie no doubt found out for yourselves, the Slimani residence is not exactly overlooked by any near-neighbours so there weren't too many people we could talk to who knew them personally. We did, however pay a visit to the nearby golf club. Now that proved a little more interesting."

"Go on, surprise me," Ross grinned.

"You tell 'em, Ginge," Sam said, leaving Devenish to continue their narrative.

"Well sir, I suggested we call at South Mersey Golf Club, based on my thoughts that Americans tend to be obsessed with playing golf. Sam agreed so we walked into the clubhouse and asked to speak to the Club Captain, figuring if anyone knew Joey Slimani, he'd be the man to talk to. The Captain, Graham Bull, was happy to talk to us about the man he thought was something of a celebrity. Slimani was indeed a member of the golf club and had told the members he was a movie producer alright, but not of pornographic films. He told them he made art films, the kind that win prizes at festivals and so on. That let him get away without having to name films they have heard of. After all, who watches most of the crap that goes under the name of 'art' nowadays."

Devenish was about to carry on but was interrupted by a sudden fit of coughing. Sam Gable took over.

"When we informed him that Slimani was in fact a well-known producer of porn movies and a former porn actor to boot, Mr. Bull was shocked, to say the least. He immediately said he would be making moves to have Mr. Slimani expelled from the club. When I told him the man had been murdered, he was shocked yet again, and almost had a fit. I got the feeling it was a bit put on though, you know, like he really knew what Slimani did, but didn't want to admit it to us in case it reflected badly on his precious golf club."

"We've never had anything like this connected to our club," he whined, as if the bloody golf club was going to be tainted by having one of its members murdered, especially as he was a porn movie producer.

"Not to mention the fact he could barely take his eyes off Sam's breasts himself, the old perv," Devenish added quickly.

"My fault, I suppose," Sam giggled, "for being born a woman."

"Sounds like a real stuck-up ould get," Ross said, using the local vernacular.

"Too right, sir," Sam agreed. "Anyway, we ascertained that he'd only met Mrs. Slimani once, at the club's President's Day function.

Brian L. Porter

"Pretty young thing," was his way of describing her, Devenish added.

"You should have seen his face when I told him she was a porn actress too," Sam could barely contain her laughter. "I thought he was going to have a heart attack."

"Me too," Devenish added. "One more thing, though, sir."

"What is it, Ginge?" Ross urged, as Devenish seemed to hesitate.

"Slimani was at the club last week, sir, on the Thursday, two days before his death. Mr. Bull told us he'd seen him with two guests in the bar, and when he checked, he found that the two men had played a round with Slimani and in accordance with club rules they had had to give their details before being accepted as guests for the day. He went away and came back with a leather-backed ledger, which proved to the club's visitors book and he was able to give us the names of both men."

Ross felt a small surge of excitement. Could it be that these were the men who must have lured Joey Slimani to his death? Or would they prove to be guilty of nothing more than being associated with the dead man?

"You got their names, then?"

"Yes, sir. Descriptions too, from a man called Dykes, who Bull called over from the bar in the clubhouse. Dykes remembered serving them that day, and I have a very good description of both here in my notebook."

"Their names, Ginger," Ross asked.

"Raymond Milland and Sydney Greenstreet, sir."

Ross groaned and allowed his head to fall forward, into his hands. Sensing all was not well, Sam Gable asked if he was okay.

"Ray Milland and Sydney Greenstreet were famous actors back in the nineteen forties and fifties, both long dead, now. Those men conned the golf club and they fell for it. That means they may well be the men we're after in connection with the murder, but those names mean shit, I'm afraid."

"Shit, sorry sir", Gable and Devenish looked a little crestfallen, Sam Gable especially.

49

"Not your fault, don't worry about it. Not everyone of your generation is into old black-and-white movies from before you were born. Sadly though, those two men could have been the killers, or maybe genuine friends of Slimani. I hope you got their descriptions."

"Right here, sir," Gable replied instantly, tapping her notebook as she did so.

"Okay, we need to circulate the descriptions and I can use them to try and find out if Trixie Slimani recognises them, when she comes in to identify her husband."

Their conversation was interrupted by the shrill sound of Ross's desk phone. Gable and Devenish moved to leave the office, but Ross made a hand motion to indicate they should stay where they were. If it was information pertaining to their case they might as well hear it sooner rather than later.

"Inspector Ross, ma friend," the voice of Doctor William Nugent boomed over the phone. "Ah have some interesting news for you."

"I take it you've got the toxicology reports back from the lab, huh, Doc?"

"Correct, and you might be surprised to hear yer man's system was heavily loaded with flunitrazepam, more commonly known as Rohypnol."

"The so-called date-rape drug?"

"One and the same. There was enough left in his system to indicate he would have been easy to subdue prior to his killer cutting the poor man's throat."

"Well, that does make things interesting, Doc, thanks. It definitely indicates this was a premeditated murder and not a spur of the moment thing, a falling out or something similar. Whoever killed Joey Slimani planned his murder meticulously and made sure he was totally compliant before finishing him off. Anything else of interest?"

"Aye, there is. His blood-alcohol level was seriously elevated. As you probably know, the legal limit for driving is 80 milligrams of alcohol per 100 millilitres of blood. Your victim showed at 95 milligrams, so he would have been well on the way to being quite intoxicated at the time of his death."

"Thanks, Doc," Ross replied. "That it?

"Not quite," the pathologist sounded almost effusive as he reeled off his list. "Mr. Slimani also had a couple of other recreational drugs in his bloodstream, namely heroin and oxycodone, an opiod painkiller widely abused in the USA, where it's often known as 'Hillbilly Heroin.' From the levels shown in the tox screen he would definitely not have known too much about what was happening to him at the end."

"Whoever did this wasn't taking any chances, were they?" Ross spoke his thoughts aloud before thanking Nugent, hanging up the phone, and relating the content of his conversation to Drake, Gable and Devenish.

Next to return to headquarters were Sofie Meyer, Tony Curtis and Nick Dodds.

"Enjoy your shopping trip?" Drake asked as the three arrived back in the squad room.

"It was interesting, to say the least," Meyer replied, smiling. "The boys seemed to very interested in some of the products on display in the establishments we visited.

"Bloody hell, Sarge," Tony Curtis spoke up before Nick Dodds could get a word in. "You wouldn't believe the stuff those shops sell. No wonder they black out the windows."

"Do you mean to tell me you've never been in a sex shop before today, Tony?" Ross surprised Curtis by walking up behind him after silently exiting his office.

"Oh, hi Boss. No, never, honest."

"Me neither Boss," Dodds concurred.

"My, my, you two do surprise me," Ross was smiling. "Did you manage to keep these two under control without too much trouble, Sofie?"

"I must say they were very diligent in their task, sir," Meyer smiled in return.

"I bet they were," Izzie Drake added.

"Oh yes, they were scrupulous in their search for films starring Trixie Mae Bluebell and Dick Hardman, and any made by Joe Slim Productions."

"And did they find any?" Ross asked her.

"Oh yes," Meyer held up a plain white carrier bag, from which she extricated five DVDs. "We were successful in finding these, sir, though the proprietor of one shop told us that we would find many more if we search the online porn sites that have sprung up recently. Apparently, many of the companies who make these films place clips from many of their movies on these sites and make them free for the public to view."

"Paul?" Ross prompted his Sergeant computer expert.

"I'm on it, Boss." Ferris replied.

"No need for you to have to sit through that stuff, Kat," Ross assured the team's admin assistant. Kat Bellamy wiped a hand across her brow and simply said, "Phew, thanks Boss. Not really my idea of fun."

"Totally understood," Ross smiled at her. "You, my dear Sofie are not getting off so lightly. You're in charge of Tony and Nick. I don't want a blow by blow account of those films you brought back. What I do want, if any of them supply the information, are the names of the actors, male and female, and directors, producers, anyone who had any connection to the dead man and his wife. I know they might not use their real names but I'm sure we can track then down if we need to."

"Very well, sir," Meyer replied. "And how long do you want us to investigate these movies?"

"Just as long it takes to extract the information we require. It may not help much but we're pretty much in the dark at present regarding motive. I think if there's anything in those films that will help us, it will be in the more recent films so ignore any that you've bought that date back more than, say, five years. I can't see anyone waiting that long to carry out some sort of revenge or whatever."

"Okay, sir. We'll do our best."

"And you two," Ross glared at Curtis and Dodds, be professional about this. No schoolboy antics, understood?"

"Yes, sir!" Curtis and Dodds spoke in unison.

Ten minutes later, Ross and Drake were holding a brief meeting in his office.

"What d'you really think happened to Joey Slimani, sir?" Izzie asked.

"At this stage, it's all guesswork, Izzie. Is his murder personal, or is it connected to the business he was in? It's easy for us to jump to conclusions and think that, just because he was in the pornographic movie business there must be something sleazy surrounding his death. But, we can't jump to that conclusion. I mean, it's not like he was some Russian gangster forcing young girls into prostitution or making them act in his movies. From what Trixie told us, these women are well-paid professionals. Okay, they like sex and are willing to do it on camera for the titivation of thousands of men around the world, but also, like she said, they earn damn good money for doing something they enjoy."

"I know," Drake turned her face up at the thoughts of what Trixie had told them. "But it surely takes a special kind of woman to want to do those things with so many men, on film, you know? I mean, anal, BDSM, getting whipped or tortured on film, it's not normal is it?"

"Not to us, no, but to them? You know as well as I do that it takes all sorts to make up this damn crazy world we live in today. I think, going back to your question, we need to try and find out who the men were that met Joey at South Mersey Golf Club last week. They may or may not be involved in his murder, but they may be aware of some reason why he was marked for death by someone. The fact they booked in to the clubhouse under assumed names shows us that, if nothing else, they didn't want to be identified."

"So, we make finding them a priority, right?" Drake asked.

"We do, Izzie. I want to see what Paul and Kat have discovered about Slimani and his business before we go any further. Then we try and find out who hated him enough to drug and sedate him before cutting his throat so deeply they almost took off his head before the train got the opportunity to do so."

Chapter 8

Background

Beckoned by Sergeant Paul Ferris, Ross strode across the room to the computer stations where Ferris and Kat Bellamy could be seen visibly working hard at their allotted tasks.

"Got something for me, Paul?" Ross asked as he was joined by Izzie Drake.

"Been looking into Joey and Trixie Slimani's backgrounds as you requested," Ferris replied. Might be an idea to get the others to hear this too."

"Everyone, come and hear this," Ross called out and the other detectives present in the room dropped what they were doing and walked across to join him and Drake in a group gathered around Ferris and Bellamy. Sofie Meyer, together with Tony Curtis and Nick Dodds, abandoned their viewing of a DVD, and Sam Gable and Ginger Devenish completed the group.

"Joseph Mohammed Slimani, born New York, March 1970, parents second generation Algerian immigrants." Ferris began. "Attended school diligently by all accounts and graduated from William Marshall High School. No trouble, popular kid, good looking by all accounts if you look at his high school photos. Cutting out the boring stuff, he was interested in cinematography from an early age but lacked the funds to do anything about his chosen career. Father was a baker and

Joey used to work nights for his dad, helping bake bread and so on ready for the next day. Don't have details of how he entered the porn industry, but at the age of 19 he appeared in his first porn movie and went on to become a regular actor through the following years. He moved to LA and his career took off. The New York police have no record of him ever being involved in any kind of trouble before he left the city. Like most porn actors Joey was probably selected not so much for his acting ability as for the size of his, erm, equipment," Ferris said, trying to spare the blushes of the female members of the team, a tactic quickly rendered redundant when Sam Gable made the comment,

"In other words, he had a big dick, right?"

"Yeah, right," Ferris grinned at her, "and he was known for his ability to sustain his performance for long periods, hence the name Dick Hardman. Seems his parents were appalled when they learned of his new career and he was asked to leave the family home. Joey moved out and within six months he'd married his first wife, Mary-Beth Jordan, a small-time porn actress. With Joey pushing her career along she became well known for specialising in films that featured BDSM elements. It was around that time that Joey made his first film, hiring a studio in L.A. by the day. All his early films featured Mary-Beth, who soon became a star in her own right. Joey was a natural at producing and directing his own movies, even continuing to appear in some of them. The marriage to Mary-Beth ended when Joey took up with one of his regular actresses, Lana Kaminski, and he and Mary-Beth obtained a quickie divorce, so he could marry his latest love interest. I spoke to a Sergeant Drexler at LAPD, boss, as you requested, and he gave me some very interesting intel."

"Okay, Paul. We're all ears, go on, please."

"Well, although the porno film industry is all legal and above board these days, Sergeant Drexler told me that there are still some connections to organised crime present in the business. Some criminal overlords, as he called them, have fingers in many legitimate businesses these days and the fact that the porno movie business is, let's say a little bit on the border between legal and sleazy, the Mob, his word, not mine, do have a few connections in the L.A. end of the market. He told me this because word was that Joey Slimani left the country in something of a hurry when he was pressured by a local crime over-lord, with certain connections, into paying them a premium for being 'allowed' to operate unhindered on their territory."

A concerted murmur spread through the group at Ferris's words.

"Sounds like a spot of extortion to me," Nick Dodds suggested.

"Totally agree with you, Nick. Nothing short of a good old-fashioned protection racket if you ask me."

"Yeah, like *'Pay up or we break your legs'* kind of thing," Izzie added.

"That's just what I thought, and Drexler kind of confirmed it. He said nobody has ever made an official complaint, of course, but the word on the street is that nobody gets away without 'paying their dues' he called it. It's not much, he explained, but it lets the pornog-raphers know that they are operating on the mob's territory and with their say so. Drexler said that, stupid though it sounds, it kind of helps the industry to police itself."

"And what did you discover about the wife?" Ross asked, feeling he knew all he needed to know about Joey for the moment.

"Kat did most of the work on Trixie," Ferris replied, so I'll let her tell you what she found. It's all yours Kat," he said, and Katrina Bellamy cleared her throat and began to deliver the results of her online in-vestigation into the life and times of the newly-widowed wife of Joey Slimani. She couldn't help blushing as she began speaking, whether from some embarrassment at her subject matter or from her natural reticence, Ross couldn't be certain.

"Trixie Mae Bluebell Slimani was born twenty-six years ago in a town called Beaver Dam, in the state of Wisconsin"

D.C. Curtis could barely repress a giggle.

"Something funny, Tony?" Ross growled at him.

"Well, sir, just the name, you know, bearing in mind the lady's pro-fession, Beaver, you know?"

"Alright, Detective Constable. Thank you for displaying your knowledge of American slang expressions. I'm sure we all know what you mean. Please, carry on, Kat."

"Of course, so, she was genuinely christened Trixie Mae, her maiden name being Wallace. Her parents, Daniel and Eileen, left the town and moved to New York when she was eight, I don't have any information on the reason for the move. Her father owned a small hardware store in the city, and the next reference I have about her was when the police had her listed as a runaway at the age of seventeen. Once she'd passed her eighteenth birthday she contacted her parents to tell them she was safe and well and working as an actress in Los Angeles. It was around that time that I found the first references to her working in the adult movie business, where her small size and ability to look younger than her years gave her a certain appeal to the pornographic film makers."

"Yeah, catering to perverts, no doubt," Dodds interrupted. A look from Ross made him clam up.

"You're probably right, Nick," Kat replied to his interjection. "Anyway, by the time she was twenty, she was pretty well-known in the business and starred in a couple of films with Dick Hardman, aka Joey Slimani. They were married when she was twenty-two and the rest, as they say, is history. She still appears in her husband's productions and specialises in certain... erm... activities that appeal to men."

"It's okay, Kat, we don't need the gory details," Ross said, sensing her embarrassment at the idea of expanding on that statement.

"Oh good, thanks. That's really about all I could find out, apart from the fact that she's made over two hundred films over the years, some as short as ten minutes, others up to an hour long, with titles such as *Gang Bang Princess*, *Back Door Pleasures* and *Hard to Please*.

"So, she's had sex with a lot of men in that time," Ross observed. "It's a good job she and her husband saw sex as a job and weren't jealous of the fact they were each sleeping around for profit."

"That is if we accept that to be true, sir," Sofie Meyer interrupted him.

"You have a point, Sofie?"

"Yes, sir. We know Mr. Slimani left his second wife after meeting Trixie, so are we to assume that neither of his ex-wives harboured any animosity towards Slimani or the women who usurped their position in his life and his bed?"

"Good point," Ross agreed. "Can we find out where the ex-wives are now, and maybe get local law enforcement in the States to contact them for us?"

"I can do that, sir," Paul Ferris volunteered.

"Okay, that's one for you then, Paul."

Ross decided they could go no further at that point and brought the proceedings to a close.

"Right people, so far we have the two unidentified men at the golf club. I want them found and interviewed. That's a priority. Sam, and Ginger, make finding those men your number one task. Speak to anyone at South Mersey Golf Club who may have seen or spoke to Joey's guests. Sofie, you and Nick go through those DVDs, learn what you can, but I don't think they are going to be much help in the investigation."

"What about me, sir?" Curtis asked, seeming disappointed to be taken off the 'viewing duty.'

"Tony, when we have Trixie brought in to identify her husband's remains and make her statement, I want you to take her butler or whatever he is, Jennings to one side. See if you can get him to talk about his mistress, as he referred to her when Izzie and I visited the house. Take him to the canteen and maybe he'll spill a little behind the scenes dirt on Joey and Trixie. You can go back to helping Sofie and Nick later."

"No problem Boss. He won't even know he's being questioned, I'll be that subtle."

"Subtle? You, Tony?" Sam Gable laughed out loud.

"About as subtle as a runaway train, more like," Dodds added.

"That's enough, you lot," Ross calmed things down.

"Tony, don't you go letting me down, you hear?"

"Trust me, sir. He won't know he's being pumped for information, I promise."

"Okay, everyone, anything else to add?"

"Yes, sir," Sam Gable had thought of something. "This is just an idea, but, based on the time I spent working with the Vice Squad, although the business we're talking about is legal as we all know, we sometimes heard of girls being imported by the traffickers to be used in the porn industry, though I never personally came across an instance of it. Do you think it might be worth me having a word with my old mates in Vice to see if they know of anything going on? You never know, Joey might have got himself involve with the wrong people over here. He'd obviously got his fingers burned back home in the States, and he might have done the same over here."

"Good thought, Sam. I'll leave it to you to get in touch with your old colleagues in Vice and see what you can glean from them, but the golf club is your priority."

"Consider it done, sir," Sam smiled at her boss.

Chapter 9

What the butler saw

The mortuary staff had performed a minor miracle in preparing Joey Slimani's remains for his wife to view in order to carry out the formal identification. Somehow, they'd managed to lay out the torso and head in such a way, that, covered by the crisp, white sheets, it would appear that she was viewing an entire body. Up to this point, she remained unaware of the gory details of her husband's body's collision with the Lime Street-bound train.

True to her word, Trixie had been brought to the morgue by her 'butler' or 'manservant', Jennings. Having been met at the mortuary by Ross and Drake, they were escorted by Izzie's husband, Paul Foster, to the viewing room, where Joey's remains lay.

On first sight of the 'body', Trixie's face drained of colour and a hand flew to her mouth in shock. Clearly, the poor woman had never seen a dead body before.

"Oh God, oh no, poor Joey." She exclaimed, as tears ran down her face. At last, her emotions gave way and Izzie Drake had to step forward and take hold of her arm to prevent her from fainting away in shock.

Ross himself asked her to confirm if... 'these are the remains of your husband, Joseph Mohammed Slimani."

"Yeah, yeah, that's my Joey," she sobbed. "He kinda looks weird," she commented, no doubt aware that the remains didn't present a typical full body shape beneath the sheets.

"Aye lassie," William Nugent provided her with an answer. "Your husband's body, as the inspector will explain, was rather disfigured by the impact of the railway locomotive and we've done our best to present him to you in the best way possible."

"Oh God," she cried again. "What haven't you told me? What's happened to Joey's body. You have to tell me."

Ross and Drake gently led Trixie away, and took her into Nugent's office, which he'd made available to them for just such an eventuality. Once they had Trixie seated and armed with a box of tissues, Ross did his best to explain the extent of the injuries caused to her husband's body.

"Trixie, listen to me, please. You have to realise your husband was already dead when his body hit the railway tracks. Whoever did this hated Joey enough to have drugged him, cut his throat, and then thrown his body from a bridge, under the wheels of an approaching train."

"No, no," she sobbed, her voice rising in decibel levels until she almost screamed, "Not my Joey. Who did it? Do you know who did it?"

"Not yet, no, but we hope you will be able to help us find his killer, Trixie."

"But, how? What can I do?"

"You can begin by telling us everything you know about the two men he met at South Mersey Golf Club two days before his death."

"What men? I dunno anything about it, who he met, that kind of stuff. If it was business, Joey never told me anything about stuff like that. He always said he'd take care of business. Me, I was just to do what I do best, you know, in the movies? He looked after everything else."

"Did you know he was meeting those two men, Trixie?"

"He mentioned something about it. Said they were contacts who could help us make some good connections with us on this side of the

Atlantic. There's a really big market for our product in Germany. Joey always said, if we could break into the German market. I wasn't too sure about it."

"Why not, Trixie?" Drake posed the question.

"Look, I know you guys probably don't think too highly of me because of what I do for a living, but the Germans, well, they can be pretty demanding sometimes and ask girls to do stuff that I'm not always very happy about, real hard-core stuff, you know?"

Ross and Drake didn't know, but they both allowed their imaginations to run riot and waited for Trixie to continue.

"Okay, I do sex for a living. I fuck lots of men, but hey, it's just sex, okay? The Germans, they often like to do stuff that's pretty painful for a woman, if you get my drift. I told Joey I needed assurances before I consider doing anything for those guys. He said he wouldn't do nothin' to put me any situation where I'd get hurt. Joey looked after me like that."

I'm sure he did, as long as there was a nice fat profit at the end of it, Drake thought.

"We're not here to judge, Trixie," Ross reassured her. "We just want to find your husband's killer."

"Or killers," Drake added.

"You think there might have been more than one of them?" Trixie looked perplexed.

"Anything is possible at this stage," Ross confirmed.

Trixie fell silent for a few seconds as though something weighed heavily on her mind. Ross and Drake waited. They knew they could often discover more by staying silent and allowing the interviewee a few seconds thinking time. That way they would often volunteer more information without further prompting.

"Joey said he had a good time with the guys he met at the golf club. He said it was very productive. I don't think they were the people he was meeting on Saturday though."

"Why do you think that. Trixie?" Ross asked.

"Well, just that if he was going to see them again, I think he'd have said something like, *'I've got another meeting with the guys from the golf club,'* know what I mean?"

"Yes, I do know what you mean, and it's a good point, though it still doesn't totally exclude them from our thoughts."

"Didn't Joey give you any idea who he was meeting before he left home on Saturday, Trixie," Drake posed the next question.

"I already told you, no. He didn't give me a clue; just said he had a business meeting. Just what are you people doing about finding his killer?"

Ross had the feeling they wouldn't get much more from Trixie Slimani. Drake asked her to describe her movements on the day he died, and she told them that after Joey left, she had Jennings drive her into Liverpool where she shopped for a couple of hours and then had him drive her to visit a friend whose name and address she immediately supplied when Izzie asked for it. She told them Jennings drove her home about 5 p.m. and she took a long bath before ordering him to phone for a take away meal from the local pizza place. She went to bed early, about ten o'clock and took a sleeping pill, (so she said) and didn't stir until the following morning. Ross hoped Tony Curtis might be getting somewhere with his chat with the butler.

* * *

"So, what's it like, working for the Slimanis?" Curtis asked the butler Jennings as the pair sat in the police canteen, where Curtis had taken him after his mistress as he called her had gone to identify her husband's body and give her statement to the police. It would take some time, Curtis told him, so why not come and join him for coffee while they waited?

"So, is that your real name, Jennings?" Curtis asked after the two men sipped their coffee in a companionable silence for a minute or two.

"Yes, it is. William Jennings, but my friends call me Bill."

"Okay, so do you mind if I call you Bill?"

"Go ahead," Jennings replied, taking a bit from one of the Danish pastries Curtis had bought and placed on a plate in the middle of the table.

"How long have you worked for the Slimanis, Bill?"

"About two years. I answered an ad for a butler. They had just had the mansion built to Mr. Slimani's own specifications and though it was a bit of a monstrosity, they seemed happy there."

"Were you trained to be a butler, Bill? You don't strike me as being the typical butler type."

"No, I wasn't but the way the ad was worded, made me think I might stand a chance."

"How so?"

"It said they were looking for someone with a young outlook, no formal training required, acting experience useful, must be good looking and willing to undertake a wide range of duties. I thought I might as well give it a go, and I was surprised to be granted an interview and even more surprised when I got the job, but hell, man, it was like no job interview I'd ever had before."

"You've got me intrigued, now. What was the interview like?"

Jennings took a moment to drain his coffee cup, wiped his mouth with the paper napkin provided with the drink, and continued.

"As soon as I got there, I knew it was no ordinary household. I mean, come on, have you seen the pictures all over the place when you walk in, right?

"I haven't seen the house myself, Bill, so go on, tell me about it."

"The entrance hall is massive, like an atrium with a grand staircase leading to the upper floors, and the walls are covered with photos and prints showing stills from some of the mistresses movies. It shocked me, I can tell you, seeing those pictures of my prospective employer's wife engaged in various sex scenes with different men."

"What did you do before this?" Curtis asked, backtracking a little so he could get a better insight of the man he was talking to.

"I had some experience of acting in a few amateur dramatic productions and I was registered with an agency that provides extras for the movie business. At the time I got the interview I was out of work, to be honest, on my uppers, mate, broke, skint."

"Okay, so, what was it about the interview, Bill?"

"Look, I'm no prude, right? It was bloody obvious they were involved in the adult film business, I'm not stupid. But, even I was surprised when Joey told me to take my shirt off. I was, like, hey, what's going on here. I remember Trixie asked me if I was shy. I told her I wasn't just, but I was a little shocked to be asked to strip off at a job interview."

"Joey said I could turn around and walk away if I didn't want the job and I thought, what the hell? I did as they asked. Trixie complimented me on my body, and I must have sounded a right prat, when all I could say was a quiet thank you. Joey then told me what I'd already guessed, that he and his wife were in the adult movie business. I thought, *Okay, so what?* and then he asked her what she thought. To be honest mate, I felt a bit like a piece of meat on display. Anyway, Joey then tells me that they often entertain other people in the industry as he called it and I would have to be very discreet about anything I saw or heard there, including the use of recreational drugs. He said I'd be very well paid for my silence and that because he was away on business a lot, and his wife had a high sex drive, I would have to help 'entertain' her when he was away. I caught on quick, I can tell you and I just gawped at her, this gorgeous young woman who was basically being offered on a plate to me. I must have stammered some kind of response because next thing, she told me to drop my pants. Bloody hell, detective, what would you have done? I was like in a trance, you know. I did what she said and when I was down to my underwear, she said 'Everything, Mr. Jennings.'

Tony Curtis, by now dry-mouthed, was busily trying to keep up with the man's narrative. He could hardly believe what he was hearing. As Jennings had said this had to be the strangest job interview, ever. Jennings carried on.

"I did what she said, and I couldn't help it, mate, with all what I'd been told, and with the thought of banging this gorgeous bird, by the time my boxers hit the deck, I had a bloody great stiffy on, know what I mean? Trixie just looked at me, smiled at Joey, and said, *"He'll do, just fine, Honey."* Ten minutes later, after telling me a few more details, including the fact I must refer to her as Mistress, I was hired on a salary you can't imagine. I've been with them since that day."

Curtis was almost open-mouthed by this time. He'd thought he'd have to pry information from this man, but instead, Jennings had opened up to him as if they were old mates. He guessed that maybe Jennings's job didn't give him many opportunities to make friends or talk to people outside the Slimani's immediate circle of friends and business contacts, so he'd been glad of the opportunity to talk to some- body, anybody, about life at *Paradise Found.*

"So, correct me if I'm wrong, here, Bill, but every time Joey Slimani went away on one of his business trips, you were bonking his missus?"

"Yeah, that's right, and all with his approval. That woman, I tell you, she's fucking insatiable between the sheets, man. Virtually as soon as the front door closed behind her husband, she'd be dragging me upstairs, and I had to call her Mistress while we were doing it, like in my contract, you know. I admit, she made me feel like a bloody porn star too."

"Sounds to me like you've got it made, Bill," Curtis observed, finding it impossible not to feel a little envious of the man's good fortune. "But, listen, what can you tell me about last weekend. We thought it a bit weird that she never reported her husband as missing until two days later and that she hadn't even heard on the news about the body found on the railway tracks."

Jennings turned a bright shade of red as he volunteered the infor- mation Curtis was looking for.

"Oh God, I still feel bad about that. As soon as Joey left for his meet- ing, she told me to meet her in her private bedroom in half an hour. I knew what was coming of course, and I was dead right. We were at it for hours, lost all track of time. Thing is, detective, she was off her head a lot of the time. I think she was high on smack or something. I'm not into drugs, never have been, which she could never understand. So anyway, she didn't let me go until late that night, around the time Joey would be expected home, I suppose, and I went to my room, took a long shower and crashed out until the next day. I never saw Trixie until I popped my head around her door at lunchtime to see if she wanted anything to eat. She was still out of it. I just left her to it. I'd no idea about Joey's plans, so I knew nothing about him being missing or anything. She woke up the next day and that's when she started to panic, because there was no sign of Joey and he wasn't answering his phone. That's when she went to the police station to report him missing."

"Bill, what you've told me is really important stuff. I'm going to ask you to come back later, after you've taken Trixie home and repeat it all again in an official statement, if you don't mind."

"Mind? Hell, no, I don't mind, not if it'll help catch whoever killed poor old Joey. I'm due a couple of hours off later, so how's about I come back then and tell you what you need to know all over again?"

"Perfect," Curtis replied, pleased that his version of 'subtlety' had worked. He would never admit that Jennings basically opened to him without any real prompting. Wouldn't do to ruin his image, after all, would it?

After escorting Jennings back to the squad room, where Trixie was waiting for him, in the company of Izzie Drake, Tony Curtis quickly informed Andy Ross of the context of his conversation with William Jennings.

Ross was pleased enough with the information he'd obtained, particularly the confirmation that Trixie had spent the weekend either in bed with Jennings or incapacitated by drugs, but he retained a feeling of intense frustration, which he relayed to Izzie Drake soon afterwards in a short, private meeting in his office.

"Bloody hell, Izzie, we're picking up snippets of information here, there and everywhere, but we still have nothing to connect a single suspect to Slimani's death. Worse still, we don't even *have* a viable suspect."

"What about the two men at the golf club?"

"For now, they are persons of interest, true. We can't class them as suspects, because we know nothing about them. Are they British, American, German, whatever. Were they friends or business acquaintances of Joey Slimani?"

"What about getting Sofie to use her contacts back home? Surely she will have some colleagues in Germany with knowledge of the German porn industry?"

"I spoke to her earlier, Izzie. She's already on it, making inquiries with her old boss. She thinks he'll be happy to help us out if he can. But, even if he does, it's a long shot whether he can come up with a link between any German porn producers and Joey. The fact remains, we're stumbling around in the dark, and I don't like it."

"Looks like we're dependent on getting cooperation from the police forces in L.A. New York and Hamburg, then, sir, doesn't it?

"Unfortunately, you could be right. I don't know why though, Izzie, but I'm beginning to get a feeling that the answer to Joey Slimani's death lies much closer to home."

"I've learned, over the years, never to ignore one of those feelings of yours," Drake replied. "So, where do we go from here?"

Chapter 10

The Manchester Connection

Sam Gable pulled up in the car park at South Mersey Golf Club. Standing just off the appropriately named Golf Links Road, just outside Birkenhead, in a beautiful setting, the club had spent 2005 celebrating its centenary, and had hosted numerous events and social occasions throughout the year. The clubhouse was impressive and was frequently used for the celebration of weddings, anniversaries, birthdays and so on, a sure sign of the popularity of the location.

"Nice place," Sam commented as she stepped from the car and pressed the locking button on the key ring.

"My Dad plays golf regularly," Ginger Devenish said in reply. He's a member at Allerton Manor Golf Club. I must ask him if he's ever played here."

"Is that where you live, Ginge, in Allerton?"

Being the newest addition to Ross's team, most of the squad as yet knew little about D.C. Devenish's home or private life, apart from the fact that he loved sailing, hardly surprising as he'd been recruited from the Port Police, where he'd spent much of his time on the Mersey, as part of the crew of one of their launches.

"Yes, I do. I'm still living at home with my Mum and Dad. They have a house near Reynolds Park, about five minutes away from Rose Lane Station. I can't really afford my own place yet, but now I'm a permanent member of the squad, maybe I can start saving for a place of my own."

"Hey, don't go knocking living with your parents," Sam said. "I bet your Mum does your washing and ironing and has a nice meal on the table when you get home at the end of your shift?"

"Yes, you're right, she does."

"Like I said, don't knock it, Ginge. What does your Dad do?"

"He's retired, Sam. He was a ship's master, captained various merchant vessels for over twenty years. Made enough money to retire at fifty-five. Now he's free to enjoy life while he's young enough to indulge himself."

"Good for him. And your mum spoils you both, I'll bet my life on it."

The flame-haired young detective smiled at Sam, before replying, "You make a good case for staying put, Sam,"

"Trust me, Ginge, you'll have plenty of time to fend for yourself when you do have a place of your own. Make the most of your home comforts while you can, mate."

"I will, Sam, thanks for the advice."

Five minutes later they were seated in the office of the club secretary, a wise-looking gentleman of around 60 years of age, white-haired but not elderly in appearance, dressed in a smart pale-yellow polo shirt bearing the club logo, embroidered on the left breast, and light brown trousers, with military-style creases. Sam had him marked as an ex-military man as soon as she saw him, confirmed as he shook hands with the two detectives, introducing himself as Major Simon Coombes.

After asking the club steward to bring teas and coffees for his guests, Major Coombes asked how he could help.

"Two men visited the club last Thursday, Major," Sam began. "They were here as guests of one your members, A Joey Slimani."

"Ah yes, our Captain, Graham Bull spoken to the police on the subject. I knew Joseph of course, he played quite regularly. I must say I was shocked and saddened to learn of his untimely demise."

"Yes, it was D.C. Devenish and I who spoke to Mr. Bull. What we need if you have such a thing, is any visual record of the men during their time here at the club. We've already ascertained that the names they gave on signing in were fictitious, but it really is important that we identify them as soon as possible as they may be among the last people outside of his home, to have seen or spoken to Mr. Slimani."

"I see," Coombes looked thoughtful as he replied. "It just so happens that we should be able to help you, D.C. Gable. Over the years, like most golf courses in the area, sadly, we have been subjected to occasional bouts of vandalism and attempted theft of equipment and so on. As a result, we had closed circuit television cameras installed, which cover the car park and the clubhouse. I'd like to be able to extend it to the driveway as well, but finances have the final word, as I'm sure you understand."

"Of course, Major. We'd be very grateful if you'd allow us to view the CCTV footage for the day in question to see if we can get a good look at the men who accompanied Mr. Slimani."

"Yes, of course. That won't be a problem. Please, enjoy your drinks, while I go and arrange it for you. Phillip, our steward, is also in charge of the CCTV equipment, as he has some experience in that sort of thing. By the way, I was very surprised when Graham told me about Joseph's occupation. Unlike Graham, however, I'm not as quick to judge people based solely on what they do for a living. Joseph, and his wife, who he introduced to me as an actress, both seemed perfectly nice, sociable people, once one got past their brash American style of speaking and lack of a few of the normal social graces. One must make certain allowances, I feel, when dealing with our friends from across the pond. As long as they abide by the club rules and adopt a sense of decorum while on club premises, who are we to judge, eh, Constable Gable?"

"Erm, yes, exactly," Sam replied, feeling the Major's comments a little condescending towards the dead man and his wife, though definitely more accepting than Graham Bull's instant condemnation of the Slimanis, on hearing of their occupations.

Within a few minutes, Gable and Devenish found themselves being ushered into a small room at the back of the clubhouse where they seated themselves in the seats provided as the CCTV footage they requested was shown.

"There," Devenish called out as the camera showed two men getting out of a Vauxhall Vectra, and being met by Joey Slimani. The three men shook hands before the two newcomers went to the rear of the Vectra, from where they extricated two sets of golf clubs. They were seen following Slimani towards the clubhouse for a few seconds before they moved out of range.

"Can we get a close-up view of the car?" Ginger asked the steward, who obliged by using the camera's zoom facility to bring the Vectra into less than sharp focus in close-up mode. "Damn, I hoped we might get the registration plate number," he added.

"Don't worry about that, old chap," Major Coombes reassured him. When they signed in, they would have had to record the car's reg. number, a rule we have so we know what vehicles are on club property in case of accidents. All to do with insurance and so on, you understand."

"Thanks, Major," spoke with relief. At least that was something. The car park camera hadn't been able to pick up any clear images of the two men, but when the film rolled on to later in the day, played in fast forward mode by the steward, it was Devenish who again suddenly shouted, "Stop, go back a bit."

The steward hit the rewind button and when prompted by Devenish, hit the play button and the film rolled again, this time in slow motion as requested by Devenish. "Stop, freeze it there," he shouted, and the film froze, showing the two men walking with Joey Slimani, into the clubhouse, in clear view of the camera.

"Got 'em," Sam Gable clapped Devenish on the shoulder. She turned to Major Coombes. "Major, do we need to go back and get a warrant, or are you prepared to allow us to take this film back to police headquarters, so we can obtain a copy which will enable us to potentially identify those two men?"

"Never let it be said that we don't do all we can to assist our police force, dear girl. Of course you may take it, provided you provide me with a receipt for it, of course," he smiled.

"But of course, Major," Sam flashed her most devastating smile back at the major who almost blushed in surprise as his stiff upper lip wavered, just a bit.

Soon afterwards, armed with the video containing the important footage, and the Vectra's registration number, copied from the club's signing-in form, Gable and Devenish set off on their return journey to headquarters. On the way, Sam initiated a trace on the Vectra's registration number which she hoped to receive information on by the time they arrived back at base.

* * *

"Well done, you two," Ross congratulated them. "Now, we might just be getting somewhere."

"Thanks, sir," Gable smiled. "Just got the news on the car too. The Vectra is a hire car. It was taken from Abbey Car Hire in Oldham on the Wednesday and returned to them on Friday morning."

"Hmm," Ross mused. "I wonder if there's any significance in the fact Slimani's body was dropped under the wheels of a Manchester to Liverpool train?"

"You mean like some form of poetic justice?"

"Exactly. Seems Joey met with two men from the Manchester area, and then ended up under a Manchester to Liverpool train. Then again, would the killer know the train was due when he tossed Joey's body from the bridge? That could have just been serendipitous timing."

"At least we have a decent image of the men," Devenish said. "We might get lucky."

"Indeed we might, Ginger," Ross agreed. Izzie Drake walked in to the office as Ross was talking to the two detectives and could see her boss was looking animated. She knew by instinct that Gable and Devenish must have brought back some good news. Ross quickly brought her up to speed, and she joined in his feeling of them having made an important step forward.

"The fact it was a hire car helps us out too, more than if it was a private car."

"It does?" Devenish queried.

"Yes, of course. They might have got away with giving false names to the golf club, but in order to hire a car, you have to produce a valid driving licence, so that should at least throw up one genuine identity."

"Of course it will," Ross responded. "If we can trace the driver, he and his friend could turn out to be pivotal to the case."

"You really think the two men had something to do with Joey's death, sir? Gable asked.

"Let's just say it would be a very big coincidence for them to meet Joey Slimani on Thursday, play eighteen holes with him, having given false names to the club, and then Joey meets with a grisly death some time on Saturday, and the hire car was returned on Friday, so they would have had to have alternative transport if they returned to Liverpool to kill Joey. I'm not a great believer in such coincidences."

"I'll get on to the car hire company right away, then," Sam Gable made a move to her desk, to make the phone call that could bring them closer to a resolution of Joey Slimani's murder.

"Ginger," Ross turned to D.C. Devenish. "Get those stills run off the golf club video and then do what you can to find out if those two guys are on our system anywhere. If you need help, get Sergeant Ferris or Kat to assist you, okay?"

"I'm on it, sir," Devenish walked to his desk, picked up the video and headed for the technical department where he could get the video copied and stills produced.

"Got it, sir," Sam Gable called across the room excitedly a few minutes later. "The name of the guy who hired the car."

"Yes, Sam, I know who you were looking for. Come on girl, out with it."

"They gave me the usual crap at first, you know, can't give out customer details due to the data protection act and so on. I just promised that if they didn't help us out, as this is a murder inquiry, I will arrange for their local council's enforcement team to pay them a visit and insist on having all their cars inspected for faults and defects and possible breach of their licence to operate. Isn't it amazing how people suddenly remember their civic duty when you give them a suitable incentive?"

"Samantha Gable, you're a wicked woman. Remind me to never get on your wrong side. Now, like I said, come on, girl, out with it!" Ross was grinning as he spoke. Sam Gable had been with the team for almost six years and was one of his most trusted and capable officers.

"The man who hired the Vectra held a UK licence, so I'm presuming he wasn't one of Joey Slimani's American connections. His name is Robert Keane, a solicitor's clerk, and the address he gave is in Failsworth, which explains why he hired a car in Oldham."

Sam's point was valid, Failsworth being a town in the Metropolitan Borough of Oldham, Greater Manchester.

"Good work, Sam. Have you checked to see if we have anything on him?"

"Yes, sir. As far as I can tell, Keane has no criminal record, but he does have a couple of motoring offences logged on the system. How do you want to handle it? We don't want to go intruding on another force's patch without letting them know we're in the area."

"No problem," Ross assured her. "I'll go and have a word with D.C.I Agostini and he'll liaise with Greater Manchester Police and fix it up for us to go and pay Mr. Keane a visit."

Sam left Ross to go and speak with Agostini, taking the time to type up the report of the visit to South Mersey Golf Club. Ginger Devenish hadn't returned from the technical department yet, but she hoped he'd be free to accompany her if they had to make the drive to Oldham to visit Robert Keane.

* * *

Oscar Agostini wasted no time in placing a call through to the Greater Manchester Police Force, after Ross presented the latest developments to him. He indicated to Ross to take seat in his office while he made the call.

"Take the weight off your feet, Andy. You look knackered, old friend."

"I am, Oscar," Ross sat down, grateful for a few moments time out. "This bloody case is driving me mad. We don't seem to be getting anywhere. So far, we haven't been able to establish a motive for Joey's murder, much less come up with even one viable suspect. I'm hoping this Robert Keane chap might be able to throw some light on things for us."

"You don't consider him to be a suspect, then, Andy?"

"At the moment, everyone's a suspect, Oscar, but to be honest we have very little to base a case on. In truth, I'd be surprised if this Keane chap is involved in the murder. If he is, he must be one of the thickest killers I've ever known. I mean, what self-respecting murderer hires a car in his own name?"

Agostini chuckled slightly, then turned to his phone and made the call to Greater Manchester. Five minutes later, he hung up and gave Ross his full attention.

"Okay Andy, your contact there will be a Detective Sergeant Ian Gilligan. He works out of Oldham Police Station on Barn Street. He'll be waiting for your people to phone to make arrangements to meet up with them and he'll accompany them when they go to see Keane. It's good, because he has the local knowledge our people don't have, so if Keane tries to do a runner, they'll need someone who knows where he might run."

Five minutes later, Ross was back in the squad room, where he briefed Sam Gable on the details of their Oldham contact. While they waited for D.C. Devenish to return, Sam phoned Sergeant Gilligan in Oldham, and arranged to meet him after lunch at the police station on Barn Street. Devenish soon returned and proudly waving a handful of copies of a grainy, just discernible 8 X 6 inch photo as he approached Sam's desk.

The two detectives quickly showed the blown-up still from the golf club video to Ross, who asked Devenish to pass the copies to Kat Bellamy, with instructions to ensure every member of the squad received a copy.

One of the men in the photo would be Robert Keane, the other mystery man remained to be identified, and that task remained a priority for Ross's team. For now, however, he watched as Sam and Ginger walked out of the squad room, making their way to pick up the pool car that would carry them to Failsworth, and, hopefully, a little light at the end of the tunnel.

Chapter 11

The Solicitor's Clerk

Something had been bubbling away at the back of Izzie Drake's brain, something she hadn't quite been able to put her finger on. Then, suddenly it appeared in her mind in glorious technicolour!

She veritably burst into Ross's office, barely knocking before finding herself standing, almost breathless in front of the D.I. as he sat at his desk, reviewing what they'd discovered so far.

"Where's the fire, Izzie?" he looked up at his friend as she slowly allowed her breathing to return to normal.

"We've been missing something," she finally spoke. "You and I both know one of the main motives for murder is money, right?"

"I've no arguments with that, but what do you mean, we've missed something?"

"Maybe this is less to do with the money involved in the adult movie business and more to do with something closer to home."

"Go on, Izzie, I'm listening."

"What if the ex-wives, or at least one of them, or even both of them plus Trixie, hatched a plot to get their hands on Joey's money?"

"Whoa, slow down a sec. You forget that Trixie will automatically get Joey's money as his legal spouse. Why would she contemplate entering into some kind of conspiracy to murder her husband when she is already his legal heir?"

"But that's just it, sir, don't you see? What if she isn't?"

"Isn't what?"

"His legal heir, that's what. So far, we've been scrambling around in the dark, trying to establish a motive for Joey's murder and the one thing neither you nor I have mentioned up to now is his will."

Ross and Drake had worked together for so many years that many people believed the pair had an almost telepathic connection. As soon as the words left Izzie's mouth, Ross seemed to realise the same, nagging thoughts had been bouncing around his brain too.

"You think there's something in Joey's will that might have made killing him now a more attractive prospect than waiting years for him to pop his clogs?"

"You never know, is all I'm saying."

"It's a good point, Izzie, but listen, if his will is already written, witnessed and validated, there's nothing anyone can do to change it, so killing him because of something in the will just doesn't make any sense."

"I hadn't looked at it that way," Drake admitted, "but what if, for the sake of argument, he left all his money to someone else and shut his wife and ex-wives out altogether?"

"Well, yes, that might be reason to generate enough anger to want him dead, especially if Trixie knew about it and it hadn't been signed yet. I think we need to find out if Joey Slimani had a will and who stands to benefit from his death."

"And the guy Sam and Ginger have gone to see is a solicitor's clerk too."

"Okay, a visit to Trixie Slimani sounds in order to me. Let's go see her and find out if Joey's lawyer is in the States or if he has one over here."

* * *

Sam Gable liked Detective Sergeant Ian Gilligan as soon as she and Ginger Devenish met the Manchester detective at Failsworth Police Station. Gilligan was tall, around six feet, Sam guessed, and possessed dark, wavy hair which he wore quite long, as it fell over his collar at the back. Dressed in jeans and a plaid design shirt, brown cowboy boots, with a denim waistcoat completing the ensemble, he reminded her of a late sixties hippie. With a ready smile and a firm handshake, he welcomed the two Merseyside detectives after they'd been admitted to the station's C.I.D. offices.

"You must be Sam and Ginger," he held a hand out in greeting. "Your Sergeant Drake phoned to say you were on your way. I can see why they call you Ginger," he laughed, as he addressed Devenish.

"I know, just can't escape the name," Devenish responded, smiling. I've been 'Ginger' or 'Ginge' since I was at primary school. My real name's Gary."

"Which do you prefer?" Gilligan asked him.

"Best stick to Ginger, Sarge. Everyone else does."

"Okay, Ginger it is, then."

Gilligan couldn't help casting an admiring glance at Sam Gable, who wore a black cotton shirt, with half sleeves, her waist enclosed in a wide black belt, teamed with slim fitting black trousers and low-heeled black shoes, perfectly highlighting her neatly trimmed blonde bob-style hair-do. The outfit showed her curves off perfectly, her figure kept in perfect trim by her rigorous daily fitness regime, a daily two-mile run, fifty press ups in her bedroom, and a weekly visit to the gym, where she never failed to attract similar attention from many of the male members. Sam always laughed to herself on the frequent occasions when a man tried to chat her up, only to be rebuffed in short measure. As soon as she mentioned she was a police officer, it tended to make most of them shy away from her. One or two had been more determined over the years but Sam had never succumbed to their approaches.

"Seen enough, Sarge?" she grinned at Gilligan, who instantly blushed in embarrassment.

"Oh, sorry Sam," he said, contrition heavy in his voice. "Most of the lady detectives we have round here are nowhere near as glamorous as you. I didn't mean to stare. Hope you'll forgive me."

As if to reinforce his point a rather dumpy thirty-something female, wearing blue jeans and a grey hoody, with a pair of trainers that looked decidedly shabby, walked through the room, pausing to wave and call "Hiya, Sarge" to Gilligan who raised a hand and called back to her, "How's it going, Fran?" Fran gave him a thumbs down signal in reply and carried on with whatever she was doing.

"I forgive you," Sam grinned at him. "It's not every day a girl gets called glamorous, not in this job, anyway."

"Don't get me wrong, Sam. That was D.C. Fran Morgan, a bloody good detective, though not blessed with your looks, if you know what I mean. She's involved in a missing child case right now. Poor kid's been missing two days. I doubt we'll see her alive again,"

"Bloody monsters everywhere you look, these days," Sam replied. "I hope she finds her."

"Yeah, she's one of four detectives working on the case. All of them are working flat out, unpaid overtime, you name it. They won't give up until they find little Beth, one way or the other."

Banter over, Gilligan led the pair from the building and was soon driving them in an unmarked Peugeot towards the registered address of Robert Keane, a mere five-minute drive from the police station. Gilligan pulled up on a pleasant, leafy avenue, trees forming an artificial archway as they grew along the grass verges that lined the street.

"Looks a nice area," Devenish commented as the three detectives emerged from the car, into the cheerless winter sun that had managed to force its way through the clouds that lay like a shroud over the Greater Manchester area.

"Yes, it is. Mostly professional people live out here," Gilligan replied. "Not exactly the upper crust of local society, but no riff-raff, if you catch my drift. There, number 40, that's where your man lives. You do realise he's probably at work?"

"Yes," Sam replied, "but as we don't know where he works, I'm hoping he has a wife who might tell us where to find him, or maybe a nice, nosy neighbour who can tell us what we want to know."

"Ah, yes, can't beat the old curtain-twitchers when it comes to gathering a spot of local intel," the Manchester detective laughed.

"Same everywhere," Sam agreed as the three of them walked through the front gate of number 40. There was a drive to the side of the smartly presented, three-bed semi-detached property, but no car sat there waiting for its owner. There was no garage, therefore the occupant was either at work, having travelled by car, or maybe didn't own a car at all, which Sam deduced would have been a good reason for hiring a car for the journey to Liverpool.

Gilligan rang the bell, positioned on the door frame to the left of the three-part glass partitioned front door. Almost immediately they could make out the approach of a figure, walking towards the door, which was opened seconds later by an attractive, short-haired brunette, dressed in a heather-grey designer jogging suit that fitted her like a glove, and emphasised the woman's curvaceous figure. Sam estimated the trainers the woman wore must have cost over a hundred pounds. Sam, at five feet six, towered over the woman, who she guessed must be not much more than five feet tall.

"Mrs. Keane?" Gilligan guessed it to be a good assumption.

"Yes, how can I help you?"

Gilligan and the others held up their warrant cards.

"Police officers, Mrs. Keane," Gilligan continued. "We were hoping to have a word with your husband."

"With Robert? What on earth could you be wanting with Robert?"

"It's just a routine inquiry," Gilligan lied. "We need to speak with Robert in order to clear something up, that's all."

Oh, well, he's at work at present," Muriel Keane replied. You can find him there if it's urgent."

"And just where does Robert work, Mrs. Keane?" Devenish asked her with a kindly smile on his face. He'd always had the ability to put people at ease with that smile.

"He's a solicitor's clerk, for Symonds, Symonds and Riley in Oldham."

"I know where that is," Gilligan said, saving them from asking directions to her husband's place of work.

"Can I ask your first name, please?" Sam asked, noting Muriel's name in her notebook when the woman answered her question. "Oh, yes, before we go, do you have any idea where Robert was during the day last Thursday? Would he have been at work all day?"

"Last Thursday? Yes, no, wait a mo," Muriel replied innocently. "Robert had booked a day off on Thursday. He'd met a nice man at the local Golf Club a while ago, an American gent, he said, and the American invited him to go and play a round at his club in Liverpool, I think it was."

Damn, Sam thought. *This is looking more and more innocent by the second. Unless the wife is in on whatever they were up to.*

"Do you know if Robert travelled to Liverpool on his own? she asked Muriel Keane, not bothering to correct her belief that her husband had been in Liverpool when in fact he'd been on the other side of the Mersey in Birkenhead.

"Oh, yes, I think so," the woman looked surprised to be asked the question. "He hired a car and drove there by himself. At least he never mentioned anyone else to me."

Gilligan looked at Sam, who nodded to confirm she'd got all she could from the woman. As Gilligan drove them from Failsworth into the centre of Oldham, Ginger Devenish, who's spent the last five minutes in thoughtful mood, reflected on their conversation with Muriel Keane.

"Curiouser and curiouser," Devenish mused from his seat in the back of the car.

"Come on Ginger, let's hear it," Gilligan encouraged him.

"Well, Mrs. Keane, as far as I could tell, was quite open and honest with us. She confirmed her husband took the day off on Thursday, that he went to play golf with an American, though she thinks it was as a friend and nothing more, and she was aware he'd hired a car to do so. Now, to my way of thinking, that all smacks of the actions of an innocent man, taking the day off work to take up a friendly invitation to play a round of golf. But…"

"A-ha, I knew there had to be a but," Gilligan smiled as he drove. "Go on mate, what's your 'but'?"

"Right, Sarge, if this was all as innocent as it appears to the casual observer, why did Keane, and the mystery third man, sign in to South Mersey Golf Club under assumed names?"

"Sorry, Ginger, I don't know the details of your case. I'm only here to ferry you guys around, basically."

Sam Gable spoke up and gave Gilligan a quick run-down on the Slimani case.

"Bloody hell, that's some shit your team has been landed with. I've heard of your specialist team of course. Everyone in the county must have heard of D.I. Ross. What's he like to work with?"

"Brilliant," Sam replied.

"I'll second that," Devenish agreed. "It wasn't long ago I was employed by the Port Police, helped out on one case and next thing, D.I. Ross asked for me to be transferred to his team, temporary at first, then permanently. He's a great guy to work for."

"Sounds like it," Gilligan said. "Wish I could be part of something like that."

"Who knows what the future holds, eh, Sarge?" Sam posed the question.

"No chance I'm afraid, Sam. My career kind of stalled a couple of years ago. I lost my wife in an accident and couldn't handle the loss for a while. I went off the rails, turned to the drink, and got in a real mess. Only my boss's intervention saved my job, got me into rehab and when I dried out, made sure I got my old job back."

"I'm so sorry about your wife," Sam said. "What happened, if you don't mind me asking?"

"Drunk driver," Gilligan replied. "Gina was only 28. She was on her way home from the shops, and some stupid idiot, twice over the legal limit came round a corner on the wrong side of the road and ploughed straight into her Mini. She was killed instantly."

"Oh, fucking hell, Sarge. I'm so sorry. I can't begin to imagine how you must have felt."

"Me either," Devenish agreed with Sam's thoughts.

"Thanks, both of you. It was five years ago, so I guess you could say I'm over the worst now, but it took a long time."

"What happened to the scrote who hit her?" Sam asked.

"He got five years for causing death by dangerous driving and two years for being over the limit, served concurrently of course. He was out in three."

"Doesn't seem fair, does it?" Devenish chimed in. "Three bloody years for taking away a life and destroying someone else's life at the same time."

"Damn right it doesn't" Sam said, real anger in her voice.

There was no time for further discussion as they now introduced themselves to a pretty young secretary/receptionist in the offices of Symonds, Symonds and Riley. After informing them they wished to speak with one of their employees she picked up the phone and after speaking to a Mr. Hartley, she informed them he would be coming to speak with them in a minute or two.

Five minutes later they were seated in the office of Charles Hartley, who informed them he was a partner in the law practice. He looked to be in his forties and wore a dark blue pinstripe suit with a crisp white shirt, and a pale-yellow tie. His hair was dark brown, showing the faintest hint of turning grey. His face was round, and had a pleasing, open visage, giving the first impression that this was man you would automatically trust with your secrets, assuming you had any to protect.

"What happened to Messrs Symonds, Symonds and Riley?" Sam inquired, and Hartley laughed politely.

"Arthur and William Symonds founded the firm in the late nineteenth century and were joined by Thomas Riley in 1909. They are long dead, I'm afraid, but Arthur Symonds was my great-grandfather, so the family tradition lives on. Now, I understand you wish to speak to Robert Keane? I hope you'll understand that as an employee of the firm, we take it very seriously if any of our people are involved in any legal matters, particularly if there's a hint of any illegal activity being involved."

"At this point we don't know if Mr. Keane has done anything illegal, Mr, Hartley," Ginger Devenish responded. "All I can tell you is that his name has come to light in connection with a murder case we're investigating."

That produced a look of pure shock on the solicitor's face.

"Murder?" he gasped, almost choking on the word.

"Again, as D.C. Devenish said, there's no suggestion that Robert Keane is directly involved in anything of a criminal nature at this point, Mr. Hartley," Sam reiterated the point. "We would appreciate having an informal chat with him, so we can clear up a couple of points, however."

Hartley leaned back in his chair, as his mind processed the information he'd been presented with, and finally, smiled again and finally broke his silence.

"I hope you won't mind if I sit in on your interview with Robert," he insisted. "Simply to ensure his rights are adhered to, of course."

"We have no objections at all," it was Gilligan who spoke this time. "But do remember that Mr. Keane is not under caution or accused of anything at this time. We are here in pursuit of our inquiries, and we hope Mr. Keane can assist us in those inquiries."

Hartley picked up his phone, spoke to his secretary, who they now knew as Millie, and two minutes later, she ushered Robert Keane into the room. Keane, five feet ten in height, about thirty to thirty-five, with what would once have been termed 'dashing good looks' rather like a thirties matinee idol, had a distinctly nervous air about him as he walked into Hartley's office.

"Please come in, Robert. This lady and these gentlemen are from the police. They seem to think you can assist them in their enquiries. I told them I would stay with you to ensure your rights are respected.

"Oh, erm, right, I see. Thank you, Mr. Hartley, but there was no need, for you to be here, I mean."

"Nonsense, Robert. You're part of the firm. I insist."

Sam Gable's instincts screamed at her. She just knew that Keane knew something but didn't want to reveal it in front of his boss. She leaned across to Gilligan and whispered her feelings to him and he nodded without replying. She was too far from Devenish to communicate with him without the others hearing, but she felt he was intelligent enough to catch on quickly.

"Robert Keane," Gilligan spoke first. I'm Sergeant Ian Gilligan, Greater Manchester Police, and these officers are Detective Constables Samantha Gable and Gary Devenish from Merseyside Police. They've travelled over from Liverpool to speak with you. I'm here as a courtesy as they are on our territory, but they will be asking you the questions. Do you understand?"

"Well yes, but, what am I supposed to have done wrong, for the Liverpool police to want to see me?"

"We're not sure you've done anything wrong, Mr. Keane," Sam began, impressed that Gilligan had introduced Devenish by his real name, rather than his nickname. "Please can you tell us what you were doing in Birkenhead last Thursday?"

"Birkenhead?"

"Yes, that town just across the Mersey from Liverpool, big place, two famous football teams, cathedrals, the Beatles, you might have heard of it?" Devenish said, sardonically.

Good for you, Ginge, Sam Gable thought. Get him on his toes, let him know we won't take any crap from him. Keane looked nonplussed and Hartley frowned.

"Well, Mr. Keane, can you please answer the question? Sam prompted the solicitor's clerk.

"Yes, I did go to Birkenhead," Keane at last replied. "I went to play golf."

"Do you usually take a day off work, hire a car, and make a seventy miles or so round trip just to play a round of golf?" Sam asked him.

"Well, no, of course not. It was just a one-off."

"And how did this one-off come about?" Devenish spoke this time.

Alternating the questioning was having a disconcerting effect on Keane.

"I, er, I met this man you see, an American chap."

"Joey Slimani," Sam stated, firmly.

"Well, yes, that's right."

"Where did you meet Mr. Slimani?" she pushed him to get to the point.

Keane looked uncomfortable. Sam had a feeling this was why he hadn't wanted his employer present during this interview.

"I...I met him online actually," he hesitated.

"Go on, Mr. Keane, we're waiting," said Devenish, quickly growing into the art of interviewing a suspect. Keane was looking guilty now, and casting glances between his boss, and the police officers, as if seeking support or encouragement from someone, anyone. The three detectives and Hartley, however, remained tight-lipped as they waited for his explanation.

"Well, you see, sometimes, at night, I find it difficult to sleep, and I sort of trawl through various sites on the internet. So, one night, a while ago I discovered a site just by chance,"

Sam Gable now felt sure she knew where this was leading and believed she fully understood why Keane was reluctant to have his boss present to hear the details of his trip to visit Joey Slimani, but, she had a job to do and so she pressed on.

"And what kind of site was it you found, Mr. Keane?"

Robert Keane hesitated, looking from Gable to Devenish and Gilligan, almost as if he was willing them to find a way for him not to reveal all in front of Hartley. Sam, however, didn't have time to waste on protecting his sensibilities.

"Mr. Keane?" she prompted, when his hesitancy became irritating to her.

Keane appeared to take a deep breath, deep down, he knew there was no way to avoid what was to come. Whether he had a job at the end of it, he just couldn't predict.

"Perhaps I should explain something first. My wife and I have been having some difficulties recently, you see. It's a little embarrassing, but, well, our sex life hasn't been all it should be. We used to have a great sex life, but for some reason, things started to go stale a few months ago."

Once again, the man fell silent, as he pondered on how best to explain his predicament to the detectives in such a way that his boss wouldn't see him as some kind of pervert or deviant, a sure-fire way to lose his job, he was certain. Symonds, Symonds and Riley certainly wouldn't tolerate any hint of scandal coming anywhere near their precious company, he knew for a fact. He risked a quick look at Hartley, whose face already bore a look of flushed concern. As though sensing the rising tension in the room, Ian Gilligan stepped in to the conversation.

"Mr. Keane, if you feel you'd rather speak with us in private, we'll be happy to take you to the station with us. You are not under any obligation to hold this interview in the company of your employer."

"Now, look here..." Hartley began, only for Gilligan to reply,

"No, Mr. Hartley, you look here, Mr. Keane has rights, and one of those rights is to speak with us confidentially if he so chooses."

"No, no, it's okay, really," Keane almost stammered. He guessed the damage had already been done and it would only make things worse with his boss if he pulled out now, leaving Hartley to think all sorts of things about him. He'd probably already decided his clerk was a sex fiend as he knew Hartley would put it.

"As long as you're sure," Gilligan reassured him. Simultaneously, the detective sergeant earned himself a whole load of Brownie points with the former Vice cop, Sam Gable, for his display of sensibility and his respect for Robert Keane's feelings, a rare commodity in many police officers, as she'd found through experience.

Keane gulped, steeled himself, mentally forcing himself to shut out the thought of Hartley being in the room, and carried on.

"My wife, Muriel, is an attractive woman, Detective, and we'd always had a good relationship, until, well, it just seemed as if the spark had disappeared from our sex lives. We sat down and tried to talk it through, to resolve the problem. We both decided we didn't want to end our marriage. We still love each other deeply, you see. I suggested to her there was a way we could both find what we needed in a way that meant we wouldn't be having affairs or cheating on each other in the real sense of the word."

"You went online to find work in the adult film industry, didn't you?" Sam Gable interrupted.

"I'm afraid so, yes I did," Keane nodded as Sam looked tellingly at Gary Devenish. "I had always held a certain attraction for women, and I thought Muriel, with her looks and high sex drive could also earn good money and solve the problem between us if she occasionally took part in the films. She thought it was a good idea, but only if I could find a proper, you know, above board, film company, were everything was professional and there was no risk to either of us. I searched for ages and found a few companies, but I was never convinced they were what we wanted."

"Until you found *Joe Slim Productions*, Gable interjected into his narrative.

"Yes," Keane confirmed. "I contacted them and received a call from Mr. Slimani. He sounded like a real professional, told me both his wife and he were involved in the business and asked me to send him photos of Muriel and myself, naked of course, to see if we might fit with his type of movies. I took some photos of Muriel and she took some of me, and I sent them to him by email. When he got back in touch I was excited and then he told me he wanted to see us both in action. I asked what he meant and he told me he needed to see us, erm…doing it, you know?"

"And you complied with that request, I take it," Gable said, in a statement, not a question.

"Yes, I bought a new phone that could take good quality video and I was able to make a short video of me and Muriel, just straight sex you understand, nothing kinky, and I sent it to Mr. Slimani. He came back to me and asked me to meet him last week. That's why I went to Birkenhead, to meet him and discuss the next stage. He wanted me to feel comfortable and not under any pressure which is why he suggested a round of golf while we discussed matters. He really is a very nice man, a proper professional."

"*Was* a nice man," Devenish now came in to the conversation.

"Sorry? What do you mean, *was* a nice man?" Keane appeared mystified.

"I'm sorry to tell you that Joey Slimani was murdered at some time on Saturday, Mr. Keane. I'm afraid there'll be no porn movie careers for you and your wife with *Joe Slim Productions*."

Robert Keane visibly paled. In fact, Sam Gable thought he was about to faint, but he managed to pull himself together and despite almost hyper-ventilating at the news, he brought himself under control and gasped "I don't understand. We just met to talk about making a film. Why would anyone kill him?"

"We kind of hoped you might be able to help us there, Mr. Keane," Devenish said, bluntly, and Sam Gable kept up the pressure by asking,

"And who was the third man?" Mr. Keane.

"I'm sorry, the third man?"

"You arrived at South Mersey Golf Club with another man," Gable said. "Who was it?"

"Oh, that was Heinrich Braun. He's a friend of Mr. Slimani's. He lives not far from me and Mr. Slimani asked me to pick him up on the way as he had business to discuss with him."

"And who is Heinrich Braun?"

"He's German, as you can guess, and is supposed to be going to direct some films for Mr. Slimani. He lives in Middleton and I called at his house to pick him up on my way to see Mr. Slimani. I can give you the address if you need it."

"Please do that," Devenish said and made a note of the address in Middleton that Keane duly supplied. "Tell me, though, what was all that crap about you and Braun giving false names when you signed in at South Mersey?"

Keane grinned, and both Devenish and Gable were becoming increasingly aware that their trip to visit the man could be nothing but a wild goose chase. If they were to believe his story and judging by the fact he kept speaking as though Joey Slimani was still alive, then this was all a big waste of their time.

"Oh, that was a bit of fun, Mr. Slimani's idea. He said the Club Captain was a real sanctimonious, stuck-up piece of shit, those were his words, not mine and asked us to do it just to see if the prick, as Joey called him even bothered to read the guest book to see who was actually playing on his precious course. As it turned out, nobody challenged us, and we left after playing with nobody any the wiser."

The experienced Sergeant, Ian Gilligan entered the conversation once again with a question Sam Gable wished she'd asked.

"One question, Mr. Keane. Why did Mr. Slimani ask you to pick up Herr Braun and ferry him to Birkenhead with you? Did Braun not have transport of his own?"

As Gable cursed herself for not thinking to ask that question, Keane replied directly to Gilligan.

"When I called to collect him, there was a black BMW on Braun's drive. He explained that Mr. Slimani had specifically asked him to travel with me so he could get to know me a little better. Apparently, he had it in mind to cast me in the film that Mr. Braun was about to direct for him."

"And did you get along with Herr Braun?" Gilligan asked.

"Mostly, yes. I confess I got a little embarrassed when he began talking about Muriel and what he expected from her in the film. He'd watched the demo video I'd sent to Mr. Slimani, you see. Hearing a stranger talk about my wife like that did give me a few uncomfortable moments, but I had to accept that was all part of the business we were getting into."

The detectives, Sam Gable in particular, could sympathise with his feelings on the matter and didn't press him further on the subject.

Sam had one other question for Robert Keane, after which she felt they could wrap up the interview.

"At any time during the day, did you get the feeling that anything was worrying Mr. Slimani, or was anything said by him or Herr Braun that would have led you to believe there was any between the two men?"

"No, nothing like that. I got the impression they were quite good friends, or at least, had a good working relationship."

"And your conversations during your time together were solely concerned with the film they wanted you and your wife to take part in?"

"Yes, although Muriel would have had a lot more involvement than me, they explained."

Gable wasn't the least bit surprised by that last piece of information.

"And you drove home after playing golf, and dropped Braun at his home again, is that right?" Devenish added.

"Yes, honestly, that was all that happened that day. Mr. Slimani said he'd be in touch soon. I can't believe he's dead. Can you tell me how it happened?"

"I'm sorry, that's all part of our ongoing investigation," Gable replied. "We may want to talk to you again in the future, your wife too."

"Oh God, Muriel is going to be so embarrassed. We hoped we could keep it all private and confidential."

"Yet you were prepared to allow your wife to have sex on film with one or more strangers?"

Keane fell silent, his face turning a bright vermillion colour as Sam's words hit home. Before he could reply, the detectives brought the interview to an end, thanking Keane for his time, and Charles Hartley for allowing them to use his office for the purpose of carrying out the interview. As they left the office, they couldn't help but hear Hartley saying "Don't go anywhere yet, Robert. I think we need a little chat, don't you?"

Sadly, Ian Gilligan closed the door fully before they could hear what they assumed would be a suitably embarrassed reply from the hapless, would-be porn star legal clerk. Soon after, they dropped Ian Gilligan back at his own station and set off on the return leg of their journey.

As Devenish took over the driving duties on the journey home, Sam, having sat in thought for a couple of minutes, ventured her thoughts to her colleague.

"You know, Ginge, some people amaze me. I know we see most things in our line of work, but I never realised just how far the tentacles of the adult movie business reached into the lives of what we might term 'normal' suburban families."

"I know what you mean," he concurred. "I'd never have put Keane's missus down as a would-be porn star. She just seemed to be so…so…"

"Normal," Sam finished his sentence.

"Exactly. Do you think they had anything to do with Joey's murder, Sam?"

"Honestly, no, but I could be wrong. I just think Robert Keane ended up in the wrong place at the wrong time and has got himself dragged into this whole sorry business through his own greed and poor judgement."

"Wonder what his boss will do. He didn't look very happy, did he?"

"I know. If looks could kill eh? Mind you, I'm not sure if Keane's done anything that could legally be termed a sackable offence, but Hartley is a solicitor and you never know what he might do, if he thinks Keane could turn out to be an embarrassment to his precious firm."

"Do you think we'll need to talk to them again?"

"I don't know, Ginge. We'll report back to the boss and who knows, we might find ourselves trekking this way again if he wants us to talk to Herr Braun. Movie director."

"I think he will, Sam, don't you?"

"Oh yes, I'm sure he will," Sam replied, hiding a slight smile at the thought she might get to see Ian Gilligan once more. She suddenly realised there was something about the widowed detective sergeant she rather liked.

Chapter 12

Love in a cold climate

Sofie Meyer, the team's on-loan German detective, holding the honorary rank of detective sergeant, though in her own country her rank would have been nearer to Inspector, sat with Detective Constables Tony Curtis and Nick Dodds, as they were joined by Andy Ross and Izzie Drake. Meyer, aided by the two D. C's had managed to pull two desks together, to form a space large enough to hold the TV and DVD player they'd set up in order to watch sections of the pornographic films they'd found in the city's licensed sex shops.

"How have our two reprobates been behaving, Sofie?" Ross asked, with a broad smile on his face, knowing that the two male detectives would have been lapping up the opportunity to study the selection of adult movies, all in the course of doing their duty.

"They have both been very diligent and attentive to their task, sir," Meyer replied, also grinning as she spoke.

"I just bet they have," Izzie Drake added, in equally jocular fashion.

"Hey Sarge," Curtis chimed in. "Me and Nick have worked really hard on this, I'll have you know."

"Of course you have, Tony," Ross commented. "I can just imagine you and Nick really working hard on these films."

The innuendo from their superior officer wasn't lost on Curtis and Dodds who both fell silent for a few seconds, until Dodds broke the silence.

"With Sergeant Meyer in charge, sir, we had no option other than follow your instructions to the letter. Anyway, these films aren't exactly my kind of entertainment."

"Really Nick? I'd have thought they'd have been right up your street," Drake said, still maintaining the light-hearted theme of the conversation. The case was serious enough, but at some point in every investigation, the team had to find ways to relieve the tension and frustration that often accompanied a particularly difficult case, with few clues and even fewer suspects readily to hand.

"No way," Dodds replied. "It might surprise you know that I actually prefer the real thing, Sarge. Penny and me have a very healthy relationship, if you catch my drift."

"Okay," Ross interrupted. "Let's get serious. Sofie, have you found anything useful, or in any way pertinent to the investigation?"

Sofie Meyer had cued up one of the videos in readiness for the presentation of her small team's report. She pressed the 'play' button on the VCR and the screen burst into life. She'd ensured the sound level was at a low level so as not to impede her report to Ross, but even so, it was impossible not to hear the sounds of sexual activity taking place before their eyes.

"This is actually the closing scene of the movie," Meyer began, and I've left it for you to see, purely because, as Nick quickly realised, this scene features our victim's wife, Trixie Mae Bluebell."

"I thought she was blonde," Ross commented as he watched the brunette on the screen performing a sex act with a well-proportioned male, whose words identified him as being African-American.

"I'm sure most of the girls in these films appear in many guises," Meyer replied. They clearly make use of wigs and make up to change their appearance to match whatever is called for by the director."

The film they were currently watching was, Sofie explained, a compilation of short scenes, all featuring interracial sex. The scene came to an end, and the screen faded to black, to be replaced by the credits.

"Now, she explained, we can see that the film was produced and directed by her husband and was made by Joey Slimani's own production company. We have noticed, from watching the other films we purchased, that Mr. Slimani appeared to use a number of regular people behind the scenes. The cinematographer in this case is a man who goes by the professional name of Paul St. George. Tony did some research and it seems this man's real name is Paul Simpson, an American who actually works in the legitimate movie industry but who apparently earns a lucrative second living working in the porn industry and his camera work is well sought after. Even in the adult movie industry there is a difference in quality between well-made productions and less professional 'skin-flick' type films as they are referred to. The film was made in L.A. in a studio which features in all of the Joe Slim movies we obtained."

She paused the movie, mid-credits before speaking again.

"We have found that Joey Slimani used virtually the same production crew for all the movies he made in the USA, so we can assume that he was a good employer and that he paid well to get the best people he could to help produce his films. The exception we found in the movies we found in the city was one film which was co-produced by Mr. Slimani and a German by the name of Heinrich Braun, a UK resident who works out of studio here in Liverpool. His studio is located in a unit on a small industrial estate near the docks. His films are marketed by a company in Germany, Ace Films GmbH, whose registered office is in Leipzig. To explain, GmbH signifies Gesellschaft mit beschränkter Haftung, which basically translates as a company with limited liability."

"Anything else of interest? Ross asked.

"Only that Mrs. Slimani seems to be a very enthusiastic participant in her movies," Meyer commented.

"I second with that assessment, Boss," Curtis quipped.

"And I'll third it," Dodds grinned devilishly.

"Alright, you pair of deviant detectives," Ross couldn't help smirking with amusement. "Why did I ever think you two could view a few scenes of pornography objectively?"

"But Boss, I swear, we were objective, most definitely," Curtis was giggling with unconcealed amusement, knowing that Ross was in a light-hearted mood.

"Oh, bloody shut it, D.C. Curtis. I might suggest to the D.C.I. that we revamp the meaning of D.C. from detective constable to deviant constable."

There was a subtle ripple of laughter from those around the desk, and as Nick Dodds turned off the DVD player on Meyer's instructions, Sam Gable and Ginger Devenish walked into the squadroom, newly returned from their investigative foray to Greater Manchester.

* * *

"So, it looks like this Henrich Braun chap might know more about Joey Slimani than anyone else we're identified so far," Ross said, after hearing Gable and Devenish's report of their interview with Robert Keane.

"That's odd, sir," Gable responded, "because the way Keane spoke, we kind of got the impression that Braun and Slimani were more recent acquaintances."

"Yeah, that's what I thought too," Devenish agreed.

"I think it's important we follow this up and speak to this Braun character," Ross decided.

"Do you want to see him yourself, Boss?" Devenish asked the question Sam was almost afraid to ask. She was thinking there could be a chance of seeing Ian Gilligan again.

"No, I don't think so," Ross replied. "You two have done a good job in speaking with Keane, and, armed with what he told you, I think you'll be in the best position to carry on where you left off with him by speaking to Braun and getting his side of the meeting at South Mersey."

Sam breathed a big internal sigh of relief, but of course, she knew Ross's decision held no guarantee she'd get to see the handsome sergeant again. Her fears were allayed a moment later when Ross picked up the phone and immediately called Greater Manchester Police, spoke for a couple of minutes to a Chief Inspector Goode, and on hanging up the phone, turned to the two detectives.

"Okay, sorted. You can go home, get a good night's sleep and get an early start tomorrow. You'll met with Detective Sergeant Gilligan again, who'll continue as liaison between us and Manchester. Between now and then Gilligan will do some digging at his end and try to find out where Braun will be during the day. There's no point you two going over there, only to find he's flown to Germany or travelled elsewhere to indulge in a spot of movie making. If he's not going to be around, Gilligan will let you know, and we can make other arrangements to interview him."

Sam Gable tried to contain the frisson of excitement that ran though her body on hearing Ross's words. It had been a long time since she'd felt anything remotely like this. After all, as she knew, she wasn't in the first flush of youth. She was a thirty-two-year-old detective, a senior member of Ross's team, yet here she was, feeling like a love-struck teenager.

Get a grip, Sam, she told herself. He's a widower, maybe still in love with his wife, or he might have a girlfriend already. Maybe all he saw in you was a fellow police officer, there to do a job and nothing more. We'll see, she thought, yes, for the first time for a long time, Sam Gable had a new goal. Whatever happened the following day, she was determined to ensure that Detective Sergeant Ian Gilligan did notice her.

* * *

The following morning dawned, a typical cold and frosty December day. Cloud cover was sparse and had led to the heaviest frost of the year so far. Combined with the streets and shops being decorated in readiness for the upcoming Christmas holidays, the city, like most around the nation, was beginning to gear down in time for the festivities, except for the country's retailers, who were collectively hoping for a last-minute sales bonanza.

Leaving Liverpool behind, with Sam at the wheel, the two detectives chatted amiably.

"You seem really happy to be heading over to Manchester again, Sam" Devenish commented. "It wouldn't have anything to do with a certain detective sergeant of our recent acquaintance would it?"

Sam couldn't believe the young D.C. had picked up on her attraction to Ian Gilligan.

"What? Why do you think that?"

"Oh, come on Sam. I'm not blind you know, and for fucks sake, in case you hadn't noticed, I am a detective, not some Scotty Road scally."

Sam sighed resignedly. Devenish was quite right of course. He was a trained observer, but then again, so was Ian Gilligan.

"Shit," she exclaimed. "D'you think he noticed too?"

"He'd have to have been, deaf, dumb and blind not to have done, if you ask me,"

"Oh fuck, I could be making a right fool of myself, Ginge. Promise you won't say anything to drop me in it, won't you?"

"Your secret's safe with me," Devenish smiled, "but if Sergeant Gilligan read your body language and sly looks of admiration the way I did, it ain't much of a secret if you ask me. and, if I may say so, you look particularly good this morning."

Sam Gable actually found herself blushing in response to Ginger Devenish's compliment. It was true, she'd gone to some lengths to look her best that morning. She normally forsook much make-up at work, only applying a little eye shadow and mascara before leaving home. Lipstick was a no-no for her at work, instead she applied a little rose-pink Vaseline to help protect them from the worst of the weather, but today, she'd risen early, sat in front of her dressing table and spent a few minutes applying a subtle shade of pink lipstick, together with her usual eye shadow and mascara and a little blusher. She's washed and blow dried her shoulder-length blonde hair and chosen a black, short skirted two-piece suit, the skirt falling just above her knees, and with a slight flare to it that would accentuate her legs and rear view for anyone who might be interested. In short, Sam looked a million miles away from her usual workaday appearance.

"I've phoned ahead, using the number Robert Keane turned over to us yesterday. Herr Braun didn't sound too pleased to hear from me, but he's agreed to speak to us at his home if we get there before noon. He says he has business appointments to keep this afternoon."

"Thanks for your foresight in setting it up for us, Sarge," Sam said, smiling at him.

"No problem," Gilligan replied, and for God's sake, drop the rank. It's Ian, okay?"

"Okay," Sam and Ginger replied in unison.

Heinrich Braun's house in Middleton, not far from Keane's home in Failsworth, was a typical three-bedroomed suburban detached house in a secluded cul-de-sac, giving him a fair degree of privacy, Sam thought as Gilligan brought the car to a halt on his drive, just behind the black BMW that Keane had referred to the previous day.

"At least, if he's got anything to hide, he won't be able to make a run for it in his car," Devenish commented as they exited the unmarked police Ford Mondeo.

Heinrich Braun answered the door promptly after Gilligan pressed the doorbell and allowed his finger to linger on the ring button just a little longer than was really necessary. He was tall, around six feet, Sam guessed, and possessed what she perceived to be bleached blonde hair, his eyebrows a non-matching brown in colour, cut in a short, spiky style that made him look more like a thirty-something punk rocker than a professional adult film producer and director. He wore grey jogging pants, white nondescript trainers, and a white t-shirt that carried a black, stylised image of a man and woman engaged in the sex act, with the words, FU*K ME printed below the image in bold red lettering.

Braun scrupulously checked the identity of each officer before allowing them across the threshold into his home. They were shown into what was clearly the lounge/living room of the property, though it resembled a miniature film studio, or perhaps, a set in readiness for filming a particular scene. Lights were arranged, as in a photographer's studio, Sam thought, at strategic places in the room, the only furniture of note being a very large sofa in the centre of the room, and a low glass-topped coffee table. A large screen television was attached to the wall above the built-in fireplace which the builders have designed in cream mock-marble. Under the bay window that would normally look out on the street stood a small table upon which stood a DVD recorder/player and several discs in jewel cases, with titles written on sticky labels in German. The curtains which hung in the window were in heavy black velvet, and all three detectives realised they made for perfect blackout curtains if the man was filming in the room. The room made Gable feel distinctly uncomfortable, especially when Braun invited them to take a seat, and she couldn't help but think of all the 'action' that had probably taken place exactly where she was sitting, especially as the large sofa was also quite low and her skirt rode up as she sat, giving Braun a more than adequate view of her legs.

"What is it you are wanting from me?" Braun asked as soon as the detectives were seated, though Gilligan remained standing close to the door.

"It's about your relationship with Joey Slimani," Sam stated. "Especially about your visit to meet him in the company of Mr. Robert Keane at South Mersey Golf Club, last Thursday."

"Yes?" was all he said in reply.

"Can you tell us the reason for your visit, Herr Braun?"

"Ja, there is no secret about it. I accompanied Herr Keane as it had been proposed by Joey, that we could use Keane and his wife in one or more of our productions. I'm assuming you are aware of the nature of my business?"

"Yes, we are," Devenish responded, feeling that Sam was slightly uncomfortable in Braun's presence. "You are a producer of pornographic films, are you not?"

"Yes, I am, and as far as I am aware, it is not against the law to make such movies, am I correct?"

"That is correct," said Devenish.

"Then why do the police wish to know my business with Joey Slimani? Have you already asked my friend Joey these questions?"

"I'm afraid we can't do that, Herr Braun. At some time on Saturday, someone murdered Joey Slimani. We are part of the team investigating his death."

As Devenish delivered the notification of Joey's death, Braun's face turned pale and the man's self-confident demeanour instantly altered. Suddenly his self-assuredness evaporated, and his voice cracked as he spoke.

"Murdered? Joey has been murdered? This cannot be. We were business colleagues, friends, you might say. Together we have made movies and made money together. Why should someone wish to harm Joey, do you know the answer to this?"

"That's why we're here," Herr Braun. "We are hoping you may be able to help with our enquiries into his death."

"But how? Why? I know nothing of this. Mein Gott, his poor wife. I must call her. She will be devastated, I think."

"Have you worked with Mrs. Slimani in the past?" Sam asked, having recovered her equilibrium.

"Yes, I have worked with Trixie on occasions. She is a very nice person."

"But she hasn't rung you to tell you of Joey's murder?"

"No, she has not. But then, why would she? She would not have thought of me at such a time."

"But wouldn't she have known you and her husband were planning to make a new movie together?" Sam asked.

"I don't know. Perhaps you should ask her."

"We will, Herr Braun," it was Devenish who spoke again. "Would you have any idea of who might have had a reason to want Joey Slimani dead?"

"I have no such ideas, no," said Braun, but both Devenish and Gable had a feeling the man was holding something back. So too did Ian Gilligan, who spoke from his position near the door.

"Was Joey Slimani afraid of anyone, Herr Braun? Had he, or perhaps the two of you, received any threats recently?"

"No, of course not, well, not as far as I am aware."

Gable gave Devenish a look that he easily understood to mean *'He's lying,'* which prompted him to quickly ask,

"Some people are apparently not too happy with Joey, people with some power in your industry, back in the USA. Are you telling me you didn't know anything about that?"

"Yes, I mean no. That is, Joey had told me yes, that he was not too popular back in the States, and that he was now working exclusively in the UK and wished to expand into the German market We have a very flourishing industry in Germany, you see."

"We know all about that, thank you," said Devenish. "We also heard that Mrs. Slimani wasn't too happy about working in the German industry."

"I know nothing about that," Braun held his arms out in a gesture of resignation. "You must speak to Trixie about such things."

It became very clear to the detectives that Braun wouldn't be saying much more to them, and a signal from the experienced D.S. Gilligan inspired Sam and Ginger to bring the interview to a close.

Outside the house, they stood for a minute or two, in conversation.

"What was it about that man that made me feel uncomfortable?" Sam queried. "I worked Vice for three years but never had a gut feeling like I did in that house."

"I think it was more the house than the man, Sam," Gilligan ventured. "It did slightly resemble a brothel on the Reeperbahn in Hamburg, I must admit."

"You've been there?" Sam asked, a little disconcerted at the thought.

"Only as a tourist. A few of us went to a beer festival there about five years ago and did the full tour of the city, including the infamous red-light district.

"Ah, right, I see," Sam felt better.

"I have a feeling we haven't seen the last of Herr Heinrich Braun in this case," Devenish ventured his thoughts.

"You think, Ginge?" Sam looked at him, seeing his determination in the look in his eyes.

"I'm sure of it. Don't ask me how or why, but something about that man makes me think there's more to his involvement than we know so far."

"Well, you guys know you can count on our support if you need us again," said Gilligan.

"I suppose we'd better be heading back then, make our report to the boss," Sam said, reluctantly.

"I suppose so," Devenish agreed.

Gilligan drove them back to the station where they prepared to collect their pool car and head back to Liverpool.

"I'll go and get the car out of the car park and meet you out front, Sam," Devenish offered, knowing it would give Sam a minute or two alone with Ian Gilligan. The Detective Sergeant slowly walked Sam out of the station and the pair stopped for a moment on the front steps.

"Well," said Gilligan, reaching out his right hand, ostensibly for a hand shake.

"Well," Sam repeated, taking his hand in hers.

Instead of shaking each other's hand, the pair just stood looking into each other's eyes for a long second, their hands getting warmer as they held each other. Gilligan pulled his hand away gently and decided to take the plunge.

"Maybe one day we could meet outside working hours, Sam. What do you think?" he asked, feeling nervous as a kitten as he did so. He hadn't asked another woman out since the death of his wife, but something about Sam Gable had made him feel more alive than he'd felt for years.

Sam's mind raced. Her heart took a little leap in her chest and her throat seemed to constrict her mouth dried up as though her tongue had swollen. She knew she'd got it bad.

"Sam?" Gilligan said, thinking he'd blown it.

"Sorry, I mean yes, that is, if you're sure. I'd love to."

"Thank God for that," Gilligan breathed a sigh of relief. "I'll call you then, okay?"

"Okay," Sam replied, turning to look at the car where Ginger Devenish sat behind the wheel, grinning like the proverbial Cheshire Cat. "I'd better go," she said.

"Mmm," Gilligan muttered, then... " Sam?"

"What?"

"If I'm going to call you, it might be an idea for you to give me your phone number."

Flustered, Sam replied, "Oh God yes, of course, sorry." She took one of her official cards and a pen from her small black leather handbag and quickly wrote her home and mobile numbers on the back. Gilligan handed her a slip of paper in return with his numbers written in clear, precise numbers.

"You'd better go then, Sam Gable," he smiled at her and Sam felt she could melt in to those eyes.

"Okay, Sergeant Gilligan," she smiled back and before she could change her mind, quickly turned and almost ran down the remaining steps, pulled open the door of the car and slipped in beside her colleague. Ginger Devenish pulled away slowly, giving her time for one last turn and wave at the good-looking Detective Sergeant.

"You alright, Sam?" he grinned at her as she finally turned to look out of the windscreen.

"Of course. Why shouldn't I be?"

"You kind of look a bit stunned," he said.

"Can we talk about the case, please Ginge, and leave my love life out of it?"

"Sure, I'm just pleased you got the result you wanted with the sarge back there."

"Yes, well, let's keep it between the two of us, ok?"

"Okay, you got it. Now, what do you think about Heinrich Braun?"

"He'd definitely get my vote for creep of the year, Ginge. There was something there, but I'm not sure what."

"I agree," Devenish replied. "Do you think he might be worth further investigation?"

"I do, but we'll have to see what the boss thinks. We don't have a shred of evidence against him as yet. But…" Sam fell silent.

"Yeah, but…" Devenish murmured as the car pulled off the motorway and they headed for the city centre, and police headquarters.

Chapter 13

A gathering of wolves?

"Heinrich Braun seems to be the only recurring name we're meeting in this case so far," Ross announced to the rest of the team, after calling an impromptu meeting, having received Sam and Ginger's report of their most recent visit to Manchester. "Sam and Ginger are both convinced the man is hiding something. Unfortunately, neither of them can put a finger on what it is that's got their suspicions raised, so for now, we can do very little apart from keep a watching brief on the man, though there is one thing we are actively involved in where he's concerned. Sofie?" He nodded in the direction of Sofie Meyer, who stood and addressed the team.

"D.I. Ross asked me to contact my colleagues back in Germany and my boss in Hamburg was very interested in the case and promised to do all he can to help. The adult movie business is a very lucrative one in Germany and like here, it is perfectly legal to make these movies as long as those who make them follow certain guidelines."

"What kind of guidelines?" Nick Dodds asked.

"Nothing too stringent," Meyer replied. "The chief requirement is that all actors employed in the films must be over the age of eighteen at the time of filming. The rest are basically rules set out to protect females in particular from any form of sexual exploitation."

"But that only covers the legal industry, Sofie," Izzie Drake raised an issue that had been nagging at the back of her mind. "We all know that, even here in the UK, there is an illegal side to the adult movie trade, with certain criminal factions being involved in producing films featuring girls that may have been coerced into taking apart, sexual slavery in fact, with many of them having been trafficked from Eastern Europe, and being forced into prostitution and maybe into these movies too."

"It is true also in Germany," Meyer replied. "Unfortunately, although our police also do their best to put a stop to such activities, the criminal fraternity will always find a way to circumvent the rules and regulations. I think we are fortunate that Mr. Slimani and his production company appear to have operated within the legal industry both in the USA and here in the UK. My colleagues in Germany are, however, now looking closely into the activities of Heinrich Braun. It seems strange to me that he chooses to make movies here in England. Why does he not produce his wares back home? Trust me, my boss knows the right people to talk to in order to discover the answers to that question."

Meyer sat down, and Ross took over the meeting once again.

"I want to know Slimani's movements after he left home on the morning of his death. If we can find out where he went, who he met, and for what reason, we may just find ourselves on the right track."

"But how the hell are we going to do that, sir?" Tony Curtis looked perplexed. "We have no idea which direction he went when he left home, so how can we trace his movements?"

"Did I say it was going to be easy, Tony?" Ross replied, and Curtis shook his head. "We might not find anything to help us, but by God, I want us to try. We know where his studio is located. Tony, you and Nick can get down there. Speak to anyone you find in the other units on the business park. See if there's any CCTV set up around the place. In a place like that, it's quite possible they have cameras set up for security purposes. You might get lucky and find some footage of Joey, if indeed he paid his studio a visit before or after his mystery meeting.

It might even be that this meeting was held at his studio. Let's give it a try, okay?"

"Okay, we're on it, Boss" Curtis replied. He and Nick Dodds were becoming quite an effective duo when teamed up together on assignments by Ross.

"Have you got anything to report, Paul?" Ross directed his question at D.S. Paul Ferris, the team's resident computer wizard, who, together with admin assistant Kat Bellamy, had been doing their best to track the histories of Joey Slimani, his company, and his three wives, past and present.

"Well, yes and no," Ferris began. "I can find nothing in the least to suggest that Joey Slimani was in any kind of financial trouble during the time he was producing films in the States. That's not to say he wasn't of course, only that if he was, it was nothing that shows up in any legitimate records."

"So, if we were being pressured or forced to pay some kind of protection money to the organised crime people in America, we'd have no way of knowing, is that what you're saying?" Drake sought confirmation.

"Exactly, Izzie," Ferris confirmed.

"Now, I had better luck with his wives."

"Better luck than Joey?" Curtis joked, raising a small peal of laughter around the room.

"Thank you for that gem of a comment, Tony," Ferris grinned.

"Anyway, I used the contacts I'd already made in the NYPD and LAPD,"

"Hark at him, sounds like something out of CSI or NCIS," Dodds quipped in response to Ferris's use of the American police force's descriptive initials.

"Since when did you two become a friggin' double act?" Ferris bit back at Nick Dodds, who held his hands up in mock surrender.

"Eh, la', it's hard work but someone's gotta do it," Dodds laughed as he spoke.

"Are you going to shut the fuck up Nick, so I can finish this report, or what?"

"Yes sir, Sergeant Ferris, sir."

"Shut up, Nick, you too, Tony. This is serious," Ross ended the banter, and Curtis and Dodds sort of shuffled towards the back of the room, in shamefaced silence.

"Right," Ferris continued, "My contacts in the States have sent me files on the lives and careers of Slimani's two ex-wives, Mary-Beth, aka Mary Honey and Lana, aka Lana Love. Nothing startling to see about either woman. Both entered the adult movie industry at a young age. The first Mrs Slimani, who I'll refer to as Mary-Beth for now, and as we know from the boss and Izzie's interview with Trixie, specialised in making what are known as BDSM movies as well as doing her fair share of straight sex stuff. For the uninitiated, BDSM stands for Bondage, Discipline and Sado-masochism, you know, sex with restraints, whips, chains, that kind of weird shit. She was obviously good at it, because at one time, she was one of the most highly paid exponents of her 'art' in the business. When she and Joey spilt up she received a fair but not exactly lucrative settlement, but bear in mind she was independently wealthy by then. The second wife, Lana, received a virtually identical settlement when she and Joey divorced, but, what struck us as being potentially significant about both of these ladies, is that their divorce settlements also gave each of them a share in Joe Slim Productions. So they were, in fact, Joey Slimani's business partners, up until his death."

Ferris fell silent while his revelation sunk in. It was Andy Ross who was first to comment.

"In other words, Paul, both women have continued making money out of Joey Slimani since their separations from him."

"That's right, sir. Now, if for some reason, one or both of them was upset about Slimani moving into the German market, perhaps thinking it might be a bad move, business-wise, which could adversely affect their financial status…"

"We might have a motive for murder," Ross adjudged.

"My thoughts exactly," Ferris confirmed. "Your turn, Kat," he turned to Kat Bellamy, who took over the conversation.

"I thought I'd see if I could track the two women down, thinking maybe one of you might want a word with them, and guess what?"

"Go on Kat, surprise us," Ross urged her on.

"Both women are here in England."

"Really?" said Drake.

"Really," Kat repeated. "Seems they both arrived yesterday. Mary-Beth flew in from LAX and Lana from JFK."

"Oh no, the sarge has got Kat doing the initials thing as well," Dodds groaned with a big stupid grin on his face.

"Nick," Ross said in an admonishing tone, bringing a mock, doleful look to Dodds's face, who did his best to pout like a naughty schoolboy, caught with his fingers in the cookie jar.

"Sorry, Boss," he murmured, amid giggles from his colleagues, who were glad to have the chance to release some of the tension surrounding the case by indulging in a little humour.

"Please, Kat, carry on," Ross encouraged Bellamy.

"Right, now, where was I? Oh yes, the two women arrived from LAX and JFK airports," Kat grinned, deliberately repeating her previous words, throwing Nick Dodds's banter back at him, not to be outdone by the gruff-voiced detective. "At present, I have no information on where they might be staying, or why they're in the UK."

"I think we can work that one out, Kat," said Izzie Drake. "Looks like the vultures are gathering. There's bound to be a reading of Joey's will pretty soon and his ex-wives, from what we've learned so far, will be sure to have arrived with an eye on what's in it for them."

"Oh great," Drake groaned. "Just what I need; another visit to Joey Slimani's private harem."

"Is it really that bad?" Curtis asked, wishing he could go and take a look at the Slimani residence.

"What, are you kidding me, Tony? My God, all those pictures on the walls of Trixie, performing in some of her movies were enough to make me feel ill, as well as wonder how some of those positions were humanly possible," this last bit spoken with a twisted grin on her face.

"I don't know," Curtis continued. "Sounds more like a pornographer's palace than a Sheikh's harem."

"Don't get me wrong, Tony, it's all that and more, but honestly la'…it's about as tasteful as a…a…" she struggled for an appropriate noun but was helped out by Tony Curtis's imagination.

"A whore's boudoir, perhaps, Sarge?"

"Yes, that's it, a whore's boudoir. Thanks, Tony."

"Anytime, you know me, Sarge."

"Don't we all, D.C. Curtis?" Ross grinned, and repeated, "Don't we all?"

Chapter 14

Friends and lovers

Ross and Drake once again found themselves seated opposite Trixie Slimani in her garishly decorated home. Izzie Drake had done her best to avoid looking at the stills of Trixie's porn film career as she'd followed Jennings the butler/manservant through the large entrance hall before being shown into the luxurious lounge-cum-sitting room. For the first time, she noticed a large mahogany sideboard at the far side of the room, on which several trophies and figurines were displayed. She couldn't help noticing that one of them resembled a large version of the famed Oscar figurine and she guessed the adult film industry must have its own version of the mainstream movie industry's Oscar Awards and that Trixie must have won the equivalent of the porn industry's version of the award. Her brain found it hard to compute just what the categories might be in such a system. Thinking of the different types of porn movies that Trixie had appeared in made her shudder a little as she imagined how embarrassed she would personally be to have to walk on stage in front of God knows how many people and deliver an acceptance speech for having won, for example, the award for 'Best Gang Bang' of the year or something similar. She couldn't stop herself from inadvertently smiling slightly at the thought.

"You alright, Izzie?" Ross asked, noticing the faraway look in her eyes. He'd worked with Drake long enough to know she was mentally somewhere else in that moment.

"What? Yes, sorry, I was just thinking of something for a few seconds. "Mrs. Slimani," she took up where the conversation had left off a minute ago, before they'd paused as Jennings had entered the room, bearing a large silver tray, with pots of coffee, tea, and a selection of Britain's finest biscuits beautifully presented. Jennings had poured, passed each of them a clean, white, linen napkin, (no paper ones for Trixie, she'd noted), and finally left them to continue their discussion. "You've just told us that you personally phoned both Mary-Beth and Lana with the news of your husband's death. Can you explain why you made those calls personally instead of allowing your husband's lawyer or the police in the States to carry out those notifications?"

"Hell, sure I can, Sergeant. Mary-Beth and Lana were not just Joey's ex-wives, no siree, they were still his friends, mine too. Where I come from you don't leave it to a stranger to deliver news like that."

"I quite understand that," Drake smiled at Trixie. "When exactly did you call them?"

"When? Hell, I called them the day you and the inspector here came round to tell me about Joey's murder. I thought they should know right away, being as they had a vested interest in Joey's business."

"In what way were they involved in Joey's business, Mrs. Slimani?" Ross asked the important question. He wanted to know if Trixie would confirm what his own team had already discovered about the ex-wives connections to Joey's production company."

Trixie was silent for a few seconds as she finished drinking the cup of coffee she held in her hand, then turned and smiled at Ross, and began her reply.

"Hell, Inspector Ross, I've told you, call me Trixie, please. When you call me Mrs. Slimani, somehow you make me feel like my Great Aunt Maud back in Wisconsin, and she's almost seventy, grey-haired and bent over with arthritis."

Better being bent over with arthritis than being bent over with some stranger doing God knows what at your rear, Izzie thought, but kept her silent thoughts to herself. Trixie continued as Ross said,

"Okay, Trixie it is. Please, go on. I don't think I could see you as a grey-haired old lady, by the way."

Izzie Drake could see Ross's point. Trixie wore a white pleated mini skirt over flesh-coloured stockings, (Drake knew a woman like Trixie would never wear tights, or, as Trixie would call them, panty-hose), a white-short sleeved blouse with a fixed raised collar, and to all intents and purposes looked like she was ready for a game of tennis, apart that is, from the drop-dead 4 inch heels on her patent leather shoes, and the fact that one serve would expose everything above the level of her skirt's hem, not ideal when wearing stockings. To offset the all-white garb, Trixie's previously blonde locks had given way to a beautiful, wavy, brunette hair, clearly a wig, and one that Drake estimated must have cost a small fortune, like everything else in *Paradise Found,* including Trixie Mae Rosebud, she thought, realising she was being unkind to the widow.

Trixie returned to Ross's question.

"Okay, see now, Mary-Beth and Lana, as I'm sure you guys have already discovered, both spent time in the business, working for Joey. They both made a real stash out of those movies and still work for other producers, regularly. When they divorced, Joey made a settlement that saw them both well looked after. I don't know all the details, but he told me that as well as a cash settlement and a regular allowance, Joey also gave each of them a share in his business. That way, they both held a vested interest in ensuring Joe Slim Productions continued to thrive."

"In other words," Ross astutely commented, "It was a good way for Joey to ensure that both his former wives would continue working for his company by making more movies, which would benefit him and help to offset the cash he'd settled on each of them, right?"

"You're a clever man, Inspector Ross. Yes, that's kinda how Joey explained it to me."

"In other words, those women had to virtually indenture themselves to Joey Slimani, in order to get a decent divorce settlement out of him," Drake commented.

"You make it sound as if my Joey was doing a bad thing, Sergeant. He wasn't. I told you before, my Joey, he was a good man, a generous man. Everyone won in those divorces, and there was nothing stopping Mary-Beth or Lana from working for other producers too. It's not like they were tied exclusively to Joey."

"Okay, we get the point," Ross replied, at the same time casting a slightly reproachful glance at Izzie Drake. He could tell Izzie was uncomfortable with the whole Slimani lifestyle, and with Trixie in particular, but he needed her to be professional in her handling of Joey's widow. "So, you informed them both of the murder and they arranged to come to England, because...?

"Because, Inspector, they both want to be here for Joey's funeral. They still cared about him, you know. You guys might not get it, but they might have been divorced but they were still friends. We all work in the same industry and its always good to get along together, so we all know each other and we're all friends, me included."

"And do you know the details of those settlements your husband made for his former wives?"

"Of course not, Inspector Ross. The details were known only to Joey and Mary-Beth and Lana. He told me the bare bones but never told me the full details of those settlements, and I never asked him."

Izzie Drake had spent a couple of minutes telling herself she had to get back on track, and fast. She'd seen the surreptitious glance Ross had thrown her way and knew he was displeased with her apparent lack of professional detachment in dealing with Trixie. Now, she was back on top of her game.

"Trixie, tell me please, if you know the details of Joey's will? I'm presuming of course that he *had* a will?"

"Yes of course. I mean, yes of course he had a will, but no, I don't know what was in it."

"I see, and did Joey have a solicitor or a lawyer, here in England?"

"Yes, he did. When we moved from the States and Joey registered his business over here, he said it made sense to have legal representation here in England. He looked up your Yellow Pages Business Directory and found a firm of solicitors in Liverpool. He told me they were real good once he'd got his business set up as a UK company, and one day he told me he wanted me to go visit them with him because he wanted us to register wills with them, just in case, and these were his words, "just in case one of us gets hit by a train one day."

Ross and Drake quickly exchanged glances that signified they were both thinking the same thing. If Trixie had been involved in Joey's murder, what better way to appear innocent than by revealing such a remark in such a way that she was effectively saying, *'I must be innocent, or why would I be telling you this?'*

The two detectives, however, had heard it all before and weren't likely to be taken in by such an obvious ploy, if, of course, that's what it was. For now though, they let the comment go.

"Yes, an unfortunate coincidental remark. I'm sure that's all it was," Ross lied, not wanting to alert her to any suspicions he may have been harbouring. Can you tell me who Joey's Liverpool solicitors are, please?" Ross asked, wanting to move the interview forward.

"Yes, Inspector," Trixie returned to the matter in question, removing a business card from the black leather purse that stood on the small side table beside her chair. Drake saw that the purse bore an unmistakeable designer label, and wondered if Ross had noticed it too. It was an item that Drake knew she could never afford and again made a statement about the lifestyle led by the woman sitting in the room with them. "Here you are," Trixie passed the card to Ross, "Joey insisted we both used the same firm."

Ross read the information on the card and recognised the name of the firm of solicitors representing the late Joey Slimani and his widow. "Hawkes and Temple, Duke Street," he read out loud so Drake could add it to her notes. "A good choice, Trixie. They've been established in the city for as long as I can remember. The card also bore the name of Michael Powell, clearly the solicitor appointed to represent the Slimanis. He passed the card to Drake, who noted the firm's telephone number and full address in her notebook, before passing the card back to Trixie.

"Do you know if Joey made any change to his will recently?" was Ross's next question, one that might throw light on any motive the widow might have had for disposing of the husband.

"I'm sure he didn't," Trixie replied, "but you can check with our old lawyers in the States," she replied, passing another business card to Ross, bearing the name, address and telephone number of Joey's lawyer in Los Angeles. "I'll call them and tell them it's okay to talk to you if you want to know the details of Joey's will. They're sure to have a copy on file."

"That will be helpful, thank you," Ross acknowledged.

"Going back to Joey's ex-wives," Drake began to shift the focus on to the subject they had really come to discuss. Everything so far had been cleverly set up to put Trixie at ease, as much as possible, before moving on to what might be a particularly touchy subject for Trixie. "When you say you're friends, just how close would you say you are?"

"Look, Sergeant, I know this all sounds like weird shit to you guys, but we are pretty good friends, you know? You need to realise that we all knew each other from working together. I did a couple of movies with Mary-Beth, while she was married to Joey, and a couple after they'd divorced, and I did two with Lana, while she and Joey were in the midst of splitting up, so we got to know each other pretty well."

"Yes, I can imagine you'd get pretty close, being involved in...doing whatever you did together in those films."

"Yep, look, I know you're afraid to ask, so I'll tell you. We did lesbian scenes together, and some threesomes, that's two girls with one guy, and a couple times, I did orgy scenes, with Lana. She's into that kind of thing, and before you ask, yes, we've been in scenes together since me and Joey got married. We're all pretty adult and civilised about it, you know?"

"I'm sure you are, thank you for being honest with us, Trixie."

"Aw, hell," she beamed at Drake, "Ain't nothin' you couldn't have found out by looking at me resume, and theirs and comparing them."

"Do you know where we can find Mary-Beth and Lana, now that they're here in England?" Ross asked next.

"Yeah, sure I know. Mary-Beth is staying at the Hotel Russell on Russell Square in London, and Lana's at the Dorchester. But you guys don't have to go to London to talk to them. They'll be here tomorrow."

"By here, you mean…?"

"Right here, Inspector. The ladies are going to be my guests until the funeral's over. They both want to be home in time for Christmas you know?"

Ross found it odd that Joey Slimani's three wives would suddenly be all together in the same house, but said nothing, apart from arranging to talk to Mary-Beth and Lana at their earliest convenience after arriving. Trixie promised to call headquarters once the two ex-wives had arrived and settled in, or at least, as she put it, "I'll have Jennings call you. He doesn't seem to have too much to do right at present, what with Joey gone and all."

Thanking her, Ross and Drake agreed to return the following day to speak to Mary-Beth and Lana and Trixie pressed a button on a pad on her side table which must have acted like a bell to summon Jennings, who appeared as if by magic within seconds to escort the two officers from the house. Ross suspected he'd been listening at the door, though was sure he wouldn't have heard much through such a thick heavy door to the living room. Ross took a moment to speak to Jennings as he and Drake stood on the threshold at the front door.

"Can I have a word, Mr. Jennings?" Ross spoke quietly after making sure he was well out of earshot of Trixie.

"Sure you can, and I told your constable the other day, call me Bill. All this 'Jennings' lark is making me feel like I'm in an Agatha Christie mystery."

Ross smiled, knowing just what Jennings meant.

"Okay, Bill it is then," Ross said.

"Yeah, well, I didn't tell him much to be honest, but if it helped, that's good."

"Actually, Bill, your information was very important, in view of what happened to Mr. Slimani. You see, what you told D.C. Curtis in effect gives Mrs. Slimani a perfect alibi for the day of her husband's murder."

"Hell, shit, I never thought of it like that. You mean the fact I was…you know, in bed with Trixie all day?"

"Yes, that and the fact you told Curtis that after you left her bedroom she was under the influence of some kind of narcotics and as far as you knew, she was 'out of it' as you put it, until the following day, is that right?"

"That's the gist of it, yeah."

"But you also said you took a long shower and went to bed early yourself, so Mrs. Slimani never called for you or requested your presence in her room any more that day or the next day?"

"That's basically it, yeah?"

"So, from the time you left her room to the next day, you didn't see her or hear from her, which means she could have left the house at some time without your knowledge. Is that also a possibility?"

"Well, yeah, I suppose so, but like I said, she was totally off her head on crack or something, so she wouldn't have been able to do much if she did creep out."

"Bill, think carefully. You told D.C. Curtis that Trixie is a regular user of strong drugs. Don't you think someone like her would know exactly how to fake being 'off her head' if she really wanted to? Especially as you admitted you're not into drugs, so you wouldn't really know if she was faking it or not, would you?"

Jennings thought for a few seconds, letting Ross's words sink in before replying.

"Here, you don't suspect Trixie of doing him in, do you? 'Cos as far as I could see from my time here, she really loved her Joey. That's what she always called him, you know, 'My Joey.'

"Bill, listen, at present everyone is a suspect until we can eliminate them from our enquiries, so I need to establish everyone's movements from the time Mr. Slimani left home to the time his body was found on the railway tracks."

The significance of Ross's words finally clicked in Jennings's brain.

"So, I'm a suspect too, is that right?"

"Like I said Bill, everyone's a suspect, but truthfully, I don't see you as having killed the goose that laid the golden egg as far as you're concerned. You told Curtis you've never been so well paid, you had Joey's permission to sleep with his wife when he wasn't around, and I'm guessing you might have been lined up to play a part or two in some of his upcoming films. Am I right?"

Jennings nodded, but qualified Ross's theory by adding, "I did agree to do a movie or two for Joey, but nothing came of it. At least he never mentioned it again. Anyway, you're right, Inspector. I was happy working here and I didn't have a motive or any desire to see Joey dead. I mean, for fuck's sake, it might be just my luck, now he's dead, for Trixie to sell this place and go back to America or something and leave me back on the dole."

Ross nodded, satisfied in his own mind that Jennings in all probability had nothing to gain from Joey's death and was in the clear, for now, at least. By the time he and Drake had returned to headquarters and checked in with D.C.I. Agostini, it was late afternoon, the sky had grown dark and the streets had become illuminated with fairy lights and the outdoor temperature had dropped until it hovered just above zero. With little more that could be done that day, Ross instructed his team to go home, get a good night's sleep and be in fresh and early the next day, when, he hoped, events might turn in their favour. As he commented to Izzie Drake as they parted from each other in the headquarters car park,

"Let's be honest, Izzie, we started with nothing, and we've still got nothing, if we're honest about it. I just hope the ex-wives can open a door or two for us tomorrow." He knew he needed to speak to his long-time partner about her unusual and overtly hostile stance towards

Trixie Slimani, but he felt it could wait until the morning. Both he and Izzie needed to rest, spend some time at home and get a good night's sleep. Things might look a damn sight more positive in the morning.

Chapter 15

Down time

"Something's worrying you," Maria Ross said to her husband as they sat in their comfortable lounge after dinner that evening. "I can always tell, when you get that faraway look in your eyes.

"Of course you can, and yes, I'm worried. Who wouldn't be? I've got a dead body, or to be precise, pieces of a dead body, belonging to a well-known producer of pornographic movies, who Doc Nugent was able to ascertain was murdered, but so far, none of my team have been able to come up with a single strong suspect."

Maria, a forty-four-year-old G.P. at a local surgery in Prescot, could often see beyond the fog that clouded her husband's thoughts when he became bogged down in a case. This time however, Ross had given her so few details about his latest case that, so far, she wasn't in a position to help or advise him. Maria decided that needed to change.

"Right, Mr. big shot Detective Inspector Andrew Ross, this is me speaking. Give! I know when you're struggling my darling husband and it's time to talk about it."

She reached across and took his hand in hers, and gently squeezed it, encouraging him to open up a little and unburden himself of some of his frustration.

"I know. I'm sorry. I haven't said much because there hasn't been much to say, but the lack of any visible motive for Joey Slimani's murder is getting to me. Up to now, we have only a very tenuous link to his previous life in the USA, and somehow, I doubt that whoever he might have upset at some time in the past would be reaching out across the Atlantic to have him done away with."

"Okay," Maria spoke softly, in a tone that suggested she was, or could be, the voice of reason that just might help her husband to clear away some of the mental fog that was hampering his investigation. "All I know so far is that your victim was a producer of pornographic movies, who'd left the States to establish a new business here after falling foul of some criminal elements over there, and that his body was found on the tracks at Mossley Hill. So, come on, what's new?"

Ross felt himself relaxing slightly and he quickly brought Maria up to date with the state of his case. He often discussed his cases with Maria, only divulging what he felt appropriate so whatever he shared with his wife could never be seen as in any way compromising his investigation. For the next ten minutes, Andy Ross gave Maria as comprehensive rundown as possible on the developments, such as they were, on the Joey Slimani case.

"You know, Andy?" Maria said when he fell silent, "It seems to me as if you might be looking at this the wrong way."

"How so, oh great and knowledgeable one?" he joked in reply.

"Well, I bet you, and Izzie especially, not to mention some of those reprobates on your team are fully focussed on the sex angle of the case, am I right?"

"I suppose you are. It's difficult not to look at it like that when your vic is a pornographer. And you're dead right about Izzie. I need to have words with her in the morning. She was close to being downright insulting to the widow today. She seems hung up on the whole porno thing."

"That's not like Izzie. I would never have marked her down as a prude. But I know you'll sort it out with her and she'll be as professional as she always is."

"So, any suggestions on how to go looking for someone with a hatred of my dead pornographer, Mrs. Ross?"

"Andy, first and foremost he was just a man, same as if he'd been a banker or a plumber or whatever. My advice is to put the sexual aspects of the case to one side and look at it from another perspective. I mean, if he was a plumber, what would be the kind of motives for someone to want to kill him?"

Ross laid his head against the back of the sofa as he thought over Maria's words. A minute passed as his wife continued to sit beside him, still holding his hand, and then, he found his voice once again.

"Maria, you're a bloody genius," he exclaimed.

"Of course I am," his wife laughed. "I'm your wife. It goes with the job, didn't I tell you that when we got married?"

"Many times," Ross laughed as well. "I guess I need regular reminders. You're right of course. Maybe we've been attaching too much importance to the adult movie business and perhaps we should go back to basics and look at the pure human aspect."

"You don't need to go that far back, Andy. You've already spoken to most of the principals in the case. What's the betting you or one of your team has already spoken to the killer. You just don't know which one it is yet."

Ross grabbed his wife's face with both hands and drew her to him in a long, sultry kiss.

"What would I do without you, Doctor Ross?"

"Not something I want to contemplate," Maria smiled at him.

"Me neither," he replied. "Now, how d'you fancy an early night?"

As Andy and Maria Ross made their way to bed, Izzie Drake lay in husband Peter Foster's arms, having fallen into bed together an hour earlier. Something had inhibited Izzie however and Peter knew something was laying heavily on her mind.

"Come on, out with it," he demanded as Izzie rested her head on his shoulder.

"Out with what?" Izzie replied.

"You're not yourself, and I know it. Don't forget, you might be Detective Sergeant Izzie Drake at work, but at home you're Mrs. Peter Foster, and I think I'm entitled to know if someone or something at work is upsetting you."

Izzie sighed. She knew that Peter knew her better than anyone, except perhaps her boss. She and Ross had worked together for so long that they were often thought by some people as being almost telepathic, able to read one another's thoughts and acting accordingly.

"I'm not sure how to put it, but I think I really put my foot in it with Andy this afternoon."

Peter looked at her with shock evident on his face.

"You cannot be serious," he replied. "You and Ross are a close as its possible to be without being a couple. What the hell did you do or say?"

"I came damn close to being downright rude to Joey Slimani's widow, that's what I did, and Andy gave me a look that told me he wasn't happy, and I can't blame him. I was out of order, and I knew it straight away. I don't know what's wrong with me. I can normally stay detached from suspects, witnesses, everyone in connection with an investigation but this time, I find myself actively disliking Trixie Slimani"

"But why? She's just lost her husband, Izzie."

"I know, and I know I should be more sympathetic. I don't seem able to control myself. Maybe it's the whole porn scene. She talks about it as if it's completely normal to do what she does."

"And what does she do that's got you so down on her?"

"Peter, honey, I'm really not sure. I can't get my head round the fact that she sees jumping into bed with one or more men and having sex in front of the camera as a perfectly normal thing to do."

Peter smiled and placed an arm round his wife's shoulders, pulling her closer to him.

"Izzie, I've never seen you like this. Come on, Babe, it's not like you're a Victorian prude, is it? We can get pretty adventurous too sometimes, can't we?"

"I know, but we're married, Pete."

"And so is she, or at least, she was until her husband was murdered, and from what you've told me he even produced films starring his wife. So, if he didn't have a problem with his wife doing it with other men, on a professional basis, why should you?"

"I don't know, I really don't. Maybe it's because her husband is dead and she just seems so self-assured, lacking in warmth, or just that she doesn't seems to be displaying any grief at her husband's death. Her reactions just don't seem normal, she's cold and emotionless, to my way of thinking anyway."

Peter paused for a moment and then gave her the best reply he could muster.

"Izzie, you've been a police officer since before we met. How many widows, widowers and parents of murdered kids have you met in that time? For God's sake, you of all people should know that different people handle death in different ways. I see it too at the mortuary when relatives come to carry out identifications or just to view a lost one after they've been laid out in the chapel-of-rest. Some are distraught, some just look sad and sniffling, and others, probably the types your widow falls into, are to all intents and purposes in total control, no flicker of emotion, not a tear in sight, and yet, I've seen them occasionally when they've left the building and the barriers come down, the tears flow and the histrionics appear. We're all different, like I said, and we each handle grief in our own way. If I was you, I'd try to cut Mrs. Slimani a little slack. You're a damn fine detective, and you can virtually read criminal's minds, but I think you need a refresher course in how to handle the bereaved.

Peter fell silent, his speech made, and he waited for his wife's response. Finally, just as he thought he'd stunned her into absolute silence, Izzie stirred and turned her head to look him straight in the eyes.

"Peter Foster, I love you, and that was probably the longest damned speech you've directed at me since our wedding day. You're a hundred percent right, too. I've been stupid, haven't I? I've allowed my petty prejudices affect my judgement. Trixie could be falling apart inside for all I know and I've been making cheap remarks at her every time we've met. I need to tell Ross in the morning how sorry I am."

"I'm sure he knows that already, Izzie. He's not stupid. He'll know the strain you're all working under and he'll probably sit you down, give you a lecture on how to handle the bereaved and it'll be business as usual from then."

"I hope you're right, Pete, I really do. If he thinks I've totally screwed up he might want to kick me off the squad."

"Not a chance," Peter replied, and then, with a devilish grin on his face, he went on, "And if he does, you've got the looks, got the body, you can always get a job as a porn star."

Knowing Izzie only too well, he leapt up from the bed just before her hand connected with the side of his head in a playful smack, and Izzie chased her husband as he ran headlong from the bedroom, down the stairs and lay, naked on the sofa, where, Peter had his own ideas of what would happen when she got there!

Chapter 16

Women of independent means

"Just what the fuck was all that about yesterday?" were Ross's first, angry words to Izzie Drake after he'd asked her to join him in his office early the next morning. She'd been expecting it, of course so his summons and instruction to close the door when she joined him came as no surprise to her. Walls were thin in the headquarters building so he deliberately refrained from blasting his friend and partner at full volume.

"I know, I know, and I'm sorry. I was out of order and please don't ask me why. I talked it through with Peter at home last night."

"And what was the outcome?"

"He said I'd lost my focus. Told me to remember Trixie's a grieving widow even though she may not be showing it, and that people react in different ways to death. He was right, and I shouldn't have allowed my personal prejudices about the porn movie industry cloud my judgement. Joey Slimani is a victim of violent crime and I have a job to do to catch his killer. His wife has to be treated with respect and compassion until and unless we find a reason why she shouldn't be."

"That it?" Ross said, curtly.

"Just about," Izzie replied, looking crestfallen.

"Like I said, I apologise. It won't happen again, sir."

She thought it wise to add his title at the end. She could only push their friendship so far.

"Sounds like Peter did most of my job for me. Did he have anything else to add?"

Izzie wondered if she should say the next bit, but her relationship with Ross was so strong, she felt it might be a way to bring the incident to a speedy conclusion.

"Well, yes. He said, that if you chuck me off the squad, I have the looks and the body to go and get a job as a porn star."

Andy Ross's face was a picture as he looked at his long-time partner. Before he could stop himself, his face broke into a smile and he began to laugh.

"Good for Peter, but seriously, Izzie, you need to get your head together before we head out there again to talk with Mary-Beth and Lana. I don't want you going off half-cocked again and insulting the very people we might need to help us solve Joey's murder."

"I know," Drake replied with a look of contrition on her face. "I honestly don't know why Trixie has managed to get under my skin the way she has done. I promise I'll be a good girl today though, trust me."

"You're lucky I do trust you, Izzie, and that Trixie didn't quite realise how insulting you were being. If she had, and taken her complaint to D.C.I. Agostini, things might have got a bit tricky for you. As it is, and I hate to say this, but if you can't leave your personal prejudices about Trixie Slimani under control, you can stay here and I'll take Sam with me. At least with her background in Vice she isn't put off dealing with women who earn their living by having sex with men."

That certainly did the trick, as Izzie pulled a face that showed her shock at Ross's words and made her realise how close she'd come to blotting her copy book.

"Sir, Andy, I've told you it won't happen again. I feel bloody awful to be honest, after all our years working together. I really feel I've let you down. I will admit, I haven't been feeling to well lately. Maybe that's why I kicked off as I did."

"You need to see a doctor if you're not well, Izzie. I need my strong right arm a hundred percent fit and raring to go when I set foot outside this building, got it?"

"Got it," she replied.

"Right then, let's forget about it and get on with the job And Izzie..."

"What?" she caught the faint glint of a smile beginning to appear on Ross's face.

"Peter was right you know. You'd make a great porn star."

Ross couldn't help laughing and Drake, realising their relationship was back to normal, picked up a small A5 notepad from Ross's desk and launched it at him.

"Bastard," she snapped at him, joining in the laughter. Things between them were okay, and she couldn't help breathing a big sigh of relief. Ross had been right about one thing, though. She knew she needed to make an appointment to see her doctor before too long, if for no other reason than to put her own mind at rest. Izzie knew her own body, and just recently, something had changed, and she'd sensed it, but up to now, ignored it. She knew she needed to be checked out, and before she and Ross left for another visit to Birkenhead, she phoned her G.P.'s surgery and managed to secure an appointment for two days hence, a minor miracle to get in so fast nowadays.

* * *

If Izzie Drake had thought Trixie Slimani looked overtly like a typical star of pornographic movies, she was certainly unprepared for her first meeting with the ex-wives of Joey Slimani. Mary-Beth Hutton, (she'd returned to using her maiden name since her divorce from Joey) looked more like a high-powered business executive than a specialist in acting in BDSM movies. The woman wore a dark navy two-piece skirt suit, the skirt cut to just above her knees, with a white blouse, and a navy neck scarf, all teamed with matching Jimmy Choo high-heeled shoes and matching bag. Her hair was a honey-blonde colour, wavy and cut to lie just below the collar of her suit jacket.

Lana Slimani, still using her ex-husband's name was also dressed conservatively in a dress in forest green, teamed with a short black jacket, and shoes by Armani. Her dress, like Mary-Beth's skirt, ended just above the knee and there was definitely nothing about either woman that Izzie could have said screamed 'porn star.' They both, however, seemed to exude wealth, and both shared the confidence and bearing that accompanied their financial status.

Izzie wasn't sure how Ross would approach the women, as, being divorced from the deceased Joey, it wasn't quite the same as talking directly to the widow. In the car on the way to Paradise Found, Ross admitted he would be playing it very much by ear. Now, seated opposite the very business-like Mary-Beth, Lana having retired to another lavish sitting room with Trixie, Ross began their first interview of the day.

"Mrs. Hutton," Ross began, only to be immediately interrupted.

"Please, call me Mary-Beth, Inspector Ross."

"Okay, Mary-Beth, we've been told by Trixie Slimani that you remained on good terms with Joey after your divorce. Is that correct?"

"It sure is. Best friends you might say."

"In that case, we're very sorry for your loss."

Very cleverly done, Izzie thought.

"Thank you, Inspector. Joey always was a good friend, even after we divorced"

"May I ask the reason for your divorce?" Ross asked.

"Of course. It's not easy to explain. I'm not sure you'll understand."

"Try me, please."

"Okay. When I first met Joey, boy, he was a looker, you know what I mean?"

Ross smiled and nodded, allowing her to continue without interruption.

"I was still at college, and he was already in the movie business. He asked me out and I said yes. Suddenly, there I was, little innocent Mary-Beth, going to all the best clubs, meeting some real groovy people, and being escorted around by this great looking guy who seemed to know everybody. I'll be honest, Inspector, I was a virgin when I met Joey, but that sure didn't last long once we started going together. I loved him, you see, and when he first suggested I might like to try out for one of his movies, I was... well, flattered I suppose, a bit scared too, you know? I mean, I knew what kind of films Joey made and the thought of taking my clothes off and having to do things in bed with a stranger was pretty daunting for a young girl with not much experience of sex."

"But you went along with it, because you loved him, right?" Drake spoke for the first time.

"Yes, Sergeant, I did. Wanna know why? Yes, I loved him, and second, he said it would just be me and him, that first time, and it was. We did a thirty-minute film about an innocent girl being taken by an older, experienced guy and having an orgasm for the first time. Of course, it wasn't really my first time, as I'd had plenty orgasms with Joey already, but there you go, that's acting for you. One thing led to another and before I knew it, I was making more and more movies and earning a lot of money. Then, one day, Joey asked if I'd maybe help him out by stepping in to replace another girl who'd pulled out of doin a BDSM shoot. You know what BDSM is, right?"

"We do, please go on," said Ross.

"I wasn't too sure, but Joey said he'd be on set, and that everything would be okay, so I agreed. Thing was, I enjoyed it. I really enjoyed it, so much that I asked Joey if I could do more. The feelings I experienced while doing that stuff got me really high, you know? Eventually, I made it a specialty. Other producers wanted to use me and I soon became well known in the industry. I know you'll find it difficult to comprehend but, there you go, I was soon known as the Queen of the BDSM movie scene."

Ross nodded sagely, and decided he had to ask the next question.

"And were you still at college while you were doing all these movies?"

"Oh no, Inspector. I'd already graduated college by then. I have degrees in Accountancy and Business management. Even though I'm still making movies, I have my own business now, and represent a lot of the girls in the business."

Izzie had already figured out that they were engaged in conversation with an intelligent woman. Being as diplomatic as possible she tried to frame her question in a neutral manner.

"And yet, you continue to make movies, even though you must make a good living from your accountancy firm?"

"Aha, do I detect an element of disapproval there, Sergeant?" Mary-Beth was smiling as she replied, clearly not offended by the question. "I bet you're a married lady, am I right?"

"You're quite correct," Izzie replied. "Okay, hear me out. You need to understand something. You're like the vast majority of women. You met and fell in love with a great guy, yes?"

Drake nodded in the affirmative.

"So, you did the whole dating thing, maybe made out a few times before you got married, but then he popped the question, you said yes, and now you live in blissful happiness, still in love and enjoying, I hope, a good, satisfying sex life and you couldn't contemplate being unfaithful to him. Am I right?"

Drake had to admit, the woman was dead on the money with her assessment of her marriage and sex life.

"Yes, you're right," she agreed.

"Okay, then try and see it my way. I was married to a gorgeous guy, but I soon discovered that I loved sex more than I loved Joey. And Joey knew it, Sergeant. In our business, jealousy doesn't really have a part to play, but Joey soon realised he was no longer giving me the kind of satisfaction I craved. In our marriage, I'd only ever had sex with other guys in front of the camera, but I started seeing another man who was also into BDSM. That kind of told me and Joey we should part, and we did."

"And it was all amicable? No bitterness or recriminations?" Ross put the question to Mary-Beth.

"No, nothing like that. Joey said we'd still be best friends and wanted me to carry on being a part of his movies too. I wasn't about to say no, Inspector. His movies sold well, and more importantly, they paid well."

"What about the so-called trouble he found himself in with some less than desirable people?"

"Oh you've heard about that? Okay, to be truthful, you should ask Lana more about that, and Trixie too. That stuff only began after we were divorced though you got to understand, there's always a hint of something about the business in L.A, like the guys with muscle trying to get a piece of the action, but it normally doesn't come to much."

Ross decided not to press her on the subject if, as she said, Lana and Trixie were better placed to give him the information, if any existed. Instead, he stayed with her personal relationship with Joey.

"Trixie tells us that you, and Lana too, are both actually part-owners of Joey's business, Mary-Beth. Is that true?"

"Kind of, yeah. You see, divorce in the States can be a messy business sometimes. We didn't want the lawyers getting rich on the back of our separation, so me and Joey, we devised our own settlement. It gave me a nice cash figure and a running share of ten percent of the profits from Joey's movies, in perpetuum. In other words, Joey and his work made me financially healthy, Inspector Ross."

"And you and Lana will be attending the reading of Joey's will, I take it."

"Yes, and his funeral as well, of course. That's the real reason we're here."

"Yes, of course. So, you can't think of anyone who might have wanted Joey dead?"

"Hell no. Joey was a pussycat, a lover not a fighter. He wouldn't harm a fly and he was straight as a die when it came to business matters. Since I heard about his death, I've gone over our lives together so many times, and I just can't think of anyone who might have wanted harm to come to Joey."

Ross let Mary-Beth return to the sitting room to join Trixie and Lana, while he and Drake spent a few minutes in conversation before sending for Lana.

"What did you think, Izzie?" he asked. He could almost hear the gears grinding in Drake's brain as she pondered her reply.

"I was pleasantly surprised by her. She definitely gave me another perspective on the whole 'porn star' scenario. Who'd have thought someone involved in that business would have two bloody degrees and her own accountancy business? She's probably a millionaire or not far off it."

"Changed your mind on the whole porn scene, have you?"

"Not entirely, no. I still find it strange that women want to do it, make these films, I mean, but if that's what they want to do and it gives then the kind of lifestyle they want, who am I to judge?"

"That's more like it, my old Izzie's back again. But seriously, I don't see her wanting her ex dead. She'd have too much to lose, financially. I know she'll still make money from the films he's already made but there won't be any more, and it will probably curtail some of her acting opportunities."

"And she has a perfect alibi," Ross added.

"I noticed you didn't ask her where she was on the day he was murdered. I kept wondering if you were going to but guessed you had a strategy."

"Nothing so devious," Ross smiled. "I had Paul Ferris make some discreet enquiries with his American contacts. On the day Joey was murdered, Mary-Beth was starring in a new production being filmed in L.A. going by the title of *Backdoor Babes, Volume 20.*"

"Right, God knows what that entailed. I mean, *Backdoor Babes.* I still can't get my head round it. A highly intelligent business woman allows herself to be tied up, bound in chains and whipped, or whatever it is they do in those kinds of films and then has sex with one or more men she's probably never seen before."

"Come on, Izzie. You've got to lose this attitude towards these women," Ross commented.

"I know, I just don't know what's come over me. I seem to have suffered from an objectivity bypass or something."

"Just make an appointment to see your doctor, okay? If you're not well, whatever it is could be affecting your work."

"I already have, honest. Did Paul manage to alibi Lana, too?"

"He did. She was at a funeral, surrounded by witnesses. So neither of the ex-wives were over here, slashing Joey's throat."

"Doesn't mean one or both of them couldn't have paid to have him killed though."

"I agree. Let's see what the lovely Lana has to say, shall we?"

* * *

Lana Slimani had a certain presence when she entered the room a minute later. The forest-green dress she wore stood out against her long, perfectly groomed blonde hair and with the light from the weak winter sunshine reflecting from it, could now be seen to be decorated with fine silver thread in the shape of holly leaves, clearly designed with the coming Christmas season in mind. As she sat opposite the detectives and slowly crossed her legs, even Andy Ross had to admit to himself that here was a woman who was totally at home with her own sexuality and who simply exuded a hint of latent erotica. Even the way she looked at him, her eyes slightly downcast but at the same time having a penetrating gaze that had him believing she could see right into his brain gave her a demure but desirable appearance. He wondered how Izzie was responding to the way Lana looked.

After answering Ross's initial questions, giving virtually the same replies as Mary-Beth to the identical questions, Lana sat quietly, waiting for the next one, which this time came from Izzie Drake.

"Mary-Beth has told us about her divorce from Joey, Lana. What was the cause of your break-up with him? she asked.

Lana showed no sign of hesitancy in her reply, delivered in the same husky sultry voice that had quickly made both detectives sit up take notice when she'd first been introduced to them.

"You might find this hard to believe, but Joey divorced me for my own safety. At the time, he was going through a bad time, financially. The movies were doing okay but production costs had risen and the cost of hiring good camera crew and paying actors and actresses had eaten into the profits. Joey knew he'd find a way to get things back on course, but word must have got out on the grapevine, and next we knew, he's being approached by a guy named Vito Trappatoni, who owns one of the biggest studios in the adult movie business in L.A. Trappatoni sent a couple of his goons round to pay Joey a visit, to tell him Vito wasn't happy that he was making too many movies, and raking in too much money, which was affecting his business. See, Trappatoni's movies were, and still are, what Joey referred to as 'Shit flicks,' low budget crap made for the mass market B grade video market. Joey told him where to get off, but Vito tried to extort money from Joey, what you people would call 'protection' money."

Ross's ears pricked up on hearing Lana's information. Could this be the reason for Joey Slimani's murder? Had the reach of what the Americans refer to as 'The Mob' have spread all the way from Los Angeles, California, to Merseyside in the UK?

"And what was Joey's reaction to this intimidation?"

"I'm sure Trixie and Mary-Beth have told you that Joey was Mister Nice Guy. He was terrified that something bad was going to happen if he didn't go along with what Trappatoni wanted. At first, he tried to talk to Trappatoni, but he wouldn't meet with Joey, he always sent Mickey Blunt, his second-in-command. Blunt told Joey he had two choices, either play ball or get out of town. Then he said Vito would make an example of someone close to Joey. Joey knew he meant me, but when his parents were killed in a fire at their apartment block in New York, he thought maybe Trappatoni was responsible for it, especially when the cops in New York confirmed the fire was an arson attack. They couldn't pin it on anyone and Joey couldn't get to talk to anyone in the Trappatoni organisation. Then, one day, I was driving home from shopping downtown when the brakes on my car failed. I was lucky. I ran off the road and rammed into a verge full of thick bushes. I escaped with a broken arm and bruising. That's when Joey got another visit from Blunt. He knew they were serious and so he came up with a plan. If we weren't married no more, Trappatoni couldn't use me as a weapon against Joey, so Joey engineered a scene in a restaurant where I publicly accused him of screwing around and shouted for everyone to hear that I was going to divorce the little rat, and sure enough, we got a quickie divorce and I left town. Joey made sure I got plenty of work with his friend, Stefan Schmidt in Hamburg. The Germans do the type of films I like doing, so I carried on making big bucks. Sure enough, Trappatoni dropped the threats against me but didn't stop hassling Joey. A small fire at Joey's studio was the final straw. He got out of town and soon after I heard he'd married Trixie. I knew her from films we'd done together. I just hoped Joey would find happiness with her. He made me a good settlement on the divorce, but there was no way we could ever get back together or Trappatoni might know he'd been conned over the divorce. So there was no problem as far as I was concerned when he married Trixie. We stayed in touch and when Joey started up his new business, he started using me again. I've starred in over a dozen Joe Slim productions, Inspector. I'm going to miss Joey, for sure."

"And did you get a share of Joey's business when you divorced?" Drake asked.

"I sure did. Joey was clever, see. That man had a head for business. Even if he'd never made another movie, we'd all never go short of money."

"So," Drake posed another probing question. "Joe Slim Productions will go on, even though Joey is no longer around to run it?"

"Of course it will, Sergeant. The three of us will make sure of that. The people who worked for Joey, on the production side, will just work for us girls instead."

"I see, thank you," Drake replied, thoughtfully.

"Just one more question for now, Lana, and I think we're done for now." Ross was keen to bring these interviews to an end. He didn't see them leading anywhere, at least, not until he knew more about the reason for Joey's murder. "I was under the impression that the adult movie industry was all legal and above-board nowadays, and yet you're telling me that Joey Slimani was hounded out of town by a thug with Mob connections?"

"I know what you must think, Inspector, but it's true. The business is totally legit, but every so often, a snake like Vito sticks his grubby little paws into it. People like him don't always use legitimate actresses like us, either. That's how they make their movies on the cheap, see?"

"You mean they force unwilling girls to make their movies, like those trafficked from Europe or Latin America as sex slaves or prostitutes," he added.

"You got it," Lana nodded her head and appeared genuinely sad. "Some of those kids ain't even eighteen, and it's sure as hell illegal for them to be making movies like that at that age, but scumbags like Vito Trappatoni don't give a shit about the law, you see?"

"Yes, thank you, Lana. I think I really do see."

Chapter 17

Christmas is coming

Detective Chief Inspector Oscar Agostini looked out across the briefing room. His entire squad was present, with the exception of D.C. Derek McLennan, who was due back from his honeymoon the following day. Ross had spent an hour in the D.C.I.'s office prior to the morning briefing and Agostini had agreed to address the team, who were currently feeling disillusioned about their lack of progress with the Joey Slimani case.

"Listen up everyone," he began. "D.I. Ross has kindly asked me to lead this morning's briefing. God knows why?" he smiled and was rewarded with a ripple of polite laughter. "Seriously, I know you've been working your backsides off on this bloody Slimani case, without much luck so far. I don't want anyone losing focus, though. The answer is out there. I'm trusting you lot to find it. You're supposed to be the best detective unit on the force, so now's the time to prove it. I have every confidence in D.I. Ross and every single one of you to find the killer of Joey Slimani, and here's an incentive for you. Christmas is drawing closer, folks, and the Super, (he was referring to Detective Chief Superintendent Sarah Hollingsworth) wants this case closed before the holiday. I don't want her suddenly cancelling leave time, because we have an open, unsolved murder on the books. You might not know this, but I'm getting more pressure from above than is good for my health, because our dearly departed adult movie producer was an American citizen and we are likely to be attracting some heat from unexpected quarters if we can't resolve the case quickly."

There were groans around the room. Nobody wanted to be stuck in the squad room or following up potentially useless leads on Christmas Day or any time over the holiday period. Agostini took a seat beside Andy Ross, who now stood and spoke to the squad.

"Thanks, Boss. Okay people, we all know just how far we've gone with the case up to now."

"Bloody nowhere," Nick Dodds grumbled.

"Not even that far," Tony Curtis added.

"Alright, Laurel and bloody Hardy," Ross quipped, "This is serious. It's Joey Slimani's funeral tomorrow and I want a good presence there. Whoever killed him might just be among the mourners, making sure he's well planted in the ground. The thing is, because he was a Yank, there's not going to be a whole load of people there to see him off, I'm guessing. So apart from the widow and his ex-wives, and the world's weirdest, or luckiest butler, depending on how you look at it, there shouldn't be too many to keep tabs on. I want photos of the mourners, Paul, you're in charge of that," he said to Ferris, who nodded, as Ross went on. "The important thing I want to do today is to talk with Slimani's local lawyer, a solicitor called Michael Powell at Hawkes and Temple on Duke Street. Sam, I want you with me. We'll leave as soon as we've finished here."

"Okay, sir," Sam Gable replied. "But where's Izzie, I mean Sergeant Drake?"

"Izzie hasn't been feeling too great these last few days. I convinced her to see a doctor and she managed to get an appointment this morning. Seems they had a cancellation just before she phoned. She'll be in later, but for now, you're with me, Sam."

"Great, thanks Boss," Gable grinned from ear to ear. She was delighted that Ross had chosen her to accompany him to talk to Slimani's solicitor, a measure, she felt, of how highly she was regarded by the D.I.

The briefing continued as Ross brought everyone up to date with the results of his meeting with Trixie and the two ex-wives.

"Any thoughts, anyone?" he invited comments.

"Sir," Sofie Meyer held her hand up to get his attention. He acknowledged her with a nod and she continued.

"I am thinking, as you have just said, that we may be looking at the case in the wrong way. So far, we have worked on the assumption that Mr. Slimani's murder is connected to the adult movie business. What if it has nothing at all to do with his business? Perhaps his murder was of a more personal nature?"

A buzz went round the room at Sofie's words. Had they been looking in the wrong place? Ross was always glad when his German loanee made the connections to his thoughts. Meyer had a sharp, incisive mind and had already proved herself to be a first-class detective during her loan spell with the team.

"Please go on, Sofie," Ross urged her.

"I have been thinking, and it seems far-fetched that this American gangster would wait until now to have Slimani killed. Too much time has passed. If he was going to have the man killed surely he would have done it back home in America. What if this is to do with some perceived transgression or argument the victim has become embroiled in since moving here to England?"

Ross noticed that the team's computer expert, Paul Ferris, was trying to attract his attention. Ferris had his laptop computer with him and Ross guessed he had something urgent to contribute.

"Hold on Sofie. Yes, Paul, what is it?"

"While you've been talking, I just did a quick internet search on our American gangster chappie. Not a nice person it would appear, but, the adult film industry seems to have been a minor part of his activities. I said that in the past tense because Mr Trappatoni is currently serving a ten-year jail sentence for human trafficking and enforced prostitution, imposed by a Federal Court just a week ago."

"Hmm, just before Joey was killed," Dodds was first to react.

"Any connection there, Boss?" Curtis added.

"I just don't see it," Ross replied. "Good lad, Paul, for digging that up. Sofie, you were saying?"

"Yes, so, perhaps, as you say, sir, we should re-evaluate our case as far as motive is concerned. Maybe Joey blackmailing someone, or being blackmailed himself, or he had insulted somebody who held a deep grudge against him. There are many reasons why people kill. He went to a meeting, his wife says, but she does not know who with. What if he had an argument with whoever he met that day and was killed in a spur of the moment act, rather than one of planned premeditation?" Sofie fell silent.

Ross, who had been thinking along similar lines, was pleased someone else saw the possibility that they'd been barking up the wrong tree.

"Good, that should give us all something to think about. Tony, Nick, how did you two get on with tracing Slimani's movements on the last day we know he was alive?"

Dodds and Curtis looked at each other, and when Dodds nodded, Curtis took it as a signal for him to speak.

"Right, sir, as you said, it was never going to be easy, and it wasn't. I'm not sure if what we've found will be any use at all."

"Let me be the judge of that, Tony, carry on."

"Okay, well, I rang the Slimani home and spoke to Jennings, the butler. He was able to tell me what vehicle Joey was driving on the Saturday morning he left home. It was his red Ferrari, very distinctive and easy to make out on CCTV, but only IF we could discover where he was going. We got a bit of luck at first. From the direction he was heading, caught on his own private cameras, we guessed he might be calling at the South Mersey Golf Club. We were right. Nick called the club and spoke to the club Captain. He remembers Joey calling at the club on the Saturday morning. He had someone with him, a German bloke."

"Braun?" Sam Gable quickly put two and two together. It was Dodds who now replied.

"Shit!" Ross exclaimed.

"No, sir, Schmidt," Dodds said, eliciting a round of laughter among the team.

"Stefan Schmidt is a German Porn movie producer," Ross replied after the others had calmed down. "Lana Slimani told me and Izzie that she did some movies for him when she split up from Joey, which was all arranged to keep her safe from the perceived threat from Trappatoni."

"So, why was he holding what appears to have been a secret meeting with Joey?" Sam able posed the question. "Surely, Joey would have told Trixie if it was just routine meeting about future productions or something like that?"

"Very good point, Sam," Ross agreed. "Paul, see if you can conjure up a photo of this Schmidt character, okay?"

"No problem," Ferris replied, and within less than a minute he'd found a full profile of the German adult movie producer. The accompanying photo was clear and showed a handsome man, around fortyish, with blonde, short-cropped hair, height unknown as the photo showed him only from the waist up.

"Well done, Paul. Now we have to find out where he is, and why he was meeting Joey Slimani."

"Sir, do you think this Schmidt could be the killer?" Ginger Devenish, who'd been silent up to that point, asked.

"I don't know, Ginger. As things stand, everyone involved in this damned case could be our killer."

"What if," Devenish went on, "Schmidt was after taking over Slimani's business, a bit like the Yanks did?"

"And Slimani wouldn't play ball?"

"Yes, sir, at least, it's a possibility, surely?"

"But according to Lana Slimani, Schmidt was a friend of Joey's who not only kept her in work when she first split with Joey but gave her a place to live and took care of her. Why would he want Joey dead?"

"Maybe he wanted Lana for himself?"

"Then he had no need to get Joey's permission or to do him in. Don't forget, Lana is free to do what she wants now, Ginger."

"Damn, I hadn't though it through properly. Sorry, Boss."

"No apologies needed. At least you're thinking about it. We need plenty of serious thought if we're to solve this case, I think." Ross spoke with a voice heavy with frustration. "Dammit, I want to know why Joey and Schmidt met on Saturday, and why Schmidt hasn't come forward to talk to us. He must know Joey's dead."

Meyer had been weighing things in her mind for a few minutes and now, she felt she might have something to add to the case.

"Sir, I have a feeling the answer to the case may lie in what you just said."

"Go ahead, Sofie. Amaze me."

"Ja, here I go. You just mentioned Herr Schmidt. We already have another of my countrymen, Heinrich Braun mentioned in connection with the investigation. Both are connected to Joey Slimani, but do we know if they are linked with each other? No, not so far. But, what if there is a link between Schmidt and Braun, a link that might give them, if working together, a motive to murder Joey Slimani?"

"You might just have a point there, Sofie. Please get on the phone to your contacts back home. I'm sure you know someone who won't mind doing a little digging around for us?"

"Of course, sir. I will call my former colleague and good friend, Silvia Houser. She knows just about all there is to know about the murky side of the porn industry in and around Hamburg."

"I won't ask how she knows so much, Sofie, but please, call her, Ross smiled as he spoke. Meyer smiled in return.

"Everyone keep at it," Ross urged his team. "Sam, let's go pay that solicitor a visit."

"Right with you, Boss," Sam Gable grabbed her handbag as she almost leaped up from her seat with enthusiasm and followed Ross from the room.

Chapter 18

Revelations by the double

The offices of Hawkes and Temple looked just as anyone would imagine a solicitor's office would look. Ross introduced himself and Sam Gable to a smartly-dressed, middle-aged receptionist, whose make-up and elegant two-piece business suit he estimated had knocked about ten years off her true age, who sat behind a functional pine desk, with a computer keyboard directly in front of her and a monitor set to one side of her workstation. One corner of the reception area was taken up by four large filing cabinets, with security bars in addition to the standard locks, obviously the receptacles for the law firm's client and court records. Pictures on two of the walls depicted calming landscapes and seascapes, designed to put clients at their ease, Ross surmised. The other wall displayed what Ross assumed to be the certificates bearing the names and qualifications of the five partners in the business. His sharp eyes quickly noted there was a Hawkes on one certificate but no Temple. Maybe the Temple connection was an old one, long dead perhaps.

The receptionist, who wore a name badge identifying her as Gloria Snow, picked up her phone and efficiently announced to Michael Powell that he had two police officers wishing to see him. In no time, she hung up, rose from her seat and asked Ross and Gable to follow her. She led them through a clear glass door, which stood sandwiched between good quality prints of typical British countryside scenes and along a short corridor, halting at a door that bore a brass nameplate, reading the name of the man they'd come to see. Gloria knocked once and confidently opened the door, walked into the office and announced the two police officers. As they followed her through the door a voice said, "Thanks a lot Gloria. Please hold my calls until further notice."

Gloria quickly and quietly departed and Ross and Gable were cheerfully welcomed by Michael Powell, who stood and walked across the spacious office to greet them, before ushering them to take a seat on a plush, burgundy leather sofa that stood against one wall, while he seated himself informally in a matching leather armchair, positioned at an angle in front of a sturdy coffee table, in mahogany, which was highly polished and was devoid of the anything except that day's copies of the Daily Telegraph, The Times and the previous day's Liverpool Echo. Ross's immediate thought was that Hawkes and Temple dealt with decidedly high-end clients, no low-lifes welcome here.

"Detective Inspector, Detective Constable, please tell me how I can help you," the solicitor spoke before Ross could utter a word. Ross couldn't detect any sign or inflection of a local accent in Powell's speech, which came across as pure 'Oxbridge,' though that didn't mean he wasn't a local man. Accents, after all, could be changed or modulated over time, as and when necessary.

"We're here to talk to you about the last will and testament of your client, Joseph Slimani," Ross announced, and Powell nodded as though he'd been expecting just such a visit.

"Yes, it was a terrible thing that happened to the poor man. Not that I knew him well, but, even so..."

"Exactly, Mr. Powell. Murder is never a pretty subject, and at present, I'll be truthful with you, we're finding it hard to discover why anyone would want to kill your client. I'm hoping there may be something in his will that might lead us in some way towards identifying his killer."

"A moment, please," Powell spoke softly and picked up his phone.

"Gloria, will you be an angel and bring me the file on Joseph Slimani, please?"

Within a minute, the receptionist/secretary, whatever she was, as Ross was unsure, knocked and entered and straight past him and Sam as she walked up to Powell, and handed him the file he'd requested, also depositing another file for his attention, on his expansive mahogany desk, which matched the coffee table, at least twice the size of her own workplace in reception. On closer inspection, Ross thought she may be younger than he'd first estimated. Her clothes and make-up were clearly designer labels, indicating a more than generous salary and Ross wondered if there might be something going on between the attractive Miss Snow and her boss, then dismissed such thoughts as none of his business. *I've been around these drop-dead gorgeous porn stars too long,* he thought, as Gloria bent forward to reach across the desk to pick up two files from what must have been Powell's 'out-tray', showing a shapely figure as she did so.

Powell opened the file, found the documents he needed and looked up at Ross and Drake.

"Well, unless I'm reading this incorrectly, I very much doubt you'll find a motive for murder here, Inspector Ross," he finally announced.

"I think I'll be the best judge of that, Mr. Powell," Ross replied, wondering if indeed, this visit would prove to be yet another dead-end in the case.

"Of course," the solicitor agreed. "I take it you'd like a copy?"

"Yes, please, and when is the will being read?"

"Tomorrow, after the funeral."

"I see," Ross said and asked if Powell would run through the main bequests of the will.

"The majority of Mr. Slimani's fortune goes to his wife, of course, but there are also very generous bequests to both his former wives, Mary-Beth Hutton and Lana Slimani. The business, Joe Slim Productions is left to his wife, but with the proviso that the two former wives both received a twenty percent share each of any and all future profits made from said business. Mary-Beth is also nominated as the company's accountant for any and all U.S. representation. Any U.K. profits made subsequent to his death are to be handled by an accountant appointed by his solicitor, i.e. Hawkes and Temple. Oh, yes, Mr. Slimani paid me a visit two weeks ago, and added a short codicil to his will."

Ross's ears pricked up at that announcement. Could this be the breakthrough they were looking for? Powell continued.

"The words that follow are Mr. Slimani's own words, Inspector.

"To my butler/manservant William Jennings who has served me well and made sure my wife Trixie has received all the service she requires in bed during my frequent absences on work related matters, I leave the sum of one million U.S. dollars, and hope that this will adequately recompense him for having to indulge Trixie Mae's more outlandish bedroom fantasies. Jennings, old boy, I never got around to making you the star I promised you could be, but I hope this goes some way to make up for my broken promise, buddy."

"I must say, that's a surprise," Ross said, "but as you say, Mr. Powell, hardly a motive for murder."

Sam Gable entered the conversation. One thing had been bugging her since the solicitor mentioned one particular word.

"Mr. Powell, earlier, you mentioned the word 'fortune' when referring to Mr. Slimani's estate. Can you tell us exactly how much his estate amounts to?"

Powell looked at Gable, hesitated for a second, and then, in a hushed voice, said, "Good question, Detective. To the nearest million, and expressed in British pounds, Mr. Slimani's estate amounts to approximately one hundred and fourteen million pounds."

Both Ross and Gable looked shocked. They knew Joey was quite well off, his years producing his highly popular adult movies made that a given, but the figure Michael Powell just revealed to them was staggering.

"How much?" Ross was incredulous.

"I think you heard correctly, Inspector. At current exchange rates, that works out at approximately twenty-four million dollars, so, as you can see, Mr. Slimani was a very wealthy man."

"And that by itself could just make him a target for murder," Sam exclaimed.

"Oh yes," the solicitor went on, "there is one other odd bequest in the will, which you may find interesting, though perhaps a little perplexing."

"Please go ahead, Mr. Powell, we're all ears," Ross urged him on.

"First of all let me explain something, Inspector Ross. Although we were asked by Mr. Slimani to draw up a new will for him, this will is essentially the same one that my client originally lodged with his American lawyers when he lived over there, a copy of which he provided us with. Since he arrived here in the U.K. he hasn't made any major changes as such, apart from the bequest to Mr. Jennings, but he did add a codicil to his original will not long before he left the USA."

Now Powell really did have Ross and Gable's full attention as he paused, almost with a sense of deliberate theatrics, before reading the codicil to Slimani's will, which had been dated some three months prior to his and Trixie's move to live in the UK.

Further to my previous bequests I do hereby add the following codicil to my last will and testament. In addition to the previously mentioned bequests I do hereby leave the sum of five million dollars to my daughter, Melita Gonzalez, to be used for whatever purposes she deems necessary to bring happiness to her life.

Michael Powell had now succeeded in bringing a look of total shock to the face of the hardened police inspector for the second time in the space of two minutes.

"Daughter?" Ross exclaimed "What bloody daughter? We've never been told about any daughter."

"I thought you'd be interested in that piece of information, Inspector Ross. I have no idea who Melita Gonzales is, where she lives, or even if she is still alive. I've tried to track her down, even phoned Mr. Slimani's U.S. lawyers, but they know nothing of her either. Nothing in the will mentions her at all apart from this one short codicil. I very much doubt if Mr. Slimani's widow is aware of the existence of this daughter of his."

Having dropped not one, but two bombshell items of information on the detectives, Michael Powell fell silent. There was nothing left to tell, and Ross quickly wound up the interview, he and Sam politely saying their thanks and goodbyes to the solicitor. Ross flashed a smile and a cheery 'bye' to glorious Gloria as he departed from the offices of Hawkes and Temple.

"If this was an Agatha Christie murder mystery, sir, I'd be thinking Mr. Powell has handed us two vital clues to the killer's identity back there, sir," Gable commented as they made their way back to head-quarters.

"You mean the money and the child?" Ross was pensive.

"Yes, sir. I saw your face when he mentioned the money Joey's left. It was a real picture."

"I'm sure it was Sam. A hundred and fourteen million pounds, for God's sake. I've totally underestimated our victim and the wealth potential of the adult movie business, that'for sure."

Ross's mobile rang, interrupting the conversation. Seeing the caller's name displayed on the screen, he excused himself to Sam, and pressed the 'talk' button.

"Izzie, good to hear from you. How did it go with the doctor?"

Sam could just hear the muffled sound of Drake's voice as Ross listened to her.

"He said what?" Ross suddenly shouted, making Sam jump in surprise. "Is he certain? Yes, yes, I understand. You're in the office now? Yes, okay, we'll see you in a few minutes."

Ross ended the call, turned to Sam whose face held a worried, yet excitable look, and said, "She's pregnant Sam. Izzie Drake is pregnant!"

Chapter 19

Trixie's tears

The squad room was buzzing when Ross and Gable walked back in after their visit to the solicitor's office. Izzie Drake held centre-stage as those team members who were present were already in the throes of congratulating her on the news of her pregnancy.

"Sergeant Drake, my office…now!" Ross shouted above the general hubbub. Izzie Drake quickly extricated herself from the back slapping of Tony Curtis, Nick Dodds, Paul Ferris and Kat Bellamy, and followed Ross into his office, closing the door behind her.

Ross wasted no time in taking hold of his sergeant by the shoulders and pulling her close into a hug that conveyed the closeness that the pair had developed over the years of working together.

"Now we know why you've been acting strange these last few days," he said as he allowed her to take a step back. "Didn't you suspect you might be…?"

"Course I did, you daft bugger," she laughed, "but I was hardly going to say anything until I had confirmation, was I?"

"Well, I'm happy for you, and for Peter. Does he know yet?"

"I phoned him before I called you. I think he fell off his office chair when I told him."

"He was pleased though, yes?"

"Once he got over the shock, yes. We didn't plan it, but now it's happened, we're over the moon to think we're going to be parents. Imagine me, a mum?"

"It might take me a while to get my head round it, Izzie. When are you due?"

"Doctor gave me a date of 4ᵗʰ July. U.S. Independence Day, and before you ask, I'll work as long as I can and once the little one's old enough, I'll be back at work."

"Damn, I thought I'd be getting rid of you at last," Ross laughed again.

"You're not getting rid of me that easily," she laughed in return. "I know there's a lot to work out, but as soon as I can, I'll be back."

"I'm over the moon for you, really I am. We've worked together a long time, Izzie and I'd hate to lose you, but you might feel different once the baby's born."

"Let's not think about it for now. July's a long way off yet."

"That's true, and we've still got a murder to solve."

"What happened at the solicitor's office?"

Ross spent the next few minutes bringing Izzie up to date with what he and Sam had learned that morning. Drake professed to being as surprised as he and Sam had been at discovering the true worth of Joey Slimani's wealth and was equally astonished by the revelation that Joey had a yet unmentioned daughter.

"You'd think if any of the wives knew about the existence of this daughter, they'd have mentioned it by now," she said, voicing the identical thoughts expressed earlier by Ross and Gable.

"Precisely. Before we go any further, I'd better go and report this latest little gem of knowledge to the gaffer. He'll be more than a little interested in your news too, so you can come with me and we'll break it to him together."

Ross and Drake had spent a few minutes bringing D.C.I. Oscar Agostini up to date on the limited progress made so far, including the results of the interview with Michael Powell. Agostini, aware that the funeral was scheduled for the following day, wanted Ross and Drake to hot-foot it over to Birkenhead immediately to speak with the ex-wives and Trixie Slimani to see if they could throw any light on Joey's mystery daughter, Melita. On being advised of Izzie's news, he congratulated her, and then, ever the professional, looked to the future.

"We'll have to look at cover for your absence when you go on maternity leave, of course, Izzie. If you're determined to come back to work, which I think is great for the squad, by the way, we might look at a temporary appointment, or maybe even a promotion from within the squad. We have at least two people I can think of who are suitable for a role as acting D.S. while Izzie's away changing dirty nappies," he grinned at his last remark.

"Oh great, thanks, sir. You sure know how to bring a girl down to earth," Drake replied, returning the grin.

"We've time to think about that anyway. For now, you two had better go and talk with those women in Birkenhead again. And maybe get Sergeant Ferris to start looking from our end, Andy?"

"No problem. If this Melita Gonzales has any kind of presence on the internet, Paul will find her."

Ross and Drake were soon on their travels again, having lingered for a couple of minutes in the squad room, where Sofie Meyer had joined the rest of the team, insisted on adding her hugs, kisses and congratulations to those of the rest of the team.

"So, Sofie thinks we're looking in the wrong places for our killer, then?" Drake said as they travelled through the Queensway tunnel that runs beneath the Mersey, connecting Liverpool with Birkenhead.

Ross, behind the wheel, replied in the affirmative.

"I have to say I had already been thinking along those lines, Izzie. Just because Joey Slimani produced adult movies we've all automatically assumed his murder must be connected to his business. Could be we've been looking in all the wrong places, which might explain why we've been unable to come up with any real leads or suspects."

"And now we've learned the man was a multi-millionaire and has a daughter that nobody seems to know anything about. Why d'you think he's kept her a secret for so long?"

"We can't be sure he has," Ross was hedging his bets on the subject for now. "It's possible one or more of his wives knows about Melita and has chosen to deliberately say nothing about her, for reasons we're not aware of."

"For God's sake, this case gets more bloody complicated by the day," Drake sighed, looking out of the passenger window at the smooth walls and the lights of the tunnel speeding past, as traffic moved at a steady 30 mph. The other Mersey Tunnel, the Wallasey tunnel has a speed limit of 40 mph. The major reasons for the difference in speed restrictions being that the Birkenhead tunnel has more bends and is 'twistier' than the Wallasey one, and the lanes in the Queensway are narrower, a mere 9 feet wide as opposed to 12 feet in the Kingsway, which in fact is comprised of two individual tunnels, each with two lanes, and each carrying traffic in one direction only. "We could do with Derek's input on this one. He's good at solving riddles."

"You're right," Ross agreed. "Derek does have a strange knack of seeing things a little different to the rest of us. I knew he was a good choice for the squad when we were first formed and he came to us as a green, rather shy and eager-to-please young bobby. Even then he could often look outside the box and once he learned to voice his opinions he became a great asset to the team."

"Sounds as if you might be talking yourself into offering him an acting sergeant's post when I go on maternity leave," Izzie voiced her thoughts out loud and Ross had to agree.

"You're right. I am, and we could do a lot worse, that's for sure."

"I agree. Derek would be perfect, or Sam, both good sergeant material."

"There's something else," Ross suddenly changed the subject as his mind once more focussed on the case. "We still haven't found out where Joey was killed. I have a feeling, if we find the site of his murder we might find something to help us find his killer. Dodds and Curtis are still doing their best to track Joey's movements on that last day. They might get lucky."

Their conversation ended as they arrived once again at *Paradise Found*. Ross's mind paused in mid-thought as he realised what a misnomer the name had turned out to be for Joey Slimani. Just as they were exiting the car, his mobile phone rang, and Ross recognised the number, and replied, "Yes Paul?" D.S. Ferris spoke quickly and passed on his news to the inspector, who thanked him and ended the call.

"Good news?" Drake asked.

"Could be," and Ross told her the gist of Ferris's news as they approached the front door.

This time, he'd requested that all three of Joey's wives, past and present, be interviewed together, and so, Trixie arranged for them all to meet in the main sitting room. Trixie, Mary-Beth and Lana all sat on an oversized sofa, which Ross thought could (and probably had) doubled as a bed on more than one occasion in this strange house of Joey Slimani's. Ross and Drake, seated opposite them on two matching armchairs, took advantage of the tea and coffee provided by Trixie and served by William Jennings, who, job done, quickly exited the room.

"I'm sorry to have to interrupt your day, ladies, but we have an important question to ask and I felt it would be easier if we asked you while you're all in one place, rather than do it in three separate interviews," Ross began.

"I gotta say, we were all pretty mystified when you called and said you had something important to ask all three of us," Trixie spoke with a worried look on her face. Was it a guilty look, Ross wondered?

"Well, let's just say that certain information has reached us and it's important we find out if it might have any significance in the search for Mr. Slimani's killer."

Ross wanted to be careful how he worded the question, not wanting to reveal the extent of his knowledge relating to Joey's will.

"I just want to know if any of you ladies can tell me anything about Joey Slimani's daughter."

The silence that followed his words was almost deafening. It was suddenly possible to have heard a pin drop in that spacious, airy room as the faces of all three women registered shock, disbelief and perhaps a little horror as they assimilated what they'd just heard. Trixie spoke first.

"Daughter, what fucking daughter? I never heard of no daughter."

"You have got to be joking," Lana added. "If Joey'd had a daughter, one of us at least would know about it."

Mary-Beth looked at Ross and the other women, but said nothing at first and then said, "Tell us more Inspector Ross."

"Does the name Melita Gonzales mean anything to any of you?"

Three blank faces stared back at him.

"You see," Drake joined in, "We have a very clever man at police headquarters, a Sergeant Paul Ferris, who has a way of discovering all sorts of things about people, especially when those people have been the victims of violent crime. His extensive investigation into the life of Joey Slimani has thrown up the name Melita Gonzales and his information is that the young lady, who just reached the age of nineteen is the daughter of Joey Slimani."

Ross's eyes were fixed solely on Mary-Beth Hutton. As Joey's first wife he felt she, if anyone would have heard of Melita, having known Joey as a teenager. It was Trixie who spoke first, however.

"But that would mean Joey musta only been about fifteen or sixteen when the kid was born."

Lana saved Ross from asking the next question.

"Mary-Beth, you knew Joey back in those days. Don't you know nothin' about this kid they're talkin' about?"

Ross noticed that both Trixie and Lana had reverted to what he assumed were their regional U.S, dialects. He thought he'd definitely got them rattled.

"Well, Mary-Beth," he added to Lana's question. "Do you have anything to say?"

Mary-Beth hesitated for a few seconds, before finally replying.

"Look, you have to believe me when I tell you that until you came here today, I'd never heard of Melita Gonzales, much less that Joey had a daughter, but I think I can put a few things together and tell you what I think happened."

"Please go on, Mary-Beth," Ross urged her. "It could be really important."

"I'll tell you what I believe. It's why I went so quiet when you first mentioned Joey having a daughter. I was putting things together in my head, you know?"

Ross and Drake said nothing, relying on their tried and trusted technique of allowing the interviewee to fill the silence. It had proved successful in the past and was about to do so once again.

"Joey and me, we were in college, as you know, when we first met. I remember one Christmas, Joey said something about it being weird that his Dad celebrated Christmas because he was, you know, not really a Christian. To be honest, Joey's Dad didn't do religion at all. He said it had caused too much trouble over the centuries in his own land and anyway, they were now Americans so they should do what Americans do, so he celebrated Christmas, Easter, Independence Day, Thanksgiving, you name it. Then Joey said something that really upset his Dad. He said, *"So why do you hate Carmen so much, Dad?"* I thought Joey's Dad was going to blow a fuse. He'd never raised his voice in front of me before that day, but he really tore into poor Joey. *"I've told you never to mention her name in this house ever again,"* he shouted at Joey. I waited till we were alone and I asked Joey who Carmen was and why his father hated her so much. Joey told me he'd had a girlfriend when he was younger, maybe fifteen, sixteen and she was of Mexican origins. Her father had died in an accident working in a flour mill and she and her brother and two sisters were being brought up by her Mom, who Joey said worked three different jobs to try and support her family. Joey's father, for some strange reason, had decided he didn't like Mexicans, and used to call them names, which I thought really odd as he was from an immigrant family himself. Joey's father forbade him from seeing the girl again, but Joey told me he continued to meet her and they dated in secret for a while until someone snitched on them and Joey's old man went ballistic and did something, Joey wouldn't say what, to make sure the relationship ended. Now, because of what you've told us, I'm assuming this Melita was the result of Joey's teenage love affair."

Mary-Beth fell silent, and Ross and Drake looked at one another, instinctively sharing a feeling that the young Joey must have fathered a child while little more than a kid himself and somehow, knew about the little girl and must have followed her progress in secret over the years and this bequest was his way of making amends for being absent from her life. Ross finally spoke, his thoughts leading him to believe that this was a tragic little drama that had taken place many years ago, but he couldn't see how it could have a connection with Joey's death.

"So, you never knew who this Carmen was?" he asked Mary-Beth. "You don't know where she lived or even if she's still alive?"

"Sorry, I don't have any idea. Her name might not even be Gonzales any more, if she maybe married again. Back then, Joey never told me her surname. He only ever mentioned the name Carmen that day at his parent's home and later when I asked him about her. We never mentioned her again during our life together, and that's the truth, I swear."

Ross believed her and realised that this wasn't helping find the murderer. Before, he could move on however, Trixie spoke up and surprised him and Drake with her next words.

"If you find this girl, Inspector Ross, I'd like to meet her, to get to know her. If she's Joey's daughter, then she's the only blood relative he has left. I'd like to help her. Maybe she's struggling through college, or maybe working in some dead-end job. I feel I owe it to Joey to do something for her."

"Yeah, go girl," Mary-Beth agreed with Trixie. "That's a great way to honour Joey, for sure. Count me in. If I can help, I will."

"Me too," said Lana. "Poor kid probably don't even know who her father was. I know Joey's father was always okay to me, but he could be a bigot at times. Even when I was with Joey, he used to put the Mexicans down, Puerto Ricans too. He seemed to hate Latinos for some reason I never found out about."

Andy Ross was quite touched by the three women's altruistic and benevolent approach to the revelation regarding Joey's daughter. He wondered what they'd think when they knew the contents of Slimani's last will and testament. He decided to push the conversation in the direction of the funeral.

"So, Trixie, while I appreciate your generosity towards Melita, if she is found, I need to ask you about the arrangements for tomorrow."

"Oh, yeah, the funeral, of course," she looked upset at the mention of the word. "Joey's being cremated at the Landican Cemetery and Crematorium on Arrowe Park Road at eleven in the morning. Trixie picked up a leaflet from the crematorium from the coffee table and showed it to Ross. There's no point having him buried in foreign soil, no disrespect intended to you guys, so I decided on cremation, and I'll have Joey's ashes returned to me and he will be with me wherever I go in the future."

"So, you don't intend to stay here?" Drake asked.

"Hell, I don't know, Sergeant Drake," Trixie said, quietly, and Drake saw a tear forming in the corner of the widow's eye. Perhaps she'd misjudged the woman. Now that her own pregnancy had been confirmed, Izzie was seeing things very differently. Trixie continued. "I just don't know what to do next, if I'm honest with you. I'm guessing Joey will leave me pretty well off, but hell, I'm too young to wear widows weeds for the rest of my life. I need to keep busy, so maybe I'll sell up and go back to the States, maybe find work in the business over there, or maybe Germany, who knows? Joey thought Germany was a hip place to be for anyone in our business, so..." she left the sentence unfinished.

"Do you have any objections to us being present at the funeral?" Ross asked her.

"No, why should I?"

"Maybe the inspector's hoping Joey's killer will show up, pretending to be a mourner," said Mary-Beth.

"Anything's possible," Ross agreed.

"Anyway, you guys will be welcome," Lana added. "There sure ain't gonna be too many there to mourn poor Joey."

"That's right," Trixie sniffed a tear away. "He ain't got no family to come over from home, and there's only a few friends and colleagues from the business who will probably show up to pay their respects. And, oh yeah, some guy from the South Mersey Golf Club called and asked when the funeral was and asked if they could be represented there."

"That was nice of them," Drake replied. "Do you recall who rang you?"

"Lemme think a minute, yeah, I remember, it was some guy called Bull, Graham Bull, said he was the club captain. I think I met him a coupla times. He said the club felt they would like to pay their last respects, seeing as how Joey was one of their members."

"And what's the agenda after the funeral?" Ross asked, and he could see that Trixie was becoming visibly more and more upset as thoughts of her husband's funeral now loomed large in her thoughts.

"We have to go see Joey's lawyer at two in the afternoon. He's going to read the will and wants us all to be there, even Jennings, he told me."

"You're not holding a wake or anything like that for Joey?" came from Drake.

"Hell, no. Who we gonna invite? Me and the girls here will come back here after seeing this Powell guy and raise a glass or two to Joey," Trixie was now visibly weeping and Ross decided enough was enough.

"Thanks for seeing us like this," he spoke softly. "We appreciate you giving us your time."

"Just do something for me," Trixie sobbed as she spoke. "Please, find the bastard who killed my Joey and put him away for a long, long time, Inspector Ross."

Ross took hold of her small hand, which was trembling now, and nodded to her. He wouldn't make a promise he couldn't necessarily keep, but he did say, "I promise you that my team and I will do all we can to make that happen, Trixie."

Mary-Beth and Lana both rose and formed a little protective shield around Trixie who appeared to have shrunk to almost child-like proportions as her emotions finally took over and her defences gave way, finally allowing Trixie's face break down into a sobbing, tear-streaked visage of misery.

Ross and Drake were mostly silent on the short drive back to police headquarters, each lost in thought as they pondered where to go from here. Drake broke the silence as they emerged from the Queensway Tunnel back onto the Liverpool side of the Mersey.

"So, Joey fathered a baby when he was a kid himself, his father, who hated anyone of Hispanic origin, probably knew about it and did something to make sure the mother stayed away from his son. Now, in death, Joey wants to finally do something to put things right for his kid. How am I doing so far?"

"Sounds about right to me, Izzie. Trouble is, as far as I can tell, although it adds another layer to this already multi-facetted case, it doesn't really suggest a motive for anyone to do away with Joey, does it? Mind you, it's a nice gesture of Trixie's to want to help the daughter, don't you think?"

"I agree, and I'm glad I saw the doctor too, because somehow, I feel very different towards Trixie and the ex-wives. Seeing her like that was humbling. She really loved him, didn't she?"

"I'm sure she did," Ross replied. "I suppose it just shows we shouldn't judge people based solely on what they do, Izzie. It's more a case of who they are that matters. Porn star or princess, they all have feelings and all deserve our respect, whether we approve of how they live their lives or not."

"Okay, okay, I know I was in the wrong for a while earlier in the case, but I promise, I'm okay now."

"I know you are. I sensed there was something wrong as soon as I saw the way you were towards Trixie. I remembered how caring and sympathetic you were towards Alex Sefton during the Donovan case," Ross said, referring to the transgender witness who Drake befriended during the recent case of the revived Lighthouse Murders.

"You're right, of course," she agreed. "I definitely wasn't myself, was I?"

Back at headquarters, as they exited the car, Ross came to a decision. "Tell you what, Izzie. It's time to change direction. It's obvious Joey met with someone else on the day he was killed. Forget German porn producers and mystery children. I think they're all smokescreens, covering up the facts we should really be looking for. Whoever it was, led him to wherever he was killed. Someone hated Joey Slimani enough to kill him and throw his naked body over the parapet of a bridge onto a railway line. We need to find that place, and when we do, we just might find the evidence we need to put a name to our killer."

"Okay, sounds good to me, but just one question. Where the hell do we start?"

Ross grinned, sardonically.

"Ah, well, I didn't say I had all the answers yet, did I?"

Chapter 20

Back to work

Sam Gable lay peacefully in the arms of her new boyfriend, Detective Sergeant Ian Gilligan, who had been instrumental in helping her and D.C. Ginger Devenish in the course of their investigation in Failsworth. The widower and Sam had felt a mutual attraction and tonight that attraction had led Gilligan to drive from his home in Oldham to Liverpool in order to cement their romantic alliance.

He'd treated Sam to a romantic dinner at her favourite Italian restaurant, Casa Italia on Stanley Street in Liverpool, where they'd spent most of the evening staring into one another's eyes while engaged in a conversation that saw them both falling for each other even more than they had so far. Sam had encouraged Ian to talk about his wife, who'd been killed by a drunk driver, and their life together. Ian admitted he found it hard to talk about the incredible loss he'd suffered, but Sam held his hand across the table and encouraged him to talk through all that had happened, how he'd turned to drink in an effort to get through his pain and how finally he'd returned to duty after a long lay-off and was still working hard to rebuild his career. When he turned the conversation round to ask Sam about her own life, she related her career so far, focussing on her time with the Vice Squad and then her appointment to the Specialist Murder Investigation Team, working under Andy Ross, where, she told him, she felt she'd found her true niche in life. Ross, she said, was easily the best boss she'd worked for, a man who valued the opinions and the input of every member of the team, and who had the most incisive mind of anyone she'd worked with in her career to date. On a personal level, she told Ian that she'd had a few boyfriends, but as yet, nothing serious.

When he drove her home later that night, he'd hardly expected to be invited in to her home, but, so relaxed and at ease did she feel with this new man in her life that Sam felt no sense of hesitation in inviting him in, 'for a coffee' which, after almost thirty minutes of kissing and canoodling on the sofa, ended with Sam rising from her seat and leading Ian by the hand to her bedroom.

After an hour spent reviving feelings neither of them had experienced for a long time, they were now lying in reflective mood as tiredness after a long working day began to take its toll on the couple.

"I suppose I ought to be making a move for home, then," Gilligan said, looking at his watch and seeing the time was approaching midnight.

"You're joking, surely?" Sam responded, pulling him closer. "There's no way you're driving back to bloody Oldham tonight, D.S. Gilligan."

"Oh, so you're giving the orders now, are you, Detective *Constable* Gable," he laughed.

"Listen to me, you beautiful man. What time are you due on duty in the morning?"

"Eight-thirtyish," he replied.

"And how long will it take you to drive just over thirty-five miles?"

"Using the motorway, maybe forty-five minutes to an hour, depending on rush hour traffic."

"So, we get up nice and early and you set off about sevenish, and bob's your uncle, you'll be there in plenty of time."

"You're a hard woman to refuse, Samantha Gable," he smiled, relaxing into the pillows as he did so, the decision made.

"And don't you forget it, Ian Gilligan," Sam replied, pulling him into a long, passionate kiss.

"What's your agenda for the morning?" Gilligan asked as they were about to drift off to sleep.

"Got a feeling I'll be going to funeral."

"Sounds like a bundle of fun," he joked and soon after, the pair drifted off into a deep, satisfying sleep, neither of them stirring until Sam's digital alarm clock woke them at 5.30 in the morning, and work beckoned the two of them.

* * *

Andy Ross walked into the squad room soon after 7 a.m. wanting to make an early start on reviewing what they knew (or mostly didn't know) about the Joey Slimani case. As he entered, he was surprised to see a figure standing in front of the white board that contained all the pertinent information relating to the case.

"Derek, what the bloody hell are you doing here at this time of the morning," he smiled as he greeted Detective Constable Derek McLennan, this being his first day back at work following his honeymoon.

"Morning, sir," McLennan smiled at his boss. "I wanted to get here early to see what I've missed while I've been away. Looks like we've got a real pearler of a case here," he said, indicating the photos and notations on the board.

"You could say that, Derek," Ross agreed. "Why don't you spend a few minutes going through the murder book until everyone gets here? Oh yes, how was the honeymoon?"

"Honeymoon was great, sir, thanks. And yes, I'll do that," Derek said, as he turned his attention to the by now heavy folder, the 'murder book' that contained everything the team had gathered so far on the Slimani case.

Ginger Devenish somehow caught the sparkle in Sam Gable's eyes as she hailed him with a cheery "Morning Ginge," and easily put two and two together, him being the only member of the squad to know about her feelings for Ian Gilligan. He corralled her by the coffee machine, for further investigation of his theory.

"Someone's looking like the cat that got the cream last night," he said very quietly as Sam retrieved her coffee from the vending slot.

"Shhh, someone might hear you," Sam hushed him.

"So, I'm right then. You really got it together with the man from Manchester," he said it as a statement, not as a question.

"You're too bloody clever, Gary Devenish," she replied, using his real name. "And yes, Ian Gilligan and I had a very nice evening together, thank you very much."

"Oh yes, and I wonder what time the handsome sergeant made his way home last night?"

Sam's blushed and that was all Devenish needed.

"Oooh, Samantha, really" he whispered in a mocking, motherly tone of voice. "He stayed over didn't he?"

"Ginge, I promise you, if you don't shut the fuck up before someone hears you, you'll be needing a new pair of balls in a few minutes," Sam smiled as she made the threat to his manhood.

"Okay, okay, 'nuff said," he laughed and walked off, having got himself a coffee, leaving Sam feeling as if everyone in the squad room had seen and heard their brief interchange. In fact, everyone had been so busy welcoming Derek McLennan back from his honeymoon that nobody had noticed her and Devenish's little performance at the coffee machine.

* * *

"Okay people," Ross called them all to order. "We're getting nowhere with this bloody case, I freely admit that, but no way are we giving up on it. We will bring Joey Slimani's killer to justice. It's the funeral today and I want a presence there. It's likely that Joey's killer could put in an appearance, wanting to see his victim finally planted in the ground. It's been done before and it could be done again. I know we're all pleased to see Derek back from his honeymoon but let's leave any interrogation on the highs and lows of his time away until later, and that's an order. Sam, I want you and Derek, Tony and Ginger with me and Izzie at the funeral. Dress appropriately and watch for anyone acting suspiciously or just anyone who looks like they maybe don't really belong there."

A chorus of agreement rippled through the room.

"What about me, Boss?" Dodds asked, having been left out of the funeral surveillance squad.

"Nick, we still need to find out where Joey Slimani was killed. I want you to go with Paul," Ross motioned to Paul Ferris, who nodded back at Ross in agreement, "and go over everything you and Tony did previously in trying to track Joey's movements. Then Paul, I want you to analyse everything we've brought in so far and try and predict where you think Joey might have gone that morning. If you have any bright ideas, follow them up, okay?"

Sergeant Paul Ferris, glad of the chance to get some hands-on investigating done readily agreed. Dodds joined the team's computer wizard and the pair immediately set to work, Dodds briefing Ferris on the progress, or rather lack of it, he and Curtis had made on their enquiry into the movements of Joey Slimani on his last day of life.

Ross was happy that none of the officers he was taking to the funeral needed to change their attire. Derek McLennan was as always dressed impeccably, in his now, 'signature' dark grey suit, white shirt and blue tie, an outfit that had become synonymous with the man within the squad. Izzie wore a dark navy skirt suit with low-heeled black shoes, while Sam Gable was dressed in a new light-grey trouser suit, complimented by a power pink blouse, and similar low heels to Izzie's.

They left headquarters in three cars, Ross and Drake in one, Gable and McLennan in the second and Curtis and Devenish in the other. Sam was grateful that Ross had put Ginger Devenish in the third car. It saved her from further discussion about her night with Ian Gilligan. So far, Devenish had kept his word about not saying a word to anyone about her fledgling romance with the Manchester D.S, and Sam was happy to keep it like that for the time being.

As Sam drove the second car in their little convoy, following Ross and Drake's Peugeot through the Queensway tunnel once again, she spent a minute asking Derek about his honeymoon, before talk turned to the current case.

"Did you manage to read through the murder book fully, Derek?"

"I did, yes. It's an odd sort of case, isn't it?"

"That's one way of putting it, I suppose. What do you think, from what you've learned so far? I know the boss is hoping you'll be able to bring a fresh pair of eyes to it. He really appreciates your ability to think outside the box, you know."

"Does he really, Sam? That's good to know. I'm glad he feels like that. You know, when I think back to when I first joined the squad and we were assigned the Brendan Kane case, I must have been such a pathetic excuse for a detective. I was really in awe of D.I. Ross and almost jumped out of my skin every time he spoke to me or asked my opinion on something."

"But that's just it, Derek. He knew you had the makings of a really good detective and that's why he kept asking you to think for yourself. He does that to encourage his officers to contribute and to really feel a fully integrated part of the team."

"I honestly thought he must have wondered what he'd been saddled with at the time."

"Rubbish! He knew you had it in you. Did you know he asked for you to be assigned to his team?"

McLennan looked shocked.

"No, I didn't, and nobody else has ever mentioned it. How do you know that's true, Sam?"

"Paul Ferris mentioned it to me ages ago, soon after you joined us. He told me the boss had requested your transfer after hearing about a case you'd investigated, something to do with a body being found in a locked garage."

"I remember that, I was helpful in solving it, yes, but I never thought it would merit me getting a move to this squad."

"Well, it did. Your D.I. at the time gave a glowing report on your contribution to the case and you could say the boss moved a few mountains to get you on his team within a few weeks of your case ending."

"Bloody hell, and I never knew about that until now. Amazing."

"Right then, come on, superbrain, what do you think about Joey Slimani's murder?"

"From what I've read, I can see why the boss thinks you might all have been too focussed on the adult movie connections. It's possible the vic was killed by an unknown assailant, someone who picked him at random for example, but the stripping of the body makes that unlikely, I suppose. It's more likely to be someone who knew him, and who might have stripped him to make some kind of statement, exactly what, I don't know. Maybe it was a mugger who liked what he was wearing and just wanted his clothes."

"What, even his underpants?"

"Yes, I agree that's not very probable either. All I'm saying is the murder could easily have nothing to do with the business he was in."

"Christ, it doesn't take you long to get back in the groove, does it?"

"Thanks, Sam. Always good to feel appreciated."

The pair laughed and Sam realised how much she'd missed having Derek around. He really did add a lot to the team, and she had a feeling he might just end up being promoted when Izzie left to have her baby, speaking of which, she wondered if Derek knew about the happy news yet.

"A baby?" Derek sounded amazed when Sam told him, just before they arrived at the crematorium in Birkenhead. "I would never have thought Izzie would interrupt her career to have a baby."

"She told me it was unplanned, but now it's happened, she and Peter are really chuffed about it."

"Well then, that's great news then. I wonder what they'll do about replacing her while she's on maternity leave."

"We'll have to wait and see, won't we?" Sam said, knowing that Derek, like her, would probably be considered for at least a temporary promotion when the time came.

"Turn here, Sam," Derek said.

They'd arrived.

Chapter 21

R.I.P Joey

The funeral of Joey Slimani was indeed a low-key affair. The small chapel at the Landican Cemetery and Crematorium in Birkenhead wasn't even half-full as his wife, Trixie and two ex-wives led the small group of mourners, the three women sitting together at the front of the room, with Mary-Beth and Lana flanking the widow, like a pair of personal bodyguards.

Behind them, dressed in black business suits, sat Heinrich Braun and Stefan Schmidt, the two German porn producers who'd both had recent business dealings with the dead man, but who both appeared motiveless when it came to the subject of his murder. In the same row sat Michael Powell, the dead man's solicitor, William Jennings, the Slimani's butler/manservant/part-time lover to Trixie and an unknown man who Ross correctly surmised was Slimani's American lawyer. On the opposite side of the room sat half a dozen men and three women, who, Ross and his people later discovered, were adult movie actors and actresses who regularly appeared in movies made by Joe Slim Productions. Seated behind the group of porn stars was a rather stiff-looking individual, the captain of South Mersey Golf Club, Graham Bull, here to pay his last respects on behalf of the club and its members.

That left just two more unknowns, who Ross would later learn were Joey's regular cameraman, Tommy Blue, and production assistant, Leo

Lassiter, both long-time associates of the dead man, who sat in the opposite row to Graham Bull.

The only others present in the small chapel were the six police officers, Ross and Drake seated right at the back, on the left, with Gable and McLennan seated similarly on the right. Curtis and Devenish stood either side of the entrance where they had eyes on the whole proceeding. Ross couldn't help feeling that, by virtue of the miniscule number of mourners, he might have overdone the police presence.

With Joey not being committed to any particular religion, the service was a non-denominational affair, with a few words being spoken by Simon Bueller, Joey's American lawyer, who, from his speech, appeared to have known the deceased for most of his adult life. Bueller concentrated on Joey's love for each of his three wives, who in turn, he said, had brought love and light into Joey's life and who remained his friends long after their respective marriages were dissolved. As for Joey's business, Bueller managed to make him sound like a cross between Steven Spielberg and Alfred Hitchcock, speaking of the 'adventure,' 'suspense,' and 'artistic excellence' of the productions he brought to the screen. Ross couldn't help wondering if Mr. Bueller had ever seen one of Joey's movies.

After Bueller's speech, Mary-Beth Hutton rose and spoke on behalf of the three wives, a good choice, Drake thought, as she was by far the most educated and erudite of the three women. Somehow, she managed to speak about Joey for just over five minutes without once mentioning his movies, concentrating instead on his life as a husband and friend to all three of the women in his life. Much to Ross and Drake's surprise, she went on to mention the fact that they had recently learned of the existence of a daughter, born while Joey was little more than a child himself and Mary-Beth hoped they would one day meet her and be able to tell her about her father.

That would be an interesting conversation, Drake thought, rather cruelly.

As the coffin finally began its progress through the curtains on Joey Slimani's final short journey to oblivion, the sounds of the nineteen sixties hit record *Spirit in the Sky* by Norman Greenbaum played over the chapel's sound system. Joey had loved the song, despite not being a religious man. He loved the idea of a great being in the sky waiting to welcome us as we passed from life into eternity.

The small group of mourners slowly filed out of the building, Trixie on the arm of William Jennings. Dressed in a tailored black dress, that hugged her waist and fell to just above her knees, and a short black jacket with a fur collar, she looked elegant and not so much like a porn actress, but more like a fashion model, Izzie thought. The two ex-wives followed, both in black outfits that were rather more conservative than Trixie's. Trixie, Mary-Beth and Lana stood together at the double exit doors, receiving handshakes, hugs and words of condolence from the small party of mourners. Being the only one, apart from the lawyers, not directly connected to the adult movie industry, Graham Bull appeared a little uncomfortable in such company and having said a few words to Trixie, made a rapid departure from the scene.

Ross and Drake finally stood in front of Trixie and the others, having left McLennan and Gable to watch the departing mourners, and to gather their impressions of their behaviour. They had instructions to look for any interaction between those present that might be inappropriate or suspicious.

"Once again, we're very sorry for your loss, Trixie," he said in a hushed tone. He hated funerals, and never knew quite what to say to the bereaved relatives, especially when their lost loved one had been the victim of a brutal murder, as yet unsolved.

"Thanks, Inspector," Trixie replied. "I don't suppose you're any closer to finding Joey's killer yet?"

"No, we're not," he spoke in all honesty. He felt she deserved that much. "We're pursuing various lines of inquiry and we hope to make progress very soon."

"I'm sure you'll succeed too," Trixie said, with strong conviction in her voice. "You strike me as a man who don't give up easily."

"You're correct in your assumption," he replied. "We *will* find your husband's murderer, I'm sure of it."

Trixie nodded, the look on her face enough to show she trusted and believed in Ross.

"I suppose you'll be at the reading of the will later," Trixie asked him. They'd spoken of it a few times and she had expressed no objections to the police being present when Michael Powell presented Joey's will in a couple of hours.

Ross was beginning to find her occasional lapses into her native New York accent quite revealing, appearing more often when she was clearly undergoing moments of stress or anxiety.

That left Ross and his people a little time to gather their thoughts, discuss the funeral and the mourners and most importantly, grab some lunch!

Izzie Drake found a convenient table under a large bay window in The Flying Horse, and she and Sam Gable claimed it while Derek McLennan joined Ross and ordered lunch. Ross chose the days 'Special' of steak pie, chips and peas, while Derek had a chicken salad. Izzie joined Ross in ordering the special while Sam decided on a bowl of winter vegetable soup with a home-made bread roll. Ross and McLennan made their way back to the table with drinks, pints of bitter for the two of them, a tonic water for Izzie, and a J20 orange drink for Sam. While they waited for the food to arrive they discussed the case.

"Any thoughts, having read the murder book and seen the prime movers at the funeral, Derek?" Ross asked and Derek looked thoughtful for a few seconds before replying.

"Yes, sir, I have, though you might not like the way I'm thinking."

"Don't worry about upsetting me, lad, you know how I work. Out with it."

"Okay, I was talking with Sergeant Ferris earlier and he told me you were thinking about changing the direction of the investigation. I agree that's the best way forward. If you don't mind me saying so, I think the investigation is too bogged down in the adult film industry. I think it's always been the easy option to look in that direction, sir, so I'm not saying it was wrong to do so, but it just seems to me that other avenues of investigation have been ignored, that's all."

Ross looked pensive. Of all the members of his team, Derek McLennan had an uncanny ability to 'see' things others might miss, an attention to detail that could often unlock a case by picking up on some small, hidden fact or omission in previous parts of an investigation. He welcomed Derek's Devil's Advocate approach which at times could seem unorthodox but had paid dividends in the past.

"I'm listening, Derek," he said as a waitress arrived at the table with the two specials. After she'd gone, Derek continued.

"Okay, sir, from the outset, as soon as you discovered Mr. Slimani's occupation, everyone seems to have assumed his death was somehow connected to his business and initial inquiries led you to believe there could be some connection with organised crime in the States, am I right?"

"Yes, you are, Derek. Please go on."

"Sir, with all due respect, I think that if the Mob, or whoever these American gangsters happen to be had wanted to kill the man, they would have done so in a way that sent out a big signal to anyone else who might cross them or upset them. The fact that you and the team are still floundering around a bit to try and substantiate a motive makes me feel that just didn't happen here. Since when, in our experience, do organised criminals bump their victims off, strip them and chuck their naked bodies over railway bridges?"

"When you put it like that, Derek, you have a point, don't you agree, Izzie, Sam"

"I certainly do, sir," Drake replied, as the waitress returned with Sam's order. Sam waited until she was out of earshot and then added her own agreement.

"That's the way you've been thinking for the last couple of days as well, isn't it sir?"

"Exactly, Sam. It's good to hear it from you as well though, Derek. Often a new set of eyes can bring a new perspective to the case. Did anything stand out from the reading all the notes, Derek?"

"Two things struck me, sir. One area that hasn't been looked at very closely is the German connection what with two of the principal players in this case being German of course, one of whom is closely connected to one of the ex-wives, the other being a close business associate of the vic. Of course, Sofie is now looking into that, talking to her connections in Germany."

"And the other thing?"

"My other concern sir, is South Mersey Golf Club."

"Really, Derek. Why?"

"The only reason I say that is that the golf club seems to keep cropping up. First you had the meeting between Joey, one of the Germans and the guy from Manchester. Forgive me if I haven't memorised their names yet. Then Joey turns up there again with the second German. My question is, why the golf club? Is there a connection between the club and Joey apart from him being an innocent member who enjoys playing golf? Could he have been connected to some other nefarious goings-on at the club?"

"Derek, you're a bloody genius," Ross clapped him on the back.

McLennan blushed a little at the effusive praise from his boss.

"Thank you, sir. I just think, with me coming in cold like this, like an outsider almost, I can see things that maybe haven't been so obvious so far."

"It's worth taking a closer look at the golf club, don't you think, sir?" Izzie asked.

"I agree, Izzie. Thanks for your input Derek. You might have given the case a new focus."

"Nice one Derek," Sam Gable added, "I always thought that lot at the club were too good to be true."

"It's only a theory, Sam," Derek, said. "I could be way off beam with it."

"Well, we'll see what a fresh look at our friends over the water gives us, eh?" said Ross. "In fact, as a fresh face to the case, I'd like you to go over there, Derek, you too Sam, as you've been there before, and this time, have a good nose around. Try talking to some of the members, see if they remember Joey, and if any of them actually spent time with him, maybe even played a round of golf with him. After all, it's unlikely he became a member of the club and never played against anybody else is it?"

"That's a good point, sir. What do you think, Derek?"

"I agree with the boss. He must have played a few rounds during his membership. Anyone got any idea how long he'd been member at South Mersey?"

Derek's question was met with a collective shaking of heads, and he made a mental note to make sure it was one of the first things they found out when they paid their visit to the club.

Lunch over, Ross strode to the bar to pay their bill and he and Izzie made their way to the offices of Temple and Hawkes, where the reading of Joey Slimani's will would soon be taking place.

Derek had suggested that there was no time like the present for him and Sam to conduct their inquiries at South Mersey Golf Club, so he and Sam headed to the Mersey Tunnel once again and were soon gobbled up by the Queensway tunnel, en-route to Birkenhead.

Chapter 22

Where there's a will

Michael Powell, out of professional respect for his deceased client, had dressed for the reading of the will in an immaculately pressed black suit, stiff collared white shirt and black tie. As he read the will, he managed to inject a degree of gravitas into his voice, which came across as being deeper and more resonant than Ross recalled from their previous conversation. Ross found himself developing a certain respect for the man, who obviously took his responsibilities to his clients, alive or dead, very seriously indeed.

Apart from Ross and Drake the only others present in Powell's office for the reading were his secretary, and Trixie, Mary-Beth, Lana and William Jennings. As he read the various bequests, the beneficiaries were mostly silent, there being little in the will to cause them any surprises. The first real reaction came with Powell's announcement of the million dollar bequest to Jennings, who'd wondered why the solicitor had requested his presence for the reading of the will. Even Joey's wives, past and present gasped audibly at the amount bequeathed to the butler, who sat stunned as the bequest sunk in.

"A million dollars? He had to be joking, right?" Lana Slimani was the first to speak.

"Joey was a very generous man," Trixie said, defending her husband's wishes, even though she too was surprised at his largesse where Jennings was concerned.

"Oh, come on, we all know what Trixie's like," Mary-Beth now spoke up, having found her voice after her momentary speechlessness. "I think we all know it's Joey's way of thanking Jennings for his service, above and beyond the call of duty."

"And just what does that mean, exactly, Mary-Beth?" Trixie sounded angry, the first time Ross had witnessed any sign of discord among the women.

"Trixie, honey, we all know Joey paid for poor old Jennings here to be available to cope with, shall we say, your slightly nymphomaniacal tendencies."

Somehow, Mary-Beth managed to say this without it sounding in any way insulting to Trixie, as though she was simply voicing an accepted fact, which, Ross thought, was quite true of course. He and Izzie had long ago worked out that Trixie was definitely a nymphomaniac. Her need for sexual intercourse was such that her work in the adult movie industry helped to fulfil her needs most of the time and it was obvious that her husband had known of her proclivities and as such, made sure, by bringing Jennings on board, that his wife's needs whenever he was away from home were tended to 'in house' as Ross put it during one their regular case conferences.

"That's not a nice thing to say, Mary-Beth," Trixie said, sounding hurt at what was, after all, Mary-Beth's statement of fact.

"Hell, girl, it's true. Don't go denying it. Nobody here's putting you down. You are what you are, honey. No-one's judging you for it. Anyway, as I said, our friend Jennings here has been well compensated for his extra duties, eh, Jennings? Trixie here has a well-earned reputation in the business for being a real good fuck."

"That's enough, Mary-Beth!" Trixie's voice had risen a whole octave as she screamed at Mary-Beth. Michael Powell's face had turned scarlet with embarrassment at what he was hearing, and William Jennings looked as if he wished the floor would open up and swallow him whole. Powell's secretary/receptionist, Gloria Snow, appeared decidedly uncomfortable, as she sat, looking askance at the tableau playing out before her eyes. All she could do was keep nervously crossing and uncrossing her legs, little realising that each time she did so, her skirt rose a little higher, until she was displaying far more leg than she would normally have considered decent. When it rose so far that her thighs were showing, Izzie did her best to surreptitiously signal to the poor woman what was happening, Gloria finally catching on to Drake's subtle hand signals and pulling her hem down, even more embarrassed at her unseemly display. She mouthed a 'thank you' to Izzie, who smiled kindly at her.

Meanwhile, the subject of this particular discussion, William Jennings, having got over his initial shock at his inordinate good luck, and having ridden out the sense of embarrassment he felt from being described as little more than a male prostitute by Mary-Beth and now, clearing his throat loudly to command the attention of the others, he asked the solicitor,

"Mr. Powell. Just how much is a million dollars in British money, sir?"

"At current exchange rates, Mr. Jennings, I estimate you should receive a legacy in the region of six hundred and fifty-nine thousand pounds, sterling."

"Bloody hellfire!" Jennings exclaimed, the sheer shock of the amount of money he'd receive, rendering him unable to say much else.

"Well, I'm sure Joey would have wanted you to enjoy it," Trixie said, supportively.

Lana, who'd refrained from saying much thus far, now broke her silence.

"Yeah, well, good luck to you, Jennings. I doubt you'll ever find a more pleasurable way of earning a million dollars."

"Lana, Mary-Beth, that's enough," Trixie was angry. "You should remember this is Joey's money we're talking about and it was up to him who he left it to. I'd rather have my Joey back than all the money in the world, so what he chose to do with it is just fine by me."

"Yeah, well, of course I didn't mean nothin' nasty by what I said," Mary-Beth now felt like a fish on a hook. She knew Trixie had quite a temper when riled and didn't want to start a public argument in the solicitor's office.

"I think you did," said Trixie, "but I'll let it go if you don't say no more about it."

Michael Powell now cast a glance at Ross, a look that held a pleading quality as though he hoped the policeman could somehow stop these terrible women, as he saw it, from making a spectacle of themselves in his office. Ross however, was interested in seeing if a real rift developed between the three women. Maybe all wasn't quite as friendly as he'd been led to believe, and if so, could there be a motive for murder hidden within the confines of their apparently sisterly relationship. Instead, the poor solicitor, who Ross genuinely felt sorry for, did his best to calm the situation down.

"Ladies, please, I hardly think this is the time or place to be holding such a discussion. Let me just say that Mr. Slimani's will is totally legal and watertight in terms of his bequests."

Of course, as Ross and Drake expected, that led the wives to another matter, that of Joey's daughter, Melita.

"And what about this daughter?" Lana questioned the solicitor. "We were all shocked when the inspector here told us about her existence yesterday, but we were all quite happy to try and make contact with her to see if she needed our help in any way, but, Holy shit, five million dollars to someone he'd never even met? How can that be right?"

"As I said, Mrs. Slimani, everything in the will is perfectly legal and binding. Believe me, I've been dealing with wills and probate matters for over fifteen years and there is nothing, I repeat, nothing to be gained by trying to overturn any of the legal bequests."

Powell's voice actually carried enough solemnity and strength of purpose that Lana actually backed away from the confrontation immediately and having done so, saw that nobody else was prepared to take on the solicitor who, it appeared, had definitely got his own fair share of steel in his nature.

Ross professed himself impressed with Powell's performance in the end. The man had some 'cajones' after all.

* * *

Being a bitterly cold day, McLennan and Gable didn't expect South Mersey Golf Club would be too busy, and they were correct in their estimate. On their arrival, having asked at the club shop if it was possible to speak to the club captain, they were advised that Mr. Bull had gone to a funeral and wasn't expected back for the rest of the day. Having attended the same funeral themselves, they both wondered what Graham Bull had planned for himself for the day. The young woman on duty in the club shop informed then she would summon the club secretary, of whom Sam had far better memories from her previous visit to the club.

The retired major, Simon Coombes couldn't have been more welcoming.

"Detective Constable, so nice to see you again. How can we help you this time?"

Sam introduced Derek McLennan and informed Coombes that they wished to speak to other members of the club in an attempt to get a better idea of the type of man Joey Slimani was.

"Ah, I see. Well, as you might guess, the weather has put a lot of people off today, and with Christmas approaching, and people being busy with shopping for the holidays and so on, we are a bit sparse on the ground in terms of members present today. You're welcome to speak to anyone in the clubhouse bar of course, but it will be pretty much pot luck whether you'll find anyone who knew the poor man."

"We'll take our chances, thank you, Major," McLennan spoke before Sam could reply. Sam then added, "We thought Mr. Bull might be here, Major. We'd have liked to have a word with him, seeing as he was at Mr. Slimani's funeral this morning."

"Yes, it was Graham who suggested he attended the funeral. He felt the club should send a representative as Mr. Slimani was one of our members. He was intending to take the rest of the day off afterwards, so that's why you won't find him here for the rest of the day."

"Right, well, if it's okay with you, we'll head for the bar and see if you have any members present we can talk to," said McLennan, in a tone that brooked no argument.

"Yes, of course. Please follow me," Coombes turned and led them from the club shop to the nearby clubhouse bar, where, the detectives were pleasantly surprised to see a good smattering of members enjoying a drink in the warm, convivial atmosphere. The bar itself was well-appointed, serving a good selection of popular beers, wines and spirits, coffee and tea, and had an extensive food menu from which members and their guest could choose from a selection of full meals or snacks, hot and cold. Predictably, the walls were decorated with prints of varied golfing scenes, a few trophies displayed in a glass-fronted cabinet, and a board with the names of past presidents of the club was positioned on a wall between the bar and lounge area.

McLennan and Gable noticed that four tables were occupied with a total of ten people, a decent cross-section, they decided. Maybe they'd get lucky.

"Joey boy, yeah, I knew him," said a man who identified himself as Frank Todd, a local builder's merchant, who was seated at a table with two companions, enjoying a drink together. "Shame about what happened to him. I take it you lot haven't caught the bastard what done him in yet?"

"Afraid not, Mr. Todd," McLennan replied. "That's why we're here today. We're hoping you and the other members might give us an insight into the man behind the public perception, kind of thing."

"Oh, yeah, gotcha. You mean, like, what he was like when he wasn't making them there porno movies of his?"

"You knew about his movie business then, Mr. Todd?" Sam asked.

"Hell, sure. Most of us who knew him knew what he did for a living. I know some of the guys here even bought some of his films, but most of 'em probably won't admit it to you guys."

Sam smiled but said nothing. Derek McLennan pushed for more information.

"Do you have any idea who might have wanted him dead?"

"Sorry mate, I can't see anyone here having a grudge against the man."

Sam remembered something and asked Todd, "Your club captain, Mr. Bull was at the funeral today, which I found a little surprising, as when we were here the first time, he wasn't too complimentary about Mr. Slimani's adult movie connections. Does that surprise you, him being at the funeral?"

"Old Bullshit Bull? No, it doesn't surprise me. He would have wanted to 'do the right thing' by attending the funeral. Joey was a member of the club after all and no matter what Bully thought about his private life, he would have put the club first. A real stickler for protocol, is our esteemed captain."

"Yeah, I'll go along with that," said one of Todd's drinking companions.

"And you are?" Sam asked.

"Mark Lee."

"Did you know the victim well, Mr. Lee?" Derek this time with the question.

"I wouldn't say I *knew* him well, but I did play a few rounds with him in the last year or so. He was fucking crap at golf, but a real fun person, always had a good joke up his sleeve to keep you laughing all the way round the course."

"And were you aware of Mr. Bull's dislike of Mr. Slimani's professional lifestyle?" Sam posed the next question.

"Hey look, don't get me wrong, Graham Bull is a pompous airbag, but there's no harm in him."

"He's right," the third man at the table said, and instantly identified himself. "Barry Clark's my name. I work with Mark. We're both firefighters, working out of the station on Dock Road. Look, it's important that you know old Bully is a bit of a religious nut, you know? One of those fanatical evangelical types, who believes totally in every word in the Bible. He's even a lay preacher for his church, somewhere across town."

"I see," Sam said, not seeing Bull's Christian fervour as being a rod to beat him over the head with. Some people, she knew only too well, took their religious beliefs very seriously. "So, you don't think he held a personal dislike for Mr. Slimani?" she asked Clark.

"I'm sorry. I didn't mean to suggest that, Detective Constable Gable. It's just that I find some of these religious types a bit of a pain in the arse, always thinking they're better than us and so on. Listen, if Heaven exists and it's full of people like fucking Graham Bull, just point me to Hell," Clark responded, and brought a round of laughter from those seated around the table.

"I'll drink to that," Todd lifted his pint glass and took a swig.

"Me too," Lee added as he drained his glass and thumped it down quite heavily on the table.

"Bit of a religious fanatic, is he?" Derek asked and received a unanimous round of replies that varied from Todd's "I should say so," to Lee's "Proper stickler for the Bible and all that God-botherer stuff."

"Would any of you say Mr. Bull was capable of hurting anyone?"

Todd actually burst out laughing, "You've got to be kidding. Bull? A killer? Thou shalt not kill and all that, know what I mean?"

"Right, of course. I hadn't thought of that," Derek replied and with that, he and Sam thanked the men, rose from their seats and made their way across the room to speak to a couple more members, who were sitting eating sandwiches and enjoying a small bucket containing freshly made chips, no frozen or oven chips allowed here, by the looks of the contents of the bucket.

The two detectives received similar responses from the two snackers and in turn, from the other members present in the bar, only two of whom admitted to actually knowing Joey Slimani, both concurring that though the American was an enthusiastic amateur, his standard of golf was pretty much at the beginner level, but the most important thing about him, they agreed, was that he enjoyed the game, and they'd enjoyed both playing with and talking to him.

McLennan and Gable decided to end their visit to the club with a final conversation with Major Coombes.

"So," Sam began, after Coombes had provided them with a welcome cup of tea each, "Joey Slimani was very much an enthusiastic member, from what we've been told. Did he play regularly, Major?"

"Hard to say, really, Constable. We don't keep tabs on our members, you know, and obviously, it would be easy for him to visit us while, say, I wasn't here, or anyone else who might have reason to note his presence. I can say quite honestly that I saw him maybe a dozen times over the last year, no more than that."

"So he maybe played once a month, would that be a reasonable probability?" Derek pressed him for an answer.

"Yes, yes, perhaps he did," Coombes agreed, for the sake of argument.

"And during his time here, did Mr. Slimani attend many organised functions at the club?" Sam asked.

Coombes thought for a few seconds before replying.

"I do seem to recall him being present at last year's President's Day, when I met his wife for the first time, and they were both at last year's Christmas dinner and dance, definitely. His lady looked extremely glamourous, I remember."

"Yes, she's a very glamorous lady," Sam agreed.

"I remember her accent actually," Coombes said. "I asked her about it as it sounded like something from an American TV programme. She said she was from New York, and that was about all we talked about as I was dragged away by another member to meet his wife."

The pair thanked Major Coombes for his time and hospitality and were soon heading back across, or rather under the Mersey, through the Queensway tunnel.

"What did you think of them, Derek?" Sam kicked off the conversation.

"I liked the members we spoke to, pretty down to earth bunch, not snobby as you might expect at some golf clubs. Good people, and helpful in their comments. I really liked their clubhouse too."

"Do you play golf?" Sam asked him.

"Sometimes. Debbie's Dad plays the occasional round and he's got in the habit of inviting me along if I'm not working. I'm probably about the same standard as poor Joey Slimani, judging by the members' comments back there," Derek laughed at himself as he spoke.

"Anyway," said Sam, "did you think their information was helpful?"

"You're thinking of something, aren't you, Sam? Something they said has set off a train of thought. I can tell."

"Yes, it has, but I want to know if you think as I do before I go shooting my mouth off."

Derek simply spoke two words.

"Club captain?"

"Yes, exactly. Graham Bull sounds like a real paragon of religious fervour, and he clearly didn't have any love for our victim."

"But as our friends back there pointed out, he's probably very much of the 'Thou shalt not kill' brigade."

"But as we both know, Derek, everyone has a point at which normal limits can be stretched beyond regular limits."

"I know. I think the boss might want to take a closer look at Mr. Bull," McLennan concluded, and in fact, when they reported the results of their interviews at the club, Ross agreed entirely with their joint conclusion.

"You've done well," he said to the pair. "You'd better follow it up. Have a word with that club secretary and get Bull's address. No point in putting it off. Go and see him and see if he gives you any vibes. He's possibly the nearest we've come to an alternative suspect since the case started. In fact he's possibly the first suspect we've really come up with. I doubt he'd kill someone over their lifestyle or occupation to be honest, but stranger things have happened."

Sam and Derek, pleased with their progress so far, stayed long enough for a coffee each, while Sam used the time to phone and speak to Major Coombes, who provided her with an address for Graham Bull. Soon after, they were again in the car, heading back through the tunnel. Derek's first day back at work was proving to be a busy one.

Chapter 23

A meeting of minds

Sofie Meyer gave one crisp knock on Ross's office door and entered the small room that served as the central hub of the team's investigations.

"Sofie, I almost thought you'd got lost. I take it you've been busy conversing with your colleagues back in Germany?"

Sofie smiled and accepted his invitation to sit.

"I have sir, but I'm afraid I have nothing that could be helpful. At least, that's how it looks to me. Heinrich Braun and Stefan Schmidt are both perfectly legitimate producers of adult movies. I was put in contact with Polizeihauptkommissar Manfred Weber, who is the same as a Chief Inspector over here. Manfred was very helpful. He runs a department that oversees investigations and complaints regarding the adult movie industry, you know, to make sure the actors and actresses comply with the law, are not under 18 for example and that those responsible for making such films are not exploitative in their employment of people. They are always on the lookout for girls who have been illegally trafficked into the country, mostly from Eastern Europe and Russia and who are often forced into making extremely hard-core movies that appeal, shall we say, to certain tastes?"

"You mean the really perverted stuff, I presume?" Ross looked angry at the thought of vulnerable young girls being coerced or forced to take part in depraved and perverted 'skin flicks.'

"Yes, exactly, sir. There are too many people who are only too willing to make such films, usually with the help and financial backing of certain criminal elements."

"And what you're telling me is that neither Braun nor Schmidt fall into that category, right?"

"Correct. Both men are totally clean. They make their films in state-of-the-art studios, have plenty of money behind them, all quite legitimate and both men are wealthy. Bearing in mind that they both worked with Herr Slimani in the making of a number of films, all of which were highly profitable, then both Manfred and I arrived at the same conclusion. Neither man had any reason to murder Joey Slimani, sir. I'm sorry it doesn't help our case very much at all."

"Don't apologise, Sofie. It helps to eliminate certain areas of suspicion, and it looks more and more as if we've been looking in the wrong places for Joey's killer. The more we delve into the background of Joey's life the more it's beginning to look as if his murder is a personal matter, rather than anything connected to his business life."

"So my inquiries with my old colleagues have not been a total waste of time?"

"Definitely not, Sofie. It's as important to clear the innocent as it is to prosecute the guilty."

"Of course, sir. I agree. So, what now?"

"Now, dear girl, we have a meeting to see what else we've learned."

* * *

The meeting, called by Ross, and which was attended by D.C.I. Agostini, who felt in need of a hands-on update on the case, saw the whole team together, in the large briefing room, one floor below the squad room. It was already late afternoon, the sun had long-since disappeared and darkness had fallen over the city. Due to the street lighting and the preponderance of winking, blinking and flashing Christmas lights that decorated street and buildings all over the city, total darkness could never be achieved in such a large city, and the streets themselves were alive with a myriad crawling headlights and tail lights as the evening rush-hour traffic began its daily, slow, yet competitive crawl for home. It was cold, and there was little Christmas cheer present in the drivers who jockeyed for position as they each tried to gain a few second's advantage on their fellow motorists. As was normal when the team met en-masse, Ross led off.

"Okay, quiet, please," and the general hubbub in the room ceased. "As you can see, D.C.I. Agostini has joined us today. Anything you want to say, sir?" he asked the boss.

"No, please go on as normal. I just want to make sure I'm up to date with whatever progress, if any, we're making with this damn case, and see if you need my help with anything. Carry on, please Andy."

"Right, everyone. We all know it was Joey Slimani's funeral this morning, which most of us attended of course. As a result of what we saw and observed, we've all been involved in certain other inquiries since lunchtime, so let's hear what we've got. Sofie, you first, if you can let the others know what you've already told me.

Meyer duly did as Ross asked and a couple of the others expressed mild surprise when she gave the two German producers a clean legal bill of health.

Next, Ross called for Devenish and Curtis's report. He'd left them at the crematorium, having tasked them with taking short statements from the small group of peripheral mourners at the funeral, cameraman, Tommy Blue, production assistant, Leo Lassiter, the American lawyer, Simon Bueller and of course, the golf club captain, Graham Bull. The two detectives had been mortified on missing out on a good lunch, but had stuck diligently to their task, finally ending up with a quick sandwich from a Birkenhead Baker's store on their way back to Liverpool.

Tony Curtis spoke first.

"Thanks a bunch for leaving us with the shitty end of the stick, Boss. We missed lunch."

The room filled with spontaneous laughter. They all knew they could count of Tony Curtis to bring a touch of humour or light relief to almost any situation.

"You poor starving detective," Ross smiled as he replied to Curtis's remark. "Just think of the weight a heavy lunch would have piled on and then you can thank me for helping to keep that body of yours in trim for the ladies of Liverpool."

More laughter, and even Oscar Agostini joined in.

"Now, do you have anything of any pertinence to this case to report, or shall we move on to discuss your dietary plans for the rest of the week?"

"Yeah, right, sir. Just thought I'd mention it, like."

"Tony, get on with it."

"Sir. So, you all left, and me and Ginge here asked the mourners to hang around a minute."

"What he means, sir, is we politely requested the people you'd identified to us if they would stay and give us a few minutes of their time," a grinning Ginger Devenish said.

"Thanks, Ginger. Now, who wants to tell this story of yours?"

Curtis cleared his throat and went on.

"A couple of them weren't too happy, well, just one of them really, that bloke from the golf club, Graham Bull. He said he was just there to represent the club and he needed to leave as he had other things to do, so I said we'd speak to him first, which we did, that is, I did, while Ginger spoke with the Yank lawyer. Bull basically repeated what he'd said when Sam first went out to the club, that he hardly knew Slimani, and that although he didn't approve of the way he earned his living, he wasn't at the funeral to pass judgement, but simply to pay his last respects on behalf of the members of the golf club. He said he had no idea who might have a reason to want to harm Mr. Slimani, and that his own contact with the man had been minimal."

"Did you manage to find out what he does for a living, besides being the captain at the golf club" Drake asked a question that nobody had addressed previously.

"Yes, he's a bloody dentist," Curtis replied.

"I take it by that reply you don't like dentists, Tony?" Ross said.

"Definitely not, sir," Curtis replied. "Who the hell would want to spend their entire working days looking into other people's mouths and causing pain and agony by the bucketful. If you ask me they're all graduates from Helga's House of Pain or some such sadistic establishment."

More muted laughter followed Curtis's last remark.

"Laughter aside people," Agostini observed, "Dentists have access to anaesthetics and other drugs, don't they? And Joey Slimani was drugged before having his throat cut, by a very sharp instrument, if I remember rightly."

"Something like a scalpel, for example," Drake said, in reply.

"My thoughts exactly." The D.C.I. nodded at Drake.

"What about the other mourners?" Ross asked.

"Nothing to be gained there, Boss," Devenish replied.

"The lawyer couldn't tell us much. Only arrived in the country yesterday, barely knew the vic. Did what he had to do from a legal standpoint and nothing else, no personal relationship at all.

The cameraman and production assistant have both worked with Joey since he came to England, the cameraman also worked with him in the States in the past. Both have cast-iron alibis for the whole weekend of Joey's murder, both working on different movie projects, one in London and one in Paris of all places. Plenty of witnesses available if we need them. That's it really, sir. Nothing else to report, I'm afraid."

Devenish and Curtis both looked quite crestfallen, both perhaps feeling they'd let the side down slightly by being unable to unearth anything on which to build a case against any of their interview subjects. Ross, however, disagreed.

"Don't apologise, Ginger. You both did ok, considering you were operating on the hoof, so to speak. Tony, I'm more than interested in this Graham Bull character. He might bear looking at in more detail. As he spoke, Sam Gable held a hand up to gain his attention. "You got something to add, Sam?" he asked.

"Yes, we do sir. Do you want to tell it, Derek, or shall I?"

"Go ahead, Sam," McLennan ceded the floor to his female colleague.

"Okay, well, sir, you asked us to visit the golf club and speak to some of the members and we found a few people who had their own memories of Joey Slimani. Some of them played an occasional round with him. It was the general consensus that he wasn't the world's greatest golfer, just someone who played for fun, really, a bit of relaxation for him, I would think. The thing is, this Graham Bull, the club captain's name cropped up once or twice in our conversations with the few members who were present in the clubhouse."

"Bull wasn't there?" Ross asked.

"No, seems he told people he was going to the funeral to pay his respects and would be off attending to some private business later. He definitely isn't the most popular person at the club, they made that quite clear."

"Not going back to his dentistry practice?" Izzie Drake picked up on that point.

"To be honest, Sarge, he might have done. Nobody seemed sure where he might be, and we didn't think we had enough to justify tracking him down there and then. Did we do wrong Boss?" she directed her question to Ross."

"No you did the right thing, Sam. You had nothing but conjecture and hearsay to go on, not enough to do anything he might construe as police harassment."

"One other thing," Derek McLennan added. "He does seem to be something of a religious fanatic, though I suppose fanatic might be the wrong word to use. He's apparently a fervent, yes, that's a better word, fervent. So, yes, he's a fervent evangelical Christian who believes strictly in the literal truth of every word in the Bible, and he's been known to criticise Joey's lifestyle more than once. Seems he felt Joey was involved in making his money from an immoral business that was designed to corrupt and deprave those who watched such filth, those are his words, as one of them members related them, not mine."

"Sounds to me like we may have a suspect, Andy," D.C.I. Agostini commented as McLennan fell silent.

"I agree sir. I think it's time we had a nice little chat with Mr. Bull."

"Oh, there was one other thing, Boss," Sam Gable said.

"What's that, Sam?"

"I'm sure, like me, you thought Mr. Bull was there officially, to pay the collective respects of the members of the golf club?

"You're going to tell me he wasn't?"

"Right. I mentioned to the secretary, Major Coombes, that it was nice of the club to send a representative to Joey's funeral, but he was surprised that we were under that impression. He said Bull being there was nothing to do with the club, it was his own decision to attend, and as far as he was concerned it was purely a private thing that Bull wanted to do, probably due to his religious beliefs, he surmised."

"So why tell you he was there on behalf of the club?" Agostini was beginning to get a bad feeling about Graham Bull, a feeling that Andy Ross shared.

"I totally agree," Ross said as he gave thought to how best to handle Graham Bull.

"Do you want us to pick him up?" McLennan asked.

"But if you do, what evidence do we have that would justify an interview under caution? Agostini was well aware that hunches might be proved right very often in the course of police work, but sadly they didn't constitute the hard evidence necessary to justify an arrest.

"None as yet," Ross spoke again, having thought careful about his next action. "I think you and I ought to go and talk to Mr. Bull, Izzie. He'll probably feel more confident on his home territory and we might find a way to trip him up, if, that is, he's in any way involved in Joey's murder. I still find it hard to believe a dislike of a man's lifestyle or how he earns his living can be a motive for murder, unless of course, our man is seriously mentally impaired."

"Okay, I agree, off you go, Andy, you and Izzie talk to him and try and get a handle on just where he's coming from on the whole matter of Joey Slimani, his life *and* his death," said Agostini.

"Let's go, Izzie," Ross said, eager to confront Bull, despite the late hour in the day. The rest of you, there's not much more we can do today. Go home, get some rest. It's been a long day. We'll meet here again first thing tomorrow, eight a.m."

Ross and Drake left the room to a chorus of 'goodnights', good luck wishes and a final cautionary word from Oscar Agostini.

"Andy, Izzie, be careful. You might just be taking hold of a tiger by the tail out there. Graham Bull could be a very dangerous individual."

Chapter 24

The house in Egremont

Finding Graham Bull's address had proved a simple task. Ross asked Paul Ferris to do a quick search of the electoral register for Birkenhead, working on the assumption their man lived somewhere close to the golf club where he appeared to spend so much of his time. Address found, though Ferris had to apply a little latitude to his original search eventually locating Graham Bull and his wife, Carol, in neighbouring Egremont, an area that forms part of the city of Wallasey, just north of Birkenhead, on the Wirral peninsular.

Ross and Drake motored into Egremont as the outside temperature seemed to plummet, and though only late afternoon/early evening, depending on one's point of view, patches of ice were forming on the roads already. Exiting the unmarked police Peugeot on the street, half-blocking the entry or exit from Bull's driveway due to a lack of parking spaces on the street, Ross and Drake instantly felt the effects of the sudden drop in temperature.

"Bloody hell, it's effing freezing!" Drake's teeth chattered as she spoke.

"Brilliant observation, Sergeant Drake," Ross replied sarcastically. "You ought to be a detective," he laughed. He looked upwards, to see a bright, star-filled sky, seemingly devoid of clouds, a sure harbinger of a heavy frost, possibly with a touch of overnight snow. Ross wished he'd brought an overcoat from home that morning. His short, Adidas padded, 'manager's-style' over-jacket didn't seem capable of keeping the creeping cold from penetrating straight through to his bones.

"Come on, Izzie," he urged her on as they covered the thirty yards or so in no time at all, though their lungs felt as if they were bursting as they reached the front door and Ross pressed the button for the doorbell. They heard the sounds of Westminster chimes coming from somewhere inside the house and then, a voice from the other side of the solid wood door called out, "Who is it?"

Ross shouted out his and Izzie's identities through the door, which slowly opened to reveal a woman he assumed to be Carol Bull. He did his best to avoid a look of surprise on his face. Carole Bull was, by his estimation, at least ten, perhaps fifteen years younger than her husband, who'd been revealed by Sam Gable and Ginger Devenish to be around fifty years of age, a fact confirmed by the woman herself after she'd invited them in and seated them in her neat and tidy sitting room, while she'd disappeared into her kitchen for a few minutes, returning with a tray containing coffee and biscuits for the three of them.

Carol Bull was thirty-four, and a youthful looking thirty-four at that. Slimly-built, she had a figure some women would kill for, though Ross and Drake both noticed a distinct lack of make-up on her otherwise extremely attractive face. Her hair was shoulder-length, blonde and had a natural curl that gave her, despite the lack of artificial 'product' a sultry, 'come-hither' look. She wore a nondescript navy-blue belted dress that almost touched her knees, and the belt accentuated her narrow waist. A plain grey cardigan helped add to the plain look she presented to the world.

"I'm so sorry, I'm afraid Graham isn't here. He was at a funeral earlier today and said he had some things to do afterwards."

"I see," Drake replied, taking the lead in the interview, as she and Ross had quickly arranged as Carol Bull had made the drinks. "Will we find him at his dental practice?"

"Oh no, he said he was going to see the pastor at church afterwards. Graham's very committed to the church you know."

"Yes, we'd heard that," Drake smiled at the woman, who appeared a little nervous, natural enough in people who weren't used to having two detectives suddenly appearing on their doorstep on a cold, dark, December evening. "Are you not a member of the church, also?"

"Well, yes, but not to the extent Graham is. To tell the truth, I go on Sundays to make him happy. I'm not really very religious, at all, but once we were married, I felt I had to go to support my husband, if you can understand that."

"Oh, yes, I can understand you doing that. I'm married too and do all I can to support my husband in his work, too."

"Yes, we do what we can, don't we?" Carol Bull replied, feeling more at ease with Izzie, thinking of her as a kindred spirit.

"So, if he went to see the pastor after attending the funeral, would he normally still be there after all this time?"

Carol Bull seemed to hesitate at that point, seeming unsure how to answer Drake's question. Ross suddenly had a hunch, and decided it was time to be more direct.

"Tell me, Mrs. Bull. Did you ever meet Joey Slimani? That was the man whose funeral your husband attended today."

The woman hesitated again. Izzie Drake instantly picked up on Ross's train of thought.

"You'd remember if you had, Mrs. Bull. Mr. Slimani was a member of the Golf Club where your husband is the club captain, and was a rather good-looking American gentleman, in his thirties, tall, with black, wavy hair."

Carol Bull did her best to appear as if she was in deep thought. Drake, however, sensed the woman was debating how to reply to her question. Finally, the woman replied in a very quiet voice, so quiet that Ross and Drake were forced to lean forward, straining to hear her words clearly.

"I met him once or twice," she almost whispered.

"Was it once, or was it twice?" Ross pressed her, sensing there was more this woman needed to reveal.

"Well, it was a few times, really," Carol Bull finally revealed. Izzie Drake felt they were on the cusp of something very relevant to their investigation and in a calm and quiet voice, she tried to encourage Mrs. Bull to go on with her revelation.

"It's alright, Carol," she reassured her. "Nobody else can hear you. Please tell us about Joey Slimani."

Carol Bull looked like a woman who was carrying a great weight on her shoulders. Whatever it was that was on her mind, she finally decided to let it out. She wasn't the type of woman who was comfortable with evasion. She looked from Drake to Ross and then back again. Neither detective said a word, giving Carol the opportunity to 'fill in the gaps' without further prompting. Realising the detectives weren't about to say anything, the woman did indeed begin to open up a little.

"You have to understand," she began, "I never ever thought someone like Joey would look twice at me."

Ross and Drake could already imagine what was coming, but they continued to play the waiting game, allowing the woman to tell her story in her own time and words. When neither of them replied to her opening words, Carol sighed, took a deep breath, and continued.

"I'm no good at lying so what I'm about to tell you is the God's honest truth. Two years ago, Graham took me to the Golf Club's Christmas dinner and dance, they call it their Christmas Ball. Pretentious isn't it? Not like it's the Lord Mayor's Ball or something is it? Anyway, I don't get to go to the club with Graham very often, he likes me to stay at home for the most part."

Izzie Drake was already building a mental picture of Graham Bull. Possessive, jealous, not wanting other men to look at his wife? Izzie could see that Mrs. Bull was in fact a very attractive woman, or at least, she would be, given half an opportunity. She currently wore no make-up, her choice, or her husbands?

"He always likes to play the 'Big I am' at golf club functions. You know, 'look at me, I'm the club captain' kind of thing. Graham likes to feel important, you see. I don't know how he got to be elected Club

Captain at the golf club. As far as I know, he's not the most popular of people, never has been."

Izzie took a moment to interrupt her story.

"Please, tell us how you met Graham, Carol."

"I worked for him, Sergeant. I'm a qualified dental nurse. Nine years ago I saw an ad for a nurse at a local practice and as I was doing a fair bit of travelling to my job in Bebington, I applied and was lucky to get the job. Graham was really nice to work for, and his patients all spoke highly of him. There was something of the old-fashioned gentleman about him, if you know what I mean. He was always polite, considerate and when, after I'd worked for him for about a year, he asked me out one day, just for a meal, he said, I was flattered and I agreed. It wasn't long before Christmas, and after he'd taken me out a couple more times, he asked me to go to the golf club Christmas Ball with him. I've not had many relationships in the past and I found it quite exciting being on his arm when we attended the ball. He was a slightly older man and he made me feel a bit like a princess that night. I was taken aback when, on New Year's Eve, he proposed to me. I said yes, and we were married in the spring.

I'd always tried to look nice and especially for Graham after we were married. The trouble was, he seemed to change once I was his wife. He didn't want me to go on working. He said no wife of his should be going out to work. I thought it was a bit of an out-of-date attitude but anyway, I gave up my job at the practice. Then he started making personal comments about my clothes and make-up, saying he didn't like me looking like a tart. I never looked like a tart, honestly. Yes, I wore skirts that were just above the knee, because everyone used to say I had good legs, and always used a bit of make-up, nothing excessive, but he made me feel like I was some kind of scarlet woman. I did what he wanted, and gradually, I seemed to go out less and less. The few friends I'd had before we got married found Graham a bit overbearing, and to be truthful, they just didn't like him. At first, I used to meet up with a couple of them for coffee and a natter in town, but gradually even those little outings dried up. I realised I'd made a mistake. Graham wasn't the man I thought he was. He'd gradually taken control of my life and it was like the only times I went out was with him, usually to club functions, especially after he was made Captain of that damn golf club."

Carol fell silent, and for a few seconds the detectives thought she'd finished speaking, but she soon began again, as if she'd just been taking a breather and had now got her second wind. Before she did, however, Ross, who had definitely got the picture by now, tried to get her to focus on the recent past, rather than giving them a complete history of what was clearly an unhappy marriage.

"Please, Carol, just tell us about you and Joey Slimani."

"Yes, of course. Sorry, was I rambling? I must have been. Like I said before, it was Christmas, two years ago. Graham introduced me to a few people, including three new members. Joey was one of them. When we went to golf club function, Graham liked me to dress up, to look good, but only because I was with him and he liked to show me off, I think. Anyway, Joey asked me to dance with him, but so did others, like Major Coombes, and I thought nothing of it. I never saw Joey again until the club held a tournament of some kind in the spring of the following year and held a big dinner at the end and Graham expected me to be there with him, and of course, I met Joey again. He paid me compliments, said what a beautiful woman I was. He made me blush. Even Graham had never spoken to me like that when we were courting. Then last Christmas, me and Graham had had a fight. I'd bought a gorgeous black dress for the dinner/dance and he hated it because it had a split up one side that showed a bit of thigh and he accused me of being a cheap tart and a whore. He slapped my face and I did my best to cover it with make-up, but Joey saw through it. He knew make-up from his involvement in the movie business."

"You did know he was in the adult movie business, I presume?" Ross interrupted.

"Yes, Graham told me a few months earlier. He said I should steer clear of the man. He said he was immoral and made money from sex, which made him nothing more than a male whore himself. I thought it was funny when he said that. He can be such a prude, inspector. Anyway, when I saw Joey again at Christmas I ignored Graham's orders and spoke with Joey, even danced with him. Later, he pulled me aside and asked what was wrong. He said he could see I'd been crying and that I was trying to cover a bruised face with make-up. I broke down and told him about Graham. Joey was all for going and confronting him but I pleaded with him not to make a fuss at the function and spoil it for lots of people. Joey said he wouldn't but only if I promised to meet him after Christmas. I did, of course, and, well, one thing led to another and we…we…slept together late in January at Joey's studio near the docks. I was scared in case anyone walked in on us but Joey said he had two studios and that this one was a kind of spare, a back-up location he kept in case the main studio was ever out of action. The affair went on for months, until a few weeks ago. I don't know how he found out about us, but one evening, Graham confronted me and accused me of having an affair with Joey. I didn't deny it. How could I? Graham had photos of us, together. To be truthful with you, I know Joey was married and we could never have been together, but I told Graham I want a divorce."

"How did that go down, Carol?" Drake asked.

"Not well. He went crazy, called me every name under the sun. Even asked if I'd appeared in any of Joey's sleazy movies as he called them. He accused me of being worse than the Whore of Babylon, asked if I enjoyed doing it on film for men all over the world to enjoy seeing my body being used by those filthy pornographic studs as he called them. I've honestly never been in one of Joey's films, and he never asked me to do that kind of thing."

"So Graham really did have a motive for wanting Joey Slimani dead?" Ross was becoming convinced they were now close to the truth.

"I'm sure Graham would never really go that far, Inspector. He has a temper, yes, but he's a committed Christian and could never murder anyone. I'm sure of it."

"There've been plenty of murders committed by Christians over the years, Carol," Drake said.

"Oh God, do you really think he could have killed Joey?"

"I'm not sure," Ross said, "but he's looking like a serious suspect at present."

"Where did he get the photos, Carol?" Drake asked. "Did he hire a Private Investigator?"

"He said he did, yes," Carol replied. The poor woman was looking pale and her hands were shaking.

"But you don't know which one?" Ross asked.

"I'm sorry, no."

"And you've no idea where he is now?" Ross was becoming frustrated.

Carol Bull simply shook her head, her face a mask of despair and defeat.

"The car on the drive, is that yours?" Drake tried to get Carol Bull talking again.

"The mini, yes. Graham bought it for me for our eighth wedding anniversary."

"So, what does your husband drive?"

"A silver Mercedes 220."

"Do you know the registration number?"

* * *

Ironically, the car and the man they sought was at that very moment parked not more than a hundred yards from where they sat talking to Carol Bull. Graham Bull had driven around aimlessly for a couple of hours after the funeral. If anyone had pressed him, he would have found it virtually impossible to recall exactly where he'd driven during that time. His route had in fact taken him south to Chester, then Wrexham in North Wales, before driving across to Crewe, where he'd stopped for a cup of tea and a sandwich in a small roadside café, before finally heading north on the M6, and then back to Birkenhead via the M56 and M53, where he'd headed straight for the Evangelical Church of St. Aidan. He'd then spent most of the rest of the day talking to and praying with the pastor, Donald Wray, before finally making his way home to Egremont, where he now sat in his car, aware that there were strangers in his house.

Having pulled up outside his home, he'd immediately noticed the unmarked police car parked across the driveway, (not that he identified it as such), and could see the head of a stranger seated in a chair in his lounge. He did, however, guess at the purpose of the visitor and had no wish to see or speak with anyone, apart from his slut of a wife, Carol. Pulling up a few yards further along the street, he decided to wait them out. He would have time to deal with the rest of his business later.

Chapter 25

Means, motive and opportunity

"That's Bull's car," Ross exclaimed, as he and Drake walked down the drive of Bull's home, having been seen to the door by Carol Bull.

"D'you think he's made us?" Drake had no sooner spoken than the engine of Bull's car was turned on, and the diesel exhaust coughed out an initial plume of fumes. "Oops, forget I spoke."

Ross was already running, attempting to catch Bull's attention in an attempt to stop him, but it was obvious the man had no intention of staying to talk to him. While he was still about ten yards from the car, it sped away from the kerb, Ross bent over wheezing slightly in the freezing air.

"Fuck!" he shouted loudly, frustration in that one word, as Drake came up alongside him.

"You okay?" she asked.

"Yeah, just not as fit as I should be, and in this cold air, my lungs are bloody screaming at me for running like that."

"Did he know who we were, do you reckon? It's pretty dark, after all."

"Damn it, Izzie. Course he knew. If he had nothing to hide, why didn't he pull up, and come striding into his house, demanding to know who'd blocked the access to his drive?"

"Good point, Boss. I s'pose that kind of makes him look pretty guilty, eh?"

"I'd say it makes him look *very* guilty."

"Want me to put a BOLO out on Bull and the Merc?"

"Yeah, do it Izzie. Our person of interest just became our number one suspect."

Once in the car, with Ross taking the wheel, Drake quickly got through to Paul Ferris at headquarters who immediately issued the 'Be on the look-out' request for Graham Bull and his car. Within minutes, every police station in the Merseyside area and beyond would receive the details of the wanted man and soon after that, every officer would be notified of the man the Specialist Murder Investigation Team wanted to speak to in connection with the murder of Joey Slimani.

On their arrival, Ross immediately set about mobilising his team. Within an hour, the rest of the team were back in the squad room, their evening off quickly cancelled by a series of calls from Paul Ferris, the squad's night duty officer. Ross quickly brought them up to date with events at Bull's home and began issuing his orders. It was still early in the evening and Ross wanted to move quickly.

"Sofie, you and Nick head to the Golf Club. Speak to anyone and everyone you can find there, especially Major Coombes if he's around. There's bound to be people using the club house for social purposes. I want to know if anyone there knows where Bull might run to. Sam, Tony, I want the two of you at Bull's home with the wife, Carol, in case he returns home, though whether he'll have the nerve to show up there after seeing us at his house is debatable. I'm not taking any chances though.

Turning to Paul Ferris, he went on, "Paul, take Ginger and go to the Evangelical Church of St. Aidan in Egremont. Talk to the pastor, his name is Donald Wray. As far as we're aware, he was the last person Bull spoke to. He may have given the pastor some indication of his immediate plans. The church will be closed now, but I looked it up and the pastor lives in a manse next door to the church.

"I'm going to see the D.C.I. and organise a warrant for Bull's house and car. If he killed Joey Slimani there's a good chance he transported the body in the boot to the railway bridge where he dumped it over the parapet. I have a feeling Mrs. Bull will probably agree to us searching the house without the need for a warrant but I want this case to be water-tight if Bull is in fact the killer. This bastard has been hiding in plain sight, behind a veneer of respectability aided by his so-called religious beliefs, but I think he's just another cold-blooded killer who's pulled the wool over everyone's eyes."

"Do we actually have any hard evidence against him, boss?" Nick Dodds asked, and everyone in the room fell silent.

"Good question, Nick and the hundred percent honest answer is, no, we don't. But what we do have is enough circumstantial evidence to bring him in on suspicion, and I have a feeling Bull isn't the type to give us too much resistance if we apply the pressure. I know it's late and you all have homes to go to, but I have a hunch we can crack this case if we can lay our hands on Bull as fast as possible. It's possible, seeing us at his home might have spooked him and made him run, but if he had no pre-planned escape plan in place if we got too close, he might now be running around like a chicken with its head cut off, not knowing what to do next."

There wasn't a single grumble from any of the team at the prospect of working late into the night. They all wanted the killer apprehended and this case had been something of a nightmare so far, with little evidence and an inability, up to now, to establish a motive. Now, based on what Ross and Drake had learned from Carol Bull they'd been presented with one of the oldest motives in the book, jealousy. Bull also had the means, through his access to drugs, and he certainly would have been able to engineer the opportunity to commit the crime, if he'd contacted Joey, and made an arrangement to meet him, ostensibly on Golf Club business. Ross felt he'd now established the three classic criteria when looking for a viable suspect. Graham Bull now ticked all the boxes.

"We're getting there, people. I can feel it. So, let's go get this bastard."

Chapter 26

Abduction

The first hint that things weren't going as Ross intended came in a call from Sam Gable. She and Tony Curtis were at the home of Graham and Carol Bull, as instructed by Ross, with the intention of being there if Bull returned home any time soon.

"Sir, I have a feeling something's not right at the Bull's home," she said as soon as Ross answered his phone.

"Tell me Sam, what's on your mind?"

"Mrs. Bull's not here, boss, and her car's still on the drive. But what has Tony and me concerned is that the lady who lives opposite the Bulls, a Mrs. Freda Tongue, just came over to see us when she saw us looking in the lounge window and asked if we were the police. She saw Graham Bull pull up in his car a while ago, maybe half an hour she thinks. He went in the house and about five minutes later he came out again. He was pushing Carol Bull from behind and was forcing her down the drive to his car. She's sure she saw the wife's hands were tied behind her back before he pushed her into the back of the car. Mrs. Tongue is convinced Carol didn't want to go with Graham and she fears she was being abducted by her husband."

"Fuck! Ross spat the word out. Why didn't she dial 999 straight away?"

"Come on, Boss, you know what folk are like. She thought it was a husband and wife thing but when she saw us she thought she should tell us"

"Well, thank God she did. It's safe to assume Bull has effectively abducted his wife, for what reason we can't be certain, but it can't be for anything good."

"Anything else you want us to do here, Boss?"

"Get a statement from Mrs. Tongue, then you and Tony had better get back here, pronto. Looks like Bull has just escalated things, big time."

As soon as he hung up, Ross found Izzie, who was busy typing up her latest report, and after bringing her up to date with Sam's information, he virtually ran up the stairs to Oscar Agostini's office. He knew the D.C.I. was working late, hoping to hear from Ross that Bull had been found and apprehended.

"If you need more men, Andy, just say so. I can let you have a dozen uniforms right away if you want them and more if necessary."

"Thanks, Oscar. Can you arrange a car to be in attendance at the Bull residence just in case Carol Bull comes home, or better still, if Bull drops her off, which I very much doubt will happen, but let's cover all bases eh?"

"No problem, Andy. Anything else I can do to help?"

"Yes, get the word out to neighbouring forces, with a description of Bull's car, in case he's decided to do a runner and is taking Carol with him. You know how these religious fanatical types can work sometimes. She might have done him wrong, but she's still his wife and wherever he goes, she goes too, unless..." he hesitated.

"Unless what, Andy? Fuck, you're not thinking what I'm thinking are you?"

"Which is what, Oscar?"

"Murder/suicide? Bull kills the unfaithful wife and then tops himself?"

"It's possible, or maybe he just wants to make his wife suffer,"

"But in either scenario, Carol Bull's toast, right?"

"Right," Ross agreed.

* * *

"Where the hell has he taken her?" Izzie Drake asked as she and Ross waited impatiently in the squad room for the remainder of the team to return, having been quickly recalled by Ross as soon as he received the news about Bull having grabbed his wife.

"Now, that's as big a question as where he killed poor Joey Slimani, assuming our belief that he's the killer is correct."

Suddenly, Ross and Drake fell silent and stared at one another, both sharing a single, terrible thought.

"He's going to kill his wife, too, isn't he?" Drake looked askance as the belief struck home.

"I think he is," Ross admitted, and we've no idea where he intends to do it."

"His friends might know," Drake postulated.

"As far as we know, Graham Bull has a limited circle of associates, Izzie, but no real friends. I'm going to phone Major Coombes. I have his home number. You can phone the pastor from his church. We must try to discover if he has any regular haunts. I know we've sent teams out to talk to them but we don't have time to wait. Call the others back. We need to rethink and regroup."

"Regular haunts, apart from the church, you mean?" Drake was totally serious in her remark. Graham Bull was surely one of the most boring men she's ever encountered.

"Not funny, Izzie. True, but not funny."

"What do we do when the others get back?"

"Until we receive a sighting of his car, or some idea of where might have taken Carol, we're shooting in the dark. We're flying by the seat of our pants now, Izzie. We can't just go running around Liverpool and Birkenhead on the off-chance we might bump into him."

Andy Ross was a worried man. If Graham Bull now realised he was a wanted man, and if he had indeed murdered Joey Slimani, it was entirely possible the man might have become mentally unhinged. Abducting his own wife from their home wasn't a good sign. Perhaps, Ross thought, Bull had intentions of finishing something he'd started when he killed Joey.

His thoughts were interrupted by Izzie Drake.

"Do you really think he might hurt his wife?"

"What, oh, sorry Izzie, I was lost in thought for a minute there. Yes, I do, and I can't help wondering if we missed something along the way, something that might have put us on to Bull sooner."

"Stop blaming yourself. None of us saw Graham Bull as a suspect, not while it looked as if Joey's death was connected to the adult movie industry."

"But, in a way, it was, Izzie, don't you see. Joey Slimani held some attraction for Carol Bull and she fell for him and went for it. If it hadn't been Joey, and maybe she'd had an affair with the postman, or a bus driver or something, maybe Bull wouldn't have reacted as he seems to have done. The thought of his wife having it off with a porn star and movie maker was something his ultra-religious mind just couldn't handle, I reckon."

Drake could do nothing but agree with the D.I. and together, they shared a nail-biting wait for the rest of the team to reappear so they could try and formulate a new strategy in the hunt for Graham Bull.

* * *

To say that Carol Bull was terrified out of her wits would probably be the understatement of the year. From the moment her husband had surreptitiously crept in to their home through the back door, and then stormed into the lounge, where a worried Carol was sitting, distractedly watching a banal game show on the TV as she waited for news of her missing husband, her life had turned upside-down. The look on his face as he walked around the sofa to stand menacingly in front of her had been enough to send shivers down her spine.

"Graham," she almost shouted his name. "What are you doing here?" and then realised that was the wrong thing to say.

"I live here, remember? Stand up, whore."

Carol obediently rose from the sofa, trying to pacify her husband at the same time.

"There's no need to call me names like that, Graham," she said, quietly. "What do you want me to do?"

"Keep still," he ordered as he pulled a length of blue twine from a pocket in his dark maroon padded jacket. As Carol attempted to struggle against him, he forced her hands behind her back where he deftly tied her wrists together. Satisfied she was suitably restrained, he pushed her firmly in the back, forcing her to walk in front of him, out of the room and into the hall, with another push forcing her towards the front door. "When we get outside, you're going to walk to the car and get in the back, where you'll lie face-down across the seats, do you understand?"

"But why, Graham? What are you going to do with me?"

"You'll find out soon enough. Now, walk, damn you, and don't try making a fuss out on the drive. I don't want any nosy neighbours thinking there's anything wrong and calling the police."

Carol had done as he'd instructed, and as soon as she'd complied by lying on the back seat, Bull had suddenly grabbed her face, forced her mouth open and gagged by a large wad of old rags. Next, Bull pulled a cloth bag over her head, rendering the frightened woman totally blind. He placed another length of twine around her neck, which he used to tie the bag in place so there was no chance of her working it loose by wriggling around. Once he was satisfied with his handiwork, and being reasonably sure they hadn't been seen entering the car, Bull closed the back door and quickly moved to the front, where he started the engine and drove slowly away from his home, hoping not to draw attention to his activity.

Carol quickly lost all sense of time, though she couldn't know that Bull was deliberately driving round in circles, avoiding his ultimate destination in a concerted and successful attempt to deceive and disorientate her. She was finding it difficult to maintain her place on the back seat of the Mercedes C Class, as she tried her best not to roll off onto the floor of the car. She felt the car slowing down and by the way it seemed to be bumping along, she guessed that her husband had pulled off the road and that they were driving over uneven ground as opposed to a tarmac road.

Eventually, the car ground to a halt, and Carol heard her husband open his door and then sensed him moving towards the rear of the car. One of the rear doors opened and grabbed hold of Carol's legs and roughly pulled her from the car, her back and head falling heavily onto the ground, winding her severely as she gasped in pain.

"Stand up, whore," Bull snapped at her, and Carol did her best to comply, though it wasn't easy, with her hands tied behind her back and her body wracked with pain from the fall.

"Hurry up," he shouted at her, and she finally managed to first get up on her knees and eventually to a standing position, her mouth still full of rags, and the cloth sack still in place.

Tears were streaming down her face as she suddenly felt Bull's hands doing something with the twine that was wrapped round her neck, which suddenly fell away and the cloth sack was pulled over her head. She could see at last, but it took a few seconds to orientate herself, in the dark and the cold.

He hadn't even given her time to grab a coat before forcing her from the house. She did her best to look around and identify where he'd brought her to, but nothing looked familiar. She could see she was in a clearing of some kind, surrounded by trees, and the only place she could think of where he might have taken her was his precious golf club, whose grounds contained a couple of small wooded areas.

"I hope you weren't too uncomfortable during our journey," Bull said, sarcastically, and then he laughed, a laugh she'd never heard before, a laugh that carried hatred and scorn in equal measures in its maniacal intensity. The fact that he'd laughed so loudly gave her cause for concern, as it meant he wasn't concerned about anyone hearing him.

"Oh, I'm sorry, I forgot you can't reply can you. Let's do something about that shall we?"

With that, she felt him touching her face, and she recoiled from him, but he placed one hand on the back of her head, and with the other he reached into her mouth and pulled the gag from its place, leaving her coughing and spluttering for a few seconds as she adjusted to being able to breathe normally again.

"Why are you doing this to me, Graham? Why are we here?"

"Why? You have the nerve to ask me why?" Bull snarled at her. She was used to him being pompous and overbearing, but this was a much more violent and vicious man than she was used to. "I thought maybe you'd like to see where your boyfriend, your lover, met his end. Oh yes, didn't you suspect, my dear little whore wife, that it was me who got rid of that piece of American slime that you regularly spread your legs for?"

Carol shook her head, tears freely flowing down her face. "No, Graham, you didn't…"

"Oh, yes I did. I made him stand right there, where you are now, made him strip his clothes off and kneel on the ground. He was drugged you see, so he couldn't resist me, and I hit him on the back of the head and then tied his hands behind his back, just like you are now. Then I walked behind him and slit his throat as easily as if I was sacrificing a goat."

"But Graham, your religion, you know? Thou shalt not kill, and all that? How could you murder a man in cold blood?"

"Ha," he laughed, "and what about, *Thou shalt not suffer a witch to live*, or *thou shalt not commit adultery?*

Carol was so cold, she could hardly think straight. Her brain seemed to be shutting down even though she knew she had to do something, or her crazy husband, and she was now certain that Graham was seriously deranged, was going to kill her, just as he'd slaughtered poor Joey.

"What do you mean, a witch? You know I'm not a witch, Graham. There's no such thing as witches, you know that as well as I do."

"Of course you're a witch. You bewitched him with your short skirts, and your smiles and your body, didn't you? Of course you did. Don't deny it, you're guilty, *guilty*," he shouted. "And you're an adulteress, as he was an adulterer. He had a wife at home, even though she was a whore too. I might even get round to exacting retribution from his other whore too, before my task is complete. I should tie you to one of these trees and burn you, as they used to do in the old days. Okay, they didn't burn them in England, before you astound me with your knowledge of history, they hung them, but I think burning would be much more exciting, don't you? It's a cold night and it would warm you up a bit, wouldn't it?" he laughed.

"Graham, I'm your wife, for better or worse, right? Okay, I did wrong, and I regret it bitterly. I'm sorry, so sorry, believe me. You're so upset, I can see that. Why don't you untie me, and we can go home, and sit down and have a nice cup of tea, and talk about it. I know we can work things out, please!" she pleaded with him.

Graham Bull approached her and almost tenderly stroked her cheek with one hand, and Carol shuddered, unsure if she'd managed to reach him. When he walked around behind her and she felt the scalpel cut through her bonds, releasing her hands, she began to relax, believing she'd managed to subdue his anger, got him to see that they could work things out, even though she knew that would never happen. That belief however, lasted no more than a few seconds, as he walked back to stand immediately in front of her, his eyes boring into hers as he spoke again.

"Strip!" he said, coldly and malevolently.

"What?" she stammered.

"You heard me, strip, you little whore. I want you just as he was before I send you to join him in hell."

"Oh God," Carol sobbed and her legs almost gave way beneath her.

Her mind raced in an effort to find some way of averting an increasingly inevitable ending to her life. A terrible smile began to play across Graham Bull's face as he delighted in the fear he could see clearly displayed on his wife's face. He was truly beginning to enjoy himself.

Chapter 27

Meanwhile

At the same time as Graham Bull was pulling his wife from the back of his car, it felt to Ross and Drake as if an age had passed as they paced the squad room, and Ross's office and even the corridor outside as they waited for the rest of the team to arrive. In fact, no more than fifteen minutes had elapsed since Drake had made the last call. They'd managed to get in touch with everyone, and expected them within minutes. Suddenly, the squad room doors burst open and Tony Curtis and Sofie Meyer hurried in to the room, to be followed closely by Paul Ferris, Nick Dodds and Gary, (Ginger) Devenish. Apart from D.C. Gable, who was in the ladies room, quickly changing into more suitable clothes for the weather, having answered the call to work dressed in casual slacks and jumper, the only member of the team absent was admin assistant, Kat Bellamy. As a civilian, Ross hadn't felt it fair to drag her in to work this late. There was nothing she could do at this stage anyway. Amid the hubbub of conversation that had begun as soon as Ross explained the situation to the assembled team, the squad room doors opened once more to admit D.C. I. Agostini. Ross had informed him of Carol Bull's abduction before he'd called in the team. Now it was time to do something, but…what *could* they do?,

"You've got all the men and women you need, Andy, authorised by D.C.S. Hollingsworth," Agostini informed him.

"That's great, thanks Oscar," Ross replied, "but where the fuck are we supposed to look for them. I'm sure Bull's got his wife somewhere where he can do something terrible to her. I have a feeling she's in mortal danger, and we missed it when we spoke to her. We should have realised her husband is a dangerous psychopath."

"You couldn't have known, Andy. For God's sake, he wasn't even a serious suspect until you knew about the wife's affair with Slimani. I wonder if his wife knew about it. She might know more than she's letting on."

"You think Trixie could be in league with Bull? Sorry Oscar, but I doubt that very much. The Slimani's marriage was more open than a whore's legs. He was quite happy for her to have regular sex with the butler, Jennings and both Joey and Trixie had sex on film with other partners on numerous occasions. Him having it off with Carol Bull a few times would hardly have caused a ripple in the context of their marriage."

"Okay, point taken, so our priority must be finding where Bull's taken his wife. Any theories?"

As Ross was talking to Agostini, he carried on thinking on his feet, and began to issue instructions.

"Sofie, get on to the station in Birkenhead and then you and Ginger meet them at Bull's dental surgery. It would be an ideal place to commit a murder, after all. He could have taken Joey there too and incapacitated him before slitting his throat. Then he could have loaded the body into his car and driven around looking for a good place to dispose of it. I'll arrange for firearms authorisation as well, so you can be met outside by a couple of armed uniforms."

"It's a good theory, Boss," said Drake, "but how could he have lured him to his dental surgery?"

"Hmm, good point, Izzie. Free dental work?"

"It's all guesswork isn't it?" Drake pondered.

"It is," Ross agreed. "I've another idea. Get on the phone to that Major Coombes guy. You've already had dealings with him. I want to know if there are any private, out of the way places on or around the golf course."

"You seriously think he'd take his wife there, at this time of night?" Agostini was intrigued by the theory.

"I do," Ross was suddenly adamant. "Everything else we've discovered about this bloody case has centred around South Mersey Golf Club. If there is a place there that offers Bull the privacy and seclusion to do what he intends to do, it would be the perfect place for him to write the last chapter of his sad little tale, if you get my meaning."

"I do indeed," Agostini agreed. "Better go make that call, Sergeant."

"Right sir," Drake extricated a business card from her purse, picked up the nearest phone, obtained an outside line and began dialling Coombes's home number.

"What does this Major Coombes do for a living, Andy? Anybody looked into him?"

"He's a structural engineer, self-employed. He served in the Royal Engineers and set himself up in business when he retired from the army. He's clean, sir," Paul Ferris piped up from his usual position, seated at his computer terminal.

Izzie was talking, and the room fell silent as everyone listened in to her conversation with Major Coombes, which she'd switched to speakerphone.

"Yes, Major, me again. I'm sorry to disturb your evening, but something serious has taken place and we urgently need to locate Graham Bull."

"Graham? Why? Has something happened to him? Wait, Carol hasn't been involved in an accident, has she?"

The words and the questions just tripped off Coombes's tongue, a natural enough reaction to a call from the police late in the evening.

"I can't go into details, Major, but it really is urgent that we find Mr. Bull as soon as possible.

"Yes, well, I don't really know Graham that well, on a personal basis, Sergeant. I can't honestly think of anywhere you might find him if he's not at home."

Before Izzie could say anything else, Ross held a piece of paper up to her, like a prompt card, and she nodded and asked a new question. "Is there anywhere secluded in the vicinity of the golf club, Major? Perhaps a place where a person could go to at night and not be easily seen from the main roads around the perimeter? Maybe a lover's lane kind of place?"

Coombes actually laughed a little at Izzie's last remark.

"Oh my Lord, you don't seriously think Graham might be involved in some sort of assignation with a woman do you, Sergeant Drake. That's just unthinkable and preposterous. It would go against all his beliefs."

"Major, please, answer the question."

Coombes caught the urgency in Drake's voice and immediately turned serious in his manner.

"Oh, I just realised. You're from the Murder Squad, aren't you? Bloody hell, you mean that Graham might be... never mind, don't tell me. Look, there are a few places around the course that might fit your criteria. There are a few small copses dotted around the course but on the far side, over by the 10th hole, there's Rendell's Wood, a fairly sizeable piece of woodland. We're quite proud of it actually as it's a real haven for wildlife. We even won an award from the Countryside Commission for our contribution to local environmental issues and wildlife conservation, something to do with hedgehogs and butterflies I believe."

Ross was fervently nodding his head at Drake as he listened to the conversation and began urging her to push for more details, giving signals by waving his arms and making hand gestures to communicate with his partner.

"Would it be possible for someone who knows the area to access Rendell's Wood, without having to cross the golf course, and to be able to park a car nearby, or even drive it into the wood from the main road?"

"Well, yes, as a matter of fact, the wood is accessible from the road that borders the far side of the course for a few hundred yards, before it turns off in the direction of Wallasey. There's a small pull-in, not an actual lay-by, but courting couples have been known to use it for, well, you know what I mean."

"Yes, I do, Major, and is there anywhere along that stretch of road where a car could pull off the road and gain entry to the actual wood, maybe a track wide enough for one car, say?"

"Actually there is, Sergeant. We call it 'poacher's pull-in,' though I don't think any poachers have ever used it. There's nothing worth poaching in the wood. The wildlife in Rendell's Wood doesn't consist of any game birds or animals worth a poacher's time, unless you count a resident population of a few hundred rabbits, who do make a lot of holes on the course, I must say. There's track that leads a little way into the wood, just far enough to make a car invisible from the road, but you'd have to know about it to find it."

"And would Graham Bull know about it?"

"Well, yes, I suppose he would."

Drake almost hung up without word of goodbye but remembered to thank Coombes quickly as she ended the call. Ross was virtually on his toes with the revelation.

"That's it. It has to be," he said, and without hesitation, gathered the rest of the team around him. "Unless I'm very much mistaken, we now have a good idea exactly where Bull has taken his wife. We need to get out there as fast as possible, but we also have to be careful how we approach the situation. If Bull hasn't already done something terminal to Carol Bull, he could be in a volatile state and it could take a very softly, softly approach to talk him out of his intended action, if it's at all possible."

"You're ready to gamble that this 'poacher's pull-in' is where he's taken his wife, then, Andy?" Agostini asked him, though he already knew the answer. He'd have made the same decision himself.

"It's our only option," Ross replied, and Agostini agreed.

"I want you to draw arms, Andy," Agostini said, gravely, "just in case."

"Agreed," Ross nodded. "Derek, Nick, you two and myself will be armed, but I don't want Bull taken down unless he leaves us with no other option, got that?"

The two detectives nodded and Ross quickly formulated their plan of action. He quickly informed his colleagues in Birkenhead that he would be bringing armed officers with him. The police station there would be closed for the night now, but he gave the on-call duty officer a full heads-up of the details of his planned operation to apprehend Bull, and that he and his team were heading through the Mersey Tunnel and would go directly to the golf course and the place known as 'poacher's pull-in.' The only problem he had, was that he'd no idea if Bull was definitely there, and if he was, how long he'd already been there and what if anything he had planned for his wife, and worst of all, if he'd already done it. Despite the imponderables, he knew they had to go for it in an attempt to find and release Carol Bull unharmed. Birkenhead were happy to leave Ross in full operational control, and he would keep them informed as the operation progressed.

"Ready?" he asked his team a few minutes later, who were now joined by Sam Gable, who was quickly brought up to speed by Izzie Drake.

A set of grim and determined faces looked back at the D.I. and after receiving confirmation by way of nodding heads and a few words to the same effect, Ross turned towards the door.

"Okay, everyone, this is it. Let's go catch ourselves a murdering bastard."

Chapter 28

Rendell's Wood

"Do I have to tell you again?" Bull snapped at his wife. "Strip, you unfaithful whore, and do it right now."

"Please, Graham, it's so cold out here."

The temperature was steadily dropping and now hovered at around two degrees Celsius. Carol was already shivering and trembling from a mixture of cold and fear.

Bull strode up to stand right in front of his terrified wife and without warning unleashed a slap across her face that sent her reeling backwards.

"I won't tell you again," he growled at her. "Get your clothes off."

Shaking with terror, Carol Bull slowly began removing her clothes, beginning with her shoes and then she reached behind her neck to unfasten the zipper on her dress, which promptly slid to the ground, leaving her wearing nothing but her bra and panties, a matching set in lacy black satin. She'd bought them, not to entice her husband, but simply to remind herself she could still be an attractive woman. Now though, they only served to fuel Graham Bull's anger.

"Look at you, all tarted up in your sexy black knickers. Who were they for? Lover boy?"

"No Graham, I..."

"Shut up and get them off, whore. You heard me. When I said strip, I meant everything. Do it, now!" he snapped at her and she trembled even more with the fear that now pulsated through her entire being.

Slowly, she reached behind her and unhooked the fastenings of her bra, which she caught in both hands as it fell from her breasts. She dropped it to the floor.

"Come on, hurry up, we haven't got all night," her husband ordered as she hesitated to go further.

The tears were running down Carol's face, stinging her cheeks as she reached down once again and slowly slid the black knickers down her legs and finally stepping out of them, leaving her totally and humiliatingly nude under the gaze of the man she once admired and loved.

Graham stared at his wife, now revealed in the bright, silvered moonlight that illuminated the clearing. The sky was clear of clouds, meaning there'd almost certainly be a heavy frost in the morning. For now, it meant the temperature was dropping by the minute. Bull was grateful for the moonlight, which gave him a clear view of his terrified wife. He hadn't dared leave the car's headlights on, just in case anyone, poacher or late-night dog walker, saw them and attempted to investigate the presence of a shiny Mercedes, parked at the end of the narrow track into the woods. He'd brought a heavy-duty torch with him but the moon was providing such bright illumination that he had no need for it.

Carol's fear was intensifying by the minute in tandem with the falling temperature. Her body shook in paroxysms of fear intermingled with the shivering brought on by the intense cold. There was no such problem for her husband who'd dressed for the occasion, wearing a black woollen pea-coat that almost reached his knees, and black watchman's cap, together with thick woollen trousers and heavy, black leather waterproof boots, as though he'd dressed for hiking in the hills of the Lake District, one of his irregular pastimes in his younger days.

"Wh…what are you going to do to me, Graham?" she spoke with a distinct tremor in her voice. She already knew what he intended to do to her, but her brain, now becoming slightly befuddled by the intense cold, was telling her to say and do anything she could think of to keep him talking to try and stave off the inevitable. She had to hope that someone would come along in time to save her.

"I would have thought that was glaringly obvious," he finally replied. The spot you're standing on is just about exactly where I put an end to your cheating, adulterer of a lover. The ground here is so porous the blood is quickly soaked up and leaves no trace. The police are probably still running round and round in circles trying to figure out where he met his demise. Don't you think it's a nice touch that you're about to die in the same place as lover boy? Your blood will mingle with what's left of his under the ground, a nice touch, I think."

Carol couldn't think of a reply. She now barely noticed the tears running down her face, falling to stain the ground beneath her feet. She tried to use her hands to cover herself and maintain a modicum of modesty, but Bull wasn't even going to allow her that small concession.

"Keep your hands by your sides," he ordered her, "and kneel down."

"What?"

"I said kneel. Are you deaf as well as stupid? Kneel down on the ground. It's time to pray."

"Pray? What are you taking about, Graham? Please, you have to stop this. You'll never get away with it."

"Don't tell me I won't get away with it. I don't want to get away with it. The Lord will forgive me for what I've done and am about to do. You're a whore, an adulteress and you've turned me into a cuckold. You deserve to die, and I aim to make sure you do. Now, kneel and pray for forgiveness and redemption."

Her body wracked with tremors, and gradually turning blue from exposure to the freezing air, Carol Bull slowly lowered herself to the ground, and knelt as instructed. As soon as her knees came into contact with the cold, damp grass, she felt as though she'd knelt in a pool of ice. The frost was already beginning to form and her resolve was fading fast.

Bull moved closer, until he was standing behind her. She now had no idea where he was or what he would do next, though she felt he was close to carrying out her execution. Bull, however, couldn't resist one more bragging session, prolonging her mental anguish and physical torment for just a little longer.

"Would you like to know how I lured your porn star to his death, little whore?"

"Graham, no, please…"

"Shut up. I'm going to tell you anyway. I used your mobile phone, yes, your own phone to lure him to meet with him. You'd left it unattended on the hall table, very remiss of you. You're so stupid, you had his number stored in your contacts. You really should have had a password to protect your personal information. So, I sent him a text message, which he would have thought was from you, saying it was imperative that he meet you at the studio. You know, the studio where you gave your harlot's body to him. How many times did you do it with him, in the space of a year? Fifty, a hundred? I bet he had great stamina, eh, Carol?"

"Please don't do this, Graham. It wasn't like that, honestly," she sobbed. "I'm so cold Graham. Please can't we go home and talk about all this?"

The absurdity of Carol's feeble attempt to dissuade him from his intent made Bull burst out laughing, an insane laughter that illustrated how close to the edge he was.

"You're delaying me, Carol. I've had enough of our little chat. Now pray, you unfaithful bitch,"

Shaking from head to foot, Carol Bull began to mumble a prayer. Not being as religious as her husband she didn't have any prayers memorised, so she just said whatever came into her head.

"Speak up. I can't hear you," Bull demanded.

* * *

"Graham Bull, armed police! Drop the blade and move away from the woman," a loud voice suddenly shouted as light flooded the small clearing, taking Bull and his shaking wife by total surprise. Ross and his team, including four uniformed firearms officers, armed with Heckler & Koch MP55F semi-automatic carbines, had quietly spent the last five minutes creeping closer and closer to where they'd heard Bull speaking and shouting, and had secreted themselves behind the trees that bordered the clearing. Ross now stepped from behind the tree concealing him, with a small megaphone in his hand, enabling his voice to carry with louder than normal volume in an attempt to intimidate Graham Bull. As he spoke two of the armed officers, looking menacing in black stab vests, with utility belts at their waists, guns pointing at Bull, joined him in stepping from concealment, along with Izzie Drake and Sam Gable who both held the powerful mobile floodlights that now showed Bull and his intended victim clearly to the officers. The rest of Ross's team and the other two members of the uniformed firearms team remained concealed behind the trees, effectively surrounding Bull. Derek McLennan had his Glock drawn, ready for use if needed, safety catch on for the moment. Ross had one other 'secret weapon' up his sleeve but wanted to keep it in reserve in case it was needed.

Bull stood transfixed by the lights, taken totally unawares by the sudden appearance of the police and the powerful, commanding voice of the man with the megaphone.

"Leave us alone," he shouted, in response to Ross's command. "This is private, between me and my wife."

"Attempting to murder your wife is not a private matter, Mr. Bull. Nor is the fact that while we've been listening to you for the last ten minutes, you've also admitted to the murder of Joseph Slimani. Give it up, now Graham. You won't be getting out of here, and you won't be allowed to murder Mrs. Bull. At the first sign of aggression from you towards your wife, these officers have orders to shoot you down. Do you want to die, tonight, Graham, or would you rather come along with us and we can talk about all this?"

Graham Bull hadn't planned for anything like this and now appeared hesitant and unsure of himself.

"I need to finish what I started," he called to Ross. "She's a whore and an adulteress, don't you see?"

"I know what you think your wife is, but that doesn't give you the right to become judge, jury and executioner in some kind of religious retribution for what you perceive as her sins. Nobody has that right, Graham. You know that. You need to calm down, drop the scalpel and walk away from Carol, and let us help her."

Behind the trees to the rear of Bull's position, D.C.s Tony Curtis and Nick Dodds stood, poised to move on the man the moment he complied with Ross's command. They were both fast and strong and were confident they could take Bull down in seconds once the woman was safe. For now, though, they had to remain silent, and play the waiting game.

Sergeant Paul Ferris stepped forward and whispered in Ross's ear. Ross nodded in agreement with Ferris's suggestion. It was time to deploy Ross's secret weapon. With Bull seemingly intransigent and a point of stalemate being reached, Ferris walked back to his position behind the trees, reappearing a few seconds later with another man beside him. When he'd visited Bull's pastor earlier, subsequently getting the recall message while at the manse, Donald Wray had volunteered to accompany Ferris to wherever Bull had been located, in case it was felt he could help by bringing his influence as Bull's pastor to bear. Although Ross had been reluctant to allow a civilian to become involved in the situation, he had to admit Wray might be of help if Bull refused to listen to police entreaties to surrender.

Now, the time had come, and Donald Wray stepped up confidently to stand beside Ross, who had to admit to himself that the man didn't exactly look like a typical churchman. Standing just over six feet tall, with a thick head of dark hair, Ross couldn't quite name the colour in the moonlight, a former Royal Navy chaplain, and built like a professional rugby second-row forward, Wray had a confident air about him that showed as soon as Ross gave him the okay to speak to Bull.

"Graham, it's Donald Wray here. Can you hear me?"

"Donald?" Bull responded immediately. "What are you doing here?"

"I've come to ask you to end this stand-off with the police before things go too far, Graham. You really need to give up that scalpel or knife you know and let Carol go. She looks frozen to the bones. Please, let her go, Graham."

"But Donald, you don't know what she's done, what she deserves."

"Listen to me," Wray's voice carried an air of authority that impressed the listening police officers. "You can't win in this situation. The Sergeant who came to see me told me all about it, Graham, so I do know what Carol's done, but it isn't up to you, me, or anyone else on this earth to judge her for her perceived sins. Only the Lord in Heaven can do that, or have you not been listening to me in church for all this time?"

Wray had carefully phrased the last question to touch on Bull's belief in the church and its teachings. He knew that Bull would hate having his belief in God's teachings questioned, and might even make him feel guilty for taking matters into his own hands.

"You're confusing me, Donald. Of course I've listened to you in church. I know what it says in the Bible about adulterers and witches too. She's both of those, Donald. She enticed that pornographic film maker with her short skirts, flashing her legs at him, and smiling at him and encouraging his attentions. She deserves to die for her sins."

"And you, Graham, are you therefore without sin?"

"Eh, what?"

"Did Jesus not teach us, Graham, *Let he who is without sin cast the first stone?* Are you without sin? We're all sinners, Graham, and that's why God sent his son to earth, to take our sins upon himself. You don't have to do this, unless you are totally without sin."

Wray appeared to be getting through to Bull, but Ross was looking at Carol Bull, and she looked to be in a bad way. Her head was lolling forward and her body was rocking slightly to and fro. He suspected that hypothermia was setting in and they didn't have much time.

"I promise you that if you surrender, nobody is going to hurt you," Wray said in an attempt to force Bull to comply.

"Why should I believe you?"

"Because the inspector here has told me he is willing to instruct his men to lay down their arms if you will agree to do as he asks."

Knowing he was taking a calculated risk, Ross called out to his men, "Lay down your arms men. Let's show Mr. Bull we mean him no harm." Ross calculated that those of his officers hidden behind Bull's position would ignore that order and only those who like him were in Bull's sight would do as he asked, which is exactly what happened. He even made a big show of laying his own Glock 17 pistol on the ground at his feet.

"See, Graham, the inspector has shown his goodwill. Won't you now do the same?" Wray pleaded with him.

Suddenly, Bull looked to the sky, then called out in a loud voice, "What should I do?" Ross suspected that in his own way, Bull was calling out to his God. It was his minister, however, who gave Bull his answer.

"What you should do, Graham, and what I'm *telling* you to do, is to lay down that scalpel, before you hurt someone with it, and to take a couple of steps away from Carol, towards me, and we can end this peacefully and leave God to make any judgements that need making with regards to sin. Do you hear what I'm saying?"

"Yes, I hear you," Bull said, and for a few seconds, it seemed to all those watching this tableau in the night playing out, as if time had stood still. Precious seconds ticked by as an eerie silence descended on the clearing in Rendell's Wood and then, slowly, Graham Bull took one, then two steps away from his wife's kneeling form, bent down and laid his scalpel on the ground, before standing up once more, still facing Wray and Ross.

The next few seconds seemed to pass in a blur. As soon as Bull had complied with Ross's instructions, Dodds and Curtis burst from behind the trees they were sheltered behind and covered the twelve or so yards between them and Bull in no time at all. Dodds hit Bull with a clattering rugby tackle that would have been at home at Twicken-ham or Wembley Stadium, taking Bull to the ground with a resound-ing 'thump' and a loud gasp from Bull as the air was knocked from his lungs. Bull may have been six feet tall and remarkably fit for his age but he didn't stand a chance against Dodds, a powerfully built fit-ness enthusiast of equal size and weight. Almost immediately his body hit the ground, Curtis followed Dodd's tackle by pinning Bull to the ground with both knees, pulling his arms behind his back and clicking a pair of handcuffs on his wrists in a move as fast as lightning.

Sofie Meyer and Sam Gable rushed forward with blankets to wrap around the almost unconscious form of Carol Bull. Ferris called for an ambulance and was promised it would be on site within ten minutes. Meyer and Gable meanwhile called on one of the uniformed firearms officers, a veritable giant of a man by the name of constable Eric Dunn, who picked Carol Bull up in his arms as though she were as light as a feather, and carried her gently, like a baby to one of the detectives' vehicles, where Sam quickly turned the ignition on and set the heater to its highest level in an attempt to warm the woman up.

"I've never felt anyone so cold and yet still be alive," Gable com-mented.

"I think Mrs. Bull is lucky we managed to find her in time, and that the pastor was able to convince her husband to put down the scalpel. Much longer and I think this would have been a second murder with which to charge him," Meyer replied.

"I agree. That pastor's a pretty brave guy, if you ask me," Constable Dunn added as he gently pushed Carol Bull's hair from her face as he laid her down across the back seat, before leaving the two women to take care of her until the ambulance arrived.

Ross, meanwhile, was standing in the clearing, looking down at the prone figure of Graham Bull, currently being pinned to the ground by Tony Curtis, who was kneeling on his back, totally immobilising him.

"Get him up lads," he ordered Curtis and Dodds, who grabbed hold of Bull's shoulders and lifted him up, placing him in a standing position directly in front of the D.I. Without any preamble, Ross formally cautioned his prisoner.

"Graham Bull, I am arresting you on suspicion of the murder of Joseph Slimani and the attempted murder of your wife, Carol Bull. You do not have to say anything, but it may harm your defence if you do not mention when questioned something which you later rely on in court. Anything you do say may be given in evidence."

Bull said nothing in reply, but merely stared into Ross's eyes, his own face devoid of any display of emotion.

"Take him away lads," he said to Curtis and Dodds, "Just get him out of my sight."

The two detective constables frogmarched Graham Bull between them to one of the waiting, unmarked police cars. They'd escort him to police headquarters, where he'd be processed and locked up overnight, prior to being formally interviewed in the morning.

Those officers still on the scene soon heard the siren emanating from the approaching ambulance and it wasn't long before it arrived, having to park on the road close to the small pull-in which was still full of police vehicles. It was met by two uniformed officers who showed them to the car where Meyer and Gable were doing their best for Carol Bull. Before long, the paramedics had taken over the care of the patient and in no time, the ambulance departed, lights flashing, as they carried the freezing, though now slightly warmer figure of Carol Bull to hospital, accompanied by Sam Gable, where she would receive a police guard until she could talk to the investigating officers.

Ross took a moment to thank Donald Wray for his assistance.

"You're welcome," said Wray, shaking Ross's hand. "I'm only pleased the whole sorry affair ended without anyone getting hurt. I just hope Carol makes a full recovery."

"Physically, I'm sure she will, but as for her mental state, after an experience like that?" Ross replied, shrugging his shoulders and shaking his head to stress the question in his words.

"Please, let her know I'm there for her if she feels she needs someone to talk to."

Brian L. Porter

"I'll do that, Pastor, and thank you again," Ross said, excusing himself, after asking one of the uniformed officers to arrange a ride home for the churchman, who was grateful for the chance, to warm up in the car on the journey home.

Meanwhile, two more vehicles arrived on the scene as Miles Booker and his forensic team, summoned as soon as Bull had been taken down, by a call from Izzie Drake, pulled up, disgorging Booker and his specialists.

"Bloody cold as hell out here, Andy," Booker commented after being shown to the scene by Ginger Devenish, who'd been detailed to meet and direct the forensic crew. He was followed by the SOCOs, (Scenes of Crime Officers), who resembled a gathering of ghostly apparitions as they trudged along the path towards the clearing, dressed in their white forensic suits and boots, carrying their cases and bags filled with the equipment they required to carry out their task.

Realising what he'd said, Booker laughed and smacked himself on the forehead with one hand.

"Yep, you got me there, mate. Right, what can we do for you? It's too bloody cold to hang around doing bugger all out here."

"From what our suspect revealed while unaware of our presence, I have every reason to suspect that we have a crime scene under our feet, Miles. According to what he told his wife, who he was holding hostage here," he gestured with his hand to where Sofie Meyer and Paul Ferris were taping off the area where they now suspected Joey Slimani had been murdered, "he murdered Joey Slimani right here by cutting his throat, and the poor bugger bled out on the ground. I'm hoping you and your people can find some trace of blood in the ground that we can trace back to Joey. Secondly, we have the suspect's car, the Merc parked over there, and I think he used it to transport the body in, to where he eventually dumped it on the tracks at Mossley Hill station. If he did, you should hopefully find traces of Joey Slimani's blood in the boot or on the seats, depending on how and where Bull laid the body on the journey."

235

"No problem, Andy. If there's blood in the ground here, it will definitely show up, and as for the car, if there's anything there, we'll find it. I presume we're okay to take it away from here, to be properly examined back at base."

"Yes, you can, Miles. But just do me favour and take a quick look and tell me if you can see anything that's a dead giveaway, will you?"

"I'll stay on for a while if you like, sir, to liaise with Miles and his team in case anything crops up," Derek McLennan volunteered.

"No you won't, Derek. You'll get yourself off home to that new wife of yours and get some sleep. And that's an order," was Ross's response.

"If you're sure?"

"Derek, go home, lad. We're done here for the night."

McLennan gave Ross a nod of agreement and turned to leave.

Miles Booker called one of his technicians across and together, they carried out a quick examination of the car seats and boot. Booker was back within a minute.

"Looks like blood in there, Andy. The boot, as you thought. We'll confirm it as soon as we can, once we get it back to base with us."

"Thanks Miles. Now, if you don't mind, we'll leave you to it. We're frozen to the bone and there's not much more we can do out here in the dark, tonight. My lot need some sleep."

"And us poor buggers don't eh?" Booker laughed again. "Just joking. Go on, get out of here. We'll do what we can and maybe have to come back ourselves in daylight. What about preserving the scene from the nosy public?"

"I've got a couple of uniforms ready to mount a guard on the scene until daylight. They'll be relieved at dawn and the scene will continue to be guarded until we can release it."

With that, Ross bade his friend goodnight as Booker moved off to supervise his team of forensic technicians. Ross and the rest of his team gratefully retired to the warmth of their cars and were soon heading back to Liverpool, under the River Mersey, looking forward to at least a few hours sleep. As Ross pointed out before sending everyone home, they still had some work to do on the case and he wouldn't be satisfied until he had sufficient evidence in the bag to ensure a conviction. Graham Bull might have verbally confessed to the murder of Joey Slimani, but as Ross was only too aware, cases based solely on a suspect's confession had collapsed in the past. He sure as hell wasn't going to allow Bull to slip through his net on this one. For now though, he and his team needed to get warm, grab something to eat, and most importantly, sleep!

Chapter 29

A window to the past

Ross kissed Maria goodbye after a good breakfast, feeling more relaxed than he had since the Joey Slimani case began. He'd soon be interviewing Graham Bull, but before beginning Bull's questioning, Ross felt he owed someone a phone call. After dialling the number, he was surprised when William, (Bill) Jennings answered Trixie Slimani's mobile phone.

"Mr. Jennings? It's Detective Inspector Ross. I need a word with Mrs. Slimani, if she's available."

"Yeah, sure, Inspector. She's just woken up. I took her breakfast up ten minutes ago. She never takes her mobile to bed with her. Hold on and I'll take it up to her."

A couple of minutes later, Trixie came on the line, sounding sleepy and bleary-eyed, which actually described her perfectly that morning. She soon snapped into full wakefulness when Andy Ross broke the news to her.

"Trixie, we have a suspect in custody. It's pretty certain he's Joey's killer. He was apprehended last night and we'll be interviewing him later this morning."

"Oh, my God. Who is it, Inspector? Is it someone we know?"

"Do you know a man called Graham Bull?"

"The guy from the golf club? Yeah, sure I know him. Bit of a weird kinda guy, what you Brits might call a bit of a cold fish. Are you telling me that worm murdered my Joey?"

"That's how it's looking at present, yes. He was caught while in the process of trying to murder his own wife."

If Ross had been able to see Trixie at that moment, he'd have seen a hand fly to her face, covering her mouth as both astonishment and realisation hit her simultaneously.

"Oh God, no. Did he tell you why he did it? Was it because he found out that Joey was helping his wife with some problems?"

That's one way of describing Carol Bull's affair with Joey, Ross thought. At least it sounded as if Trixie might be aware her husband was sleeping with Carol Bull, which would make his job a little easier. Trixie's next words actually stunned him, not something that was easy for anyone to do with his years of experience.

"That poor woman had a terrible marriage you know, Inspector. Her husband kept her so downtrodden and had an intense jealousy of her even talking to another man. We met her at a couple of golf club functions you know and Joey got on well with her. He felt a little sorry for her to be honest. She got talking to him once, after she'd maybe had one too many drinks and she admitted she was finding it real difficult to cope with his insane jealousy. I told Joey he should try and get her to meet him somewhere private. It sounded to me as if she needed a darn good sex session to give her some self-respect back. I said to him, "Hon, go give her a good time. Maybe if she feels wanted by a man again, she'll pluck up the courage to stand up for herself. He's nothin' but a bully. Fuck her, make her feel like a real pretty woman again, Joey," is what I told him, "but be discreet, you know what I mean?"

Ross was astounded at what Trixie was telling him. It was clear she knew all about Carol Bull's affair with her husband. In fact, the way she was telling it, she and Joey planned the whole thing as a kind of therapy for Carol Bull.

"At least I was relieved of the odious task of telling the grieving widow her husband was bonking someone else's wife," he related

Trixie's words to Izzie Drake when she joined him in his office soon afterwards, armed with two coffees, which she placed on his desk as she sat down in the visitor's chair.

"I have to say, the Slimani's are one of the weirdest couples I've ever encountered, and that's without actually having met the husband, at least not when he was alive," Drake responded after hearing the story. "I'm not sure my provincial Liverpudlian upbringing prepared me for dealing with people like them," she smiled, imagining what her Mum and Dad would think if she told them about the way Joey and Trixie lived their lives together.

"Not the sort of people you'd want to take home to meet your parents, eh, Izzie?"

"You reading my mind, or what?" she said in astonishment.

"Why, what…oh, is that what you were smiling about?"

"Yeah, can you imagine my Dad's reaction to meeting Trixie?"

Ross, who'd met Drake's parents a couple of times, laughed out loud.

"You poor Dad would probably take one look at her in her little ra-ra skirts and drop dead from an instant heart attack," he joked.

"You're probably right. Trixie would probably try to drag him off to bed and we'd end up arresting my Mum for assaulting her with a frying pan or something."

The two of them sat laughing together, then fell into a few moments of silence as they did their best to enjoy their coffees, which Ross was sure were mixed by a team of sadistic taste goblins, prior to being placed in the office coffee machine.

"Well, Drake broke the silence. "You ready to talk to our killer yet?"

"I'm just waiting for a preliminary report from Miles Booker. Hopefully he's got enough for us to hit Bull with hard evidence so we're not solely reliant on a confession. You know how ropey it can be building a case on nothing but the word of a killer."

"Yeah, a clever barrister can play all kinds of tricks in court and pull a confession to pieces and leave us with nothing."

"Exactly," Ross said firmly. "So I want to go to the CPS, (Crown Prosecution Service) with a case they can be confident of winning."

"Stupid, isn't it? We catch him in the act of attempting to murder his wife and hear him admit to killing Joey Slimani and we still have to go through all the evidence gathering as if last night never happened."

"I agree, Izzie, but that's the system we have to work under and at least it keeps us on our toes, eh?"

At that moment, as if by magic, Ross's phone rang and he hurried to answer it. Much to his relief, it was Miles Booker.

"Miles, good to hear your voice this morning. Got anything for me?"

"You might say that, Andy, old son. The blood in the boot of Bull's car is a match for Joey Slimani's. There was a pair of wellingtons in there as well, with bloodstains on the soles and on the sides, also Joey's. Looks like Bull wore them during the murder and sloshed around in the blood before it permeated into the ground, which, my friend, tested positive for blood and we're testing it right now. And here's a little extra for you. One of my lads found a mound of earth in the clearing that looked like something was buried there. We dug a little and came across Joey Slimani's clothes, and before you ask, I had the list of what he was wearing on the day he disappeared in my car. I've had it with me since the case started, and the shirt we found was monogrammed with Joey's initials too. I'd say you have enough to put Mr. Bull away for a long time, Andy, and that's before we finish testing the earth samples."

"Miles, I love you, mate," Ross was ecstatic. "Now all we need to do is get a few answers from Bull and we can wrap this bloody case up."

Graham Bull looked more than a little haggard by the time he sat in Interview Room 2, opposite Ross and Drake. A uniformed constable stood by the door, more as a matter of routine than from any threat from Bull, who was looking cowed and defeated. Sitting beside Bull was his solicitor, Gerard Newman, from the firm of Newman, Kirk, and Robb, one of the city of Liverpool's older legal establishments. Gerard was the third generation of lawyers from his family to be a partner in the firm, and was, by a happy coincidence, a member of Bull's golf club! In his navy-blue three-piece suit, white shirt and red tie, teamed with highly polished black leather shoes, Newman looked every inch the legal eagle. Ross doubted there was much he could do for Bull in his current situation however, not with the mounting evidence against his client.

After Ross started the obligatory recording of the interview and identified himself, Drake, Bull and Newman, and even mentioning Constable Hewitt as being in attendance, (Not taking any chances with this one), he addressed Graham Bull.

"Good morning Mr. Bull. I trust you slept well."

Bull glared at Ross and grunted something indecipherable. Ross let it pass.

"You do know why you're here, I presume?"

"I'd be stupid not to, wouldn't I?" Bull spoke for the first time.

"For the record, Graham Bull is charged with the murder of Joseph Slimani and the abduction and attempted murder of his wife, Carol Bull. I must inform you, Mr. Bull that we now have significant evidence to go to trial with or without your confession. I ask you now if you have anything to add to what you said last night?"

At that point Gerard Newman interrupted.

"I have instructed my client to say no more on this subject, Inspector Ross. If you have any further questions, I ask that they be directed through me."

"Now, you listen to me, Mr. Newman. Your client is charged with two major offences. Neither murder nor attempted murder are to be taken lightly and we have every right to question your client. If he chooses to exercise his right to silence, that's fine, but I am not required, while questioning him, to direct those questions to you, so please don't try my patience so early in these proceedings."

Newman blushed and shuffled uncomfortably in his chair. He hadn't expected the policeman to be so dismissive of him.

"Are we now on the same wavelength, Mr. Newman?" Ross asked the man.

"Er...yes, we are," Newman replied.

"Good. Now, since your arrest last night," he addressed Bull, "we have uncovered evidence that you carried the body of Joseph Slimani in the boot of your car, and we have found the victim's clothes where you buried them after murdering him, as well as traces of Mr, Slimani's blood in the ground where you cut his throat and where he subsequently bled to death in front of you. You were also witnessed by me and a number of other police officers abusing and threatening to kill your wife, after having first abducted her by force from your home in Egremont. Do you have anything to say to me?"

Bull remained silent. Clearly, his solicitor had briefed him on how to handle the interview and it looked as if they were going to have a problem eliciting any information from him. Izzie Drake stepped in, using a different tack.

"Of course, we will have a lot more evidence against you when your poor wife is well enough to talk to us." When the police had finally managed to reach Carol Bull the previous night, she'd already reached the second stage of hypothermia. She'd had a slow, weak pulse, her breathing had slowed down and she was suffering from a lack of co-ordination, was sleepy and displayed extreme confusion. Drake continued. "How you could have subjected her to such treatment with temperatures hovering around freezing point, I just don't know. I was under the impression you were a good man, Mr. Bull, a regular church-goer and a highly religious person. All I can say is that your behaviour last night displayed a complete lack of Christian feeling towards your wife. In fact, I'd go as far as to say you behaved as though you were being influenced by Satan more than Christ."

Izzie's words at last brought a response from Bull, who suddenly tried to leap up from his chair, attempting to reach across the table to get to Drake, who calmly held her ground, as Ross stood up and placed one open hand into the middle of Bull's chest, halting him immediately. A push saw him slump back into his chair beside Gerard Newman.

"Mr. Newman," Ross now spoke firmly to the solicitor, "I suggest you speak to your client and inform him that if he continues to exhibit such violent behaviour during questioning, I will not hesitate to have his ankles shackled to the table to prevent him attacking my sergeant. Is that clear?"

"Y…yes, of course Inspector Ross," Newman replied, his face having turned ashen as he witnessed Bull's show of aggression. He now realised this was not the mild-mannered though rather pompous club captain from the golf club he was dealing with, and being more used to cases involving civil litigation as opposed to violent crimes, he began to believe he might be out of his depth in having answered Graham Bull's plea for help.

"Interview suspended at ten-forty a.m.," Ross announced for the benefit of the recording. "to enable Mr. Newman to confer with his client." He and Drake exited the room, taking Constable Hewitt with them, who took up guard outside the interview room, leaving Bull and his solicitor to confer in private for a few minutes.

"We're going to grab a quick coffee," Ross announced to Hewitt. "I'll get someone to bring you one too, while they talk in there. I want Bull to sweat a little, so there's no rush to get back in there. I take it coffee's okay with you, is it?"

"I'd prefer tea if you don't mind, sir," Hewitt replied sheepishly.

"Okay, tea it is, lad. Don't be afraid to state your preferences. I don't bite…much."

Ross laughed and clapped the young P.C. on the shoulder. Hewitt breathed a sigh of relief as Ross and Drake moved off along the corridor. He was still young enough and green enough to feel a little intimidated in the presence of a senior officer, though he knew Ross to be a fair man, with a great reputation for success, and was held in high esteem by those who worked for him.

Ross and Drake took their drinks into his office where they sat and relaxed for a few minutes.

"Nice touch there, Izzie, accusing him of being in league with the Devil," Ross complimented his sergeant. The pair had interviewed many suspects together and worked great as a team.

"Thanks," Drake replied with a smile. "I had a feeling that might get a response from him. He's so fired up with thinking he's got God on his side. I guessed he'd baulk at the suggestion he had the Prince of Darkness in his corner."

A knock on the door interrupted their conversation, followed by the head of Paul Ferris.

"Can I have a word?" he asked.

"Come in, Paul. What is it?" Ross beckoned him in with a wave of his hand.

Ferris entered the office and closed the door, leaning against it as he spoke.

"Just had a call from Sofie, sir. She's at the hospital. She's been there for an hour, having relieved Sam and sent her home to get some sleep. Apparently, Carol Bull regained consciousness half an hour ago. She'd slept well, having been sedated by the doctor to make sure she had a comfortable night. Seems she is ready to talk and give us a full statement. She's really had it with Bull according to Sofie and is definitely not going to try and excuse or defend what he did. She intends divorcing him as soon as possible and Sofie has pulled the uniformed guard in to the room they've got Carol in to witness the statement she's insisted she's fit to give us, a state fully corroborated by her doctor, Sofie added. Just thought you'd want to hear the news right away."

"Cheers, Paul. That's made my morning. Gives us a bit more ammunition to use with the CPS in ensuring they go ahead with all the charges against Bull."

"You don't think his brief is going to try and go for an insanity plea, do you?" Drake suddenly asked.

"That had crossed my mind too," Ferris said, and Ross frowned as he contemplated the possibility.

"I think he might," Ross mused, "but I doubt a man like Bull will allow Newman to take that path. He's so goddamned convinced he was in the right to do what he did, he'd argue like hell if Newman tries to get him to plead that he's insane. I want you to do something for me, Paul. Do a full background check on Bull. I want to know if he's had so much as a parking ticket in his life. I've had a feeling building in me that there's more to this bastard than meets the eye."

"No problem, Boss," Ferris replied as he left, leaving Ross and Drake to finish their drinks before heading back to continue their interview with Graham Bull.

"Where'd that suddenly come from?" Drake asked, puzzled at Ross's words to Ferris.

"Looking into Bulls past? I tell you, Izzie, since we picked him up last night, something's been bugging me, and it just came into my mind. We have this bloke who suddenly kills his wife's lover, then tries to kill his missus, but we're supposed to accept he's never previously put a foot wrong in his life? I suspect there's more to Mr. Graham Bull than meets the eye. If he's such a religious fanatic, how do we know he's been totally lily-white up until now?"

"Bloody hell, that's stretching things a bit, isn't it?" Drake was a little stunned. "You really think he could have been in trouble in the past?"

"No, but I think he may have got away with stuff in the past that was never brought to official attention."

Five minutes later, Ross and Drake were back in Interview Room 2 with Bull and Gerard Newman. After restarting the recording and once again identifying those present, Ross re-opened the interview.

"So, Mr. Newman, has your client got anything to say to us in the light of his previous conduct?"

"My client feels your sergeant deliberately provoked him by her outlandish comments about the Devil and I must say, I tend to agree with him."

"Oh, do you? So it's okay for him to make rash statements about the fact he sees himself as doing God's work but we're not allowed to state that to us, and I might add, most normal people, his actions seem to be more those associated with the exact opposite of Godliness, that is, his actions have been Satanic in nature?"

Newman looked lost, as though Ross's words had left him confused. Ross decided to press home his advantage.

"Mr. Newman, putting aside the fact you're a solicitor representing Mr. Bull, are you expecting me to accept that you personally believe that the murder of one person, followed by the attempted murder of another, can be justified as being the work of God?"

"Erm, well, under normal circumstances..." he hesitated.

"What, Mr. Newman? You were about to say no, weren't you? You see, even you can't find a way to justify your client's actions, can you. So I put it to you that we, and my sergeant in particular, is perfectly entitled to allude to a Satanic connection between your client and his crimes."

Graham Bull positively exploded from his chair, and it took Ross, P.C. Hewitt and Izzie Drake to restrain him on this occasion. One he'd been subdued, Ross summoned two more constables and Bull was dragged, screaming to his cell.

Newman was left, standing in one corner of the interview room, looking bewildered and stunned by what had just taken place.

"You okay?" Ross asked the solicitor.

"Er, yes, I think so."

"If I were you, I'd get off back to my office and have a nice cuppa. We'll let you know when your client is to be interviewed again."

"Yes, thank you," Newman spluttered as he rushed from the room and out of police headquarters as fast as his legs would carry him.

"I reckon he found out something new about his golfing buddy in there," Drake said as she and Ross sat once again in his office a while later. Ross had stopped in the squadroom to bring his team up to date, and also received a welcome boost when Tony Curtis walked in bearing a statement from Carol Bull. He'd rushed across to the Royal, where Carol had been taken by the paramedics, after Sofie Meyer called to say she'd taken a statement from Carol Bull. He handed it to Ross who quickly read through the document, written in Sofie's ultra-neat handwriting, smiled, and passed it to Drake.

"That should make sure he goes down for life," she grinned as she finished reading Carol's damning indictment of her husband.

* * *

Over the next twenty-four hours, Sergeant Paul Ferris and admin assistant Kat Bellamy, ably backed up by Sofie Meyer and Sam Gable, launched an in-depth look into the past of Graham Bull. He'd studied at the UCL Eastman Dental Institute at University College, London, where he obtained his degree in dentistry. After working for a couple of dental practices in his home town of Stafford, he'd eventually opened his own practice in Hereford, where he'd lived and practiced his trade until he left the city abruptly in 1990, finally turning up once again in Birkenhead, having purchased the practice there from the retiring incumbent. Soon after, he'd met Carol Dunham, who first worked for him as a dental nurse, before becoming Mrs. Bull ten years previously, as she'd told the detectives who'd interviewed her.

Finally, Ferris found what he was looking for, spent a few minutes on the phone, and was soon knocking on Ross's door again, this time with a laptop in his hand.

"Okay, Paul, I know that smug look. You've got something for me, haven't you?"

"You could say that," Ferris smiled. "It seems our Mr. Bull only found religion after being virtually run out of town when he was in Hereford."

"How so? Come on, you bloody sadist, don't keep me waiting," Ross grinned at his computer expert.

"Okay, Bull worked for a dental practice called Knight and Butler, and while he was there, he started dating one of the nurses, sound familiar?"

"This is starting to sound like a case of Déjà vu," Drake said, waiting for the rest.

"Yep, so, one day this nurse decides to dump our friend because he's getting a tad too possessive. Bull takes it badly and starts following the girl around and when she finds a new boyfriend, our man corners him outside a pub one night and gives him a beating."

"Was he charged?" Ross asked.

"No," Ferris looked disgusted. "Bull's parents were quite well off and they convinced the lad not to press charges."

"In other words, they paid him off," Drake said, disgust on her face.

"You got it," Ferris replied, sharing her disgust.

"And you got this where?" Ross asked.

"From my cousin Ron. When I learned about Bull being in Hereford as a young man, I rang our Ron. He's an investigative journalist down Hereford way, not a great one, but competent enough. Our Ron married a local girl and lives in a village called Credenhill, about six miles from the city and has always worked hard at what he does.

"So we know Bull's got a temper, not just now, but historically. It tends to lend credence to our theory that all this religious stuff he keeps spouting is just a smokescreen, but one altercation with a love rival in a back alley behind a pub years ago doesn't add any real meat to the bones of our case."

Ross knew however, that Paul Ferris wouldn't have come battering his door down for something he was sure to know wasn't conclusive proof of anything. Ferris's next words confirmed that suspicion.

"Ah, but there's more," he said, with a note of triumph in his voice. Ron told me that about two months after the business with the new boyfriend, the dental nurse actually disappeared without a trace."

"Bingo!" Ross exclaimed with a note of satisfaction in his voice. "Did your Ron know anything more about the case?"

"No, not really. It seemed to be one of those cases that was in the headlines locally for a few days, then, you know how it is, something else came up that was more newsworthy and interest died away. But, undeterred as they say, I rang C.I.D. at Hereford and got lucky. A D.S. who worked the case back then is still there. He's a D.I. now and he was happy to talk to me. When I told him we had Graham Bull downstairs, charged with murder and attempted murder, he hissed through his teeth, I could tell by the sound, and said he was glad someone had nailed the bastard at last. You see, Bull was suspected of being involved in the disappearance of the dental nurse, Joanne Perkins, but they could never prove anything. D.I. Watson is going to email me as much info as he can on the case and is happy to talk to us again if we think he can help. He promised he'd get it to me within the next hour or so."

"Paul Ferris, I could bloody kiss you," Ross smiled as he spoke.

"Er, no thanks, Boss," Ferris laughed, holding his hands up in mock horror.

"Yeah, me too," Drake added and rose from her seat, walked up to Ferris and landed a kiss on his cheek, before returning to her seat.

"That was from both of us," she said and Paul Ferris grinned back at her.

At a team briefing held soon after Ferris had brought the latest information to Ross, the D.I. addressed a hastily convened gathering of his team.

"Right, listen very carefully,"

"I will say zis only once," Curtis giggled, mimicking the fake French accent of a character from the popular TV show, 'Allo Allo.'

"Thanks for that, Tony," Ross glared at the eternal joker in the pack. "Okay, I'll start again. Now we've got Graham Bull in custody, he's not proving very talkative. I have a feeling his brief is going to try and go down the insanity path, but, thanks to Pal and Kat, we're on the trail of something else Bull might have been involved in some years ago. I want everyone not already engaged in other matters to work on probing every aspect of Bull's life."

"How did we catch on to this other crime, sir?" Ginger Devenish asked.

"Good question, Ginger. To be honest, it was a hunch, a piece of inspired guesswork you might say. I had a feeling that Bull couldn't be quite as squeaky clean as he appears, not when he possesses such warped thinking and violent tendencies. I guessed he might have one or two little skeletons in his closet and, lo and behold, it looks as if I might be right in that assumption."

"Come on, Gaffer," Dodds urged him, using a form of address he only used when he was feeling frustrated. "Out with it, or is it so secret, we're not allowed to know?"

"Shut up, Nick, and listen."

"Sir," Dodds replied, sheepishly.

"Anyway, it looks as if I was right. We have a missing girl in Hereford from the time Bull worked as a dentist down there. I'm waiting for information from one of the officers who investigated the case. Meanwhile I want you to learn everything there is to know about Bull. I have a hunch he's been hiding in plain sight for years. If he was responsible for the death of another woman, I want him brought to justice for it, is that clear enough?"

A chorus of agreement went around the room as Ross and Drake made their way back to his office. A few minutes later, Paul Ferris once again appeared in the doorway, holding a file he'd just collated from the email D.I. Charlie Watson of West Mercia Police in Hereford had sent to him.

"Sir, here's the info from Hereford, but listen, I've got D.I. Watson on the line on my phone. I left him hanging on as I thought you might want to talk to him."

"Good man, Paul, and yes, get back out there and transfer him to my office number."

A minute later, Ross was talking to Charlie Watson, who spoke with a mild West Country burr in his voice.

"D.I. Ross," he said.

"Andy, please, and thanks for calling."

"No bother, and just call me Charlie. Look, I know you're holding Bull on a murder charge, but your Sergeant Ferris said you're delving into his past, and I've got to tell you, I always had Bull down for the disappearance of Joanne Perkins, but I could never find any evidence to back up my suspicions. That case has haunted me for years, Andy. I still revisit it from time to time, even visited Joanne's parents a couple of times just to let them know their daughter hasn't been forgotten. If I can help you nail him, I'm your man."

"Thanks, Charlie. What made you suspect Bull in the first place?"

"Right, you already know about the fracas he got involved in with Joanne's new boyfriend after she'd dumped him, right?"

"Yes, please carry on."

"So, about four weeks after that little contretemps outside the pub, Joanne left work one evening, and never made it home. She lived with her parents in Kington, about twenty miles from the city. She used to commute in her mini. When she didn't arrive home by 9 p.m. they called us and we put a call out for the car, which was later found, parked up and locked in a little lay-by not far from her home. Joanne was never seen alive again. When we investigated, we learned that Graham Bull hadn't given up on getting her back and even when she went on a couple of casual dates with another young chap, just drinks and the cinema type of thing, Bull kept hanging around, watching her, following her when she went out and it put off the new chap who buggered off sharpish-like."

"So Bull was stalking her," Ross commented.

"Effectively, yes. She'd told a friend, Anna Cross about it but never made an official complaint. She just thought Bull would get fed up in the end. I don't think he did get fed up. As far as I was concerned, he thought if he couldn't have her, no one else could. That's about all I can tell you, Andy. We did our best to track her final movements on that last day but nobody saw hide nor hair of her after she left work. I think Bull waylaid her, made her pull over into the lay-by or made a plea to her to meet him there to talk or something, and he took her from there and killed the poor girl."

"I tend to agree with you, Charlie," Ross said, as Watson fell silent.

"If you can think of anything that might help us, I'd be glad of it," said Watson.

"I don't know what I can suggest after all this time, Charlie... unless, hang on a minute, do you know if Bull was a member of any golf clubs during his time in your neck of the woods?"

"Golf? Now you come to mention it, I think he mentioned something about a golf club during one of the interviews we had with him. Let me check."

A pause was followed by the sound of D.I. Watson busily tapping away on a keyboard and he was back on the line in a minute or so.

"Yes, here we go. I don't know much about golf, or whether he was a member or not but he mentioned playing at Riverside Golf Club regularly. He must have thought it made him sound a bit upper class or something because it had nothing to do with the investigation. But hang on, why did you ask about golf, Andy? Am I missing something here?"

"Charlie, I think the bastard was playing you. We found our first vic's body on a railway track but Bull had killed him in a wooded area on a golf course, and he would have murdered his wife in the same place if we hadn't worked it out and got there in time to save her. I think he was taunting you. I could be wrong but I'm guessing you just might find Joanne Perkins' body somewhere on or close to that golf course you mentioned."

"Fuckin' hell," Watson thumped his desk, which Ross heard clearly and knew it for what it was, having done the same thing many times over the years. "You really think he was mocking us by virtually telling us what he'd done and where he'd buried her?"

"He's an arrogant bastard, Charlie and I wouldn't put it past him."

"I've got to go and talk to my chief about this Andy. Can we keep in touch, on this one, mate"?

"I'm counting on it, Charlie, because if we can nail him for another murder as well, we might secure a whole life sentence on the arrogant little sod."

Izzie Drake had heard most of the conversation between Ross and Watson and as they talked it through afterwards, she agreed that their chances of securing their conviction would be greatly enhanced if they could nail another murder on Graham Bull, who still sat in his cell, unknowing and in blissful ignorance of the continuing investigation into his past life.

Chapter 30

Second charge

After three days of regular interrogations, Graham Bull continued to be intransigent and totally non-forthcoming with Ross and Drake, even a session with Oscar Agostini had failed to elicit a response from the prisoner. Ross had the feeling that even Bull's solicitor, Gerard Newman had become tired of his client's uncooperative attitude towards himself, even though he was doing his best to help the man.

Ross wasn't worried as by now, they had Carol Bull's statement and various investigations by his team had found what could only be called a few character flaws in the dentist. Bull's current dental nurse, Anne Sloan, had provided a statement to Tony Curtis in which she stated that Bull could occasionally make her feel uncomfortable in his presence, as though his eyes were staring straight through her clothes, undressing her mentally. His receptionist, Patricia Smith told Sam Gable that she'd fielded several complaints from clients, including women who had also felt uncomfortable in Bull's chair, even though they wouldn't or couldn't always clarify their reasons for saying so. It was becoming clear to Ross and his team that Graham Bull had been a long-term and dangerous predator and had used his so-called religious beliefs to enable him to mask his true personality.

Just as things had grown quiet in the squad room and as Christmas drew ever closer, the days growing colder and his team growing bored with the inactivity, the phone on Andy Ross's desk rang just as he'd settled down with his sergeants, Izzie Drake, Paul Ferris and Sofie Meyer for a brief case conference.

He picked the jangling instrument up impatiently, and heard the voice of Charlie Watson, the Hereford D.I. based at West Mercia Police's Bath Street station in the beautiful West Country cathedral city.

"Andy?"

"Yes, it is, Hello Charlie, how's everything?"

Ross could tell Watson had something important to tell him. How, he wasn't sure, but he guessed this was no social call.

"We've found her, Joanne Perkins, or at least, we found what's left of her. You, Andy Ross are my new best friend. How the hell did you know he'd taken her to his bloody golf club to kill her and bury her?"

Ross was stunned by Watson's revelation. Although he'd given him the tip about the golf club, he hadn't expected it to bear fruit quite so quickly and decisively.

"Well done, Charlie. And it was just intuition on my part, based on how our case panned out in the end. I just had an idea he might have done this, or something like it, before and it looks like I was right. How did you find her so fast?"

"My gaffer hates having unsolved mysteries on the books, so when I went to him with what you'd told me, he authorised the use of a forensic anthropologist. It just so happens we have one living close to the city, and she turned up with a team of six students, all keen to help her in her search. She had some kind of ground penetrating radar gizmo with her that enabled her to search for buried bodies and such like. She's helped us in the past so the gaffer had no hesitation in calling her in again."

Something clicked in Ross's personal memory banks. He had a feeling he knew who Watson's forensic anthropologist might be.

"This forensic expert of yours wouldn't by chance be Doctor Hannah Lewin, would it?"

"My God, yes, it is. Do you have psychic powers up there, Andy?" Watson joked.

"I wish I did, Charlie, but no. It's just when you said she'd helped you guys in the past, it triggered a memory. Hannah helped us out a few years ago when we had a set of bones discovered when an old dock was being drained for development and Hannah was a friend of our pathologist, who roped her in to help. I thought she was based at the university in Cambridge though, not in the wilds of Herefordshire."

"She was, but she got married and moved down here, she works freelance now but she's still on the Home Office's retained list so gets called in whenever they need her."

"Good for her. Please say hello from me when you see her and give her my congratulations on her marriage."

"Of course I will, mate. In fact, when I mentioned we were kind of linked to a case up there in Liverpool, she mentioned that she'd helped out on a case up there some years ago."

"Well, at least I can one hundred percent count on the fact you're getting the best information possible. She was brilliant when she was up here."

"Same here, Andy. So, she wandered into the woods that border the golf course, with three of her helpers and within an hour she struck pay dirt. She discovered the decomposed remains of a young woman, the sex was apparent due to certain characteristics of the bones, she said, and she confirmed the remains had been in the ground for between ten and twenty years, which puts them right in the missile of our time frame. While she was unearthing the poor girl's remains, her other students managed to locate what looked like a shallow grave, but it was actually where the killer had buried the girl's clothes, separately from the body. We cross-referenced what we could identify from the clothing with what Joanne was last seen wearing on the day she disappeared and there's no doubt, Andy, it's her. Hannah's examination will continue at the morgue of course and she's confident she will be able to give us a positive I.D. There's one more thing, too. Joanne was wearing her white uniform dress when she left work on the day she disappeared, and it was found in the bundle of clothes we found, and we got lucky. There was a small blood stain on it, and Hannah is certain she can pull a DNA sample from it. So all we need is a blood sample from yer man, and we've got him."

"Great work, Charlie. I can't believe how fast this is all coming together. Fancy a trip to Liverpool?"

"Really all your good work, Andy. I've just followed your lead, mate, and yes, have blood sample kit, will travel," he laughed.

Ross was delighted with the news, and now felt he really had the measure of Graham Bull. Before he and Charlie Watson ended their call, Watson made arrangements to travel up to Liverpool, to interview Graham Bull. The net was finally closing on the man who thought he was too clever to get caught.

Ross, Drake, Ferris and Meyer sat and congratulated themselves. Bull wouldn't know what hit him when this latest development was presented to him.

* * *

The majority of Ross's team had completed their Christmas shopping by the time when, three days later, they welcomed the arrival of Detective Inspector Charles Watson and Detective Sergeant Maggie Riley of West Mercia Police to their squad room. Ross carried out the necessary introductions and D.C.I. Oscar Agostini came down from his lofty tower to meet the visitors.

"Bloody hell, Andy, you've got a real good home from home here. Our entire C.I. D. department doesn't have this much floor space, and you're just one branch of the detective division up here."

It was Agostini who replied.

"Well D.I. Watson, Merseyside Police covers a much larger Metropolitan area, but your place is just as important to the nation's policing no matter how big or small it is."

"Kind of you to say so, sir," Watson said, clearly proud of his part in the big picture of policing the United Kingdom.

Ross liked the West Mercia detective. Watson was shorter than he was, at about five feet eight, some might even describe him as diminutive. He looked to be in his late forties, with a full head of dark brown hair with eye to match, and he wore a dark charcoal suit that Ross was sure would have Marks & Spencer labels inside. Maggie Riley stood a couple of inches shorter than her boss, was slimly built, with shortish blonde hair cut in a neat bob. Penetrating blue eyes looked out from her round face and she exuded intelligence, Ross thought. As her name suggested, she spoke with a faint Irish accent and it was quite obvious where her antecedents originated from. They had come armed with the results of Hannah Lewin's tests on the remains discovered in the woods at Riverside Golf Club and soon, the two Hereford detectives were seated in an interview room, with Ross and Drake in attendance, facing Graham Bull, who looked perplexed and a little nonplussed at seeing the two new arrivals, and his solicitor, Gerard Newman, who quite frankly, looked as if he'd rather be anywhere else than in that room at that moment. As usual, a stony-faced uniformed constable stood, sentinel-like by the door.

"Well, Mr Bull, here we are again," Ross began. "Anything more you want to say to us, yet?"

"My client has nothing further to say to you, Inspector Ross. I must inform you that I will be pleading that my client committed these offences due to temporarily being of unsound mind as a result of discovering the truth about his wife's infidelity."

"I see," said Ross. "So, your client is effectively saying that he's never had these feelings before and this was an aberration caused purely and simply by the recent affair between Mrs. Bull and Joseph Slimani, is that right?"

"Yes, that's what I just said, isn't it?"

"And was this your client's idea or your professional recommendation to him?" Drake added.

"I don't think that's relevant," Sergeant. "I've told you what's happening and that's all you need to know."

"Okay," Ross spoke again. "I've introduced D.I. Watson and D.S. Riley, but you may not realise, Mr. Bull that you have met D.I. Watson previously, though he was a detective sergeant back in those days."

Bull remained silent, barely acknowledging Ross's presence.

"I see," Ross continued. "Does the name Joanne Perkins mean anything to you, Mr. Bull?"

Both Ross and Drake noticed a slight tic that appeared in Bull's eyes at the mention of the name. It was only minor, but it was a giveaway.

"Mind gone blank, has it?" Ross was beginning to enjoy himself. "Perhaps this will remind you," he said as he produced a photograph of Joanne Perkins from the file Paul Ferris had produced from Watson's earlier email. "You worked with Joanne when you were employed as a dentist by Knight and Butler. She was a dental nurse, a pretty girl as you can see, not someone you'd easily forget. Ring any bells?"

Ross nodded to Watson, who took over at that point.

"I interviewed you twice when Joanne disappeared, Mr. Bull, surely you remember that? You were adamant you knew nothing about Joanne's disappearance but your work colleagues, including your boss, Mr. George Knight, were equally adamant about you having a 'thing' for Joanne. You asked her to go out with you on numerous occasions, didn't you? Trouble was, Joanne knocked you back every time, didn't she, because she saw through your nice guy routine. Like the other young women at the practice, she found you a bit creepy and wanted nothing to do with you. The day she disappeared you said you were playing golf when she vanished into thin air, but at the time, I didn't tell you what time she went missing. So how could you know what time you needed and alibi for? I questioned you a second time because of that anomaly but unfortunately we were unable to produce sufficient evidence with which to hold you."

Newman interrupted.

"This is all very interesting, Detective Inspector, but just what, if any relevance does this have to the current case against my client?"

Ross re-entered the conversation at this point.

"Ah, now this is where things become interesting, Mr. Newman. Since he was arrested, your client, has, through your good self, insisted that his recent crimes were a one-off, an aberration caused by the shock he felt at discovering his wife's infidelity with Mr. Slimani and you confirmed this not five minute ago, correct?"

For the first time, Gerard Newman felt a suspicion that Ross was about to hit him and his client with something they weren't expecting.

"I believe that's what I said, yes," Newman sounded a little less confident.

"Please, Charlie, feel free to carry on," Ross handed over to Watson again.

"I have to inform you," Watson said to Bull, "that late yesterday afternoon the decomposed remains of Joanne Perkins were discovered, buried in a shallow grave in the woodland adjacent to, and forming part of the property of the Riverside Golf Club, and close by, we also found a second burial site containing the clothing worn by Miss Perkins on the day she disappeared. We have sufficient forensic evidence to link her murder to you, and I am therefore officially charging you with the murder of Joanne Perkins."

As a stunned Graham Bull and a speechless Gerard Newman sat in a state of shock, Charles Watson cautioned Bull, and Ross felt a deep sense of satisfaction as he spoke once more, after Watson had finished.

"I suppose that was another of your sudden 'aberrations' too was it?" he looked at Bull, who stared back at him, a look of defeat finally appearing on his face, as he leaned across to whisper something to his solicitor.

"I'd like to request a recess, Inspector Ross," said Newman. "My client wishes to confer with me in private if you don't mind."

"I don't mind at all. Mr. Newman. Take all the time you want. Just inform the custody officer when you're ready to recommence our little chat won't you?"

Newman nodded. He knew now that his proposed defence strategy had just been blown out of the water. No jury would ever believe that Graham Bull had acted out of a sense of passion, fuelled by temporary insanity, not once they knew he'd already committed premeditated murder over ten years ago. This was not going well for Newman or his client. He, as well as Ross and the police investigators, was yet to learn that things were about to lurch from bad to worse for Graham Bull.

Chapter 31

End game

Ross, Drake, Watson and Riley were taking a well-earned break from the interrogation of Graham Bull, enjoying coffee and tea in Ross's office, which was now appearing very cramped. That feeling intensified when a knock on the door was followed by the appearance of Gary, (Ginger) Devenish, who squeezed himself into the cramped space, bearing a sheet of paper which he carried as if it was as valuable as a solid gold ingot.

"Sorry to disturb you, sir, but D.S. Meyer said I should tell you about this as soon as you were free."

"That's okay, Ginger. What have you got?" Ross smiled at the newest member of his team.

"Well, you wanted us to probe Bull's past, and Sergeant Meyer gave me the task of looking into Bull's student days, to see if anything came up."

"Don't tell me he was up to his tricks when he was a bloody student?" Ross could hardly believe it.

"Make of it what you will sir, but in his first year at dental college, Graham Bull was admitted to hospital following a severe beating he received while making his way back to his digs one night."

"So you're saying he was the victim in this case?"

"Yes, but I dug a bit deeper, and it seems no charges were laid against the two lads who beat him up, who were caught in the act, so it seems. The official records are scant on the incident as Bull refused to press charges against the two assailants, who as it turns out, were brothers, but get this, they had a sister who was studying at the dental school alongside Bull."

"I'm thinking I can predict what you're going to tell me next, Ginge, but go on anyway."

"I'm giving you the shortened version here, of course, but I spoke to a couple of people at the dental school and I was passed on to a bloke called the Resident Advisor who was there when this happened. The two lads who assaulted Bull did so as a warning because the guy had been harassing their sister. Bull didn't press charges because if he had done, the girl was ready and willing to lay charges of sexual harassment and sexual assault against Bull which would have probably led to him being kicked out of the university and would have been the end of his dental career. The chap told me this in confidence, but when I put a bit of pressure on, saying this is a murder investigation, he gave me the name of the girl. I said we wouldn't use her name publicly or name her in court or anything like that, but it would help in our questioning of Bull as a murder suspect. So, the girl's name is Claire Holliday, and I looked her up and she's now a successful orthodontist in private practice in Oxford. That's about it, sir. I don't know if you want me to contact her?"

"That's great work, Ginge, well done. I don't think we need to drag the past up with Miss Holliday but it gives me something else to hit Bull with. It all goes to prove that the man has been a sexual predator since he was a student and it helps to shoot his defence full of holes. He won't know we're not going to call Miss Holliday so when I add this to everything else, I'm pretty sure our man is going to forget playing the insanity card and go for a straight admission of murder and attempted murder, especially as there's now DNA evidence to implicate him in the Hereford murder. You've done great work in tracking that down, Ginge. We'll go and hit him with it in a few minutes."

Devenish was pleased his work had been appreciated by his boss and departed as Ross and the others decided to continue their interrogation of Graham Bull. He'd had long enough to talk with his solicitor.

Sure enough, once faced with the alleged long-ago sexual assault on Claire Holliday, even though no charges had been forthcoming, Bull capitulated, through his solicitor, with Gerard Newman informing Ross, and Charles Watson, that his client would be pleading guilty to the murders of Joey Slimani and Joanne Perkins, and the attempted murder of his wife, Carol Bull. Ross was particularly pleased for Carol Bull, who would be saved the trauma of having to testify in court. Before he came to trial however, Bull would change his mind, and his plea. Newman engaged an eminent Q.C. (Queen's Counsel), who insisted they could go for a not guilty verdict. Bull jumped at the chance.

Charles Watson and Maggie Riley, also delighted to have cleared up the disappearance of Joanne Perkins, returned to Hereford, having excused themselves from joining Ross and his team in a celebration drink that evening. It was a long journey home and they needed to report to their own superiors, and get things moving on their own murder case against Bull.

Ross and Watson both felt that the Crown Prosecution Service would probably elect for a single trial for Bull, so it was important that both Merseyside Police and the force from West Mercia ensured their paperwork was watertight and that nothing could go wrong or be taken advantage of by a tricky, clever barrister once the two cases were tried before a judge and jury.

With Bull safely behind bars, and inquiries ongoing to ensure he stayed there, Ross and Drake at last found the time to pay an important visit, to talk to Trixie Slimani. Ross felt she deserved a fuller explanation of what had transpired.

"So this Bull guy, he's some kinda weirdo?" Trixie said after Ross and Drake together had given her as full a picture of the outcome of the case as they could.

"That's one way of putting it," Drake replied. "He's a predator, Trixie. He's also narcissistic, meaning he thinks only of himself and what he wants. Other people are just there to serve his needs."

"Wow, a real crock of shit," said Trixie.

"He'll definitely undergo psychiatric evaluation while he's awaiting trial, but there's no doubt he knew exactly what he was doing and there's no way he can plead insanity, as he was planning to do."

"What a bastard," Trixie's voice shot venom in each word. "Tell me something though, Inspector Ross."

"If I can, of course."

"Well, you say he killed a girl years ago and left her buried on a golf course, and he would have buried his wife, poor thing, on the course here, as well, so why did he dump my poor Joey's body on that damn railway track instead of burying him on the South Mersey course too?"

"I have a theory about that, Trixie and I'm sure, when he eventually talks to us, as I'm sure he will, he'll confirm it."

"I'm intrigued. Let's hear it."

"Okay, he wanted Joey dead, but he didn't want anything to lead back to him. If he'd buried Joey on the course, and the body was discovered, there'd be questions asked and everyone at the club wou ld have been under suspicion. He'd have known we'd do background checks on all club members and we'd have been sure to find out that he has been a member of another golf club in Hereford and that a woman he worked with down there had mysteriously disappeared. He was intelligent enough to know that we would have gradually pieced it together until the clues all pointed at him. So, instead, in a way, I think Joey played into his hands."

Trixie's eyes gawped and she gave a sharp intake of breath.

"He did? How?"

"Joey, from what we've learned, played occasionally at the club and wouldn't usually be seen there twice in one week, as he was the week before his death. Those meeting he held at the club gave Bull an idea. What if he made it difficult for Joey to be identified after killing him? Joey was American after all, so Bull could take a calculated risk that his fingerprints wouldn't be on record over here as long as he hadn't committed a crime, and he'd read enough crime thriller books over the years to know how professional hitmen work. The book shelves at his home proved that. His wife confirmed he enjoyed reading that kind of thing. So, he knew he had to make it hard to identify the body, long enough to delay the police in their initial investigation so what better way than to remove his clothes and all trace of I.D. and then deposit Joey's body in a public place as though making a statement, which would almost certainly lead the police, once they identified the body, as he knew we would, into believing his death was connected to the adult movie industry. Devastatingly simple really."

"But how did he know you'd identify Joey so soon?"

"He knew you'd report him missing when he never came home from the 'meeting' he lured Joey to at the studio. It was there he drugged Joey with a powerful sedative, bundled his body into his own car and cool as a cucumber, kept your husband in that car boot all day, unconscious from the drugs, and then drove to Rendell's Wood after dark. There, he taunted and eventually murdered Joey, I'm sorry, but you did ask, and then buried the clothes and just drove to Liverpool and how would you Americans say, 'mosied around' until he found a promising place to dump the body. I'm sure it was no coincidence he threw Joey's body from the bridge as that train approached. He saw it coming from a long way off on that straight track and then quickly hoisted the body out of the car and threw it over the parapet, after first making sure there was nobody around. He was hoping the train would help to make the body hard to identify and his plan was going well for a while, but we're not as stupid as he seems to think we are. That's about it, really, Trixie. I'm sorry if it's upsetting to hear, but you did ask and I think we owed you the truth, at the very least."

"No, it's okay, Inspector, really. I'm just glad you caught the murdering bastard in the end. Tell me please, how you first latched on to the evil asshole."

"I'll let Sergeant Drake explain that one to you as she was one of the first to agree with my theory that we were being led up a blind alley. Go on, Izzie, please," Ross said, allowing Drake to take over the story.

"Sometimes, clever people can be too clever and overplay their hand. To begin with, everything seemed to point to Joey's death being connected in some way to the industry you both worked in. We found links to the German porn industry, to the American connection with a certain underworld figure who had threatened Joey, and at one time we even suspected you, Mary-Beth and Lana might have conspired to have Joey killed."

Trixie gasped in shock, "What? You thought I might have..."

"Only for a short time, Trixie. You must understand that everyone is a suspect to begin with in a murder case and you'd be surprised how many murders are committed by those closest to the victim. But, as we investigated Joey's life and talked to various people, we came to one inescapable conclusion. Joey Slimani was liked, loved or respected almost universally. We couldn't find one person who wished him harm or who had a bad word to say against him, except a certain man at the Golf Club who made a big thing about Joey being involved in the porn industry."

"Graham Bull," said Trixie.

"Correct," Drake agreed. "That still didn't make us suspect him of anything, but on the day of Joey's funeral, who should turn up un-expectedly but Graham Bull. We believed he was there as an official representative of the golf club, him being the club captain of course but we later discovered he wasn't there on the club's behalf. We had to ask ourselves a question. Why would Bull attend the funeral of a man he had admitted he didn't like and whose lifestyle represented everything that Bull resented in his guise as a committed Christian? In other words, had he simply turned up to gloat at the death of the man he despised? But that was still too simplistic, so, we started look-ing deeper into Bull's life and slowly but surely, we put the pieces to-gether until we arrived at the conclusion that Graham Bull was your husband's killer."

"I gotta say, you guys have done a great job. I feel real bad for his wife though. My Joey tried to help her feel less like a piece of used up trash and more like a desirable woman, and he ended up dead."

Izzie felt she had to say something, but was unsure how to diplomatically voice her thoughts. She ploughed on anyway.

"Well, Trixie, you need to understand that not everyone has the same attitudes towards sexual intercourse as you and Joey. You must be aware that the vast majority of people would view what Joey and Mrs. Bull were doing as being an extra-marital affair and that such things can cause great harm to a marriage?"

"Yeah, I guess you're right," Trixie was forced to agree. "Sometimes I guess we forget that everyday nine to five type of marriage stuff. But still, Joey didn't deserve to die."

"No he didn't Trixie. We are really so sorry and we mean that."

"I know that, Sergeant and thank you. I'm just pleased you managed to save his poor wife before Bull killed her too."

"Or anyone else," Ross spoke again.

"Anyone else?"

"Yes, I think it's only right we should tell you that when we arrived at Rendell's Wood, and while we were getting into position to take Bull down he was boasting to his wife about getting away with Joey's murder and he expected to get away with killing her too, though God knows how he thought we wouldn't put the pieces together by then, We'd seen him speed off from his house earlier and we were on to him by then. He even mentioned your name too as he bragged to his wife."

"Me? You don't mean he was intending to come after me too?"

"Who knows, Trixie? Maybe he fancied you but knew you'd never look twice at a man like him, so put you on a list to be dealt with later."

"Jesus H Christ, that makes me nauseous, Inspector. It's a shame you guys don't have the death penalty over here, because I'd sure as hell like to see that perverted bastard fry for his crimes, believe me, I would."

Ross nodded, and said nothing. Personally, he wasn't a supporter of the death sentence, always being aware that over the years, there'd been too many miscarriages of justice that had seen innocent men and women executed in the UK. Posthumous pardons were all well and good but couldn't bring the innocent back to life, or ease the grief of their families.

After saying their goodbyes to Trixie for the time being, Ross and Drake headed back to headquarters where a mountain of paperwork awaited them in connection with the Joey Slimani case. For now, they could relax a little, though. The hard work was done and like the rest of the team they still had lives to live beyond the arduous and at times frustrating world of criminal investigations.

"I've got to do some Christmas shopping, before its too late," Drake said, as they covered the few miles back to base, glad, they hoped, to have seen the last of *Paradise Found*. It would be up to others to organise the witnesses when the time came for Graham Bull to face trial for his crimes.

"What are you going to get for Peter?" Ross asked, glad to be able to talk of more mundane matters.

"I haven't given it much thought yet," Izzie replied. "I'll think of something though. I always rely on a spot of last-minute inspiration. How about you? You got something in mind for Maria?"

"Yes, as a matter of fact I have. She's dropped enough subtle hints about a coat she'd like. For once, I've listened, even though she probably thinks I haven't and first chance I get, I'll buy it and hide it in my office until I can sneak it into the house."

"I suppose you'll want me to wrap it up for you, as usual?"

"But of course. What are sergeants for after all?" he grinned across the car at her from the driving seat.

"Bloody chauvinist," she laughed.

"Hey, don't knock it when I pay you a compliment. Nobody wraps presents like you do, Sergeant Drake."

"And nobody knows how to creep round me like you do, Detective Inspector Ross," she smiled a big smile, the first in a long time, or so it felt.

As they pulled into the car park at headquarters and alighted from the car, they both looked up as a flurry of light, white flakes fell from above, the first snowfall of winter, light and powdery, it would never settle, but it put them both in a better mood as thoughts of Christmas replaced thoughts of blood, death and dismembered bodies.

Chapter 32

Life goes on

Christmas came and went in a blur for Andy Ross, Izzie Drake and the rest of the Merseyside Special Murder Investigation Team. Though it was cold, there was no snow, so no picture postcard White Christmas, though a heavy frost in the morning on Christmas Day did give the city a white frosted coating. Ross's wife, Maria, was delighted with the camel coloured Cashmere coat her husband bought her, congratulating him on his ability to succumb to a mere two or three dozen hints about what she'd like under the tree. In return, Ross received a full set of DVDs, featuring the films based on his favourite horror author, Stephen King's works. The only downside for Maria was being forced to sit and watch *Carrie*, which she'd seen on numerous previous occasions, with her husband.

Izzie Drake solved her quandary about what to buy her husband, Peter, by presenting him with a voucher for his favourite DVD store. Peter, a film buff, was over the moon with his gift and Izzie loved the beautiful sapphire pendant on an 18 carat gold chain that he'd surprised her with.

Most of the team, being single, spent Christmas with their families, though Sam Gable was the odd one out, having been invited to spend the holiday with her new boyfriend, Detective Sergeant Ian Gilligan at his home in Oldham. For Sam, it was a romantic, peaceful and very happy time, and Ian had cooked an amazing, traditional Christmas dinner, after which he presented Sam with a gold bracelet, complete with a tiny pair of gold handcuffs attached. Sam thought it was the most gorgeous present she'd ever received. Showing a coincidental meeting of minds, she'd bought Ian a pair of cufflinks, also with a handcuff design on them.

Sofie Meyer had returned to her home in Germany, having been granted a full week's leave and after spending the holidays with her family, she would return to Liverpool on New Year's Eve, to allow Paul Ferris to spend New Year at home with his wife and son. This would be Sofie's last Christmas as part of Ross's team, as her two year attachment to the squad would end in the summer of 2006.

* * *

At least, Sofie would still be with the team in order to see Graham Bull tried and sentenced to two concurrent life sentences for the murders of Joanne Perkins and Joey Slimani and to twenty years for the attempted murder of Carol Bull, who had started divorce proceedings soon after Bull had been remanded in custody soon after his arrest. The trial was short, with Bull finally attempting to achieve some sort of absolution by pleading not guilty to all the charges, claiming diminished responsibility. His solicitor, Gerard Newman, had engaged the experienced barrister, Sir Miles Darley to represent Bull in court, but even his eloquence, during his only real contribution to the defence in an impassioned plea for leniency, based on the infidelity of his wife, failed to sway the jurors, who sat, stony-faced throughout the proceedings. Ross, with all his years of experience knew what the outcome was going to be even before the judge sent them out to consider their verdict.

Ross and Drake once again met D.I, Charles Watson and D.S. Maggie Riley from Hereford, who'd arrived to give their evidence in the Joanne Perkins case. Unlike their visit to Liverpool, this time the two Hereford officers took the time to get together in a local pub near the court in Manchester, where the trial took place.

"A satisfying result in the end, Andy," Watson exclaimed, as the four of them raised their glasses in a toast to the judge for his stiff sentencing.

"Perfect, Charlie," Ross replied. "It was a pleasure working with you, however briefly, you too Maggie," he addressed Riley too.

"It's always good to meet our colleagues from other forces," Drake added. "It's great we can cooperate closely without point-scoring off each other."

"You're right there, Izzie," Watson agreed. "I can recall, not too long ago either, when if two forces had to work together on a case it would virtually end up in fisticuffs."

"You're not wrong, Charlie," Ross acknowledged as he drained his glass, saw the others also low on alcoholic beverages and said, "Another drink anyone?"

* * *

Trixie Slimani had looked like a million dollars when she'd arrived for the trial, eager to see her husband's killer being put away for a long, long time. She walked into court, head-held high, on the arm of Bill Jennings. Trixie wore a plum-coloured skirt suit by Versace, with matching heels that served to accentuate her shapely legs, and every head turned as she passed, as those in attendance strove to get a good view of the widow. Jennings had clearly been spending his legacy, as he too wore a suit that probably cost more than two months of Ross's hard earned wages.

In a brief conversation on the steps of the courthouse, before the detectives had left for their short get-together with Watson and Riley, Trixie had informed Ross that she'd decided to sell *Paradise Found*, and move back to the USA. She'd decided to take over the running of Joey's film production company, in partnership with Mary-Beth and Lana and Joe Slim Productions would henceforth be known as Joe Trix Productions. Bill Jennings, she said, would be going to the States with her where he would be her personal assistant and bodyguard. *At least that sounds better than butler or manservant,* Ross thought, when he realised Jennings would probably be filling exactly the same role in New York as he had in Birkenhead.

On a more personal note, Drake asked if she'd heard anything from Joey's daughter, Melita.

"Mary-Beth spoke to her not long ago," Trixie replied. "Being a tax and financial consultant she offered to help Melita to invest her legacy wisely. The kid has her head screwed on, for sure. She's using some of the money she inherited to open a dog rescue and sanctuary. Seems she's animal mad. Hey, though, even though she never knew her father, she's grateful to him for leaving her the money, and she's going to call her sanctuary, *Joe's Place.* Cool huh?"

"That's really nice, Trixie," Drake admitted, pleased that something good had materialised out of the whole sorry tale of Joey Slimani's murder. Ross and Drake shook hands with Trixie and Bill Jennings on the court house steps and watched the pair walk away, arm in arm, looking almost like a happily married couple. "D'you think she'll marry him, next?" Drake asked Ross, who gave the question some thought for a few seconds before replying.

"I think Trixie likes being married, Izzie, so it wouldn't surprise me at all if she isn't Mrs. Jennings before long. Good luck to 'em, I say."

"Yeah, me too. Despite what I thought about her earlier in the case, she's actually a nice person, not the hard-faced cow I first thought she must be because of her being a porn star."

"That was just your hormones being all scrambled up before you knew you were pregnant,"

"I know. I'm glad we parted on good terms with Trixie. I hope life works out for her from now on."

"I'm sure it will," Ross predicted. "Trixie Slimani is a survivor, I guarantee it."

"Talking of survivors, did you know Carol Bull has a new job?"

"Now, how did you know that? Wait, don't tell me, Derek."

"But of course. You know that every bit of gossip from the whole of Merseyside seems to gravitate to Derek's encyclopaedic brain."

"Okay, do tell."

"This was all down to Derek's new wife, Debbie. Seems she came home from work one evening and told Derek she'd met a new dental nurse at work. Carol Bull is working in the Dental Clinic at the Royal and is in the process of changing her name, reverting to her maiden name, wanting to dissociate herself as much as possible from Bull. She actually approached Debbie in the canteen, having seen her name badge and asked if she was related to a detective on the Force in Liverpool. At first, like you, I thought our Derek's all-encompassing tentacles of knowledge had spread to Birkenhead as well," She laughed, and Ross joined in.

"I'm pleased for her, let's hope she can put the emotional trauma of her time with Bull behind her and start again, like Trixie's having to do," Ross said as the pair motored back to Liverpool as dusk fell across the landscape of Greater Manchester and the shadows slowly lengthened. It had been a long day. Most of the team had left hours ago and would already be relaxing at home. Sam Gable had only travelled as far as Oldham, where her fledgling romance with Ian Gilligan was blossoming nicely, week by week.

"Look," said Drake, as they negotiated one of the roundabouts that led them into the city centre. "Tulips," and sure enough, the grassed area of the roundabout's central reservation displayed a profusion of the ubiquitous harbingers of Springtime, in countless colours, brilliantly lit by the lighting positioned to highlight them by the clever council workers who'd planted them.

It really felt as if the cold, dark days of winter were behind them, along with the case of the mangled body on the railway tracks at Mossley Hill. Unbeknownst to the two detectives, Detective Constable Sam Gable had received a phone call notifying her that her father had been taken to hospital after suffering a heart attack. As both she and Ian had already shared a bottle of wine between them that evening, Sam took the fastest option open to her as driving was out of the question. With Ian by her side, and after a quick taxi ride into Manchester, she considered herself fortunate to be just in time to catch… the last train to Lime Street.

Dear reader,

We hope you enjoyed reading *Last Train to Lime Street*. Please take a moment to leave a review in Amazon, even if it's a short one. Your opinion is important to us.

Discover more books by Brian L. Porter at

https://www.nextchapter.pub/authors/brian-porter-mystery-author-liverpool-united-kingdom

Want to know when one of our books is free or discounted for Kindle? Join the newsletter at http://eepurl.com/bqqB3H

Best regards,

Brian L. Porter and the Next Chapter Team

About the Author

Brian L Porter is an award-winning author, whose books have also regularly topped the Amazon Best Selling charts, fifteen of which have to date been Amazon bestsellers. Most recently, the third book in his Mersey Mystery series, *A Mersey Maiden* was voted The Best Book We've Read This Year, 2018, by the organisers and readers of Read-free.ly.

A Mersey Mariner was voted the Top Crime Novel in the Top 50 Best Indie Books, 2017 awards, while *Sheba: From Hell to Happiness* won the Best Nonfiction section and also won the Preditors & Editors Best Nonfiction Book Award, 2017. Writing as Brian, he has won a Best Author Award, a Poet of the Year Award, and his thrillers have picked up Best Thriller and Best Mystery Awards.

His short story collection *After Armageddon* is an international best-seller and his moving collection of remembrance poetry, *Lest We Forget*, is also an Amazon best seller.

Three rescue dogs, three bestsellers!
In a recent departure from his usual thriller writing, Brian has written three successful books about three of the eleven rescued dogs who share his home, with more to follow.

Sasha, A Very Special Dog Tale of a Very Special Epi-Dog is now an international bestseller and winner of the Preditors & Editors Best Nonfiction Book, 2016, and was placed 7th in The Best Indie Books of 2016, and *Sheba: From Hell to Happiness* is a UK #1 bestseller, and award winner as detailed above. Earlier in 2018, Cassie's Tale was released and instantly became the best-selling new release in its category on Amazon in the USA.

If you love dogs, you'll love these three offerings which will soon be followed by book 4 in the series *Saving Dylan*.

Writing as Harry Porter his children's books have achieved three bestselling rankings on Amazon in the USA and UK.

In addition, his third incarnation as romantic poet Juan Pablo Jalisco has brought international recognition with his collected works, *Of Aztecs and Conquistadors* topping the bestselling charts in the USA, UK and Canada.

Brian lives with his wife, children and a wonderful pack of eleven rescued dogs. He is also the in-house screenwriter for ThunderBall Films, (L.A.), for whom he is also a co-producer on a number of their current movie projects.

The Mersey Mysteries have already been optioned for TV/movie adaptation, in addition to his other novels, all of which have been signed by ThunderBall Films in a movie franchise deal.

Look out for the 7th book in the Mersey Mystery series, *The Mersey Monastery Murders*, coming soon.

See Brian's website at http://www.brianlporter.co.uk/

His blog is at https://sashaandharry.blogspot.co.uk/

From International Bestselling Author Brial L Porter

The Mersey Mysteries

A Mersey Killing

All Saints, Murder on the Mersey

A Mersey Maiden

A Mersey Mariner

A Very Mersey Murder

Last Train to Lime Street

The Mersey Monastery Murders (Coming soon)

Thrillers by Brian L Porter

A Study in Red - The Secret Journal of Jack the Ripper

Legacy of the Ripper

Requiem for the Ripper

Pestilence

Purple Death

Behind Closed Doors

Avenue of the Dead

The Nemesis Cell

Kiss of Life

Dog Rescue
Sasha
Sheba: From Hell to Happiness
Cassie's Tale
Saving Dylan (Coming soon)

Short Story Collection
After Armageddon

Remembrance Poetry
Lest We Forget

Children's books as Harry Porter
Wolf
Alistair the Alligator, (Illustrated by Sharon Lewis)
Charlie the Caterpillar (Illustrated by Bonnie Pelton)

As Juan Pablo Jalisco
Of Aztecs and Conquistadors

Many of Brian's books have also been released in translated versions, in Spanish, Italian and Portuguese editions.

You might also like:

Murder on Tyneside by Eileen Thornton

To read first chapter for free, head to:
https://www.nextchapter.pub/books/murder-on-tyneside-cozy-
crime-mystery

Manufactured by Amazon.ca
Bolton, ON

23189146R00176